A LIFE OF HER OWN

irst published in 2001 by
Marino Books
An imprint of Mercier Press
16 Hume Street Dublin 2
Tel: (01) 661 5299; Fax: (01) 661 8583;
e.mail: books@marino.ie

Trade enquiries to CMD Distribution
55A Spruce Avenue
Stillorgan Industrial Park Blackrock
County Dublin
Tel: (01) 294 2556; Fax: (01) 294 2564
e-mail: cmd@columba.ie

© Dee Cunningham 2001

ISBN 1 86023 132 2
10 9 8 7 6 5 4 3 2 1

A CIP record for this title is available
from the British Library
Cover design by SPACE
Printed by Cox & Wyman, Reading,
Berks, UK

A LIFE OF HER OWN

DEE CUNNINGHAM

DEDICATION

To Leah, Sam and Sadhbh, whose coming has brought extra joy into my life.

ACKNOWLEDGEMENTS

My thanks to Katie Donovan for giving me a glimpse into the fascinating world of journalism, and to John Collins for sharing with me his own priestly experience and insights. I must stress, however, that the characters depicted as working in both newspaper and parish in *A Life of Her Own* are products of my imagination and do not exist outside the covers of the book. My thanks also to my five children and their partners for their unfailing support and belief in me. I am especially indebted to Cliona Cunningham for her invaluable comments on the manuscript, and for the ideal working environment and generous hospitality which she and her husband, Tom Avonts, provided in their Belgian home at crucial stages during the writing of this novel. And, finally, I would like to express my appreciation of Jo O'Donoghue and all the team at Marino Books. It has been a pleasure working with them.

ONE

As Cathy descended the steps of the Ha'penny Bridge the street lamps were casting spirals of light into the river: great, glittering spirals that plunged and wriggled down through the dark waters of the Liffey. Normally she'd have stopped to admire them, but tonight, because of what had happened earlier, she just wasn't in the mood. The quays were quiet. There were very few cars to be seen on streets that a few hours earlier had been choked with traffic. She could hear her high heels clicking over the concrete as she reached the pavement and saw the lights from the archway ahead reflected slickly on the damp roadway. Crossing the narrow street with the February wind blustering around her ankles, she looked forward to getting in out of the cold, even if it was only for the short length of the covered passageway. For a moment she thought longingly of the warmth of the pub she'd left behind, wondering if she'd made a mistake.

She could worry about that later. No time now for regrets. Quickening her pace, she went up the steps and under the Merchants' Arch. In the daytime, the narrow passageway with its tiny shops on either side always gave Cathy the feeling that she'd stepped back in time, back to those medieval days when it had been a busy thoroughfare. In her imagination she would people it with shoppers dressed in motley garb and hear the cries of the street sellers. But tonight she saw nothing romantic about the passageway. Its deserted air didn't tempt her to linger. Despite her haste, she couldn't help but notice the young man sitting on the ground against one wall. Eyes closed, head thrown back against the brick, in his outstretched hand he held a plastic cup. Propped up near his feet was a dirty piece of card with 'homeless' scrawled on it in large uneven letters.

A common enough sight nowadays. Yet Cathy checked her stride. She wanted to move on but found she couldn't. The hopeless way the boy sat there called for her sympathy. How awful to be reduced to that level. And at such a young age. He was just a few years younger than her, probably still in his teens. His thin face was covered in a light stubble and lank hair swept the collar of his stained sweatshirt. So young. Surely somewhere there was a mother or a father who cared about him?

But then, Cathy's own father was dead. And she didn't see much of her mother these days. So perhaps it wasn't so strange. Perhaps he was from the country, like herself, but hadn't been as lucky as she'd been in getting a job, making a life. She felt a pang of guilt. A moment ago she'd been feeling sorry for herself but now she realised how little she had to worry about compared with someone without even a roof over his head. Talk about putting things into perspective. Her hand went to her shoulder bag. Not that the money she'd give him would do anything about his homeless state, but it might buy a hot meal or a night in a hostel.

'I wouldn't,' a voice said quietly beside her. 'He'll only spend it on drugs.'

Cathy whirled in surprise to see a man, dressed casually in black leather jacket and dark jeans, standing there, watching her. With a vague sense of alarm she said: 'I didn't hear you come up.'

'I'm sorry.' He made a gesture of reassurance. His eyes were kind, his voice gentle. 'Didn't mean to startle you.'

'That's OK.' Cathy recovered from her fright. 'It doesn't matter.' She turned to look again at the youth who sat motionless, eyes still closed, arm still outstretched in appeal. 'Isn't that just awful?' She began fumbling in her bag again.

'Yes, it is.' Out of the corner of her eye she saw the man shake his head and give a small shrug of defeat. 'A bottomless pit, I'm afraid.'

'But we've got to do something.' Cathy turned to him indignantly. 'We can't just do nothing.'

'No, we can't do nothing. But I think you're wasting your money.'

Her indignation grew. 'Don't you think I should be the judge of – '

Just then someone gave her a shove from behind. She felt herself being pushed, felt her bag strap sliding from her shoulder.

'Hey!' She made a grab for the bag. She felt the tug

on the strap as it cut into her hand and saw the stranger move forward, a look of alarm on his face. Then someone pulled hard and yanked the bag from her grasp. Her arm was thumped, knocking her backwards. As Cathy staggered, fighting to save her balance, she had the confused impression that the passageway was full of people. She heard a voice raised in protest. Then her legs went from under her. She fell to the ground. Her hands scraped over the concrete, taking her weight. For a moment she lay in a daze.

'Are you OK?' She heard the concern in the stranger's voice. As he helped her to her feet, their bodies brushed. Her face pressed briefly against the leather of his jacket, and she caught the faint tang of aftershave mixed with cigarette smoke. Something about the way he held her made her want to stand there a little longer. Instead, she shook his hands away, stepping back slightly in embarrassment. She looked up to meet two concerned eyes studying her.

'Did you hurt yourself?'

'I'm not sure.' Glancing quickly around, she saw that they were alone in the passageway except for the homeless youth who was still stretched out motionless, like a waxwork tableau. 'What happened? Who were they?'

'Kids. I tried to stop them but they were too quick for me.' He looked at her ruefully. 'I wasn't even able to break your fall.'

'It wasn't your fault.' Shaken by the speed of what had happened, Cathy found herself talking to him as if they knew each other well. 'I can't quite take it in.'

'Are you OK?' he asked again.

She quickly inspected herself. Apart from an enormous ladder in her tights and a few superficial cuts and scratches on her shins, there didn't seem to be any serious damage. Her right hand was beginning to throb but the skin was unbroken. 'I'll live, I suppose.'

'Well, that's a relief,' he said. 'I know it's not much consolation to you, but it could have been worse. Had you much in it?'

She looked blankly at him. 'Oh my God! My bag! They took my bag!'

'I know.' His glance was sympathetic. 'What did you have in it? Money? Credit cards? Keys?'

Cathy tried to think, but her thoughts were in a jumble. She shook her head. 'I just can't seem to think straight.'

'You've had a bad shock,' the man said. 'Look, what you need is to sit down and give yourself a chance to recover. How about a cup of coffee? Then I'll go with you to report it to the guards.'

Her hand was beginning to throb; her legs ached. The prospect of coffee was a welcome one. Hesitating, she glanced at him uncertainly. She saw a man in his thirties, well built, with dark brown hair and a sympathetic face. She thought the leather jacket was like something a biker would wear, but there was nothing rough or threatening about him. All the same, he was a stranger, even if he did have a pleasant voice. After what had happened it was foolish to take chances.

As if he had guessed what she was thinking, the man smiled, offering a hand. 'I'm Stephen Brown.'

Reassured by his firm handshake, she smiled back. 'Cathy Carmody.'

'We can go to the guards first if you like,' he said. 'The nearest station is only five minutes away.'

Again she hesitated. 'Well, I . . . '

'Look.' His voice was patient. 'I'm only trying to help. Tell me to buzz off if you want.'

She found herself wavering. After the fright she'd had, the last thing she wanted was to handle this on her own. She studied his face, seeing nothing but friendliness in it. If he was prepared to walk into a police station with her, he was probably genuine. She decided to trust him.

'OK. Thanks. I'd love a coffee. But maybe we should get the guards over with first.'

'Right. The garda station it is.' He smiled reassuringly at her. 'Let's go.'

As they moved away, Cathy glanced back at the homeless youth, still apparently carved in stone. The man beside her gave a resigned sigh. 'OK, OK,' he said, digging into the pocket of his jeans. As the coin chinked in the cup, the beggar's eyelids moved a fraction, then were still.

'Happy now?' Stephen Brown asked.

'Not really.' Cathy found herself wondering if the beggar knew the bag snatchers. She sighed inwardly. Was anybody what they seemed to be? 'Like you said, it's a bottomless pit.'

'You can forget about the cash,' the desk sergeant said. 'The credit cards might turn up, but to be on the safe side, you'd better cancel them. Anything else?'

'The keys to my flat.'

'We're always telling women not to carry keys in their handbags.' The sergeant had a narrow, lugubrious face and a reproving air. He reminded Cathy of a nun who had taught her at school. 'Better still, don't carry a bag at all.'

She felt a rush of exasperation. 'What am I supposed to do?'

The desk sergeant shrugged, chewing the end of his biro. 'Men manage.'

As her exasperation grew, she heard Stephen ask: 'Any chance you'll find the thieves, Sergeant?'

'Divil a bit.' The policeman shrugged again. 'A lot of them are known to the guards. Kids as young as seven or eight. But unless you actually see them do it . . .' His hands gestured defeat. 'Better get your locks changed. They might have older brothers.'

'Great,' Cathy said. 'That's all I need.'

'Look, we get this all the time.' His narrow features softened momentarily. 'At least you weren't injured.' His tone grew brisker. 'Sorry we can't be of more help.' He turned away. 'We have your phone number.'

'Come on,' Stephen said. 'Let's get that coffee.' He headed over to the door and waited for her to catch up. 'He's right. You could have been hurt. Pity they couldn't have been more help, though.'

'Doesn't surprise me.' Her exasperation had gone,

leaving her with a flat, empty feeling. 'It's been that kind of day. Everything has gone wrong for me.'

'Sorry to hear that.' He held open the door. 'We'll go over to Bewley's and you can tell me about it.'

'Are you sure? I think I've taken up enough of your time.' She glanced at him doubtfully as they came out on the steps of the police station. 'Besides, you must have made other plans.'

'Nothing I couldn't change,' he said easily. 'While you were talking to the guard I made a couple of calls on my mobile. On the other hand...' He gave her a quizzical look. 'Maybe you're meeting someone?'

Cathy shook her head. 'I met him earlier.' She felt her face redden. 'The thing is, we had a row . . . '

She saw him grin. 'It just hasn't been your day, has it? How about that coffee?'

She found herself warming to him. 'OK. I'll ring my flatmate from there.'

'She's out.' Cathy said, as she put down her mobile phone. 'I left a message.' She picked up the mug of coffee and sipped it appreciatively. 'God, I needed this.'

'I got you some ice. That hand looks painful.'

'That's really thoughtful of you.' She stared at him in surprise. 'How did you manage that?'

'It's slack this hour of the evening.' He glanced around the half-empty restaurant. 'The woman at the counter was very helpful.'

As she took the plastic bag of ice cubes, it occurred to Cathy that he was the kind of man who would always find women helpful. She gasped slightly as the chilly bag touched her burning skin. 'Are you a doctor or a nurse or something?' She wouldn't have been too surprised if he was. There was something about him that commanded trust.

Stephen shook his head. 'But I've done a bit of First Aid.'

'Lucky for me I met you.' While she was adjusting the cold compress, Cathy studied him covertly. Nice eyes. Good build. And that smile of his. It really transformed his face. Not, of course, that she was remotely interested. As of tonight, she'd given up on men. But that didn't mean she couldn't sit and chat with one, did it? 'I think I'm due a bit of luck,' she said with a slight shudder. 'After the day I've had.'

'So you were saying.' He cocked an enquiring eyebrow. 'Want to tell me about it?'

Still feeling bruised after her row with Alan, Cathy looked at him doubtfully. Men could be such shits. Yet there was something about this one that invited her confidence. Maybe it was because he was just that bit older. She remembered the way he'd held the door for her when they were going out of the police station and the unhesitating manner in which he'd insisted on paying for the coffee. It made her feel – well, *cherished*. He came across as a really nice guy. And there was no harm in talking, after all. It would be good to get it off her chest.

'I've just broken up with my boyfriend.' To her surprise, she found herself pouring out the whole story.

'And so you walked out of the pub and left him?' Stephen smiled at her across the table. 'Good for you. He sounds like a real two-timer. A man like that doesn't deserve a lovely girl like you.'

'It's great that you can see my point of view,' Cathy said. 'That was one of the problems with Alan. I see that now. With him there was only one side. His. Even if he hadn't been unfaithful, there still would have been problems. But, you're right, he *was* a two-timer. God, I could kick myself.' She felt her face grow hot. 'That weasel! How could I have been such a fool?'

'*He* was the fool,' Stephen said.

'Thanks.' She felt heartened by the admiration in his eyes. 'But it still hurts.'

'It always does when someone lets you down. But people make mistakes – do things they're sorry for afterwards.' He looked at her speculatively. 'Maybe if he . . . ?'

'No chance! Once I heard about that other woman, I knew it was over. I could never trust him again.'

She saw him nod. 'Everything depends on trust. If you haven't that in a relationship – '

'You've nothing.' Cathy looked at him eagerly. 'That's just the way I feel.'

His eyes met hers. There was silence for a moment. Then Stephen asked: 'Was the ice any help?'

She looked at her hand in surprise. She'd forgotten about it while they were talking. 'The pain's gone.' The ice had melted in the plastic bag. As she poured the cold water away into her empty coffee mug she felt a rush of gratitude. 'Do you know something? You're a great listener. Your wife's a lucky woman.'

He smiled faintly. 'I'm not married.'

'Well, your partner then?' A man like that was bound to have someone. The nice ones always did.

'No partner either,' he said equably.

'Oh?' In spite of herself, Cathy felt a stirring of interest. 'No, don't tell me.' She grinned at him. 'You've been working on an oil rig for years.'

Stephen smiled again, shaking his head.

'Just come out of prison? Stranded on a desert island?'

He burst out laughing at this.

'I know, I know.' Cathy was laughing too. She tried to think of something even more outlandish. 'You entered a monastery at the age of eighteen?'

She saw his smile fade. 'Not exactly.'

'What's that supposed to mean?' She stared at him in surprise.

He looked uncomfortable. 'Perhaps I should have said . . .'

'What?'

He gave her a sheepish smile. 'I'm a priest.'

Cathy felt a sharp pain in the pit of her stomach. 'What kind of priest?'

'A Catholic priest, of course.' He seemed surprised. 'What other kind?'

'Isn't that just typical? For your information, there are Anglican priests and Buddhist ones, to mention but a few.'

She saw his face redden. 'You're right, of course. I wasn't thinking.'

'You're not the only ones in the universe, you know.'

'I never thought we were.' He gave her a puzzled look. 'Why are you so angry?'

'I'm not angry.' But she heard her own voice rising above the hum of the restaurant and noticed a woman at another table glancing curiously at her. She said more quietly: 'What makes you think I'm angry? I was surprised, that's all.'

'No,' Stephen said. 'It's more than that.' His eyes were troubled. 'You don't think much of priests, do you?'

She forced herself to meet his gaze. 'No,' she said evenly. 'I don't.' She glanced at her watch. 'Thanks for all your help, *Father*. You've been very kind. But I can manage for myself from now on.' She got to her feet, feeling a kind of triumph at the stunned look on his face. But the pain in her stomach was still there.

'Wait!' Stephen stood up too. 'Look, I don't know what the problem is. But I can see you're upset. If you don't want my help, I won't force it on you. At least let me give you the money for a taxi. A loan,' he added quickly. 'You can post it back to me if you want.'

She waited in silence while he wrote down his address and took the two pieces of paper with a curt nod of thanks. As she walked away from the table, in her mind's eye she could still see the look on his face.

What was all that about? Stephen shook his head in bewilderment as the girl moved away across the restaurant. He felt shocked at the speed with which it had happened. One minute they were laughing together, the best of friends. The next she was glaring at him as if he were Public Enemy Number One. It didn't make sense. Of course, some people had a thing about the clergy: he came across them sometimes. They were usually older people who'd left the Church and still associated it with the authoritarian ways of their youth. The worst you would encounter in someone Cathy's age was an amiable indifference. Unless they happened to be junkies looking for a fix. But that was a different matter. Sometimes women pretended to be disappointed when they heard he was a priest and would make half-laughing comments about the waste of a good man, but these would be women past their prime, wryly good-humoured about disappointed hopes. Not like Cathy, who had the kind of face and figure that men noticed. He could see heads turning to watch her as she threaded her way through the tables towards the exit. He smiled wryly to himself. No, someone like Cathy definitely wouldn't be interested in the likes of him. Whatever the reason for her anger, that wasn't it. As she disappeared from view, he felt a pang of regret. He'd never know now. Pity it had to end that way.

Still, a man in his position had no business even thinking like that. Put her out of your head. Start thinking about the sermon you've to write for that wedding at the weekend. As he felt in his pocket for cigarettes, he remembered that he was trying to give them up. He sighed in resignation and opened a stick of chewing gum instead. A poor substitute for nicotine, but better than nothing. He decided to have another cup of coffee before heading for home. Caffeine was bad for you too, but a man was allowed some vices. When he came back from the counter, his mind was safely on Saturday's sermon. But then his eye fell on the wet, crumpled bag that had held the ice cubes, and he found himself thinking of her again, wondering if she had got home safely. He remembered that he had given her his phone number. Would she get in touch with him? It didn't seem likely. All the same, he couldn't help hoping she would.

TWO

How could she have been so rude? Cathy asked herself as she got into the taxi. How could she have stormed out of the restaurant like that? The man was only trying to be kind. She felt a twinge of embarrassment at the memory of Stephen's stunned expression, and wondered what had come over her to react in the way she had. But she didn't want to think about that now. The important thing was to get home. She gave the taxi driver the address, and leaned back in her seat with an exhausted sigh. What an evening! It would be a relief when it was over. But at least the journey wouldn't take long. That was one of the advantages of having an apartment close to the city centre. At peak time, of course, it could take anything up to an hour, but this late the traffic was light and she'd be home in fifteen minutes.

And it wasn't the only good thing about it, she thought, as the taxi made its way through the well-lit streets. Apart from its convenient location, the apartment was the nicest place she'd lived in since she came to Dublin nearly six years before. She recalled the sense of jubilation which she and her friend Liz had felt the previous summer when they moved into the bright, modern apartment. After a succession of cramped, dingy bedsitters, they were finally able to afford somewhere decent to live. Both of them felt their careers were taking off. Cathy had recently been promoted to manager in the computer shop where she worked and Liz, a journalist, had just signed a new contract with a national daily newspaper. The sky was the limit. 'Next stop the editor's chair,' she recalled her friend saying jubilantly. 'And a wealthy boyfriend for you, Cathy.'

Not that she wanted a man with money. Just someone she could depend on. And Alan had seemed to fit the bill. Cathy frowned to herself, peering out the window as the taxi crossed the canal and headed up the Rathmines Road. He was good company, had a steady job and was an attentive lover. The kind of man her mother would have called 'good husband material'. It just showed how wrong Mum was. He was nothing but a deceitful two-timer. Cathy was still smarting over the slimy way he'd twisted and turned in his attempts to avoid being found out, blaming everyone but himself for his actions. And the sickening thing was that when they'd first started seeing each other, he'd seemed so genuine.

How could she have been so wrong about him? Was it because she was a bad judge of people? Liz sometimes told her she was naive. But was it really naive to expect people to be straightforward and sincere? Cathy didn't think so. It was the way she'd been brought up, after all. Just because Alan had been a liar there was no reason to give up on the human race. Most people were OK. But what about the ruffians who'd snatched her bag? Stephen said they were kids, she reminded herself. Maybe they didn't know any better. God only knew what kind of homes they'd come from, what kind of parents they had. That was the kind of thing her father would have said. He had been such a forgiving person. The trouble was that she didn't feel ready to forgive anyone at the moment. Not Alan, and certainly not the kids who stole her bag. She thought again of Stephen, wondering if he would be shocked at her attitude.

Priests were big into forgiveness, weren't they? But when you thought about it, he hadn't tried to make any excuses for the thieves. And he was the one who'd said she shouldn't give any money to the beggar. Funny sort of priest. If he really *was* a priest. What about those jeans? And that leather jacket? Maybe it was just a line, like blokes pretending to be married when they weren't. And not married when they were. Could you trust any of them?

Just as it occurred to her that her thoughts had gone full circle, she realised that the taxi was backing into the narrow mews where she lived. She saw the lights on in the downstairs apartment and breathed a sigh of relief. Thank God, Liz was home. She'd have money for the taxi. Then she remembered the twenty pounds the priest had lent her. It was still in her jacket pocket where she'd thrust it on leaving the café. As the driver counted the change into her hand, she thought briefly of Stephen's face when she'd left him at the table. Again, she pushed the memory firmly to the back of her mind.

She could worry about that later. Right now the important thing was to get indoors and put her feet up. Maybe have a hot shower.

The lights of the taxi receded from the mews and disappeared down the street. Cathy rang the doorbell. When she heard movements inside, her heart began to thump. She suddenly remembered what the sergeant in the police station had said about having the locks changed. Maybe it wasn't Liz inside after all. Maybe it was the thieves! For God's sake, get a grip, she told herself. If it was thieves, they'd hardly come to the door, would they? All the same, there was no sense in taking chances. She stood well back from the doorstep, waiting cautiously as the door swung open. She sighed with relief at the sight of Liz standing there, her head swathed in a towel and her face covered in a white clay mask. The tiny hallway was wreathed in steam from the nearby bathroom. A flowery scent filled the air.

'Oh, it's you!' Liz said through stiff lips, trying not to disturb the mask. 'What happened your keys?'

You can forget about that shower, Cathy told herself. If Liz had been having one of her lengthy baths it would be hours before the water heated up again. But it didn't matter. She was too tired anyway.

'Why didn't you pick up the phone? I've been trying to get through for ages.' She pushed past Liz without waiting for an answer, went into the living room and collapsed on the couch. 'Don't tell me.' Kicking off her shoes, she stretched her legs out with a grateful shudder. 'I forgot. It's Monday night . . . '

She saw Liz nod gingerly.

'... and you gave your phone number to some guy on Saturday night and you don't want to talk to him now?'

The other woman's eyes gleamed like two dark circles in the white face mask. Despite her exasperation, Cathy gave a half-hysterical giggle. 'You look like a mummy from a horror film.'

'Mind what you're saying.' Liz grinned and grey fissures began appearing on the mask's whiteness. She put her hands up to her face. 'Back in a sec. Then we can talk.'

'Wait, Liz.' But the other woman had disappeared out the door.

Cathy felt tired and on edge. While she waited for Liz to return, she glanced quickly around the room to reassure herself that everything was in place, that nothing had been taken. It was a relief to see the Monet prints side by side on the wall, just above the framed charcoal sketch which one of her sisters had drawn of the bungalow back home. And the family group was still there: a younger Cathy beaming out at her, her parents and sisters caught forever in time. The clock was ticking away on the little mahogany writing desk that had belonged to her father. Beside it lay a couple of books she'd left there that morning. The long plum-coloured velvet curtains Liz had picked up for half-nothing at a country auction were drawn cosily across the patio doors. The television was silent in the corner. Everything was where it should be.

Stupid to feel relieved. After all, it was her bag that had been stolen. The apartment was OK. Nothing else was gone. Yet something else had been taken, she knew. Her peace of mind. Her trust in the order of things. It might take a lot longer to restore those than to replace the credit cards or the locks on the door. Still, it was good to be home. Good to have someone to talk to. That is, if Liz could settle in one place long enough to listen.

A movement in the doorway. Her friend was back, her face pink and glowing without the mask. She removed the towel from her head and began rubbing at her short hair until it stood up in black spikes around her face. She grinned at Cathy, inviting her admiration.

'Well, am I beautiful, or what? Listen, I hope you're not hungry, because I ate the last of the bread.' She gestured at the archway which led to the tiny modern kitchen. 'The ham too.' She pulled a wry face. 'Got an attack of the munchies earlier. God! I'm such a pig! But not to worry –'

'Listen, Liz . . .'

' – the Spar on the corner doesn't close till eleven. And, seeing as you still have your coat on – '

'Liz . . . ' Cathy felt suddenly exasperated. 'Will you shut up for a minute and let me get a word in.'

'I know, I *know*,' Liz looked penitent. 'It was my turn to buy food. But you've no idea the day I've had. I've been trying to chase up a story. But I was let down. My editor has been such a shit about it.' Her mouth twisted sadly. 'I don't think he's going to renew my contract.'

'Oh, Liz!' Cathy momentarily forget her own problems. She knew that Liz's ambition was to be made permanent on the staff of the newspaper. 'What will you do?'

Liz shrugged. 'Cross that bridge when I come to it. What the hell!' She grinned at Cathy. 'Maybe I'm overreacting.' Her eyes narrowed. 'Listen, I wasn't expecting you home. I thought you were meeting Alan.'

'I was. And I did.' Cathy's voice was crisp. 'Alan's history.' To her surprise, she realised she didn't care.

'I don't *believe* it! So you finally gave him the bullet.' Liz looked at her in admiration. 'I never thought you'd do it.'

'I mightn't be as tough as you, Liz, but I won't let anyone make a fool of me.'

'Good for you, kiddo. Although it seems to have taken a lot out of you.' Liz looked speculatively at Cathy's legs, which were propped up against the arm of the sofa. 'What happened your tights?' She reached out and plucked at the ribs of laddered nylon. 'Did Alan do that? I must say he never struck me as the violent sort.' Speculation turned to amusement. 'Or was it done in a fit of passion?'

'You can stop laughing, because it isn't funny. No, Alan didn't do that. I fell.' Cathy felt suddenly close to tears. 'You're not the only one who's had a bad day. My bag was snatched. Keys, money, everything.' Her voice broke on a sob. 'I kept trying to get through on the phone and you wouldn't answer . . . '

'Your bag? You're kidding!' Liz stared at her, open-mouthed. 'When did it happen? Where?'

'A couple of hours ago. In town.' She shook her head distractedly. 'I can't believe it either. But it happened.'

'God! That's just awful. I never *realised*.' Liz showed her concern. 'I didn't mean to slag. But you know me. Anything for a laugh. Listen, tell us, were you hurt? God, there's a bruise on your knee.'

Her sympathy was like a balm. Cathy's spirits began to rise. 'I'm OK now. I got a fright at the time. Luckily, this man came to my rescue – he brought me to the police station . . . '

'A man?' Liz's interest was aroused. 'Was he good looking?'

Cathy sighed. 'Is that all you ever think of? Actually he wasn't bad, but . . . '

'The plot thickens.' Liz raised her eyebrows. 'Hang on a sec. I'll put the kettle on for a cup of tea. Then you're going to tell me *everything*.'

Liz could be a good listener when she wanted. She gave her full attention to the story, interrupting occasionally to ask a question or clarify a point. It was a side to her Cathy didn't see very often. Liz was probably like that when she was working. Although she was impressed by the other woman's professional attitude, Cathy had a sense of doubt. Liz was a journalist, after all, and her work was very important to her.

'You're not going to put all this in your paper, are you?'

Liz shook her head. 'Mugging stories are two-a-penny. Of course, the tabloids might be interested in the priest angle. Particularly if he made a pass. But we're not a tabloid,' she said sanctimoniously. She darted a quick glance at Cathy. 'Did he come on to you?'

'Of course not.' Cathy was shocked. 'What a filthy mind you have.'

'It isn't me has the filthy mind.' Liz chuckled. 'But you were lucky, really. Not about the bag being taken. That must have been awful. But to have met that priest. You could just as easily have been picked up by some kind of conman.'

'Do you think priests aren't conmen?' The words were out before Cathy could stop them.

'God, it's not like you to be so cynical!' Liz looked taken aback. 'But you've a point there, kiddo. All that pie in the sky. You'll-get-your-reward-in-heaven lark. I don't believe a word of it. "Seize the day" is my motto. But – '

'I didn't quite mean it that way . . . '

' – I've always put you down as being religious. I don't know why. It's not as if you bothered with Mass or anything. It's more your attitude. You can be a bit *soft*.'

'Thanks very much.'

'No, don't get me wrong.' Her expression was affectionate as she looked at Cathy. 'It's one of the things I like about you. But take tonight, for instance. If you hadn't been so worked up about some junkie sleeping rough – '

'We don't know he was a junkie.'

'Come on, Cathy.' Liz's eyebrows rose expressively. 'Get real. Most of that crowd are addicts of some kind. Believe me, you're wasting your sympathy. Now, if you'd been paying more attention to yourself . . .'

'I wouldn't have got mugged? Is that it?' Cathy looked at her incredulously. 'Are you saying it was my own fault?'

'God, no,' Liz said hastily. 'Where did you get that idea? All I'm saying is that sometimes you can be too kind for your own good. That's why I was surprised when you started getting cynical. What have you got against priests, anyway?'

The speed of the question disconcerted Cathy. 'Nothing, nothing. Just a general observation. Some of them don't strike me as being sincere, that's all.'

'There are a lot of hypocrites around.' Liz nodded. 'Mind you, it's not just the priests. But this guy, Stephen, was all right, wasn't he?'

'Yes.' She looked down at her hand and saw that the swelling had gone. The ice cubes had done their work. 'He was very kind.'

'It's easy for a man to be kind to a girl with your looks.' Liz gave a cynical cackle. 'Probably fancied the pants off you. If you'd looked like a dog, it'd be a different story.'

'Don't be ridiculous.' She had a sudden memory of his hands helping her to her feet. 'He was just doing the Good Samaritan act.'

'Oh yeah? Funny he never mentioned he was a priest.'

'Well, he did at the end. He wasn't trying to hide it.'
Cathy wondered why she was defending him.

'You liked him, didn't you?'

'He was OK, I suppose.'

'Sounds to me like you fancied him.'

'No, I didn't.' She was amazed at her own vehemence. 'But even if I did, what'd be the point? The man was a priest. In case you hadn't heard, they take vows of celibacy. They're not supposed to go out with women. End of story.'

'OK, OK. I get the message.' Liz threw her hands up in defeat. 'You don't fancy him. That's official. But it's not quite end-of-story, is it? What about the money he lent you?'

'I forgot about that.' Cathy felt in her jacket pocket. 'He gave me his address.' She smoothed out the scrap of paper. 'Probably some monastery somewhere.' A thought struck her. 'But he couldn't have been a monk. His head wasn't shaven. In fact, he had lots of hair. *And* a leather jacket.'

'Cool. Had he a Harley Davidson nearby? Are you sure he was a priest?'

'Nothing cool about where he lives,' Cathy said. 'Looks like an ordinary housing estate.'

'You can say that again.' Liz peered at the address written in squiggles of black biro. 'That's kind of a rough area, if it's where I think it is. I knew a bloke once who came from around there. In places like that they eat their young.'

'Maybe you *should* be writing for the tabloids, Liz.'

'Don't look at me like that, kiddo. I'm only telling you what the man said. Anyway, what are you worried about? All you have to do is put a cheque in an envelope. The postman will do the rest. He probably gets danger money.'

'Yes, I suppose.' Cathy was doubtful. 'I wish now I'd been nicer to him. He must have thought I was really rude, walking out on him like that.'

'I wouldn't lose any sleep over it,' Liz said. 'He's a professional do-gooder, remember. He'll get extra heavenly points. Anyway I'm sure he's used to meeting a lot worse than you.'

'You're probably right. But – '

'But nothing. Trust Auntie Liz, she knows about these things. Tell us, are you hungry? Do you fancy a burger and chips?'

'God, yes.' She suddenly remembered that she hadn't had anything to eat since lunchtime. 'But I've no money.'

'Yes, you have. You've the change from the twenty pounds, you eejit. But you'd better hold on to that. It'll be a few days before you get your new credit card. The burgers are on me. And what's more, I'll even go down to the chipper and get them.' Liz went over to a wall mirror to check her reflection and ran a comb through her hair. 'Will I get coleslaw too? And to hell with the diet.'

'To hell with the diet,' Cathy said absently. 'Will you be OK on your own?'

'There's always plenty of people out on the street

at this hour. But don't worry, I'm armed.' She held up a small can of hairspray. 'Good as a guard dog. Try and stay awake till I come back with the food, will you?'

'I'll do my best. Listen, Liz, I owe you one.'

'You can lend me that new top of yours next Friday night.'

'Ah, Liz. I haven't worn it yet.'

'Well, then, those black fuck-me high heels. They do things for my legs.'

'You fight a hard bargain,' Cathy groaned. 'Some friend you turned out to be.'

As the door slammed behind Liz, Cathy recalled with a smile their first meeting four years before. The lease was up on the bedsitter she was renting and she'd answered an advertisement to share a house in Terenure with three others. It was a good house; there'd been a lot of people after it. By the time she got there, the room was taken. As she trudged despondently down the garden path, she saw a dark-haired girl around her own age pushing open the gate. Although it was a mild evening in April, she wore a long trench coat over boots and a black beret which was perched rakishly on her thick, shoulder-length hair. Liz told Cathy afterwards that this was how she thought journalists dressed.

'Am I too late?' she called out, as if they were old friends. 'I suppose *you* got it?'

'No,' Cathy said as she came up to her. 'I missed it too. It's gone.'

The other girl grimaced. 'What the hell! Who needs

it anyway?' She glanced at the neighbouring houses. 'Suburbia! Yuck!'

'I thought it would be nice,' Cathy said wistfully. She liked the estate, with its well-kept houses. The gardens were bright with daffodils and other spring flowers. The trees lining the roadway were beginning to put out leafy shoots. Children played on an open green area. 'Reminds me a bit of home.'

'That's just it.' There was a wealth of meaning in the laugh Liz gave. 'Like I said, who needs it? Anyway.' Her voice was decisive. 'It's miles from the nearest pub.'

'I never thought of that.'

'Not many people do.' Her eyes gleamed. 'Until it's too late.'

Cathy laughed. She fell into step with the other girl. After they'd exchanged names, they walked together towards the bus stop. By the time the bus came, she'd learned that Liz lived in a small town not far from Dublin and had just got herself a job in the city.

'In theory,' Liz said. 'In *theory*, I could get the bus in every day. And home again in the evening. It's what my mother wants. But what good would that be? The city's where the action is.' Her eyes danced as she looked around the dimly lit lounge bar. 'Nightlife! Opportunities to meet new people.' She gave a wicked grin. 'I mean men, of course.'

'I'll drink to that.' Cathy's spirits had begun to lift. She'd recovered from her disappointment over the house. Liz had an air of excitement about her that was infectious. 'And to your new job. What is it exactly?'

'Hard to say. Kind of general duties, if you know what I mean.' A shadow crossed her face. 'It's not one of the big dailies. That's the next step. But it *is* a newspaper. A weekly one. You know, the kind they put through your letterbox. The money's crap – I'll probably have to go waitressing as well – but it's a foot in the door.'

Cathy nodded. 'You have to start somewhere. I'm in an office but I don't intend to stay there.' The optimism with which she'd left home in County Cork two years before began to rekindle. Liz was right. The city *was* full of opportunity. 'I think I'll do a diploma at night. Get more qualifications. Another string to my bow.'

'Attagirl!' The other girl's dark eyes twinkled. 'God, I can't wait to come and live here. Can't wait to leave that one-horse town.' She gave a melodramatic groan. 'Sometimes I feel stifled by it.'

Cathy smiled sympathetically. 'That's exactly how I felt before I left home. But big places can be lonely.' She pictured the large, impersonal office where she worked. 'It 's not all that easy to make friends.'

Liz laughed. 'I've already met you and I haven't even moved yet.' There was something irrepressible about her, Cathy thought. Like a rubber ball, ready to bounce back. But there was more to the other girl than that, she suspected. Studying the vivid face opposite her, she sensed that beneath the bubbly personality lay a determination to succeed that matched her own. What kind of a friend would Liz make?

'Look! You can be lonely anywhere, kiddo,' Liz said. 'In your own family even.'

'That's true.' Cathy thought back to the years at home after her father died. Although Mum had done her best, she never seemed to have as much time for her as Dad would have had. And her older sisters had been caught up in their own pursuits. She felt a sudden sense of fellowship with Liz.

'Welcome to Dublin.' She lifted her glass in salute. 'I'll help you find somewhere, if you like.'

'Why don't we look for a place together?' Liz asked. 'I think we'd make a great team.'

For the first time in two years, Dublin seemed a much less lonely place. A warm, positive feeling took hold of Cathy. The past couple of years had been difficult ones. But now it was time to put them behind her. Time to move on.

Until tonight, she'd never looked back.

Examining memories was like reaching down into a lucky dip. You never knew what you might come up with. She couldn't seem to stop after she'd unwrapped the first one. Meeting Liz had been a turning point in her life, for the better. But there had been others that had not been so good and she didn't want to dig them up. Her thoughts skated over the surface of these memories the way your fingers scrabbled through the lucky dip, feeling the shapes, putting off making a choice. And then, abruptly, she grasped one and pulled it into the light.

She found herself thinking of her father. He'd have been dead for thirteen years on 7 August next. The date was easy to remember because it was the day after her birthday. She'd been twelve. A skinny kid with a suntanned face and long brown hair with golden highlights in it. At least, that was the way she looked in the photograph hanging on the apartment wall. She glanced up at it now to see the birthday girl standing between her mother and father, with her two older sisters sitting on the grass in front of them. A happy family group, caught and preserved forever. It had been taken by her mother's sister, Aunt Helen, in the back garden of their home in the small town where they lived at the time, not far from Cork. Out of range of the camera, the other guests – mostly girls from her class at school – sprawled around on the lawn watching them.

Also out of range, but in Cathy's line of vision, was the new bicycle which she'd been given by her parents that morning. Mountain bikes were in that year. Several girls she knew had them and Cathy was thrilled with her present. As she took up her position for the photograph, her eyes sought out the bike propped against the back wall of the bungalow. Her gaze passed admiringly over its sturdy frame, its bright, painted mudguards, its gleaming bell, and she had a sudden vision of herself, dressed in her new school uniform, skimming down the hill to secondary school, her books packed into the capacious basket in front of her, her head held high.

An exciting yet scary vision. Scary because second-ary school, which she was starting in three weeks' time, was an unknown world. She was leaving the certainties of childhood behind her. Leaving the primary school – where she'd had the same teacher all year, and where she knew everyone in her class – to enter a world of strangers. Some of the girls in class with her would be going too. But there would be many unfamiliar faces. She wouldn't know any of the teachers. And, she realised with a pang of apprehension, none of them would know *her*.

What made it even worse was the fact that her parents wouldn't be there. Both of them were teachers in the primary school. Although Cathy's father had never taught her and she had only had Mum for a year, way back in senior infants, she'd always taken their presence for granted. They had been an integral part of school life ever since she was tiny. And now she was heading off into a new world without them. Wouldn't anyone feel a bit scared?

Still, it was exciting too. Going to secondary school meant she was growing up. People couldn't treat her like a child any more. She'd be as good as Noreen and Detta. Not that she foresaw much help from her older sisters in coming to terms with her new world. Noreen, studying for her Leaving Cert, would be too far removed to have any time for her during school hours. And as for Detta . . . well, hadn't she made it brutally clear that someone fifteen, going on sixteen, wouldn't be seen dead hobnobbing with a mere first year?

I'll manage without her, Cathy thought. She was old enough to cycle to school on her own. And with a bike like that, she couldn't wait to start. While the photograph was being taken, she was so caught up with her own thoughts that she barely listened to Aunt Helen's shouted instructions.

'Say cheese, everyone. Oh, Cathy, you didn't smile.' Her aunt sighed impatiently. Helen, an imposing woman in her forties with a decisive manner, was every inch a hospital sister – a complete contrast to Louise, Cathy's mother, who was slender, willowy and vague. 'You weren't looking at the camera. I'll have to take another one.' Helen threw Cathy a stern look. 'This time, pay attention.'

Her father chuckled. 'You listen to Matron.' Cathy grinned back, aware of the friendly rivalry between him and his sister-in-law. But Dad could be bossy too. Earlier on he'd been a real live wire, dashing around, cajoling people into posing for him, even when they were camera-shy like Mum. He'd shot a lot of pictures of Cathy, blowing out the candles. Larking about on the grass with Noreen and Detta. Having her face licked by Jeff, their black-and-white mongrel. After he'd taken a group shot of Cathy with her classmates, he had suggested that Helen take one of the family.

'You too, Louise.' He summoned Cathy's mother, who was passing by with a plate of birthday cake in her hand. 'No sneaking out of it.'

'Now, John, you know I *hate* having my picture taken.' She looked at him pleadingly. 'Must we?'

'Yes, Missus, we must.' He gave her a mock stern glance. 'Come on, now, and do what you're told.'

'If you say so, John.' She sighed, handing the plate to one of the guests.

Anyone would think he was some kind of tyrant. Cathy felt a pang of irritation with her mother. Dad liked his own way but he was never dictatorial. She couldn't understand why Mum felt she had to play up to him. There was no place in the 1980s for that kind of 'little woman' act. When she grew up, Cathy would want a man to treat her as an equal. Otherwise she wouldn't be interested in marriage.

Not that she wanted to get married. Not for years and years, anyway. Noreen and Detta were always giggling over fellas, but Cathy wasn't interested in men. She'd rather have a bicycle any day. Her irritation evaporated at the thought of her new possession. Waiting for Aunt Helen to take another picture, her eyes strayed to it again. She felt her father's arm across her shoulders and his fingers gave her arm an affectionate squeeze.

'Look at the camera, Cathy. This is an important birthday for you.' His voice was thoughtful suddenly. 'In its own way, a milestone.'

But Cathy only half-heard him. As soon as the picture was taken, she shrugged his arm away and scampered over the grass to examine the new bike again, her heart full of the thrill of ownership.

If only I'd paid more attention to him, she thought now as she gazed at the photograph. If I had only realised. But how could she? How could anyone at that party? How could they have known that less than twenty-four hours later, on the main road to Cork, his three-year-old Fiesta would have a head-on collision with a lorry coming out of a dangerous bend? That Dad would be killed instantly and the other man badly injured? It transpired that it was the lorry driver's fault: he had been too far over the line. But knowing that wouldn't bring Dad back. Nothing would.

But why was she thinking about it now? She'd got over all that years before. It had happened half a lifetime ago. Although she occasionally thought about him, there were times when she couldn't remember what he looked like, or how his voice sounded. Yet at other times he seemed very close. Like now. She gazed probingly at the photograph, as if by examining her father's features she could somehow learn more about him.

Dad would be in his early sixties now, but in the photo he was forever forty-nine. Still youthful. Still had his hair. Tanned and fit-looking in a short-sleeved polo shirt and casual trousers. A gleam of humour in his eye. He'd been a man with such enthusiasm for life, she recalled. A great sense of fun. But he'd had a serious side to him too. He hated injustice and had a strong social conscience, often espousing causes where other people would be indifferent. She heard him say once that his sense of humour was the only thing that saved him from being a fanatic. She wondered how true that was. All she knew was that he'd been on his way to an Amnesty International meeting in Cork the day he'd been killed. What a waste. Cathy felt her eyes fill with sudden tears.

But what had brought this on? Why start thinking

about her father? Into her mind came the image of the man she'd met earlier. He hadn't looked like Dad. He was much younger, anyway. And taller. But she remembered the warm, safe feeling she'd experienced in Stephen's company. There was something solid about him. Something good.

It's just your imagination. Someone you met for such a short time. You know nothing about him. She imagined how Liz would laugh if she told her of her feelings. Or if she didn't laugh, she'd make too much of it. 'So you did fancy him,' she'd say. Which wouldn't be true. But try explaining that to Liz and you'd be met with a sceptical grin. Liz was a dear. But when it came to men she had a one-track mind. Better not say anything to her. There wasn't any point.

Because nothing was going to come of it, she told herself as she heard Liz coming in through the hall door. He'd been a nice man who'd helped her when she was in need. If there were more people like him, the world would be a better place. Tomorrow she'd send back his money with a thank-you note. And that would be that.

THREE

A bell woke Stephen abruptly. He reached through the darkness for the clock on his bedside locker, his fingers pressing ineffectually at the alarm button until his tired brain registered that the ringing sound came from the telephone. He grabbed the receiver and fell back against the pillows.

'Yes?'

'I hope I didn't disturb you, Father.' The carefully modulated voice of Breeda Cullen, the church sacristan, sounded in his ear.

'What?' Stephen felt stunned with fatigue, having spent most of the night with a dying parishioner. He glanced at the window, where a watery light was filtering through the gaps in the curtains. 'What time is it, anyway?'

'Just gone seven-thirty, Father.'

'God, Breeda, I'm only in bed since five. Can't it wait?'

'Did you know you're saying the early Mass?'

'No, I'm not!' He sat bolt upright, instantly awake. 'I'm saying the ten o'clock. Father Mulvey's on early rota this week. You know that.'

There was a hesitancy at the other end of the line. 'He's put you down for today. I assumed he'd have told you.'

No you didn't, Stephen thought. Old man Mulvey's coming the hound again. That's why you're ringing me. He stifled a yawn. 'What about Father Hennessy?'

'Father Brendan's away on a course.' The sacristan was apologetic but firm. 'I'm afraid there's no one but you.' A note of urgency sharpened her voice. 'And the early birds will start arriving any minute.'

'Great. Just great.' He felt sorry for himself suddenly. What in God's name had possessed him to become a priest? You were expected to be at everyone's beck and call and have no life of your own. And now it looked as if you weren't supposed to get any sleep either. And what was it all for? So that power-hungry characters like Father Dan fucking Mulvey could throw their weight around under the guise of doing God's will? It's not as if anyone appreciates what you're doing. You must be some kind of masochist to put up with it. It hit him suddenly that he was beginning to think like his own father, who had no love for the clergy. No, Dad, you're wrong. He remembered the look of peace on the face of the dying woman he'd anointed a few hours earlier and thought of other deathbeds where his presence had brought comfort. What I do *is* useful. As he reached for the light switch, he spoke quickly into the phone.

'Let there be no panic, Breeda. I'm on my way.'

When he had time, he liked to walk to the parish church from the dingy housing estate where he lived, a journey which took him past row after row of similar houses with cramped, featureless gardens set in roads, crescents, drives and avenues, all with a common name, like variations on a theme. Although there was nothing uplifting about the route, especially not on a dank, grey February morning like this, he always felt that the fifteen-minute walk helped prepare him for saying Mass. But there wasn't time today. As Stephen dashed to his four-year-old Nissan Primera parked on the concrete strip outside his front door, he waved briefly to his next-door neighbour, a middle-aged man in stained overalls who was loading an old fridge into a battered van in his own driveway. Then he backed the car into the road, just managing to avoid a teenage boy in a greasy anorak and tattered jeans who'd appeared from nowhere. Before Stephen could say anything, the youth mouthed something and held up two fingers, then loped away on thick-soled runners.

'Nice to see you, too.' Stephen grimaced as he straightened the steering wheel and revved the engine. There was a time when something like that would have bothered him. It no longer did. There were worse things than the insolence of the young. But he knew that some of his older colleagues, those already having difficulty adjusting to a world which had lost its respect for priests, would see it as part of a general malaise affecting society.

Who knows, maybe they're right, he thought. But Stephen didn't have time to ponder questions like that. He turned the corner and drove quickly through a network of roads until the high, domed roof of the parish church came into view. Indicating right, he went through the gate into the paved churchyard. St Mary's, an imposing building set in its own grounds, had been built at some point in the 1930s, a time of great piety and packed churches. According to older parishioners, weekday masses had been well attended throughout the fifties and sixties and even into the seventies, but since then, the numbers had gradually fallen. Today, in the second month of the new century, Stephen knew he'd be lucky to find more than a dozen people in the church. And none of them a day under seventy. He gave a resigned smile as he saw an elderly man, accompanied by a woman of around the same age, shuffling up the front steps to the main door. Sometimes it seemed as if half his parishioners had one foot in eternity already. It was only a few hours since he'd administered the last rites to one of their neighbours. How soon would it be before he buried this pair?

Lack of sleep was making him morbid, he told himself. What he needed was a strong cup of coffee to get the adrenalin going. But it would have to wait. As he parked the car at the side of the church near the sacristy, he glanced at the dashboard clock. Made it, with a few minutes to spare. Better get a move on, though. God, how he hated the feeling of being rushed. There'd only been enough time to throw on his clothes and have a quick shave before jumping into the car. And now he'd another hasty dash through the drizzling rain. Slightly breathless, he arrived in the sacristy to find the sacristan, a dark-suited woman in her fifties, waiting for him, a long-suffering look on her face.

'One of those mornings, Father.' Although she was married, with two teenage sons, Breeda Cullen had a prim air to her. With her short, greying hair and severely cut suit she looked more like most people's idea of a nun than either of the parish sisters, who usually dressed more casually. 'The altar server is down with flu. There wasn't time to get anyone else, but I'll do the responses.'

'Fine, Breeda.' He wondered if there was any point in asking why the parish priest wasn't saying the early Mass. It wouldn't be the first time Father Mulvey had changed arrangements without informing anyone. After a year in the parish, he should be used to his superior's high-handed ways. As he hastily robed himself in his Mass vestments, he said, 'Don't tell me the boss has got flu as well.'

'Not to my knowledge.' Breeda's careful voice gave nothing away. Stephen sometimes wondered how someone with a similar background to his own came to be living in a working-class parish, but they weren't on close enough terms to ask. Hers was the kind of personality which discouraged intimacies.

'Well, I presume he'll be saying the ten o'clock Mass.'

She gave him a distant look. 'I presume so. It's gone eight, Father.'

How did an old tyrant like Dan Mulvey manage to inspire such loyalty?

'I know, I know. It won't hurt them to wait a minute or two.' He shot her a rueful grin. 'All six of them.'

'You'll find there's a few more than that, Father,' she

said in a self-righteous voice. 'Anyway, "Where one or more of you are gathered together in My name...".'

'Those are my lines, Breeda.' He grinned again, this time in mock reproach. 'You'll be wanting to say Mass next.'

To his surprise, her expression grew thoughtful. 'Would that be such a bad thing, Father? Women are needed in the ministry.'

'You'd better not let Dan Mulvey hear that.' Stephen picked up the chalice and paten that waited for him on a side table. 'You wouldn't want to bring on an attack of paranoia. Not a pretty sight,' he warned.

Breeda looked unperturbed. 'Father Mulvey's a bit old-fashioned,' she said, without a glimmer of a smile.

'You can say that again!'

'But we're in a new century now.' As she held open the door that led to the altar, her eyes met his levelly. 'Never underestimate the power of the Holy Spirit, Father.'

'No.' Stephen felt somehow rebuked. 'I try not to.' He came out into the chancel of the lighted church, glanced down at the nave and saw about a dozen people scattered throughout the first ten rows. The rest of the church was empty. Hardly worth getting out of bed. He was immediately shamed by the thought. Not one to be held by a priest about to perform the holy sacrifice of the Mass. Breeda was right, it had nothing to do with numbers. He tried to compose his thoughts and knelt for a moment in silent prayer at the foot of the altar steps. There was some coughing and shuffling in the benches behind him. After a moment, a hush fell over the high-ceilinged church. As always, before saying Mass a feeling of awe came over him. By the time he turned to address the small congregation, he'd become completely caught up in the Mystery that lay ahead.

He hadn't always felt that way. When he was a kid, once the excitement and the novelty of his First Communion wore off, he didn't want to go to Mass any more. OK, maybe on Sundays. But weekdays? During the school holidays? Forget it.

'Well, I like going,' Mum said. 'And Jack does too. Don't you, Jack?'

But Jack didn't count. Jack was three years younger than Stephen and couldn't bear to let Mum out of his sight. Why she wanted to bring him to Mass was a complete mystery to him. There was no comfort in it. He grew bored quickly and spent most of his time in church kicking the seats and wailing that he wanted to go home. Stephen sometimes wished he could do the same but he knew he was supposed to give a good example. He could – and did – voice his objections, however.

'Why should I? Daddy doesn't go.'

His mother looked defensive. 'Daddy's got to work.'

He refused to be put off. 'He doesn't go on Sundays, either.'

Mum glanced around as if afraid of being overheard. But there was nobody in sight. Everyone else had gone into Mass, leaving the three of them standing on the pavement. 'It's because he's a non-Catholic.'

'He doesn't like being called that, Mum.'

'OK, a Protestant.' Taking his hand, she glanced over at the church, from where strains of organ music were drifting. 'But you're a Catholic. And you have to go to Mass.'

'Only on Sundays,' Stephen said swiftly. He knew *that*. 'Haddie, Haddie, Hie!' He shook her hand away and danced around in triumph. 'I don't have to go. It's not a sin.'

He saw a look of exasperation cross his mother's face. She tightened her hold on Jack, who was pulling at her other hand, and turned away. 'Sometimes, Stephen, you can be a tiresome boy.'

Now that he'd won, the victory was no longer sweet. He hated when that cool note came into his mother's voice.

'It's OK, Mum. I'll go.'

'No.' She shook her head. The organ music had died down. 'It's too late.' Pulling Jack after her, she walked ahead of Stephen towards the gate, the determined set of her head and shoulders a mute reproach to him.

'Sorry, Mum.' Anxious to get back into favour, he followed hastily. 'I was only joking, Mum.' He pulled at her sleeve. 'We could still go.'

'No. I won't be late. It's not respectful.'

'But, Mum . . . '

'Listen, Stephen.' She stopped at the gate and gazed sternly down at him. 'If we don't show respect for God's house, we respect nothing. Don't ever forget that.'

He looked back at her, abashed.

'No, Mum, I won't.'

Sometimes he and Jack played at saying Mass, fighting over which of them would be the priest, which the congregation. It was the kind of game you played on wet days when Mum outlawed Cops and Robbers or Martians versus Aliens because the noise would wake Gillian, their baby sister, from her nap. Play something quiet, she'd say. And they'd ransack the wardrobes for dresses that looked like vestments. When Gillian reached the toddler stage she was included in the game, sitting uncomprehendingly on the carpet, her mouth open like a baby bird's while Stephen or Jack as the celebrant ceremoniously popped a peppermint into it.

Jack was the one who got the biggest kick out of the game. And was the most inventive. Once, he put a shimmering skirt over his shoulders like a cape, a high tea cosy on his head and, brandishing a walking stick belonging to his father, pretended to be the Pope. He made Stephen and a boy called Mark who lived nearby carry him around the dining room on a chair while he rained blessings on the populace, as he'd seen on television. But Mark, a delicate boy, suddenly got a stitch in his side and dropped his end of the burden, causing the Papal chair and its occupant to crash to the ground. The noise alerted Mum. Concerned for her dining-room suite, she immediately banned the Vatican Game. Undismayed, Jack quickly recovered from his fall. He made the Pope a bishop and sat on a throne in the corner, demanding obedience from his subjects.

Early on, Stephen realised that, where he liked the ritual, the donning of the vestments and the saying of the prayers, Jack liked the power. This irked him sometimes. As the elder brother, he felt *he* should be the one giving orders. The priestly game often ended in a thumping match, which he usually won, being the bigger and stronger of the two. But in a year or so, the brothers lost interest in the game and never played it again. After a visit to the theatre, Jack decided he was going to be a famous actor. Stephen was torn between wanting to be an astronaut and following in his father's footsteps as a construction engineer. Although his ambitions soared spacewards, he had a streak of practicality in him which made him think that the latter career was a more likely one.

He was not long in secondary school when the idea first occurred to him that he might become a priest. The school was run by a religious order and from the first day he set foot in it, Stephen was impressed by their self-discipline and dedication to the priestly life. Despite the fact that the school buildings, set in spacious, well-kept grounds, had, in a previous existence, belonged to wealthy owners, and that most of the pupils came from comfortable middle-class backgrounds like his own, the priests themselves had a simple, unostentatious lifestyle. Although some were more likeable than others, they all seemed to him to be saintly men serving a cause greater than themselves. And their lives, though orderly and down to earth, managed to convey a deep sense of the spiritual. It was this combination of practicality and other-worldliness that appealed to Stephen. Something in his nature welcomed it. As he grew older, another part of him rebelled against the idea. He tried to express something of what he was feeling to Mark, who was still his friend, although they attended different schools. They were both sixteen and spent a lot of time talking about the nature of existence.

'Religion is dead,' Mark said definitively. 'In fact, God is dead. Or so Nietzsche believed.' His features hadn't changed much since childhood. He was still fine-boned, with a thin, questioning face and soft dark hair that fell lankly over his ears.

'But what do *you* believe?' Stephen asked.

'Nothing,' said Mark. 'And everything. Sometimes I think Nietzsche may have been right.' His voice lost its sureness. 'But then again, maybe . . . '

'You're a great help.'

'Sorry. But why be a priest? We're in the 1980s, Stephen. The post-Christian era. By the end of the century, the churches will be empty.'

'I'm not sure you're right,' Stephen said slowly. 'But even if you are, it just makes it more of a challenge.'

Mark looked sceptical. 'But what about women? Sex, that kind of thing?'

'What about it?' Stephen felt defensive suddenly. 'Look, I never said I was going to be a priest. I just said I was thinking about it. It's a career option, like any other.'

'Well-paid, too.' Mark gave a sly grin.

'Come on, you're no one to talk. Philosophy isn't exactly a lucrative profession. And priests do useful things. They don't sit around on their backsides all day ruminating on the meaning of life.'

'Good for them.' Mark stared at Stephen for a moment with a furrowed brow. 'It's not because of your father, is it?'

Stephen felt his face grow hot. 'What do you mean – my father?'

'Because he's a Protestant. You wouldn't have this crazy idea about making up to God for him, or something?'

'You can be an awful asshole at times. Where did you get that idea?'

It was Mark's turn to redden. 'Just something you said years ago. Look, forget it. You were only a kid. People change.'

'You haven't.' Stephen punched him lightly on the arm. 'You're still an asshole.'

'And you're not?' But there was no acrimony in Mark's voice.

'Maybe I am, if I said a stupid thing like that.' He met Mark's eyes squarely. 'Look, if I do decide to enter the priesthood – and I haven't made up my mind about it – but if I do, it won't be because of my parents. It'll be for me. No one else.'

'Are you sure about that?' Mark looked unconvinced. 'Your mum's pretty religious, isn't she?'

'That's true. But she doesn't know anything about

this. No one does. It's something I have to work out myself.'

'Well, I won't tell anyone.'

'Thanks.' Doubt tugged at him suddenly. 'It mightn't come to anything. It's just an idea. Maybe it's what I want. I just don't *know*.'

'If it's right for you, you'll know.'

He wished he had Mark's confidence. 'Maybe.'

'There's no maybe about it.' Despite his delicate features, his friend had a toughness about him that often surprised Stephen. He smiled encouragingly. 'Find out what you want and go for it.'

Stephen suddenly felt as if a burden had been lifted from him. He smiled back at Mark.

'OK, I will.'

That was sixteen years ago. Mark now lectured in philosophy in an American university. And Stephen had been working as a curate in the Dublin diocese for nearly nine years.

He wondered what made him think of Mark after all this time. As he removed his vestments in the sacristy after Mass, Stephen thought back to that conversation. *Find out what you want. And go for it.* It had worked out the way Mark had said it would. *If it's right for you, you'll know.* And he had known. By the time he'd sat the Leaving Cert exams, he'd been sure. But that was all water under the bridge. He didn't believe in looking back, or dwelling on things. Live in the present. That's what he told the people he counselled. Live in the here and now. Because now is all we've got. Except for eternity, of course. But maybe that would be one big now. Who knows? Stephen certainly didn't. All he knew at the moment was that he could do with a cup of coffee and a couple of hours' sleep. He didn't have time for the latter so he'd have to settle for the coffee, strong and black. And maybe something to eat. But before he headed back to the house for breakfast, he'd an errand to do.

The parish office was a modern one-storey building in the church grounds. When Stephen looked in the doorway, he saw Sister Dolores, the parish social worker, a thickset woman in her forties with fuzzy ginger hair and a homely, unmade-up face, sitting on the edge of a desk talking to Mary Grimes, the secretary. Both women stopped their conversation and looked at him.

'Sorry to interrupt, ladies.' Stephen kept his voice light. He would have preferred to find the secretary on her own. He liked Mary, the younger of the two; she was always friendly and helpful. But he never felt quite at ease with Sister Dolores. Although he'd been working in the parish for nearly a year, she always managed to make him feel he was still a newcomer. He took a folded sheet of paper from his jacket pocket. 'I've a couple of items for Sunday's news-sheet. Hope I'm not too late.'

'No, you're all right, Stephen.' Mary flashed him a smile. She was an attractive young woman, fashionably dressed in a sweater and skirt that showed off her shapely figure, in contrast to Sister Dolores, whose bulky form was clad in an acid-green tracksuit and Adidas runners. As she took the piece of paper, she glanced over at a side table, where an electric kettle was coming to the boil. 'Want a coffee?'

Before Stephen could answer, Sister Dolores said: 'God, Mary, you should know better than that. Only the best of Colombian coffee for Father here. None of your nasty instant. Isn't that right, Stephen?'

He felt his face grow hot as he remembered the grin she'd had last week when they bumped into each other outside Bewley's and she'd noticed the packet of coffee beans in his hand. At the time, she'd made some remark about exploitation and the Third World. He might have known she'd bring it up again. Dolores never missed a chance to have a go at him.

'That's right.' He hid his embarrassment under a smile. 'I'm off to make some now.'

'Grinds his own beans. What do you think of that, Mary?' An instructive note crept into the nun's flat voice. 'It's the only way to bring out the true flavour.' She laughed dryly. 'No doubt about it, some people would teach you how to live.'

Not quite knowing what to say to this, Stephen looked at her pleasantly, while Mary, glancing from one face to the other, smiled uncertainly. Then Sister Dolores heaved her bulk off the edge of the desk and planted her feet on the floor. 'Better get moving. I've work to do, even if nobody else has.' She turned to Stephen. 'By the way, Eileen's out for your blood. Seems you stood her up last night.'

Conscious of the look of interest on Mary's face, Stephen said stiffly: 'I wouldn't put it quite like that. Sister Eileen and myself were supposed to be at the same meeting but something came up and I couldn't get there.'

'Well, it's her you should be telling, not me.' Sister Dolores padded past him to the door. 'I'll be back around three, Mary, if anyone's looking for me.'

'Right, Sister.' As the door banged behind the nun, Mary looked at Stephen. 'Don't mind her. Underneath she has a heart of gold.'

'You could have fooled me.' Stephen gave a wry smile. 'Did you ever get the feeling someone didn't like you?'

'Who? Sister Dolores?' He read the surprise on Mary's unguarded face. 'No, no, you're imagining it. I've told you, she's a great character. The poor people love her.'

'I don't doubt you, but . . . '

'Sister Eileen and herself are so different. Yet they're the best of friends.' Mary shook her head in wonderment as she went back to her desk. 'Sure you don't want that coffee?'

'No, thanks.' Stephen was half way out the door. 'I'm going home for something to eat. If Sister Eileen comes in . . . '

'Don't worry, I'll tell her.' Her eyes lit up with laughter. 'Sister Eileen on the warpath! That'll be the day!' He heard her giggle as he closed the door.

'Mmm. That coffee smells good.' There was a smile on Sister Eileen's face as she stood on the doorstep, her cheeks glowing from the raw February wind.

With her beautiful eyes, and her dark hair coiled loosely in a bun at the back of her head, she reminded Stephen of a Madonna in a painting. He half-expected to see a few cherubim clutching the skirts of her long, navy raincoat. As always, he was pleased to see her and found his face breaking into an answering smile. 'You're just in time for a brew,' he said.

He held the door open in the narrow hallway, and she stepped past him, automatically heading down the short passageway to the kitchen. As he followed her tall, erect figure, Stephen felt a pang of nervousness. If what Sister Dolores had said was true, he might have offended Sister Eileen. And that was something he'd never want to do, not in a million years. She was the closest friend he'd made since coming to the parish. Better sort this out at once. He couldn't bear the thought of any awkwardness between them. In the kitchen, he glanced at her enquiringly. But Sister Eileen was taking off her raincoat, and her smooth, rosy face was impossible to read.

Stephen took a quick breath. 'I'm sorry I let you down last night. But – '

'You didn't.'

'– something came up and I– '

'There was no commitment.'

'Still, I said I'd go, and – '

'Listen, Stephen,' Sister Eileen held up a shapely

hand. 'You said you were about God's work.'

'Did I?' He was taken aback. 'I'm not sure I put it quite like that.'

'Not in so many words. But it was obviously important.' Her dark eyes examined him intently. 'It was, wasn't it?'

He remembered the scene in the alleyway, the shocked look on the girl's face. 'Yes, it was. Something that came up out of the blue.'

Sister Eileen's eyes never left his face. 'Want to talk about it?'

He remembered her clean, flowery scent. The way her hair had brushed against his face as he was helping her to her feet.

'Not really.' He looked uncomfortably at the woman opposite him. 'It's . . . '

'Confidential?' The nun nodded. 'I understand.' She smiled gently. 'You and I are in the same business, after all.'

'That's true. I suppose you *could* call it confidential.' He felt relieved when he saw her nod. He didn't know why he was reluctant to tell her about the girl. He only knew that he was. 'The less said about these things the better. The thing is . . . I felt bad about cancelling at the last minute.' Even as he said it, he knew this wasn't true. At the time, he'd been so caught up with the desire to help the girl that he hadn't considered Sister Eileen's feelings. It was only when Sister Dolores had mentioned them that he'd begun to feel guilty. As he looked at her, his sense of guilt grew. 'I hope you're not too angry with me.'

'Why would I be?' She gave a light laugh. 'Haven't I told you I don't mind?'

'It was something Dolores said.'

He was surprised to see a look akin to embarrassment cross her face. 'Oh, you mustn't mind Dolores.' She shot him a quick glance. 'What did she say?'

'I got the impression that I was in the doghouse.'

'With *me?* Because of missing the meeting?' She gave a baffled laugh. 'I don't know where she got *that* idea from.'

'So it's not true?'

'Well, of *course* not.'

Good old Eileen! He might have known she'd understand. Dolores was a different matter.

Almost as if she could read his thoughts, Sister Eileen said, 'Honestly, Dolores can be funny at times. It's that sense of humour of hers.'

'I must say I never noticed it. The sense of humour, I mean.'

'Oh, she has one all right. Believe me.' She shook her head, half-laughing. 'Just wait till I see her.'

Stephen shook his head too, but more in bewilderment than amusement. Women were hard to figure out at times. 'Well, as long as you and I understand each other.'

'Well, of course! Now, what about that coffee?' Still smiling, Sister Eileen began looking around the small kitchen, obviously wondering where to put her raincoat. As she made to drape it over the back of a chair, Stephen took it from her.

'I'll hang this up.'

'Don't bother. I won't be stopping long.'

'It'll only take a moment.' He hung the coat in the narrow cupboard under the stairs. 'One advantage of living in a small house,' he said as he came back into the kitchen. 'Everything's close to hand. Although it can be claustrophobic at times.' He smiled wryly. '*And* painful, when you bump into things.' Which happened often enough. Even after a year, he still couldn't get used to living in such a confined space. His last posting had been in a large, echoing parochial residence which he'd shared with the parish priest and another curate. 'But it's good to have my own place. And I do have privacy.'

'There is that. But . . .' Sister Eileen looked doubtful, ' . . . I like to spread myself. I wouldn't be as tidy as you.' Sitting at the table, she glanced around the kitchen. 'I think you must have been a seaman in a previous existence, Stephen. Everything's so neat.'

'You have to be, in a house this size.' He headed over to the filter coffee-maker sitting on a worktop and poured two steaming mugs of coffee. 'Besides, I just don't have many possessions.'

He saw a gleam of amusement in Sister Eileen's eyes.

'Unlike the rich young man in the Gospel?'

Stephen wasn't sure if he liked the comparison. 'Well, unlike him I have a few vices.' As he put the mugs down on the table, he glanced over at the coffee-maker, a present from his mother the previous Christmas. He gave a little sigh of satisfaction as he inhaled the aroma.

'And this is one of them.'

'Careful, you're taking too much pleasure out of it.' Sister Eileen raised an ironic eyebrow. Her eyes searched the table. 'Still off the cigarettes?'

'Yes, but only just.' Stephen groaned. 'Even the mention of them makes me want to light up.' He looked piteously at her but she stared at him, unmoved.

'Weren't you the foolish man to start smoking in the first place?'

'Thanks for your sympathy. What were *you* in a previous existence? Slave-driver in a galley ship?'

She frowned slightly. 'If Father Mulvey were to hear you . . .'

'I know, he'd indict me for heresy. But you brought up the subject, not me.' He grinned at her. 'You ought to be ashamed of yourself, Sister. The Church takes a poor view of reincarnation.'

Sister Eileen went pink. 'The Eastern religions have a lot to teach us,' she said evasively. 'Funny, though, to be talking about previous existences. Sometimes I can't remember a time when I wasn't a nun.' She shot him a tentative look. 'Does that make me sound old?'

'Come on.' He was only two years younger, after all. 'But I know the feeling.'

'I was thirty-four last November.' Her voice was ruminative, as if she spoke more for her own ears than for his.

'I know.' He'd taken her to the cinema to celebrate and given her a copy of the Tao-te-Ching as a present. 'What else is new?'

'I'm twelve years in the order,' she went on, as if he hadn't spoken. 'I did a degree in college first. So I wasn't exactly a child when I entered . . . '

Unlike Stephen, who had gone into the seminary at eighteen.

'And yet . . . ' There was a faraway look in her dark eyes. 'Sometimes I feel as if the years before I entered are like a dream and the last twelve years are the only reality. But just supposing I had to give up being a nun, would I look back on those years and feel they'd been a dream too?'

'"I do not know whether I was then a man dreaming I was a butterfly,"' Stephen quoted, '"Or whether I am now a butterfly dreaming I am a man."' He glanced thoughtfully at her. 'You're not thinking of leaving the order, are you?'

'What? No, of course not. I couldn't imagine any other life.' She laughed gently. 'There I go again. But seriously, Stephen, I wouldn't want to be anything but a nun. I know it's what God wants me to do.'

He nodded. There was silence for a few moments as they drank their coffee, each busy with their own thoughts.

'Did you ever have doubts?' Stephen asked.

'Doubts? At the time, do you mean? Or since?'

'Over the years.'

He saw her considering the question carefully. She smiled. 'No, I've never had doubts. Of course, I did the right thing by not entering straight from school. Those few extra years in the world have stood to me. I think in the past a lot of people entered too young; they didn't always know what they were giving up.'

'Maybe,' Stephen said. 'It's not the same for everybody.'

'That's true. Some vocations need to be cherished early. I can only speak for myself.'

There was something serene and untroubled about Sister Eileen. He studied her smooth, unlined face, noticing her dark eyes and the graceful way her black hair was coiled into a knot at the back of her neck. She had a calmness about her that most people found reassuring. A solid kind of beauty that many men would find attractive.

'You must have turned a few heads at college,' he said tentatively. 'Were you never tempted?'

'There were men, yes.' She gave a faint smile. 'But nothing serious.'

All at once, into Stephen's mind came the picture of another face, younger, even more beautiful, with a quality of vulnerability that aroused his protective instincts. He felt troubled by the memory and tried to banish it. He looked down at his coffee mug for a moment.

'And how about you, Stephen?' He glanced up to find Sister Eileen watching him with lively interest.

'What?' He found it hard to focus on what she was saying. 'Doubts about my vocation?' He shook his head. 'Like you, I've never had them.'

'I'm glad, Stephen.'

'Of course, I have other doubts. Sometimes I wonder if what I do makes any difference.'

'In the lives of the parishioners, you mean?'

'Yes. But I'm thinking mostly of the ones who stay away.'

'In ever-increasing numbers.' Sister Eileen nodded. 'You've got to remember that this is a poor parish. It has huge unemployment, drug-pushing, broken families with parents in jail, young people dying of Aids, you name it. You know, Stephen, it's very hard to preach the gospel message to people like that.'

'Yes. But they're the ones who need it most.'

'Well, that's what we're here for.' Her voice had a confident ring to it. 'And we *are* reaching some of them.'

'Not as many or as quickly as we should. We're into the twenty-first century now, Eileen.' He looked at her earnestly. 'If the church is to survive, it has to make changes in the way it goes about things.' He sighed. 'Try telling that to the parish priest.'

'Father Mulvey's a good man, but a little set in his ways.'

'He's an ostrich with his head buried up to his backside.'

She gave a reluctant laugh. 'But you get on well enough with him, don't you?'

'Oh, we're civilised about it,' Stephen said gloomily. 'But sometimes I get a bit frustrated. Talk about a closed mind. I don't know how you put up with him.'

She nodded sympathetically, but refused to be drawn further. 'God never gives us a cross but he gives us the means to carry it.'

'Dan Mulvey is a cross, all right.' Stephen drained

his mug and stood up from the table. 'But I'm damned if I want to carry him.'

'That's the trouble with crosses,' Sister Eileen said.

The parochial residence was a well-kept house and garden adjoining the church grounds. It was comfortable in an old-fashioned way, with a polished mahogany hallstand in the tiled hall and antimacassars on the high-backed chairs in the seldom-used front parlour. When the middle-aged woman who came in every day to cook and clean for the parish priest showed Stephen into the small study, he saw a real coal fire burning in the hearth. Father Mulvey, a white-haired man in his sixties, sat behind his desk, reading a leather-covered breviary.

'Hope I'm not interrupting, Dan.'

'Not at all, not all.' The parish priest put down the book. 'Come in, Stephen, come in.' He had a round, ruddy face and a hearty manner. 'I was just about to have some tea. Bring another cup, will you, Betty.'

'Not for me, thanks,' Stephen said, but he knew that when the tea came, he would be forced to accept a cup. He sat down, facing the desk. 'You wanted to see me?'

'That's right. But we'll wait for the tea first.' Father Mulvey left his seat and went over to the fireplace, where he put more coal on the fire. 'That's a cold one today, Stephen. Real brass-monkey weather.'

He wondered why the parish priest had sent for him. It wouldn't be to apologise for getting him out of bed the other morning, that was for sure. Father Mulvey was like God: he never explained his actions. God, or some kind of medieval monarch. At the start of every week, he would meet briefly with the two curates and the parish sister who made up what he liked to call 'the team'. There was no discussion: each was given their tasks for the coming week. 'Brendan, you do the early Mass. Stephen, you're on duty. Sister Eileen, will you take Rosary in the old folks' home? I'll hear the children's Confessions in the primary school.' No discussion. And no comeback. If for some reason he decided to change the tasks midweek, that was up to him. He was the boss, after all. And if he wanted to keep Stephen in suspense as he fussed around with the fire-irons, that was his prerogative too.

While Stephen was thinking this, Betty arrived with the tea tray. As he'd predicted, Father Mulvey wouldn't take no for an answer and insisted on pouring a cup for him, putting the milk in first to protect the china.

'OK,' Stephen said as the door closed behind the housekeeper. 'What's up, Dan?'

He saw the other man frown. 'There are going to be a few changes around here. That's what's up.' No longer affable, his manner had become acerbic.

Stephen was surprised. 'I thought you didn't believe in change?'

'Well, you know my philosophy – if it ain't broke, don't fix it. And it has worked well. Very well indeed,' Father Mulvey said with satisfaction. 'I've been running this parish for close on fifteen years and we've never had any trouble.' His face clouded over. 'Until now.'

'Trouble?' Stephen pricked up his ears. Had some brave soul in the Ladies' Altar Society challenged one of the boss's diktats? That'd be the day. Or maybe an altar boy had been caught listening to a Walkman in the sacristy – practically a mortal sin in the parish priest's book. No, judging by his expression, it was probably a bit more serious than that. 'Don't tell me they've found more needles in the church grounds. I've been on to the police about it but they say they can't . . . '

'No, no, Stephen,' the parish priest said testily. 'Nothing like that.'

'What, then?'

Silence for a moment. Stephen was surprised. It wasn't like Dan Mulvey to be at a loss for words. Then the older man said reluctantly: 'It's Brendan. He's . . . ' there was distaste in his voice, ' . . . been very foolish.'

Foolish? He pictured Brendan Hennessy, the senior curate, and wondered what kind of folly he could be capable of. A mild-mannered man in his early fifties, he carried out his duties in the parish in a quiet, caring way, never pushing himself forward or getting involved in any kind of controversy. His only interest, apart from his ministry, was his weekly game of golf. What could he have done?

'Now, this is between ourselves, Stephen.' Dan Mulvey's voice was tense. 'The Church has had enough scandals. We can't afford for this to get out.'

Scandal? Stephen's heart missed a beat. Brendan had always struck him as a decent sort. But you could never tell with people. Not nowadays. 'Oh, God, he hasn't been messing around with the altar boys? Or the kids in the primary school? Not the little girls?'

'Nearly as bad.' Dan Mulvey shook his head. 'He's got himself mixed up with a woman.'

Stephen was dumbfounded. Brendan, with a woman? It was hard to believe. 'One of the parishioners?'

'No, she doesn't live in Dublin. Some small town outside it. It seems he met her playing golf. He's a member of some club in Kildare or Navan or somewhere.'

'I know.' Brendan's weekly golf game was a sacrosanct affair, never to be missed whatever the weather. Stephen was beginning to realise why. A thought struck him. 'Is she married? Or very young, maybe?'

Dan Mulvey frowned. 'A widow around his own age, I believe.'

'Oh, well then.' Stephen heaved a sigh of relief.

'What do you mean, "Oh, well then"?'

'She's a grown woman. It's not like it's little children, or young girls. When you said "scandal", I – '

'What's the difference? It's all lust, isn't it? Sins of the flesh.'

'There's a huge difference,' Stephen said.

'Well, I can't see it. Broken vows are broken vows.' Father Mulvery's face reddened ominously. 'Don't tell me you're going to start making excuses for him.'

'Of course not.' Again he pictured the senior curate's mild, inoffensive face. Hardly the stuff of romance. 'I just can't see Brendan . . . Are you sure they're not just friends?'

Dan Mulvey snorted. 'He wants to marry her.'

Stephen's jaw dropped. He stared speechlessly at the other man.

Dan Mulvey gave a tight-lipped smile. 'Now you see what we're up against. Bloody women! They're the cause of all the trouble in the world, going right back to Eve.'

Stephen found his voice. 'Is he leaving the priest-hood then?' He was surprised to feel a sudden pang of loss.

The parish priest glared at him. 'Who said anything about that?'

'But – '

'If every priest left the priesthood because of a carnal lapse, there wouldn't be too many of us around. Just because the devil puts temptation in a man's way it doesn't mean he has to give in.'

'But if he loves this woman . . . '

'Love, my arse!' Dan Mulvey gave a bark of derision. 'It must be the most abused four-letter word in the English language. No, the word you're looking for is lust. L-U-S-T.' He spelled it out with relish. 'The poor eejit thinks he's in love. You'd expect him to have more sense at his age. But there's no fool like an old fool. And of course once that woman got her hooks into him . . . '

'So what's he going to do?'

'What?' The parish priest frowned at being interrupted in mid-sentence. 'Well, the bishop has suspended him from parish duties and ordered him to go on retreat, get spiritual guidance. There's a place over in England set up specially for this kind of thing.' He gave a grunt of satisfaction. 'They'll soon talk that nonsense out of him.'

'What about the woman?'

'What about her?' Dan Mulvey shrugged. 'She's hardly my responsibility.'

'I suppose not,' Stephen said slowly. 'But supposing Brendan has other ideas? What if he doesn't want to go?'

A hard look came into the other man's eyes. He shrugged again. 'If he has any sense, he will.'

Stephen's face was troubled as he left the parish priest's house. He just couldn't believe it. Brendan Hennessy, of all people. The last person you'd expect to do something like this. He pictured the soft-spoken senior curate. Who'd have thought he had it in him? He'd always struck Stephen as being a conscientious priest, if a trifle unimaginative in his approach. Hardly the sort to kick over the traces. But then, how well did he really know him? Although they'd been colleagues for almost a year, he realised that he knew very little about the man, outside their life together in the ministry. All he'd ever learned from an occasional chat over a couple of beers was that Brendan played off a handicap of eighteen and followed snooker championships on television. Stephen had a vague recollection that he'd said his mother had died a few years previously. But no other personal details had been offered – and none had been looked for. Brendan was obviously a very private man, not given to confidences, and Stephen had no wish to pry.

Now it looked as if that privacy might be blown wide open. 'If the papers get hold of this, we're in big trouble,' Dan Hennessy had warned. But how do you keep something like this quiet? As he parked the car in his tiny driveway, Stephen was filled with doubt. There was bound to be speculation about the senior curate's sudden departure. Parishioners would ask questions, put two and two together and come up with all sorts of outlandish answers. And journalists were always on the lookout for gossip. Gone were the days when there was an unwritten rule not to look too closely into the affairs of the clergy. The scandals over the last few years had put paid to that. Nowadays, the slightest hint would be enough to have reporters descending like hyenas on the parish, asking questions, printing articles full of surmise and innuendo, reopening old wounds. It didn't bear thinking about.

It was essential to get things into perspective. Compared to some of the recent scandals involving clerics, Brendan's lapse from grace was a fairly minor one. And according to the parish priest, prayer and counselling would help him to see the error of his ways. After all, as it said in the Liturgy, 'Thou art a priest for ever according to the order of Melchizedek.' It was a sacred calling, and Brendan wouldn't turn his back on it lightly. He thought of something Dan Mulvey had said. 'It's his age, Stephen. A kind of madness comes over some men at fifty. They're usually trying to prove something to themselves. I've seen it happen before. Fortunately, it doesn't last long They get over it, accept their lot and settle into contented middle age. Brendan will too. You'll see.'

He should have felt reassured by this, but as he turned the key in his front door a sense of gloom descended on him. Probably caused by fatigue, he told himself. Brendan's predicament wasn't his worry. The important thing was to keep things running smoothly in the parish until he'd trained in this rookie priest who was being sent as Brendan's replacement. 'It's up to you to do a bit of hand-holding,' the parish priest had said peremptorily. 'I haven't time for that kind of thing.' Stephen smiled wryly to himself and stepped inside the door.

A pile of correspondence lay on the floor of the hallway. Junk mail mostly – a few begging letters. As he sorted through them, he felt a sense of disappointment. Glancing over at the answering machine beside the telephone he saw the red light blinking. His spirits rose as he pressed the button marked 'New Messages', but they fell again when he heard Sister Eileen's gentle voice. What was the matter with him? What had he hoped for? It was stupid really, but he had thought Cathy might have got in touch. Why would she? At least to send back the twenty quid he'd lent her. No, it wasn't the money. He'd always been too honest to deceive himself, and he wasn't going to start now. He pictured the look on her face that night in Bewley's when he told her he was a priest. He tried to define that look, struggling for a moment to pin it down. Disappointment – anger, maybe. And something else. In his work as a counsellor he saw a lot of pain. He could be wrong, of course – it had been such a fleeting impression. But even if he was right, what business was it of his? She wasn't a client asking for help, or a parishioner needing spiritual guidance. Put tritely, she'd been a damsel in distress and he had gone to her aid. Not Sir Galahad, more the Good Samaritan. It was part of his calling, after all. Theirs had been a chance encounter, unlikely to be repeated. And some instinct warned him that it was better that way.

He told himself to forget her, thinking that he had far too much on his plate to have time for her. He'd a busy weekend in front of him. He picked up the phone and dialled Sister Eileen's mobile number. She'd probably heard about Brendan's absence and wanted to talk.

As he waited for her to answer, his eye fell on the bundle of junk mail he'd thrown on the hall table. He knew Cathy wouldn't get in touch now. She's had all week to send back that money. Maybe it was just as well. The money didn't matter, he told himself. What was twenty pounds when it was a question of safe-guarding your immortal soul?

FOUR

The morning after the bag snatch, Cathy woke early. She had slept fitfully, drifting in and out of troubled dreams, several times regaining consciousness with a dry mouth and a thudding heart. Although there was an hour to go before her alarm clock went off, she knew she wouldn't get back to sleep. She found herself reliving the attack of the night before – saw again the dimly lit archway, felt herself being thumped and thrown to the ground, heard the footsteps of her assailants as they ran from the scene. Round and round in her head the images went.

It was no good. Better to get up and start the day. She headed for the bathroom, taking care not to disturb Liz, who was asleep in the next room. When she stepped under the hot shower, she noticed her leg was still throbbing from the fall and there was a soreness in her right hand. It would have been worse, she knew, if it hadn't been for the ice cubes Stephen had given her. At the memory of her rescuer, Cathy's heart lifted. She knew it was going to take some time to get over the attack, but with people like him around, she could tell herself that the world wasn't such a bad place. Pity he was a priest. But did it matter? She was finished with men – for the time being, anyway.

After her shower, she towelled herself dry, her mind busy with the day ahead. A lot to be done, and not only the usual heavy workload in the office. Because of the stolen bag, phone calls had to be made. She listed them as she went back to the bedroom. Better get to it soon. Maybe it was a good thing she'd woken early. It would mean that she had a head start on the day.

The shower had given her fresh energy. She dried her hair and dressed quickly. By the time a sleepy-looking Liz, wearing an oversized nightshirt with *Life's a Bitch* emblazoned on the front, stumbled into the living room, her short, black hair standing up like a cockscomb, Cathy was preparing to leave for work. She'd been on the phone to cancel the stolen bank and credit cards and arrange for new ones to be sent out and had left a message on the landlord's answering machine about changing the locks, and another one at the police station for the sergeant who was dealing with her complaint. She checked her reflection in the wall mirror, shook out her newly dried hair into a shining bell around her face, and turned to smile at Liz.

'I'm off. I think I have everything covered.'

Liz gave a gigantic yawn, dug a spoon into a bowl of low-sugar cereal and wrinkled her nose thoughtfully. 'Will you bother about the priest's twenty pounds?'

'What do you think I am?'

'No need to jump down my throat.' Liz looked aggrieved. 'All I meant was, he probably wouldn't miss it.'

'You don't know that. But even if it's true . . . '

'Oh, don't mind me. What do I know?'

'Ah, Liz. Don't be like that.'

'Sorry, kiddo.' Liz looked morosely up from her cereal. 'I think I got out on the wrong side of the bed.' She smiled mollifyingly at Cathy. 'I'm not at my best first thing in the morning. You should know that.'

'If I don't now, I never will.' Cathy returned the smile. 'But listen, Liz, I have to send that money back.'

'As soon as you get your new credit card.'

'No, I don't think I should wait till then. I'll go to the bank at lunchtime. '

'Please yourself.' Liz gave her a resigned look. 'But I don't know what your hurry is.'

'I just want to make sure I don't forget.' Bad enough to have been rude to the man. Cathy didn't want to be thought dishonest as well.

But when she queued up at the bank during her lunch hour, she discovered to her dismay that her account was low. A couple of hours before she'd been robbed, she'd gone to a cash machine and taken out money to cover her living expenses for the week. The second withdrawal left a big hole in her account. Damn those thieves, Cathy thought as she moved away from the counter. A week to go till pay day. She'd need to watch her spending until then. She hated the thought of being overdrawn and was always careful to stay within her means, unlike Liz, who lived a hand-to-mouth existence at the best of times, and was always in the red for the last week of every month.

If only she hadn't withdrawn that money. If only

she hadn't taken the short cut through Merchants' Arch. She really should have had more sense at that hour of the night. But it was pointless to indulge in regrets. All she could do was make sure it would never happen to her again. Before she left the bank, she put the cash into an inside pocket of the heavy skiing jacket she'd deliberately selected before setting out that morning and buttoned down the pocket carefully. She had told Liz earlier that even if she had to carry all her possessions distributed throughout the coat, she wouldn't bring a handbag into the city until she felt safe again.

'And when will that be?' Liz had asked. 'You can't wear that for the rest of your life.' She rolled her eyes dramatically. 'Put enough stuff in the pockets and you'll look like the Michelin man. It does nothing for your image.'

'Who cares about that?' Cathy had snapped. But now, remembering her friend's words, she found herself glancing into shop windows, trying to glimpse her reflection. Michelin man, indeed! It would be funny if it wasn't so unflattering. Still, maybe Liz was right. She smiled ruefully as she saw her reflection in the mirrored angle of a shop window. The bulky jacket was definitely more suitable for a country hike than Grafton Street at lunchtime – and, let's face it, not in keeping with the image of the smart young businesswoman which Cathy had worked so hard to foster. But that wasn't what worried her as she examined her reflection. What was really disconcerting was the panicky expression on her face, the pair of frightened eyes staring back at her. She thought of something her father had said not long before his death, the time his car was stolen by joyriders when he was visiting friends in a Cork suburb. Although the police later recovered the car and it hadn't suffered serious damage, the robbery had unsettled the whole family, particularly Cathy's mother. 'Cork's no longer safe, not like when I was growing up there.' She threw a pleading glance at Cathy's father every time he set out for the city. 'Maybe you should leave the car at home, John. Go by bus.'

'Or give up going altogether?' It was obvious to Cathy her father hadn't much patience with this way of thinking. 'Is that what you're saying?'

She saw her mother's look of hope. 'Maybe till things settle down.'

'Till joyriders stop joyriding, and thieves pack in the business? Listen, Louise.' His voice was suddenly earnest. 'A wise man said, "Never take counsel of your fears." The day you do that is the day you give up. And *they* win.' He gave her a kindly glance. 'Do you understand what I'm trying to say?' Although her mother looked doubtful, Cathy knew what he meant.

Remembering his words now, she felt a sense of resolve. Dad had been right. You couldn't give in to your fears. He'd always faced life with courage and determination, and she'd do the same. She wouldn't let some sneak thieves dictate to her how to live. She wasn't going to give up carrying a handbag because of the snatch, but she'd be more alert in future. As she turned away from her reflection, she knew her eyes were no longer frightened. And her back was straight as she strode through the lunchtime crowds.

And another thing: she wasn't going to torment herself over what some stranger might think if she didn't return the loan straightaway. She knew she was honest. That's what mattered. She'd send the money back as soon as it was convenient. If Stephen Brown didn't like it, he could lump it. In the meantime, she proposed to banish all thoughts of him and last night's mugging from her mind.

But this was impossible to do. When she entered the small office at the rear of the shop, she was greeted by Martina, her assistant, who said there was a message from the police sergeant she'd dealt with the night before, asking her to ring back. 'But don't get your hopes up,' the other woman said. 'The guards are useless, if you ask me.'

Cathy paid no attention to this. Martina, a sharp-featured woman in her forties, could always be depended on to take a pessimistic view of things. Without waiting to take off her jacket, Cathy picked up the phone and rang the police station. When she heard the clipped tones at the other end of the line, her spirits rose. But to her disappointment, the sergeant had no news for her. When he'd rung earlier, he'd merely been responding to the message she'd left that morning. What could you expect? His voice was resigned. The thieves were long gone. How did you trace people like that? Where would you even start? The guards on the ground might have their suspicions. But pinning the crime on someone was another matter. Forget about it. As for the money, forget about that too.

Cathy thanked the sergeant and put down the phone. She stared hard at the wall behind her desk. Tears pricked at her eyelids. It wasn't just the disappointment over the handbag, but the memories the conversation had brought back. Her thoughts were interrupted by Martina's flat, reedy voice. 'I knew you wouldn't get any joy out of that lot.' As she turned around, Cathy saw the older woman's look of gloomy satisfaction. 'I told you about that time my brother's house was broken into . . . '

Cathy sighed inwardly. She was beginning to wish she'd kept the story of the mugging to herself. Jason, the salesman in the shop, had been sympathetic without being pushy. But Martina had made a meal of it, dredging up every disaster that had happened to relatives and acquaintances within living memory until Cathy was sick of listening to her. The older woman was hard to take at the best of times. But today, as she stood there obviously enjoying every minute of the drama, she was downright unbearable.

'Shouldn't you be gone for lunch?' Cathy glanced pointedly at her watch and then at Martina's coat, which was hanging on the back of the office door. As she started to remove her own jacket, she remembered what her lecturer on the personnel-management course had said about the importance of maintaining good staff relations. With an effort of will, she smiled at the other woman. 'I won't hold you up.'

'There'll be nothing worth eating by now.' Martina shrugged.

God give me patience! Cathy struggled to keep her manner pleasant. 'It was your own decision to take the later lunch. But if you want to go on the early one in future . . .'

'Not much point. Everywhere's too packed. You'd have no comfort.' Martina gave a sigh of resignation as she buttoned her coat and dragged a furry leopardskin hat over her faded blonde hair. 'I'll just have to take my chances.'

'You do that,' Cathy said, turning away. Never lose your temper with a subordinate. Another piece of advice from the personnel course. It's unprofessional and shows poor management skills. As she picked up some papers from her desk, she recalled the confident young lecturer and wondered how he'd cope with Martina. Probably have a nervous breakdown. She smiled wryly to herself as the door banged and she heard the shrill tones of the other woman addressing Jason outside in the shop. There was no point in letting it get to her. There were worse things in life.

The phone rang. It was Paul Kinsella, her boss, calling from his other shop.

'Hi, Cathy. How's business?'

'Brisk, Paul. A lot of enquiries about the new Pentium III processor.'

'Great, Cathy, great. But we need more than just enquiries. We want action, Cathy. Sales.'

'Yes, Paul.' She grinned to herself. He was obviously in one of his 'captain-of-industry' moods. When he opened the new store six months previously, he'd made Cathy manager of the city-centre shop and normally he left the day-to-day running to her. But every so often, he seemed to feel it necessary to brush up his high-flyer image. 'Sales will come, Paul, trust me.'

'That's *my* spiel, Cathy.' She heard the smile in his voice. 'What I tell my bank manager. But you're right, things are going well at the moment.' Paul Kinsella had every reason to be pleased with himself. Still in his twenties, he'd two thriving shops to his credit. 'How's Martina behaving herself?'

'Funny you should ask . . . '

'Don't tell me. Giving you a hard time?'

Cathy gave a resigned sigh. She cast her mind back to what Paul had told her eighteen months before, when she'd joined PK Computers.

'I promised my father I'd keep Martina on when I took over the stationery shop. Besides, what grounds would I have to get rid of her? Her work's OK. I tried sending her on a people-skills course but it was a waste of money.' Paul had given a heartfelt sigh. 'I don't know how my da put up with her for nearly twenty years.'

Recalling this, Cathy said, 'Her bark's worse than her bite, Paul. Nothing I can't handle.'

'Good girl. I knew I could depend on you.' His voice grew crisp as he moved on to another subject. 'Now, about those sales figures for January . . . '

After she got off the phone, she realised she hadn't

told Paul about the bag snatch. Not that he'd given her a chance. Sometimes conversation with him was like being run over by a steamroller. He was easy to work for and had loads of personality, with a good sense of humour. But he was a young man in a hurry – he'd probably be a millionaire by the time he was forty – and all he thought about was business. Well, maybe not quite all. Cathy smiled to herself as she remembered the first time they'd met.

It was one of those noisy, uncomfortable parties. Too many people, most of them in an advanced stage of inebriation, crowded into too small a space. When a skinny young man with a bony face and a receding hairline pushed his way towards her, she gave him a quick, dismissive glance. Some women might find that odd mixture of youth and maturity attractive, but not Cathy. Nor did she go for the fast-talking salesman type. The only thing in his favour was that he was sober. She'd get rid of him politely, she told herself. But he was impossible to rebuff. Much to her surprise, she found herself agreeing to go with him to a late-night cafeteria, where, over chicken burgers and chips, she listened to the saga of Paul Kinsella's path to success.

'When Da retired, I phased out the stationery and began stocking computers. Haven't looked back since.' His face darkened. 'But finding good staff is a problem.'

'So I believe.' Cathy was eager to get into the conversation. 'I'm doing a diploma in personnel management at night. I'm nearly finished the course.

One of the things they've told us . . .'

'Then you'll know what I'm up against.' But she sensed he wasn't really listening. He glanced at his watch. 'I'll drive you home.'

'No need. I'll get a taxi.'

'It's OK.' He grinned at her. 'You're quite safe. I have to be up early. Saturday's my busiest day.'

Talk about fancying himself! When he asked to see her again, she refused. He took it well. 'Shot down before I got to first base. No hard feelings, though.' When he pulled up at the house in Harold's Cross where she and Liz had a tiny flat, he gave her his business card.

'Good luck with the diploma. Let me know when you get it. I might have an opening.'

Chance'd be a fine thing. Cathy had no intention of contacting Paul Kinsella. She was after a position in a big international company, not in some small computer firm where the boss might make a pass at her. But months later, after several fruitless job interviews, she realised that even though she'd graduated with distinction from the evening course, the gap between a big personnel department and the office she was in was too large to bridge with one leap. She needed some practical experience in a smaller milieu. Maybe PK Computers was the place for that.

'Great timing!' Paul was delighted to hear from her. His assistant manager had just left. He needed a replacement straightaway. At the interview, he told her he was expanding the business. 'Strictly between ourselves, I'm opening another outlet next year. I'll want someone I can trust to run the shop here. Of course, I'm not promising anything . . . '

'I'm not either,' Cathy said. Although it would get her out of a boring job, she found herself hesitating. The experience would be useful, it would look well on her CV. But one thing troubled her. She took a deep breath and looked him straight in the eye.

'We need to define our relationship.'

She saw his face redden. But he didn't evade the question. 'You mean because I came on to you once?'

'Yes. I need to know why you're offering me the job.'

'You don't pull your punches.' She heard the admiration in his voice. 'You and I will get on.' She saw that he'd quickly got over his embarrassment. 'Listen Cathy, where business is concerned I don't mess about. OK, so I asked you out and you told me to get lost. But that's water under the bridge. I think you can do this job.' He glanced down at her CV. 'You have computer skills and you strike me as being good at handling people. The rest you can learn. And you needn't worry about me coming on to you again. It's the quickest way to lose staff. One of the first lessons my da taught me.' He gave her a winning smile. 'So what do you say?'

Cathy smiled back. He might look young but his head was screwed on the right way. It wasn't the job of her dreams. But it might be the first step on the ladder. 'OK, it's worth a try.' I'll give it six months, she told herself. Then move on.

A year later, she was still there. She'd found it hard

going at first but gradually, as she learned more about the business, she grew more interested in it. The more Paul got caught up in his plans for the new shop, the more responsibility he delegated to her. By the time he opened the second premises, Cathy was manager of the first in all but name. When he offered to make this official, with an appropriate increase in salary, she didn't take long to decide.

Maybe a small outfit wasn't such a bad thing. Particularly when you were in charge. She got on well with the other staff – Jason, the salesman, and Billy, the service engineer. The only fly in the ointment was Martina. But she'd learned how to deal with her. Cathy didn't rule out eventually moving to a larger firm, but there was no hurry. It would be nice to have a bit of stability for a while. And the promotion meant she could afford the rent of that new apartment Liz was talking about. All in all, life was on the up and up. Not bad, she told herself, for someone who'd be twenty-four in a few weeks.

Now, six months later, she found herself musing over the way a chance encounter, a random decision can change your life. If she hadn't gone to that party – if Paul Kinsella hadn't given her a lift home – she wouldn't be working for PK Computers today. And if she'd accepted his offer of a date, she might be his fiancée now, not his employee. Although that was extremely unlikely. Even if she'd gone out with Paul, their relationship would have been fleeting. Not enough chemistry. She liked and respected him, but she knew she'd prefer him as an employer than as a lover. It didn't take a genius to know that Paul was the centre of his own universe. His needs would always come first. The woman who loved him would have to put her own life on hold.

No way! Cathy told herself. She needed to come first in a man's life. She wouldn't share him with another woman, or play second fiddle to his business. She wanted a friend as well as a lover. Dream on, she told herself while she signed some letters Martina put in front of her. Where are you going to get a man like that? Then she smiled wryly to herself as her mother's voice sounded in her head.

'I don't know, girl. Only God knows the answer to that one.'

Think of your mother and that night you find yourself phoning her. A triumph of optimism over experience, Cathy told herself later. Because, as usual, comfort was not forthcoming.

'You were mugged! Oh God, Cathy!' Her mother's voice could be heard several octaves higher at the other end of the phone, then keening away into the distance. 'Vincent! Cathy's been mugged!'

She heard her uncle Vinnie's gruff voice in the background. 'Don't be upsetting yourself, Louise.' He came on the phone. 'What happened you, girl?'

'I'm OK, Vinnie.' Although he'd been married to her mother for nearly six years, Cathy had never called him 'Dad'. 'My bag was snatched last night. But I'm fine now.'

'I see.' She could almost hear the cogs of her uncle's mind turning laboriously as he digested the news. 'They get much?'

'Some cash. Credit cards.' For her mother's sake she found herself playing the whole thing down. 'More of a nuisance than anything else.'

Uncle Vinnie was a man who hadn't much truck with credit or Laser cards. He knew all about cheques, though. The monthly cheque from the creamery, subventions from the EU. 'How much cash?'

'Not much. Will you put Mum – '

'So you're all right then.' She read the relief in his voice. She wasn't coming looking to him for a loan. *As if she would!* Uncle Vinnie was as tight as the proverbial drum. And Mum wasn't much better. Cathy had long ago learned to rely on her own resources.

'Yes, I'm fine.' No point in mentioning the bruised knee, the sleepless night, the sheer horror of it all. Except on occasions, where her mother was concerned, sensitivity wasn't one of her uncle's attributes. She pictured his stolid, weather-beaten face and powerful shoulders, his blackened fingernails. She thought of her handsome, vital father. How could two brothers be so different? Unconsciously, her voice sharpened. 'Will you put Mum on again, please?'

'Right so. I'll say goodbye then, Cathy.' Uncle Vinnie seemed unperturbed by his dismissal. Of course, he had a hide like a rhinoceros. Probably dying to get back to his slow perusal of the racing column or the farming page of the newspaper. Had he bothered to get his reading glasses fixed or was he still using a magnifying lens, she wondered, remembering the last time she'd visited the farm. How could someone as educated as her mother bring herself to marry a man like that? Surely she must be sick of him by now?

But Louise had other things than her marriage to worry about when she came back on the line.

'I *knew* no good would come of you working in Dublin. I said it then and I'm saying it again.'

'I'm nearly six years here, Mum. It's the first time anything like this has happened.'

'Only a matter of time, girl.' Funny how sing-song her mother's voice became when she was excited. 'That city is no place to live. Cork's bad enough, but Dublin's gone to hell altogether. To *hell*.'

Hell isn't a place. It's a state of mind. She banished the thought hastily. Not something to share with Mum. She kept her voice reassuring. 'Dublin's no worse than anywhere else.' Why had she rung? She might have known it wouldn't do any good. Move on to something safer. 'How's everything at home?' Not that she thought of the farm as home. Home was a white bungalow with green shutters, a big, grassy garden at the back, and a sloping front driveway too steep to cycle up on your bike. She recalled the time one of her sisters had attempted it, falling off and skinning her knee. 'How's Detta?'

Her mother laughed indulgently. 'Give her a pair of wellies, a cow to milk and she's as happy as– '

'A pig in shit?'

'Oh, now! I'd have put it less crudely. But . . .'

Not for the first time, she found herself marvelling at her mother's casual disloyalty towards her older sister. If it wasn't for Detta, she couldn't have kept on teaching after she'd married. Mum never had any interest in the farm, Cathy remembered. All she'd wanted was a man to look after her. And she'd got one in slow-moving, tight-fisted Uncle Vinnie, whose only saving grace was that he was devoted to her. He'd got in return not only the woman he'd always wanted, but also a ready-made daughter in Detta, the niece he had most time for. Cathy recalled the alacrity with which her older sister gave up her office job in Cork, moving in with the newly-weds to look after the rambling old house and help Vinnie run the farm. But then, she'd cherished a dream of country life ever since childhood holidays. So Detta was another one who'd got what she wanted.

Hadn't Cathy too? She'd got away from home and gone to Dublin, the city of her dreams, to her first job and the start of a new life. Once she left home, did it really matter whether Mum lived in the town or a few miles outside it? As long as she was happy – wasn't that the main thing? But her mother's happiness had no bearing on the way Cathy felt. The loss of the family bungalow had been a devastating blow to her, like losing part of the past. Nowadays, whenever she went home on a visit she felt the pain of that loss again. Lately it had been easier not to go.

As if she read Cathy's mind, her mother said

reproachfully: 'You haven't been near us since Christmas.'

'Bad weather. Pressure of work.'

'I don't know where I went wrong.' The keening note came back into Louise's voice. 'My family are scattered to the four winds. My eldest daughter's lost to me. First Saudi Arabia, and now New York.'

'I thought Noreen was coming home in the summer?'

'For how long? Till the wanderlust takes her again? As for *you*, it might as well be America, for all we –'

'I can't come next weekend,' she broke in hastily, although she had made no definite plans. 'But I'll see . . .'

'The following one, then.' For all her gentleness, Louise was impossible to deter once her heart was set on something. 'Detta will meet the train.'

'OK.' Cathy gave a long sigh of defeat. 'The following weekend it is.'

After she put down the phone, her knees began trembling so much that she collapsed on the living-room couch. Get a grip, Cathy. Your bag was taken. It's not like you were raped. But the thought brought no comfort. It was a pity she hadn't been able to tell Mum how she felt, but it would have been a waste of time. Her mother always took bad news personally – as if she, not the other person, was the one deserving sympathy. Although she could get worked up over whatever mishap had occurred, she seemed unable – or unwilling – to offer any consolation. There had been no point in expecting any. Cathy was annoyed that she had even thought of looking for it.

She felt a sudden sense of desolation. Her eyes filled with tears for the second time that day. What's happening to me, she wondered. I'm turning into a real cry-baby. It could have been worse. There was no need to go to pieces. She would get over it. It was a pity Liz wasn't there to help put things in perspective, but she was out covering some event for her paper – and afterwards, doubtless, she'd be off to the pub with her journalist friends. Cathy'd be lucky to see her at breakfast the following morning.

Liz wasn't the only friend she had. What about Finola, or Janet? The three of them had been close at one time when they worked together, but they hadn't seen much of each other since Alan came along. It must have been a couple of months since she'd talked to Finola. Why not ring her and catch up, arrange to meet. She dialled the number and waited eagerly until Finola's mother answered. 'Sorry, dear, Finola went to Australia last month. She's gone for a year. I thought you knew.' As she put down the phone, Cathy realised that it was over six months since she and Finola had seen each other. What about Janet? She took a long time to answer her phone, and it wasn't Janet's voice Cathy heard, but that of an aggrieved young man who'd run all the way downstairs from the top-floor flat. She'd moved, he said tersely. He couldn't remember exactly when. And no, he'd no idea where.

Oh God! Cathy stared blankly at the wall of the apartment. Monet's 'Waterlilies' looked blankly back at her. It was the sort of thing magazine articles warned you about. Just recently she'd read one that stated baldly, 'Don't abandon your friends just because you're in a relationship. You never know when you'll need them.' But she hadn't abandoned them. They just drifted apart. Once she'd started seeing Alan, she'd stopped going to discos with Finola and Janet. After that there'd been no pressing reason to stay in touch. If they'd been real friends, it would have been different. But the only thing they had in common, she realised now, was that they all wanted to meet men.

The desolation descended again. She felt isolated, adrift on a sea of loneliness. It was like that first year in Dublin, that terrible time when she was friendless and desperate. It was better not even to think of it. The past was past. She'd moved on since then. She had a good life now. OK, so she'd no boyfriend any more. But he was no loss. She needed to put it all behind her – not just the row with Alan, but last night's bag-snatching, the encounter with the priest, everything. Move on. The loneliness would pass. If Liz were here she'd tell her to go and have a soak in the bath, her blanket remedy for heartache, man trouble or worries over weight gain. That was to be followed by an early night. Things would look better in the morning. They always did.

As she turned on taps in the bathroom, she thought again of Liz. There was someone who seldom suffered heartache over men. She was much too tough. 'Treat them mean and keep 'em keen.' It seemed to work for her. But she never kept any of them long; she wasn't interested in steady relationships. Her career was too important to her. 'Love and ambition don't mix,' she often said. 'Travel light and take your pleasure where you find it.' And that philosophy wasn't confined to men – she treated other people's possessions just as casually. That expensive jar of bath crystals Alan had given Cathy for Christmas was almost empty. But you couldn't stay annoyed with Liz for long. She was a good mate. She might borrow your last pair of tights without asking, or work her way through your bath salts, but she would never move in on your man or betray a confidence.

Not that Cathy went in for heart-to-heart talks. Not even with Liz. There were some things better left untold. Some things so private and personal that she couldn't imagine talking about them – she wouldn't know where to start. Just as well, probably. Because there was no one who'd understand. As she stared unseeingly at the water rising up the sides of the bath, she thought of the man she'd met the previous night. He'd been kind. And understanding. Why had she been so horrible to him?

Maybe she should ring him. It would be polite to thank him. And nice to hear his voice again. But she'd better do it before her bath. Impulsively she turned off the water and hurried into the living room. What had she done with his phone number? She'd normally have written it into her address book. But that had been stolen with the bag. After a frantic search through coat pockets and spare handbags, she was about to give up when she spotted a sheet of folded paper tucked under the clock on her father's old writing desk, where she'd put it for safekeeping the previous night. Relieved, she snatched it up. His writing wasn't easy to read – more like a doctor's than a priest's.

But what did she know about priests? Or about this man? Suddenly her haste left her and she stared doubtfully at the phone. Maybe it wasn't such a good idea. Maybe she should just post back the money, as she'd originally planned. What was the point of ringing him? Why this illogical desire to hear his voice? The desolate feeling which had never quite left closed around her again. It was like a weight pressing on her head, a hot pain in her stomach. God, she was really going to pieces.

This is stupid. She reached for the phone, began tapping out the number and heard the ringing at the other end. But once again doubt clutched her. In a panic, she slammed down the receiver before anyone could answer, then sat staring at the phone with a thumping heart. She stared at it for a long time without moving, while in the bathroom the water cooled in the half-filled bath, completely forgotten.

'Did you ever hear from that priest?' Liz asked one night during an ad on television.

'Why should I?' Cathy kept her voice casual.

'I thought maybe when he got the money.' Liz stared hard at her. 'You *did* send it?'

She felt defensive suddenly. 'You're behaving like my mother.'

'Have it your own way.' Liz shrugged, popped a square of chocolate into her mouth and turned back to the television. 'Movie's on again.'

Cathy said nothing. Why hadn't she sent the money? If she left it any longer, it would be embarrassing.

This time she didn't slam down the phone after the first ring. This time she waited, rehearsing explanations, framing apologies. When the machine answered, she didn't know whether to be relieved or disappointed. A bit of both, maybe. At the beep, her heart began to thump and her mouth went dry. *Go on, you fool! Say something.*

At last she forced herself to speak, stumbling slightly over the words. When she hung up, she noticed that her hands were shaking.

FIVE

Stephen was surprised to hear the girl's voice on the answering machine. A week had gone by since the night of the bag-snatching. Not that he'd forgotten her. Even before she said her name, he knew who it was. Ignoring the other messages waiting, he replayed the tape and listened again to the soft, hesitant voice.

He'd been to the theatre with Sister Eileen. A peace offering, to make up for missing the lecture with her the previous week. Eileen had said it wasn't necessary, but some obscure feeling of guilt made Stephen insist. He'd his doubts about the Shakespearean comedy she'd chosen – his own preference would have been for something more modern – but to his surprise it was a sparkling production that held his attention throughout. And Eileen had been pleasant company. He loved the theatre and quite often went on his own, but during the evening he came to the realisation that a good play was even more enjoyable when you'd someone to share the experience with. A pity he'd gone back to her place for coffee. Apart from the fact that he'd had to endure Sister Dolores's verbal sparring – what had that woman got against him? – it was probably too late now to return Cathy's call. He hesitated and glanced at his watch. Definitely too late. She'd probably be asleep.

But there was no rush, was there? He recalled her voice on the tape. The way it had faltered once or twice. Was she under some kind of stress? Not for the first time, he wondered what it was about this girl – young woman, really – which made him want to help her. I'm a priest, he told himself. *Feed my lambs. Feed my sheep.* It's what I'm supposed to do. Yet there was nothing sheepish about Cathy. He recalled the spark that lit up her eyes when she taxed him with not wanting to help the beggar that night. He sensed a passion about her, an idealism that provoked his admiration.

Steady on, Stephen, let's not get carried away. If she was anxious to talk to you, she'd have rung before this. No need to read too much into the phone call. It was just what it set out be – a thank-you message, long overdue. And an apology for the delay. Now that she'd got it off her chest, there was no need for him to return the call. But she *had* left a couple of telephone numbers. Maybe she expected him to get in touch. Tomorrow or the day after would be soon enough. There was no rush.

'PK Computers. Good morning. How may I help you?' The voice was crisply efficient. For a moment he wondered if it was the same girl.

'Cathy? This is Stephen Brown. I got your message last night.'

'Hello, Father. Nice of you to ring back.'

'Was there something I could help you with?'

'Not really. I just wanted to apologise for the delay . . . '

You took your time about it. Astonished at his own reaction, he took refuge behind a screen of false heartiness. 'No need. No need. You're a busy woman.' Aware that he sounded like the stereotypical priest in a television drama, he gave a nervous laugh. *Shut up, Brown. Get out before you make a fool of yourself.* She didn't echo his laugh.

'Not that busy.' Her voice was rueful. Her professional manner dropped away. 'I don't really have an excuse. I think I just kept putting it off.'

He was disarmed by her honesty. This was the Cathy he remembered. He forgot about cutting short the phone call, cast aside the hearty-priest persona and said in a more normal voice, 'Tell me, how are you? Have you recovered from your ordeal?'

'I think so.' He thought she didn't sound sure. 'Although I haven't been sleeping since it happened. But that isn't why I rang you. I wanted to arrange about sending back the twenty pounds you so kindly ... '

'Oh, that.' He'd forgotten about the money. 'Listen, there's no rush.'

'But there is. I should have paid it back before this. I don't know what you must think.'

'I knew you wouldn't forget.' Was that true? Did it matter? The main thing was, she hadn't ...

Silence fell between them. Like him, she must be wondering what to say next. He knew with sudden clarity what he should do. Tell her to post the money back. He put the thought aside. 'Have you talked to anyone about the mugging?'

'A few people.'

'I mean, really talked?'

'Maybe I should put it behind me, not dwell on it.'

'Sometimes it helps to talk things through.'

'I suppose.' She sounded doubtful. 'But who?'

'I could give you the name of someone.'

'Like a counsellor, you mean? No, thanks.'

'Just as you like.' He hesitated. 'But if I could be of any help?'

'You?' He heard the surprise in her voice. 'What would you do? Pray over me?' She gave a harsh little laugh. 'Teach me the error of my ways?'

He tried not to feel offended. 'I do a bit of listening as part of my work. I just thought . . . maybe as a friend?'

'A friend?' She was quiet for a moment. He waited, mentally crossing his fingers. Suddenly it was important to him that she'd say yes. After an age, he heard her sigh.

'I could do with someone to talk to, that's for sure.' Another silence. Again he waited. When she spoke, her voice was decisive. 'OK, why not? It'd be nice to have a chat and say thank-you in person.'

'That's great.' Stephen was surprised at his own sense of relief. 'The next question is when?'

'How about tonight?'

'Tonight?' His smile faded. 'I don't think I can.' He hadn't visited his parents in weeks. His mother was expecting him. 'How about tomorrow? No, wait a minute, tomorrow night's a bit tricky too.' He didn't usually arrange counselling sessions for Friday nights, but the client had been adamant, insisting she couldn't make it earlier in the day. He wished now he'd been firmer about it. 'That brings us up to the weekend.'

'I know.' He heard the animation go out of her voice. 'You've Confessions, evening Masses.' Although her tone was casual, he could sense her disappointment. 'Let's leave it.'

'No, wait.' He'd ring Mum and arrange to call out some afternoon the following week. 'I can meet you tonight.'

'If it's too much trouble, forget it.' Cathy's voice was stiff. He was suddenly reminded of the girl who'd glared at him across the restaurant table. 'You were the one to suggest it, not me.'

'That's right, I did,' Stephen said equably. 'And it's no trouble at all. Now what time would you like to meet?'

He was smiling again after he put down the telephone. There was something very nice about Cathy. He sensed an innocence about her, a simplicity. Under the sophisticated veneer, he suspected she was really just a country girl. A couple of heart-to-heart chats and he felt sure he'd get to the bottom of whatever was troubling her. Then he'd help her sort things out. As he headed to the kitchen to have some long-delayed breakfast, he found himself humming a fragment from a favourite opera. At times like this he felt very glad to be a priest.

'I prefer this to the other place,' Cathy said. The coffee shop was smaller, with more intimate lighting, and a wine bar at one end. He had the feeling she wanted no reminders of their previous meeting, when she'd left so abruptly. 'I'm going to have a glass of wine. What will you have?' She smiled at him across the marble-topped table. 'My treat.' She'd already given back his twenty pounds. It was the first thing she'd done when they met. 'I think it's the least I can do, don't you?'

'No need.' It embarrassed him to have women buying him drinks. It had taken years to discourage his mother from doing so. *I'm not a child, Mum. And I haven't got a vow of poverty.* But he knew that wasn't why Cathy wanted to pay. He liked that kind of independence in a woman. Even so, when the waiter came with their order, Stephen waved her money away. 'You can get the next one.'

She eyed his cappuccino. 'Do you ever drink alcohol?'

'On social occasions.'

'What's this, then?' Her eyes narrowed. 'A counselling session?'

When he saw her frown, Stephen gave a rueful smile, hoping desperately that she wasn't going to walk out on him again. He put out a placating hand. 'To tell you the truth, I don't know what this is. Strictly speaking, I'm not supposed to be out in public with a beautiful young woman like you.' He shot her a quick glance, inviting her laughter. 'Or in private, for that matter.' She stared back at him, stony-faced. *That went down like a lead balloon.* He tried again. 'I have to watch my step, keep a clear head.' He wondered if it sounded as feeble to her as it did to him. It was the kind of patronising act he'd seen older priests pull, trying to hide their misogyny. Unable to meet her eye any longer, he glanced around the wine bar and saw a couple at another table holding hands. He averted his gaze hastily.

What in God's name am I doing here? When he glanced back at her, he sensed she was wondering the same thing.

'Look, Cathy – '

'No, *you* look, *Father.*' Her words had an icy precision to them. 'I wasn't under the impression you and I were on a date.' Her chin lifted disdainfully. 'I assure you, that's the last thing I need. But neither do I want you to be practising some sort of therapy on me just so you can feel good.'

'That's a bit harsh.'

'Is it?' She gave him a long, considering look. Although he met her gaze, he squirmed inwardly, unused to being weighed up and found wanting. What had made him dismiss her as a naive country girl? If he wasn't feeling so uncomfortable, he might have smiled at his own presumptuousness. What had they had been told in counsellor training? *Don't judge. And never underestimate the client.* He should have remembered. Of course, Cathy wasn't a client. But he'd been treating her like one.

'Look.' Shifting his gaze imperceptibly, he admitted

defeat. 'I understand what you're saying . . . '

'Do you?' He saw hope tussle with doubt in her eyes. 'Really?'

'I think so. I'm sorry if I came across as being patronising.'

'You did.'

'It's an occupational hazard, I'm afraid. Although a friend of mine says it's part of my nature.' He smiled wryly. 'Something I need to watch.'

He was rewarded for his honesty when he saw the tension leave her face. But he was unprepared for the riposte that followed.

'So you do have friends?'

'A few,' he said equably, refusing the challenge. 'If I'm lucky, maybe I'll make another tonight.

When she smiled, her whole face lit up. 'Maybe we'll both be lucky.'

'My father had a lot of friends. He was a wonderful man. So caring, and *good*, in a non-preachy way. I really admired him.'

'I wish I could say the same about mine,' Stephen said unguardedly. When he read the question in her eyes, he found himself backtracking hastily. 'Don't get me wrong, my father's OK. But I obviously don't feel the same way about him as you did about yours.'

'Because mine died, you mean?' She wrinkled her nose thoughtfully. 'You think maybe I put him on a pedestal?'

'You tell me.' Stephen was relieved at having shifted

the emphasis away from his own affairs. His relief vanished when he saw her eyes flicker. *What have I said now? Give me a counselling session any time. At least there you know the rules.* 'Look, you don't have to answer that . . .'

'No, it's OK.' To his surprise, she decided not to take offence. 'Maybe I do idealise him. But that's only natural, isn't it? I was only twelve when he died.'

'A bad age to lose your father.'

'Is there a good age?'

'I don't know.' Just where was this conversation heading? This must be how the early sailors felt when they were about to enter uncharted waters. He tried to scramble back onto dry land. 'Tell me about your mother.'

Cathy gave him another of those long, unsmiling looks.

'Tell me about yours.'

'Dad was a Protestant,' Stephen said. 'Still is. Apparently there was a lot of pressure on him to turn when they got married. But he wouldn't budge. He had a bit of a closed mind.'

'Sounds like a man of principle.'

'Yes, well, that's one way of looking at it, I suppose.' He felt a pang of irritation at the approval in her voice. She'd have a different attitude if she knew the full story. 'Principles mean different things to people. It hasn't always been easy for my mother, living with a non-Catholic.'

He saw her eyes widen in sympathy. 'Does he make it difficult for her?'

'Not exactly. I don't think he ever tried to interfere. It's more his attitude. He's inclined to knock all religion.'

'It's not a crime,' Cathy said thoughtfully.

'No, of course it's not. At the end of the day, people must follow their consciences . . . ' *That is, if Dad had such a thing.* 'But my mother's faith means a lot to her. All she ever wanted was a bit of support when we were growing up.'

'"The family that prays together, stays together".' He saw a gleam in Cathy's eye. 'She sounds like my mother. Even now when I go home for the weekend she expects me to go to Mass with her.'

'But you don't?'

Her chin shot up determinedly. 'I wouldn't give her the satisfaction.'

He suppressed a smile. 'I suppose there's always one parent we react to.'

'Is that what you think? That I don't go to Mass to spite my mother?'

He felt himself redden. 'I didn't make that assumption.' But he knew he had. 'Why don't you go then?'

He saw her face close over. 'I have my reasons.'

'OK.' He couldn't keep the challenge out of his voice. 'Name one.'

She didn't flinch. 'I don't believe any more. Is that good enough for you?'

'I see.' He hid his surprise. He should have seen that one coming. He wanted to ask more questions. But if these were uncharted waters, they'd just hit a reef. Proceed with caution from now on. He kept his voice bland. 'That's as good a reason as any, I suppose.' He laughed lightly to defuse the tension that had sprung up. 'Maybe you and Dad would have something in common.'

Cathy laughed too. Then her face grew thoughtful. 'Ever since the mugging, I just can't stop thinking about my own father.'

'Something like that can reopen old wounds.'

She nodded. 'And not just my dad – other stuff as well.'

'What kind?'

'Nothing important. Things I haven't thought about in years, like when I came to Dublin first. It was a big adventure, but at the same time kind of scary.'

'Must have been,' Stephen said. 'Cities can be lonely places.'

'Yes.' Her face was suddenly bleak. She stared past him unseeingly.

'You said "nothing important", but I think it was.' Despite his best intentions, he began to probe. 'Something happened, didn't it?' His eyes sought hers. 'Had it anything to do with a priest?'

'What are you talking about?'

'I know you've something against priests,' Stephen said doggedly. 'I just thought, maybe . . . '

'You're doing it again, aren't you,' Cathy cried. 'And then you wonder why I don't like priests. You're all the same. You think you know it all.' He saw dislike on her face. 'And you ask far too many questions.'

'In other words, mind your own business.' Stephen hid his dismay under a note of rueful amusement. But inwardly he was cursing himself. Why hadn't he the sense to take his own advice? 'I'm really sorry, Cathy. I didn't mean to pry. I was just interested, that's all.' He gave her a conciliatory smile. 'From now on, you can ask the questions.'

'I'm not sure I want to.' Cathy didn't return his smile. The anger had left her face, to be replaced by a tight, guarded look. She drank the last of her wine and put the glass down decisively on the table. He watched her as she began looking around for her handbag. Stephen felt a terrible sense of failure. And of impending loss. If she walked out, he knew he'd never see her again. There was no time to analyse these feelings. He just knew he didn't want it to end like this.

'Don't go.' He put out a supplicating hand. 'Please stay and have another drink.'

She looked at him, her eyes cold. 'Why should I?'

But in the end she agreed to stay. 'Just for one drink.' This time a mineral water. *She* was the one who needed to keep a clear head. Although this was said without a smile, Stephen laughed as if it had been funny. Trying to keep things on a lighter footing, he described a mildly humorous incident involving the parish priest and an elderly parishioner and was rewarded by a reluctant chuckle. Emboldened, he went on to regale her with stories of his schooldays, describing teachers and pupils he'd known – some of them noted for their eccentricities. From schooldays, the conversation turned to holidays and soon he found himself telling Cathy about summers spent in Kerry and west Cork with his parents and brother and sister.

He recalled one time when he was about twelve setting out in a small motor boat with his father. The coastland was broken up into numerous bays separated by rugged peninsulas. They'd headed out into a bay one dull August afternoon, hoping to make it past the point of a promontory and back again before nightfall, but the headland stretched so far out to sea that it seemed it would take forever. At one point, as the small boat crept along, Stephen looked back over the greenish-grey waves and saw that the coastline had dwindled to a faint smudge. The long, craggy finger of headland still stretched inexorably away to their left, an endless vista of sea and sky melding into each other at the horizon.

Suddenly it seemed that he and his father were the only two people left in the universe: two tiny dots on a vast, inhospitable ocean. There was no sound except the laboured chugging of the engine. He experienced a moment of pure terror. Then his father, without saying anything, nosed the bow up through a trough in the waves. The boat described a wide, sweeping arc and headed back in the direction of the shore. Stephen could still remember the shudder of relief that coursed through him at the sight of that distant landfall.

'If it was me, I'd have been scared out of my wits.'

Cathy had followed the story with close attention, her face alive with sympathy. 'Did your father know? Is that why he . . . ?'

'I don't think so.' He was surprised at her question. It presupposed a sensitivity on his father's part which Stephen felt sure didn't exist. 'I'd have died rather than let him see my fear. Mum always said Dad didn't know the meaning of the word. She often nagged him about driving the car too fast, but he never took risks where boats were concerned. Dad didn't turn back that day because of me.' Stephen shook his head decisively. 'He probably realised that he'd bitten off more than he could chew. Decided to head for home while the light still held. I'm sure I was the last person he thought of.'

'All the same. You were only twelve.'

'What difference did that make? When I was half that age Dad still expected me to keep a stiff upper lip.' His expression softened at the sight of her dismayed face. 'You want to think the best of my father because of the way your own was. A waste of time, believe me. But there's no need to feel sorry for me.' He smiled reassuringly at her. 'He wasn't a bad father. In fact, compared to some of the stories I've heard over the years, I think I probably had an idyllic childhood.'

'Me too. Did you ever go out in a boat again?'

'Not that holiday. But I went sailing off Dun Laoghaire a few times after that. I grew up in Blackrock, not far from the sea. My parents still live there. Dad had a skiff for a while but he got rid of it a few years ago. Jack and I never shared his enthusiasm for messing around with boats. And Gillian had no interest at all.'

'She's the youngest?'

He nodded. 'Around your age.'

'Are you good pals?'

'Yes, I think we are.' Stephen found himself marvelling at the easy rhythm of the conversation. After that prickly start, who'd have thought Cathy would turn out to be such a good listener? 'But I've never told Gillian about that day in the boat. Never told anyone.' He shook his head in wonder; his eyes met hers. 'Until now.'

'I'm glad you told me,' Cathy said softly.

'So am I.' Without stopping to think about it, he said, 'Want to do this again?'

She looked startled. 'Meet for a chat, you mean?'

'Oh, God, yes. I hope you didn't think . . .'

'No, of course not.'

Although she smiled, he felt awkward, and thought he should spell things out. 'That is, if you can spare the time from all those boyfriends.'

She gave a snort of derision.

'You know what I mean.'

'Yes.' She gave him a level look as she got to her feet. He stood up too. The colours of springtime were in her eyes, he saw. Light green with a darker fleck. And were echoed in the wool of the sweater which clung gently to her body, hinting at the shape of the firm, young breasts underneath. 'Yes, Father, I know exactly what you mean.'

I wonder. As his eyes studied her, desire gripped

him, arousing his senses, taking him by surprise. *Sweet Christ!* He stepped back quickly, masking his growing confusion with an explosive laugh. 'For God's sake, will you call me Stephen!'

To his relief, she seemed unaware of his embarrassment. 'All right then, I will, Stephen.' She smiled. 'How does that sound?'

Despite his growing discomfort, he loved the way she said his name.

How did you describe someone like Cathy? He drove home through the night-time traffic. Where would you even start? Already over the past couple of hours he'd had to revise his original estimate of her several times. There was a lot more to her than met the eye. *God, but she was pretty! That face. That figure. The man that gets her is in for a treat.* He recalled those hazardous moments in the wine bar. Just thinking about them brought on his arousal again.

Watch it, Stephen, you're in dangerous waters. Looks like we've struck another reef. But if he ran aground, it wouldn't be because of Cathy's reticence to talk about herself but because of his own concupiscence. The word made him smile. It conjured up his own past, back to his days in the seminary, when the word was constantly on the lips of his spiritual director, an arid priest in his fifties who always gave the impression that the sexual act was the result of a bit of bad plumbing on the part of the Almighty. God couldn't make a mistake, of course, but even He might be capable of an error of judgement. How much simpler life would be for everyone if He'd devised a less messy way of propagating the species. You see, concupiscence was the big problem.

Why couldn't he just call it simple lust and be done with it? But the spiritual director had been one of the Dan Mulvey school of theologians. A man who delighted in biblical concepts. *The sin of Adam. Daughters of Eve. The woman tempted me.* Although it had to be nearly ten years since he'd last heard the director's sonorous voice, the rolling phrases echoed through Stephen's head. Carnal knowledge, concupiscence, and their evil ally, the occasion of sin.'

The woman tempted me? As he slowed down for a red light, he saw Cathy's smile and heard her soft voice. But he'd been the one to suggest another meeting, not her. He should have had more sense. Maybe it wasn't too late to change his mind, though. Maybe it would be better not to see her again – wiser, anyway. But he didn't need to decide about that right now. He'd more pressing things to think about. With Brendan Hennessy gone from the parish and the new young curate still trying to find his feet, Stephen's workload had increased. Things would get even busier with Lent coming up. The parish priest was a lazy sod at the best of times. He'd have to come up with some plan to make old Mulvey shoulder more of the burden. *Better put your thinking cap on, Stephen.* But his thoughts were as wayward as his body had been earlier. As he waited patiently for the traffic light to change, his mind went winging back in time. Back to the first girl with whom he'd ever made love.

Her name was Barbara. Somebody at school's sister, or cousin – all those years later he couldn't remember which. But he'd never forget those dark eyes, the long black lashes sweeping the perfect, oval face, and that shiny black hair which you could gather up in handfuls, burying your face in its silkiness, drowning in its sweet scent. She was slightly older than he was, having just started college, while Stephen was still in Leaving Cert year at school. Not a good time to begin getting interested in girls, that was what his mother said.

But when was a good time? He was seventeen, for God's sake. Some of his classmates had been going out with girls since they were fourteen. Of course, what Mum didn't know wouldn't kill her. He'd already had some brief skirmishes with the opposite sex over the previous summer. Nothing serious. A few shifts after school discos, some eager exploratory gropings in the shadow of suburban walls – and then, of course, there was the never-to-be-forgotten night of the barbecue on Killiney Strand when he could have gone all the way. But didn't. The girl had been willing; it had been Stephen who'd turned away before things got out of hand. Too risky, he'd said. Which was true enough. But as he lay on the sand, struggling with his emotions, the shadowy outlines of other couples heaving and tussling around him in the glimmering darkness, he knew what had really caused him to draw back from the ultimate sin had been the image of his mother's horrified face flashing into his mind at the wrong moment. And as if Mum wasn't bad enough, she'd managed to conjure up Uncle Jimmy as well. Father Jimmy, her priestly brother, Stephen's boyhood hero, who'd served out on the African missions until ill health brought him home prematurely. Although it was some years since he'd heard Jimmy's voice, it sounded softly in his head, blotting out the hissing of the sea against the shingle and distancing him from the muffled yelps of laughter and the odd shout of derision that rose up from the shadowy clumps of bodies around him. *Forget all this,* the voice said. *God's work is more important.*

Next day, of course, he cursed himself for being a fool to have been so close to the unknown and to have turned it down in favour of a different sort of mystery. He was not likely to get such a chance again. But to his amazement, he did. A few months later he met Barbara. And then he was glad he'd waited.

It started innocently enough. She invited him to her Debs' ball in September. Even Mum was pleased about that. *It's a rite of passage, Stephen. Enjoy it.* By now, his mother knew he was thinking about the priesthood, and approved of the idea. 'Although I'd like him to experience something of life before he goes in,' he overheard her tell a friend. 'But not too much, or he might change his mind.'

Looking back, he realised that her fears were justified. His first night out with Barbara had been one of pure delight. The start of it had been a bit of an ordeal, when he'd sat making self-conscious conversation with her parents in the ostentatious sitting room of their house in Monkstown. Behind their backs, her brat of a younger sister sniggered at him in his rented tuxedo and made-up bow tie, her malicious little eyes lingering on the rough white patches on his neck where he'd cut himself shaving. But from the moment Barbara walked in, smooth creamy shoulders rising from the shimmering blue of her wild silk dress, dark eyes sparkling, with her gleaming hair pulled back in a coiled black chignon, the enchantment began.

The next day he'd no precise memory of how the hours had passed, what the meal had been like or what the other young people with them had said. He remembered the disco afterwards – the insistent beat of the music, his hands around her narrow waist, her hair, which had worked loose from its chignon, tickling the side of his face, the softness of her breasts against his shirt-front. He didn't try anything on the way home, content to walk hand in hand in silence through the early morning suburbs under long avenues of trees, treading carelessly on the first fallen leaves, drifting dreamily past front gardens bright with late roses and the gold and amber of early autumn. A few cars passed them, a laden milk float.

At her gate, he glanced along the gravelled driveway at the windows of the sleeping house and drew her into the shelter of an overhanging hedge. He heard her gasp of pleasure as he kissed her for the first time on the mouth. Her lips were soft and yielding to begin with but, as their excitement grew, soon became as demanding as his. His hands were pressed into the small of her back, moulding her body close to him, but now she drew slightly apart and, taking one of his hands, placed it on the soft swell of her left breast. As he fingered her nipple through the stuff of the dress he felt it stiffen abruptly and found his own passion mounting. He bent to kiss her again, thrusting his tongue between her lips. She pulled away from him.

'No, Barbara! Please!' But his protests were tinged with relief. His passion, although exhilarating, was frightening. As he stepped back, struggling to master his feelings, he knew that never in his life before had he felt so out of control. He gave her a sheepish smile. 'I'm sorry.'

'Don't be. I want it too.' In the shadow of the hedge, he saw her eyes gleam. Suddenly she seemed light years his elder. 'But not here.'

'You mean . . .?' His spirits rose; his body leaped in urgent anticipation. 'But how?'

'I'll think of something.' She squeezed his arm. 'Leave it to me.' Again he had that sense of a huge age gap between them. She gave a conspiratorial grin. 'My cousin has a flat.'

Her cousin, some kind of businessman, had a job that took him away from Dublin a lot. He was hardly ever there during the week. Complaining that she couldn't study at home, Barbara had persuaded him to give her a key to his studio flat. In return, she kept an eye on the place for him, put out the rubbish and fed the cat: a brindled grey tabby who followed them around closely as if suspecting them of wanting to steal something.

'Are you sure this is OK?' Stephen watched Barbara select a bottle of red wine from the rack fixed to the wall of the tiny kitchen. He found himself glancing around uneasily, half-expecting the cat's owner to arrive in at any moment.

'We'll get him another one.' She rummaged in the drawer for a corkscrew. 'Anyway, he won't mind. He has a soft spot for me.'

Wouldn't anyone? She was wearing jeans and a close-fitting fine-rib sweater that defined her narrow midriff and small, swelling breasts. He was finding it difficult to keep his hands off them. Her hair was done up in a loose knot again tonight. He imagined himself undoing it, letting the shiny black tresses slip and slide through his fingers. As if she guessed his thoughts, she grinned at him, handing him the bottle to open. 'Let's have some vino first, get ourselves in the mood.'

'I think I'm in the mood anyway.' But he opened the wine, sniffing it appreciatively before pouring some of it into the two glasses she'd set out on the worktop.

'That's not the first time you've done that.' She threw him a quizzical glance. 'I think you're a bit of a connoisseur.'

'I'm not.' He gave a self-deprecating shrug. 'But my father is. Among other things.'

'Oh?' Barbara came up close to him and touched her wineglass lightly against his cheek. 'What kind of things?'

The glass felt cold against his skin. He hoped she couldn't hear the thumping of his heart. His mouth went dry. 'He fancies himself as an expert on women too.'

She moved the glass, held it to his mouth. 'Like father, like son?'

'Not really.' In his confusion he drank clumsily; wine ran down his chin. 'I'm sorry.'

As swift as any cat, she put out her pink tongue and lapped the liquid from his chin. 'How's that, then?'

He felt an exquisite shudder go through him. 'I don't think that's the first time *you've* done that.' As he bent to kiss her parted lips, he said: 'I think maybe you're a bit of a connoisseur yourself.'

Her mouth twitched with amusement under his. 'I think maybe I am.'

One wall of the living room was taken up with the poster of a Gauguin nude. The floor was dominated by a large divan bed covered in a Spanish blanket of garish design. The cat, which had settled down on a nearby rocking chair, watched them with an aloof wariness.

'He fancies me, you know.'

How to get that sweater off in one swift movement? It couldn't be done. He fell back on humour again. 'Who, the cat?'

'No, silly, my cousin Garry.' A quick glance from those dark eyes of hers. 'I think he'd like to . . . *you* know . . . '

'Wouldn't we all?' He ran his hand despairingly over

the back of the close-fitting sweater. 'You're playing games with me, Barbara. It isn't fair.'

'No, I'm not. I can be a bit of a bitch. But I'm not a tease.' She drained her glass and put it on the floor, swung her legs up onto the Spanish blanket and fluttered her eyelashes at him. 'The trouble with you . . . ' – her tone was conversational as she began drawing the sweater upwards – ' . . . is that you're in too much of a hurry.' As her head emerged from its folds, she gave him a sardonic smile. 'Maybe it's because you're just a kid . . . '

'Mind who you're calling names.' But it was impossible to take offence when your whole attention was riveted on two swelling globes barely covered by a couple of scraps of black lace. In a voice he scarcely recognised as his own, he heard himself murmur: 'I'll show you who's a kid.'

'I hope so.' She took his hands and guided them behind her back to open the clasp of her bra. With a quick movement, she shrugged herself out of it, leaving him holding the scraps of lace in his hands. Her breasts were small but rounded, the nipples standing up like pink raspberries.

'Oh God, Barbara!' He made a lunge forward.

'No, wait, don't touch yet.' She reached her hands upwards and with another quick movement, tossed her hair free from its knot. The long, black tresses slid down over her shoulders, ebony against the cream of her skin.

'Wait,' she warned again.

'Barbara, *please*.'

Her hands tugged at the zip of her jeans. Her dark eyes never left his face as she deftly wriggled out of the faded denims and kicked them away onto the floor. All that was left now was a triangular scrap of black lace at the base of her smooth, rounded stomach. She drew it slowly downwards over her thighs, a satisfied little smile playing about her mouth, 'You like?'

He eyed her naked body with awe. Never in his life had he seen anything so beautiful. He felt all his senses respond to the sight.

'Oh God, yes.' He felt his mouth go dry again and heard his voice thicken. 'I *like*.'

It was only the following day that he thought of his immortal soul. Waking up in his own bed with the beginnings of a headache, the sour taste of wine on his tongue, he remembered all the things the priests at school had said about sin and damnation. Things he should have thought of last night. Guilt gripped him suddenly. *Oh, God! What had he done? What would Mum say?* He panicked for a moment, then lay still. She won't find out, he told himself. I'll make sure she doesn't. As for the priests, what did they know about anything? Had any of them ever seen beauty like Barbara's? Or known what it was like to be in love? He doubted it. Dried-up old men, that's what they were. Fools. With all their talk about heaven and the next world, they'd forgotten how to live, truly live in this one. You wouldn't catch Stephen making that mistake – no way. His guilt evaporated, speedily forgotten. From now on his motto would be *Carpe Diem,* seize the day. Live now. Worry about it later.

But later has a way of catching up with you. Eventually. At first everything went like a dream. No questions were ever asked when he told his mother that he was off to Mark's house to study. Why would there be? He had never given her cause to worry before; why should she suspect him now? And sometimes it wasn't just an excuse and he actually did study with his friend, because Barbara had a way of ringing up at the last minute. Her parents were going out; she'd have to babysit her little sister. Or it was the wrong time of the month. Once or twice, alarmingly, she cancelled because Garry, her cousin, was due back in a couple of hours' time.

'It's OK, he doesn't suspect a thing,' she said the next night that she and Stephen were able to be together. 'You're not the only one supposed to be studying, remember.' Sprawled naked on the divan, her body languid with satisfaction, black hair spread out against the gaudy colours of the blanket, she echoed the pose of the figure in the poster on the wall above. But Barbara was more perfect than any Gauguin nude, he thought, her features more delicate. She was Snow White before she ate the poisoned apple. She was Thumbelina rising from a lily pad. But not a version that any child's book of fairy tales would ever show. He found himself smiling at the notion. Imagine a parent's horror at an illustration which pictured those small but voluptuous breasts, that narrow waist, the whiteness of her stomach against the luxuriant blackness of her bush. No, Barbara's body was only for grown-up eyes. His eyes. He felt a fierce pride of ownership suddenly. His smile vanished. The idea of someone else gazing at it was . . . unthinkable.

'There's no danger that he might walk in and find us, is there?'

'Now, you mean? Tonight?' She smiled lazily. 'No, he's in Dusseldorf. Don't worry. Relax.' She rolled over on her stomach and reached out an enquiring hand.

'Dusseldorf? How do you know?'

'He makes out a list for me. He's a very organised person.'

'I see.' Somewhere at the back of his mind a little doubt niggled. 'How old is Garry, anyway? He sounds a bit weird.'

'Weird? No, he's actually quite boring.' Her hand had moved again, in long, stroking movements. He felt a tremor run through him. 'I think someone is beginning to wake up. Yes, I do believe . . . ' She smiled into his eyes. 'But I can stop this if you'd rather just talk.'

'No, no.' He felt another tremor. All his nerve endings seemed to be concentrated under her finger-tips. He forgot his doubt – if it had been a doubt. 'Please, don't stop.'

But if Mum had no inkling of what was going on, his brother Jack had.

'Did you get lucky yet?'

'Get lost.' Stephen tried to concentrate on a

Shakespearean sonnet. *When to the sessions of sweet silent thought.* 'Listen, I could do with a bit of silence around here . . .'

'You can tell me.' Jack refused to be put off. At fourteen he'd already discovered girls and was always eager to initiate a discussion about them. He gave a conspiratorial grin. 'I might be able to give you a few tips.'

Where did he get all that confidence from, Stephen wondered. Jack was a constant cause of surprise to him. He might be three years younger, but even when he was a kid he always seemed to know more than was good for him. He sighed and put down his book.

'Oh yeah? You and who else?'

'Laugh if you want to.' Jack shrugged. 'It's your loss.'

There were times when he made Stephen feel the younger of the two. 'At your age I was more interested in soccer. OK.' He gazed challengingly at his little brother. 'What makes you think you know more about women than me? Tell us, have *you* got lucky yet?"

Jack smiled, gave a little shrug. He had looks that women had been drooling over since he was born – glossy, dark curls, a well-shaped nose and not a pimple in sight. 'Maybe I have, and maybe I haven't. I'll tell you one thing I know, big brother, that you don't.'

'And what's that?'

'There's none of them worth breaking your heart over,' Jack said smugly, and dodged out of the room before Stephen could think of a retort.

'So you're going to do engineering after all,' Mark said one day at the beginning of December. 'Like your Dad?'

'He's in construction,' Stephen said. 'I was thinking more of computers. That's where the future lies.'

'People will still want houses. And factories.' Mark had a tendency to indulge in argument for its own sake, Stephen noticed. Maybe he thought that was how philosophy students spent their time. 'But you have a mind above all that, haven't you?'

'Not really.' He found himself reddening. 'I want to get a decent job when I finish college. Maybe even get married.'

His friend looked surprised. 'Married?'

'Well . . . some day. Don't you?'

'Oh, sure, some day,' Mark said. His eyes narrowed. 'What happened to all that stuff about wanting to serve mankind?'

'Yeah, well,' he said, giving a sheepish smile. 'That was before . . . '

'Barbara?' Mark grinned. 'I get it, Stephen. Nothing like a bit of pussy to help you get your priorities right. Once you realised what you'd be giving up . . . '

'Don't talk about Barbara like that.'

'Sorry. I forgot you were in *love*.'

'Cut that out, will you,' Stephen said sternly. 'Look, Mark, joking aside, the application form for university has to go in before the end of January. And you heard what the career-guidance teacher said. The choices we make today . . . '

' . . . will affect the rest of our lives. I know, Stephen.'

Mark's thin face grew serious. 'It worries me, too. But isn't it a bit soon to be talking about marriage? You only know Barbara a few months.'

'I never said ... I was just talking in general ... You're the one who...'

'Fair enough.' But he could see by Mark's face that he wasn't really convinced. 'And another thing, what about your mum? Does she know yet? That you've changed your mind about being a priest?'

His mother had received his decision calmly. 'Well, if that's what you want, Stephen.' It was impossible to read from her face how she actually felt. 'I'm sure you've given it a lot of thought.'

'Well, yes.' He felt relieved yet oddly disconcerted by the equanimity with which she'd taken the news. 'I thought you'd mind.'

'Mind?' She frowned slightly. 'You weren't thinking of becoming a priest to please me, were you?'

'No, of course not, but ... '

'And I certainly wouldn't want you to do anything you weren't absolutely sure of. The priesthood is a huge commitment, Stephen.'

'I know.'

'And if you have doubts, it's better to come out with them now than wait till six months after you've gone in. But you know, Stephen,' she looked at him thoughtfully, 'it's only natural to have some doubts. Even poor Jimmy wasn't 100 per cent certain at first.' A wistful look came over her face. 'Funny, really, when you think what a saint he was at the end.'

'Uncle Jimmy?' Although it was three years now since his uncle's death, Stephen still felt sadness at the mention of his name. How much worse it must be for Mum. At the same time, he suspected it sometimes helped her to talk about her dead brother. 'He's the last person I'd have accused of having doubts.'

'Strange, isn't it?' His mother nodded. 'But you didn't know Jimmy at seventeen, of course. You wouldn't think it to see him later on, but he was quite wild at your age.'

'Jimmy, wild? I don't believe it!'

'Oh, yes.' She shook her head and gave a little reminiscing smile. 'That summer before he entered the noviciate he must have gone out with a dozen different girls.'

'Girls?' He gazed at her warily.

'Why not?' She gave him a bland look. 'He was a normal teenager. With all the urges boys his age have. Quite innocent, of course. I don't think he got up to much.'

He kept his voice light. 'How do you know?'

His mother laughed. 'I knew my brother. He enjoyed a bit of fun but that's all there was to it. When I say Jimmy was wild, he wasn't *that* wild.' Her lips tightened. 'He was brought up to have respect for girls.' She gave Stephen a level look. 'Just as you were.'

He tried not to look away. 'Times change, Mum . . .'

'Maybe, but morality doesn't. Even if you're not going to be a priest, you're still subject to God's law.

Don't forget that, Stephen.'

He squirmed inwardly under that unwavering gaze. 'No, Mum, I won't.'

Imagine Uncle Jimmy going out with girls like that. But it was all quite harmless, Mum said. You wondered why he bothered with sex if he wasn't going to experience it properly. Or improperly, if you agreed with Mum's point of view. But rightly or wrongly, it all sounded a bit sad. Particularly so when you realised that poor old Jimmy had only another fifteen years of life left to him. Fifteen years of study and celibacy, before he snuffed it. Not that anyone could have guessed that at the time. Poor Jimmy, shifting girls like mad, never really getting to know any of them. What a pity he hadn't met someone like Barbara. Who knows, he might even be alive today. But at the very least, his last fifteen years on earth would have been different ones. At least he'd have lived.

At the mention of Barbara, Stephen felt his whole being flood with joy. What a girl! Mark was right, of course. Marriage was a long way down the road. But it was no harm to have goals. It made it easier to concentrate on his studies when he knew that some day they'd have a future together. Because she was the right girl, the only girl for him. He knew that, deep down. How wonderful that she felt the same way. At the thought that he'd be seeing her that night, he felt his senses quicken in anticipation.

He arrived at the studio flat in good time. Someone had hung a holly wreath over the doorknob; carol music sounded from an upper landing. *"Tis the season to be jolly, Tra-la-la-la-la . . . '* He found himself humming along with it as he waited for her to come to the door. As the tune changed to 'White Christmas', he wondered what was taking her so long; she usually answered on the first ring. Could he have got there before her? No, he could hear sounds of someone moving around inside the flat. Ah, here she was now.

The door was pulled back abruptly to reveal a black-haired young man in his twenties, bare-legged under a short, striped dressing gown which gaped open to reveal a hairy chest and crumpled red silk boxers. He held a bottle of wine in one hand and a corkscrew in the other. He grinned at Stephen.

'If you're collecting for something, you're out of luck.'

Oh, God! The cousin. Why hadn't Barbara phoned?

He thought of pretending he'd come to the wrong flat, then decided that it would only arouse suspicion. Better bluff this one out. He thought rapidly, drew himself up to his full height, which made him slightly taller than the man in the doorway, and embarked on an involved explanation concerning a missed lecture, borrowed study notes. 'So, if you see Barbara, will you tell her . . . '

'Listen, why don't you tell her yourself.' The black-haired man had an open, friendly manner. And he looked much younger than Barbara's description of him. Before Stephen could say anything, he shouted back over his shoulder. 'Bar! One of your friends from college.' As the young man turned back again, he gave Stephen a half-embarrassed smile. 'Give her a moment. The place is a bit of a mess.'

'I think there's been a mistake. It was your cousin Barbara I was looking for.'

'No mistake,' the young man said cheerfully. He glanced back over his shoulder again. 'Bar! What's keeping you?'

Of course it was a mistake. Anyone could see it was a mistake. But the other man, though he seemed a decent enough bloke, obviously wasn't too bright. But supposing it wasn't a mistake? Suddenly something boiled up inside Stephen's chest. Without stopping to think, he shouldered aside the young man in the dressing gown and ran down the short passageway into the living room.

It was strange, really. In all the times he'd worried about someone bursting in on them in the flat, it had never occurred to him that he himself might be the one who did the discovering. It was years later before he saw the irony of it. At first the scene looked harmless enough. The cat was asleep on the rocking chair. Barbara was sitting on the edge of the divan, glancing through the pages of a magazine. It took a moment for him to notice that her blouse was slightly askew and her feet were bare.

'Oh, hi, Stephen.' She tried to smile. Her gaze darted nervously from him to the young man behind him and then back again. 'What brings you here?'

'You needn't bother pretending,' Stephen said

coldly. 'I know what's going on.' Anguish ripped through him suddenly. 'Barbara, how could you?' He was unable to keep the tremor out of his voice. 'How could you do it?'

'Do what?' the young man asked. 'What's going on, Barbara? Who is this guy? What does he want?'

The girl ignored him and looked instead at Stephen with a smile that was half-apologetic, half-embarrassed, the sort you'd see on the face of a child who'd been caught misbehaving but hoped the grown-ups wouldn't be too hard on her. She gave a little shrug of defeat. 'I tried to ring, but you'd already left.'

He said nothing. With a dreadful clarity, he saw that her blouse was buttoned wrongly, the top button not in its corresponding buttonhole, but in the one below. With that same clarity, he could see that she was wearing nothing under the blouse, the fabric straining over the curve of her breasts. His blood pounded in his ears. And for a moment time stood still, lengthened, turned into a lifetime. A lifetime of staring at that top button, of watching the smile become meaningless on her face. A lifetime trapped in a moment's frozen grasp. Then, mercifully, time speeded up, came back to normal. The blood quietened in his ears. He heard his own voice.

'You bitch, Barbara!' He found himself choking over the words. 'You fucking bitch.' His face twisted with contempt as he turned away.

'Hold on a minute.' He heard the bewildered voice of the young man in the dressing gown. 'For God's sake . . .'

As Stephen gazed at him, stony-eyed, he saw realisation beginning to dawn on the young man's face.

'Barbara?' There was a kind of plea in his voice. 'Jesus! Barbara!'

'Oh, shut up, Garry,' Stephen heard the girl snap as he headed for the door. 'You're no help at all.'

'This can't go on, Stephen.' His mother's face was troubled as she watched him push away his plate. 'Why won't you tell me what's wrong?'

'Nothing's wrong.' For a moment he had the sensation that he was at the bottom of a dark pit and that his mother was looking in at him over the edge. He glanced down at the table and the moment passed. 'I'm just not hungry, that's all.'

She looked sceptical. 'Are you worrying about the Leaving Cert?'

'Starving yourself won't help.' His father put down his newspaper and stared at Stephen. 'Draw up a study plan after Christmas and stick to it. In the meantime, lighten up, will you. There's nothing worse than people who go around feeling sorry for themselves.'

'That's not like Stephen . . . '

'Everyone gets exam nerves, son. The secret is not to give in to them.' His father's voice was brisk but not unkind as he got up from the table. 'What are you worrying about, anyway? You're good enough to get the points for engineering.'

'I'm not worried about that,' Stephen said. Engineering, the Leaving Cert, the future – all of it seemed so trivial at the moment. Everything was pointless. It would all end in death, anyway. And the sooner the better. 'Leave me alone, will you. I'm OK.'

'Fair enough.' His father shrugged and left the room. But Mum wasn't content to leave it at that.

'It's not the exams, is it?'

He found it hard to meet her eye and said nothing.

'Look, if you won't talk to me, talk to one of the priests at school,' she said. 'Didn't you tell me you have a one-day retreat at the end of the week?'

He'd forgotten about that. 'It's just a chat for the sixth years.'

'Well, then.' Mum's face was hopeful. 'While you're at it, you could talk about your vocation.'

Stephen looked at her bleakly.

'What vocation?'

It was too late for that. Too late for everything. He was back in the dark pit. And there was nothing anyone could do about it.

'But what's happened to make you change your mind?' Father Maeliosa took a log from a brass container near his chair and placed it carefully in the blazing hearth. Outside the small sitting room, a chill December rain gusted against the windows; inside, the fire gave out its comforting warmth. 'You were so keen on the idea when we talked about it before the summer.'

'That was a long time ago.'

'At your age, yes. A lot can happen in a few months.' Some of the boys said that Father Maeliosa was pretty old. He could be up to eighty, maybe. But the eyes which studied Stephen were as bright and penetrating as a ten-year-old's. 'So what are you thinking of doing instead?'

'I don't know,' the boy said dully. He turned away from that keen, blue-eyed gaze. 'Nothing, really. I mean . . . what's the use?'

'What's the use?' The old man's voice was thoughtful. 'That doesn't sound like you, Stephen.'

The log crackled in the grate, sending shadows flickering up the corners of the room. He tried to think of something to say, but the words wouldn't come.

'I've known you since you started secondary school,' the priest said reflectively. 'A good student. I've always thought highly of you.'

Not any more. Not if he knew.

'Other boys might talk like that. "What's the use? No point to life." But not you, Stephen. What's happened to change you?'

'Nothing.' He waved his hands helplessly, avoiding those penetrating blue eyes.

'Whatever it is, you can tell me.'

Stephen hesitated, glancing at the shadows dancing up the walls.

'Between ourselves,' the quiet voice pressed him. 'Nothing you tell me will leave this room, I promise.'

All at once he ached to unburden himself. At whatever cost. With a little sigh he turned to look into the older man's face, bracing himself against the condemnation he was sure he'd find there. To his relief, he saw no reproach. Only compassion.

'You're not the first young man to be taken in by a woman's wiles.' Father Maeliosa's smile had a touch of sadness to it. 'I dare say you won't be the last. We men are frail when it comes to the temptations of the flesh.'

'I thought she loved me,' Stephen said. The priest had turned out to be a surprisingly sympathetic listener and quite unshockable. What a relief that had been. 'I see now I was only fooling myself.' That was the most painful part of it. He kept remembering the scene in the room, the black-and-grey tabby asleep in the chair, the embarrassed smile on Barbara's face. It was the coldness behind that smile that got to him every time. 'If she'd even looked sorry, if she'd even pretended to care . . .'

The priest nodded. 'But don't judge all women by her, Stephen. There are decent ones out there too. Women like your mother. Some day you'll meet a nice girl, get married, settle down . . .'

'Married?' He was filled with sudden revulsion. 'I'm never getting married.'

'You feel that now. But in time . . .'

'No.' Stephen shook his head. 'I could never trust anyone in that way ever again.'

'Maybe you're wiser than you know.' Father Maeliosa pursed his lips thoughtfully. 'If you put your faith in earthly love, you're doomed to disappointment. Take it from me, Christ is the one person who'll never let you down.' He gave Stephen a shrewd look. 'But I think you've already found that out for yourself.'

He met the old priest's eyes levelly. 'Yes, Father, I think I have.'

Father Maeliosa took out the purple stole he wore when hearing Confessions. 'Now, if you kneel down and say a good Act of Contrition, I'll give you absolution.'

Stephen hesitated. Could it be that simple? Scarcely daring to hope, he looked at Father Maeliosa. 'Just like that?'

'Just like that,' the old priest said firmly.

Just a few sentences and the slate was clean. *Say a Rosary for your penance. Go, my child, and sin no more.* When he closed the door of the room behind him, he felt light-headed with relief. The dark pit was a thing of the past, its memory fading rapidly. As he nodded to a classmate leaning against the plinth of a large statue of St Joseph, he had to resist the smile that was threatening to break out on his face. He waited until the other boy had gone into the priest's sitting room before he allowed himself to feel the joy that surged over him. He felt like a kid again after his First Confession. Only better.

What had he known at that age about sin? About God's mercy? He wanted to dance down the dimly lit corridor, waving to all the statues. He wanted to run across the quadrangle in the driving rain shouting out a chorus of *Adeste Fideles.* Instead he took the bus to the nearest MacDonalds and bought himself a Big Mac with a double helping of fries, washed down by a giant Coke. As he ate, his mind was full of what had taken place in the small sitting room. The noise and bustle of the crowded restaurant faded into the background as he found himself going back over everything that Father

Maeliosa had said.

Human beings are weak and sinful. Only God is perfect. *Lead us not into temptation*, we pray in the Our Father. But sometimes God allows these temptations in order to test us. If that was the case, Stephen had said ruefully, then he'd failed the first test. He hadn't even put up a fight. Even worse, he'd let Uncle Jimmy down. But he wasn't to look at it that way, Father Maeliosa said. If he was going to be a priest, it wouldn't be because of a promise made by a distraught fourteen-year-old at the deathbed of a beloved uncle, taken too young; it would be because he believed it was what God wanted him to do.

But God wouldn't want him now, would he? Not after what Stephen had done. 'Don't you believe it,' the old priest had chuckled. 'Have you never heard of Saint Augustine?' He'd led such a dissolute life, his poor mother had despaired of him. But once he renounced the pleasures of the flesh, he'd gone on to be one of the Fathers of the Church.' And what about Saint Ignatius Loyola, founder of the Jesuits? He was an officer in the Spanish army. 'And those lads were no choirboys, believe me. No, you're in good company, Stephen.' Father Maeliosa had advised him not to make any hasty decisions when they parted company. 'Say your prayers and sleep on it.'

That night, Uncle Jimmy came to him in a dream – one of those vague, fragmentary dreams that are so difficult to piece together afterwards. They were playing chess at the kitchen table, that much he remembered.

Jimmy seemed to be winning; he had taken most of Stephen's pawns. 'You're not dead, after all.' The boy was overjoyed. But his uncle just smiled and shook his head. Soon Stephen understood that Jimmy was going away, back to heaven to be with God. 'Take me with you,' the boy cried. 'I've made my Confession. I'm ready to go.'

His uncle shook his head. 'God doesn't want you, Stephen. Not yet. You've things to do on earth.'

Stephen felt tears of disappointment. 'What things?' He put out his hand and clutched Jimmy's sleeve. He knew he was dead. Yet his arm felt real. With a thrill of surprise, he felt the flesh of the arm and the bone under it. He's alive, he thought. He's really alive. Suddenly the arm vanished away to nothingness under his fingers and he woke up. It was still night. Despite his disappointment at losing his uncle again, he found himself smiling into the darkness. It was so good to be alive. He couldn't bring Jimmy back, but he could live his life in a way that would make his uncle proud of him. A few nights later on Christmas Eve, as he knelt at midnight Mass with his mother and Jack, Stephen renewed his resolve.

Although he vowed after Barbara he'd never give his heart to another woman, he made no promises for his body. The summer before Stephen entered the seminary, he and Mark went on holiday to Crete. Mark was content with a couple of brief romances during the fortnight but Stephen brought a different girl back to their apartment every night. Afterwards, when he came home to Ireland, he could remember few of their faces and none of their names. Not that he wanted to.

'Talk about an orgy.' His friend was filled with horrified admiration. 'You don't do things by halves, do you?'

'This is going to have to last me a long time,' Stephen said. Although he pretended to Mark that he'd enjoyed every minute, the memory of his escapades sickened him. *I did it for Jimmy*, he told himself. Afterwards, looking back, he asked himself if that had been true.

And now he was waiting at a traffic light, wondering if it would ever change. But it wasn't the same set of lights he had been stopped at when he began thinking about Barbara. With a shock, he realised that this traffic junction was quite near to his house. He'd driven most of the way home on automatic, as it were, while his mind had been otherwise occupied. A dangerous thing to do. He was horrified at his own lack of attention, knowing that that was how accidents happened.

On the other hand, there were other ways for them to happen, he reflected as the high dome of Saint Mary's came into view. A bag snatched in a lighted alleyway. A beautiful young woman needing help. A sidelong glance in a wine bar that had set his senses racing; the stirring up of old memories, best forgotten. He thought about what Father Maeliosa, since gone to his reward, had said about the frailty of the flesh. *You're in good company, Stephen.* But it was one thing to say that to comfort a remorseful teenager nursing a bruised heart, an idealistic youth appalled at the acting-out of his own desires. But for a thirty-two-year-old man, well schooled in celibacy and self-denial, it was a different matter altogether.

But how true was that? Did one ever get used to celibacy? It was an unnatural state, after all. He drove past the dark bulk of the parish church, glancing over at it from force of habit, picturing the empty pews, the hushed tabernacle. 'I may be one of your anointed, Lord,' he found himself praying, 'but please don't forget, I'm still a man.'

And the man wanted to see Cathy again. Even though the priest warned him he would be making a mistake.

SIX

'So you're seeing him again?' Liz glanced quizzically across the breakfast table at her. 'Is that wise, do you think?'

Cathy gave a careless shrug. 'Just friendship, Liz.'

'Friendship with a man? Can't be done. It's a myth.'

Cathy was nettled by the other woman's air of omniscience. Without stopping to think, she said, 'There was this boy I grew up with. We were pals for years . . .'

'Yes?' She saw a speculative gleam in Liz's eye. 'Until?'

Why did I have to bring that up? 'Nothing. It was a long time ago.'

'Can't be that long. If you were such pals, why didn't you mention him before? What happened?'

'Nothing. I told you, it was years ago. To get back to what you were saying . . .'

'Platonic friendships?' Liz was instantly diverted. 'They don't work. Not unless there's a big age gap.' She looked dubious. 'And even then – but of course he's quite a bit older, isn't he?'

'Not that much,' Cathy said. 'He's thirty-two.'

'Eight years.' Liz pursed her lips. 'There's a lot to be said for older men. More finesse.' She gave a knowing grin. 'More money too. But a priest?' She shook her head. 'You wouldn't know what you'd be getting into.'

'Even if he wasn't a priest, I'd feel the same way.' Cathy was adamant. 'After Alan, I'm in no hurry to get into another relationship.'

'OK, I believe you where thousands wouldn't.' But being Liz, she couldn't leave the subject alone. 'When are you seeing him again?'

'I don't know if I will. I'm in two minds.' Cathy sighed. 'He's one of those people who think they can solve everyone else's problems.'

'Sure, what problems have you got? Well, I know you were mugged but you've got over that. What else is bothering you?' Liz could be insensitive at times, Cathy thought. She abandoned the toast and got up.

'I promised my mother I'd go home this weekend. But I don't feel up to a family reunion. And the thought of the hordes on the Friday-evening train doesn't help.'

'Well, you can't say you have the flu. You used that excuse a few weeks ago. What is it about families?' Liz looked rueful suddenly. 'I put on ten pounds at Christmas. Comfort eating. Would you blame me, with relatives like mine?' Her face cleared. 'Why not go down tomorrow morning? That way you only have to spend one night there. Get the afternoon train back on Sunday.'

'Don't get me wrong,' Cathy said hastily. 'They're not that bad. It's just that I feel I don't belong there any more.'

'Tell me about it.' Liz gave a dramatic shudder. 'You should meet my family. The original ugly duckling, that's me. Trouble is, I'm still waiting to wake up and find I'm a swan.'

'I know the feeling,' Cathy said.

The train was five minutes late getting into Cork station, but her sister arrived even later, strolling down the platform as if she'd all the time in the world. As they exchanged hugs, it struck Cathy that life on the farm seemed to suit Detta. She'd never worn that contented air when she worked in a solicitor's office. A pity she didn't get a good haircut and invest in some skincare. Twenty-seven was too young to start letting yourself go. Not that Detta had ever believed in style – not even in the days when she needed to dress more formally.

'Will you look at the cut of you.' Her mocking gaze took in Cathy's smart trouser suit, her new leather bag. 'Every time I see you, you've a different outfit.' She, as usual, wore grubby cords and an ancient waxed jacket.

'Wouldn't do *you* any harm,' Cathy said. 'When are you going to donate that jacket to a museum?' She laughed as she followed her sister's stocky figure out to the station yard, where her car, a battered-looking Cortina Estate, was half-blocking an exit. It looked as if it had been abandoned rather than parked.

They drove along the quays past the grey hulls of ships docked along the quayside. Cathy watched the sunlight on the water, noticing the way it scattered in myriad dancing fragments on the surface. On the opposite quay, the windows of the tall buildings had been turned to gold. Ahead of them they saw the sloping roofs, spires and domes of the city as it climbed the surrounding hills. As always when she saw this panorama, Cathy had a sense of homecoming. Although she'd grown up in a small town about twenty miles away, her grandparents had lived in Cork. When they were alive, she and her sisters had often stayed with them in their tall old house on College Road. The city held many happy memories for her.

Detta, however, was in no mood for nostalgia. 'Don't know how anyone lives here,' she said as they joined a swarm of cars crossing the bridge and negotiated a maze of narrow side streets. 'Traffic in Cork is worse every time I come in. I just have to pick up Vinnie's reading glasses from the opticians. Then we'll head for home.'

Cathy would have liked to stroll down Patrick Street and have a coffee in one of their old haunts, but she knew her mother was expecting them. Soon they left the city behind and drove swiftly along winding country roads. As always when approaching her uncle's farm, she had the feeling she was heading into alien territory. All too quickly the hedges and ditches flashed by. She saw leafless trees pencilled against a wintry sky, red-roofed barns and five-barred gates, and wrinkled her nose at the ripe smell of manure. Then they left the road and travelled over a rutted track, the old Cortina whining as they climbed between hedges of thorns that scraped and rattled against the sides of the car.

'Nearly there,' Detta said cheerfully. A slate roof and weathered gable appeared above a hedge. They turned a corner, and the austere lines of the old farmhouse, with its grey plastered walls and narrow sash windows, came into view. They drove past the small, railed garden in front and headed into a large yard, surrounded by barns and other outbuildings. As the Cortina rattled over the cattle grid, two black-and-white farm dogs rushed out to circle the car, barking noisily. Cathy saw her mother's slender, white-headed figure emerging from the back porch. Despite the tension that gripped her, she felt her spirits rise in anticipation.

'I thought you were coming last night.' There was a look of reproach on Louise Carmody's gentle face.

'I'm here now. That's the main thing.' As Cathy hugged her mother, she felt half-afraid of crushing her. 'You've got thin, Mum.'

'Oh, now, girl.' Her mother's voice was arch. 'You know what they say – you can never be too rich or too thin. Will you look at the style! What are Detta and I like compared to you?'

'Oh, Mum! You look wonderful.' When Cathy was growing up, Louise had dressed in long flowing skirts, her abundant black hair hanging loose, or in a plait over one shoulder. A romantic style, the child thought, until she became a teenager and saw to her embarrassment that her mother had begun to look like an ageing hippie. It was a relief when Louise had at last cut her hair. Now completely white, its simple, short style showed off her dark eyes and delicate bone structure. At fifty-seven, she'd relatively few wrinkles and looked a few years younger than she was. 'I hope I look as well when I'm your age,' Cathy said, smiling.

'You've nothing to worry about, child. You get better looking by the day. Isn't that right, Detta?'

'Oh, a real beauty.' Detta's lip curled. She turned to Cathy. 'Mum'll catch cold out here in the wind. Go and do your nattering inside.'

Something happened to her as soon as they came within the vicinity of the farmhouse, Cathy noticed. She became the bossy older sister, proprietorial of Mum. Still, she was right about the wind. Its shrill whine gusted down from the upper reaches of the mountain, blowing up dust and tossing the heads of the unopened daffodils scattered in clumps around the edges of the yard. She took her bag from the boot of the car. Feeling like a hypocrite, she said, 'How's that husband of yours?'

Louise looked pleased. 'He's been dying to see you all week.'

'Pull the other one, Mum.' Sometimes Cathy thought that the older woman lived in a world of her own devising, seeing only what she wanted to see. With a resigned laugh, she followed her mother into the farmhouse.

'Well, Cathy girl?' In the low-ceilinged kitchen, Vinnie was at the table, finishing his meal. He didn't get up from his seat but gave her the glimmer of a smile. 'Train got in OK?'

'I'm here, amn't I?' She glanced at the cheap magnifying glass lying beside the newspaper in front of him. 'Detta collected your specs. It's a wonder you didn't get a new pair while you were at it.'

'Erra, girl,' Vinnie shrugged. 'Is it made of money I am?'

Old cheapskate. 'I thought you'd be out gallivanting on a grand spring day like this. Chasing bullocks, or strangling the odd chicken.' But Vinnie stared back impassively, refusing the challenge. Louise was the one who spoke.

'Listen, girl, that fella wouldn't know the meaning of the word "gallivant".' Her mother had a special voice around him, Cathy noticed. She always seemed nervous whenever the three of them were in the same room, as if something unpredictable might happen. The man should have carried a government health warning, she thought indignantly. After nearly six years of marriage, Mum was turning into a parody of an old country-woman. She saw Louise raise the gas under the kettle. 'Cathy, have you eaten?'

'I had lunch on the train. But I'd love a cup of tea.'

'The fire's lit in the parlour.' Detta began clearing the table of soiled dishes. She gave a sardonic smile. 'In your honour.'

That was something, anyway, Cathy thought. It was the one room in the house she liked. She found the kitchen, with its mixture of cheap modern units and old wooden furniture, depressing. Its narrow windows never seemed to get the sun, and the faded oilcloth that permanently covered the table gave it a sleazy look. She shot a glance at her uncle in his heavy corduroys, his suit jacket worn shiny at the cuffs, smoke trailing from the cigarette in his cupped palm. What was good enough for previous generations was obviously good enough for him. But Mum knew better than that.

'Cathy and I will have the tea inside.' Louise began setting out cups and saucers on a tray. 'We have a lot of catching up to do.'

'Oh, don't mind us plebs,' Detta said, grinning at her uncle. 'Anything's good enough for us, isn't it, Vinnie?'

'That's right, girl. No peace for the wicked.' He got up from the table and padded in stockinged feet to the back door, where a pair of dirt-caked wellingtons stood. Cathy saw he'd holes in both heels of his socks. She was glad Mum wasn't doing his darning, anyway. 'Leave the dishes till later. I want you to take a look at that heifer . . .'

'Right so,' Detta said. After she and Vinnie left the kitchen, Louise raised an ironic eyebrow.

'That pair just love mucking around in wellies, discussing the price of cattle.'

'Don't you think you rely a lot on Detta?' Cathy felt a sense of unease. A woman came in during the week to help with the housework, but it struck her that her sister had a heavy workload. 'She can't have much time for a social life.'

Louise looked surprised. She handed the tea tray to Cathy. 'Don't you worry about Detta. She'll be fine.' Opening the door leading to the front hall, she gave a playful smile. 'Now, girl, I want to hear *everything*.'

Not even as a child had Cathy told her mother everything. As she followed her into the front room of the farmhouse, she found herself doing a quick mental edit.

Once Louise had heard the details of the break-up with Alan and had got over her disappointment that her daughter had turned down what sounded like a 'good catch', the conversation moved on to local gossip, of which she had plenty to offer. Cathy knew by the time her visit was over she'd have heard a litany of deaths and illnesses, not to mention the doings of delinquent offspring of neighbours and acquaintances within a fifty-mile radius of the farm and beyond. When the catalogue of acquaintances ran out, there'd be stories gleaned from newspapers, television and radio. Louise was morbidly fascinated by other people's misfortunes. And not just in real life, in literature too. Cathy could remember as a child watching her endless rereading of the doomed love affair between Catherine and Heathcliff in *Wuthering Heights*. And *Casablanca* had always been Louise's favourite film. As she drank her tea by the parlour fire, Cathy let the flow of information gently wash over her while she took in her surroundings.

Unlike the kitchen, the parlour was attractive, with a mahogany fireplace and two long, narrow sash windows set into the the thick wall of the farmhouse. Framed in red velvet, they looked out over the small front garden, a large red geranium in a brass pot brightening each deep embrasure. Cathy liked the room because it contained so many reminders of her childhood. The gilt overmantel mirror above the fireplace had hung in her grandparents' house in Cork. And the satinwood piano, seldom played nowadays, conjured up the image of Granny Riordan's neat white head and erect back. She was only ten when the stately old lady had died, but she could still recall the warmth with which visitors were welcomed in College Road. Grandad had been a professor of modern languages. Even after he retired, university colleagues, visiting academics and students from other lands came to their gatherings. Cathy remembered a warm June night when she'd stayed awake to listen to her grandmother playing a Chopin prelude. Lying upstairs in bed, she was filled with wonder as the golden notes rose upwards through the hushed house.

How could someone like Louise, who'd grown up in that atmosphere, be happy living in the country? Her first husband, Cathy's father, had been brought up here but had left as soon as he finished school, going away to train as a teacher, leaving his younger brother Vinnie to inherit the farm. Although John Carmody often said he was basically a son of the soil, he'd been educated, intelligent and witty. Cathy remembered his love of books and paintings, his appreciation of beautiful things. Some of the modern watercolours and oils hanging on the parlour walls had belonged to him. Louise had brought them to the farm when she married Vinnie. A few poignant reminders, Cathy thought, of the life her mother had shared with her father.

'Do you ever miss Dad?'

She saw Louise's smile fade, her face suddenly vulnerable. 'Why do you ask?'

'You were so happy together. Even when I was young I knew you were very much in love.'

'We were.' She got up and went over to draw the curtains across the windows. Cathy waited, gazing pensively into the fire. When she regained her seat, Louise said, 'I think of him always. But life goes on. And Vinnie's a good man.' She gave a wistful smile. 'They were brothers, after all. You mightn't think it, but there's a lot of your father in him.'

Cathy frowned. 'You could have fooled me.'

'We all see what we want to see,' her mother said gently. 'When you meet the right man, you'll understand.'

'I doubt that.'

Louise sighed. She gave Cathy a sidelong look. 'Detta and I went back to the bungalow last week. That nice couple who bought it are still there.'

Cathy leaned forward to stir the fire. As sparks showered up the chimney, she asked, 'Did they keep the flowering cherry? And the Canadian maple on the back lawn?'

'They haven't changed a thing. We met some of the old neighbours.' She saw her mother hesitate. 'Fergal's parents were asking after you.'

'The O'Reillys?' Cathy forced a smile. 'Does she make visitors take off their shoes before they walk on the carpet? Is the father still chasing kids out of the garden?'

'A lot of the neighbourhood children are gone,' Louise said thoughtfully. 'Anne O'Reilly's working in England. I don't think she comes home much.' She gave Cathy an oblique look. 'You heard Fergal was sent to west Cork?'

She felt her throat go dry. 'They say . . . they say he'll make a good priest.'

'That's all Jacinta O'Reilly ever wanted.' Louise gave a short laugh. 'Detta and I were just saying . . . '

'Mum,' Cathy said sharply, 'don't drag that up again. It was his own decision.'

'But you were such good friends when you were growing up.' Louise looked baffled. 'People called you "the Siamese twins". When you went away, you kept in touch. Letters. Meetings during the holidays. Then it all stopped. What happened, Cathy?'

'We just drifted apart.'

Louise looked unconvinced. 'You two were made for each other. Even after he went to the seminary, the first day home for the holidays, he'd come looking for you.'

'That was six years ago. People change.'

'You wouldn't still be carrying a torch for him?'

'Mum!'

She saw a speculative gleam in her mother's eye. 'You don't seem to have met anyone since.'

'What about Alan?'

'He wasn't good enough for you, was he? Sometimes I think you expect too much from people.' She looked at Cathy and sighed. 'I'm afraid Fergal has spoiled you for other men.'

'Like my namesake spoiled it for Heathcliff in *Wuthering Heights?*' Cathy asked scornfully. 'Mum, you're such a romantic. Don't worry, I'm not going to pine to death over Fergal O'Reilly. He's not the only fish in the sea.' She hesitated, wondering if she should say anything about Stephen. *No, better not. Mum would be sure to get the wrong idea.* 'I put him behind me years ago. Why are you so anxious for me to meet someone? What about the others?'

'Detta's not interested in romance.' Louise shrugged. 'As for Noreen, if that one ever settles down, I'll put an ad in the *Examiner*. But I've high hopes for you, Cathy.'

'Which no doubt will be disappointed. Look, Mum, when I meet the right man I'll tell you. But believe me, Fergal O'Reilly was not him.'

'He was such a beautiful little boy.' Louise's face was dreamy in the firelight. 'Those blue eyes, that blond hair.'

'Yes,' Cathy said. His beauty wasn't something she'd questioned as a child. When you saw a rainbow arcing across a rain-soaked sky or noticed the motes of dust dancing in a sunbeam, you accepted these things as part of the wonders of nature. 'A pity boys have to grow up.'

Her mother's eyes were suddenly alert. 'He hurt you, didn't he, child?'

Oh, no, Cathy thought. Her mother was like a dog trying to suck the last bit of a juicy bone. 'Just leave it, will you, Mum.' She picked up the teapot and poured out more tea. 'As you said yourself, life goes on.'

That night, as she tried to settle down in the spare room, sleep was slow to come. The wind keened around the farmhouse. A dog howled somewhere in sympathy. Images surged over her, no logical pattern to them.

She was a small child, counting the money she and Fergal got for their First Communion, laughing because she had more. She saw him smile, pretending not to mind. Then the pair of them took turns riding a two-wheeled bike, while Dad showed them how. They were studying for their Leaving Cert, hearing each other's French translations. They did a twenty-four-hour fast for Concern, shuddering at the taste of the watery soup. They clowned together at the school disco, at ease with each other. Yet aware.

Just as the images began to blur, she heard his voice. 'No matter what happens in the future, Cathy, we'll always be there for each other.' She was catapulted into wakefulness. She sat up in the darkness, her mind suddenly clear. No hope of sleep now. A door into the past had opened. A road she had vowed never to go down again was beckoning and she felt powerless to resist its pull.

Six years before, when Cathy went to Dublin first, she stayed in a small red-brick terrace house with her sister, Noreen and two other nurses from the nearby hospital. After a few weeks on the bedsitter trail, replying to advertisements, she eventually found a place of her own. A compact bedsitter at the top of an old three-storey house in Drumcondra, not far from the

Archbishop's palace. It wasn't the place of her dreams, Cathy told herself the first night she moved in, too excited to sleep after Noreen and her friends had gone. But at least it had its own bathroom, tiny though it was, and she could manage the rent. If she walked to work, she could save on bus fares, and maybe bring in sandwiches for her lunch.

She'd already found a job as office junior with a firm of chartered accountants on the second floor of a narrow, nineteenth-century house overlooking the north quays. It was a dusty rabbit warren, smelling of mildew and the occasional rank odours of the river at low tide. Cathy shared the main office with Sinéad, the senior typist, and Mrs Dunne, the boss's middle-aged secretary. From her desk, she could see the upper storeys of the buildings on the opposite quay. If she stood by the copier machine and craned her neck, she could glimpse the sun glinting off the grey waters of the Liffey.

The accountants worked at the back. The poky offices with their dark, panelled partitions and crammed filing cabinets reminded her of a Charles Dickens serial she'd seen on television. The first time she went into one she pictured its occupants in wing collars, sitting up at high desks, poring over ledgers with quill pens. The head of the firm, James O'Donohue, wouldn't have been out of place in a nineteenth-century setting. A Scrooge of an employer, fawning on his wealthier clients but being brusque with the staff, he was a stickler for timekeeping and liked to dictate everything that went on, down to the smallest detail.

Even his sons were afraid of him, according to Sinéad. It occurred to Cathy that Jimmy, the curt, unfriendly brother, would be just like his father in a few years' time. But Peter, the younger of the two, soon struck up an acquaintanceship with her.

'Settling in OK?' He looked up from his desk and grinned. His brother was out and they were alone in the office. Other mornings Peter had kept his eyes on his computer, giving a muttered thanks when she placed his post in front of him. Today he was relaxed and confident. 'Bit of a change from Cork, isn't it.'

'Culchie land, you mean?' Cathy was tired of hearing snide comments from the two other women in the office. 'Believe it or not, we do have computers, and buses, and . . .'

'OK, OK.' He put up his hands. 'I get the message.'

He was kind of attractive, even if his ears stuck out. He had alert blue eyes, and if his face was too sharp to be handsome, he had an engaging smile. If his brown hair was any shorter, he'd be a skinhead. It looked strange with the dark blue shirt and matching silk tie. 'Are you into punk rock? Or have you just been let out of the army?'

'The Gestapo, actually. "Ve haf ways of making you talk." To tell you the truth, I did it to get up my old man's nose.' He shrugged. 'He made me get rid of the ponytail. So I said to myself, "if it's short hair you want . . ."'

Cathy grinned as she turned away. 'He certainly got that.'

'Hang on a minute,' Peter said. 'Listen, the city can be a big place if you don't know your way around. Maybe I could . . .'

'Maybe.' Talk about a fast worker. She smiled as she kept going. Noreen had warned her against guys like that. And nobody needed to tell her that being asked out by the boss's son was one of the oldest clichés in the book. I wasn't born yesterday, Cathy told herself.

But Peter proved a difficult person to put off. And Cathy was lonely. Apart from Noreen and her friends, she knew no one in Dublin. After turning him down several times, she agreed to meet him for a drink. It wasn't really a date, she told herself as she got ready. She'd make that clear from the start.

'So there's a boyfriend back home?' It was hard to tell from his smile if he was surprised or disappointed. Probably neither. He struck her as being the kind of guy who prided himself on having everything figured out. 'No problem.' His tone was easy as he sipped his pint. 'Do you go home every weekend?'

'Not really. He's away at college.'

'I suppose it's handier for him to come to Dublin.' Peter smiled knowingly. 'Now that you have your own pad.' A look of envy crossed his sharp features. 'You country people know all the angles.'

'Not really, 'Cathy said again.

She saw his eyes narrow as he studied her face and comprehension dawned. 'I get it. He hasn't been up to see you yet.'

'No.' She looked away from the alert blue eyes. 'It's hard to explain.'

Peter's lip curled. 'The silly bollix.'

She felt her face redden. 'It's not Fergal's fault.'

'Well, whose is it, then? OK, students don't have much money. But what's wrong with hitching?' He stared at her with undisguised admiration. 'I'd hitch halfway across Ireland if I had you at the end of it. What's the matter with the guy?'

Finding it difficult to meet his gaze, she looked down at the table. 'He . . . he's in a seminary.'

'For priests? Ah, come on, you're winding me up!'

Cathy looked at his astonished face, and shook her head.

'Let me get this straight,' Peter said slowly. 'He's going to be a priest, right? But he's still your boyfriend?' He gave a baffled laugh. 'What'd be the point?'

She bit her lip. 'He probably won't stay. It's his mother . . . '

'Ah, come on,' Peter said again. 'Not in this day and age.'

'It's not just her. He kind of likes the idea himself, but . . . '

'I get it.' She saw his face clear. 'He wants you too. What a nerve!' But there was no admiration in his voice. 'So what's he going to do?'

'He's going to have to choose,' Cathy said. 'I've told him that. He's giving it a year. That way he can be fair to everyone.'

'Ah, come on . . . '

Ignoring the disbelief on his face, she hurried on. 'He's going to make his decision in the summer holidays before he has to go back for his second year.' When she saw his eyebrows rise, she tried to smile. 'It's only another few months.'

'Well, it's your life.' Peter drained his glass and got up from the table. 'But it's the weirdest thing I ever heard.'

'You don't have to go.' Cathy felt a stab of disappointment. He was good company, even if she'd ruled out anything happening between them. Besides, she didn't relish being dumped in a strange pub, having to walk home through unfamiliar streets. It was too late now to regret telling him. 'We can still be friends.'

'Who said anything about going?' He grinned at her. 'Just getting another round.' He glanced at the lager left in her glass. 'Same again?'

He really had an infectious grin. She smiled in relief and fumbled for her bag. 'Let me get this.'

'There'll be other nights.' He grinned again. 'Something tells me you're going to need friends. After a story like that, you're not safe to be let out on your own.'

'Thanks a lot.' Cathy's chin went up. But it was difficult to take offence. As she watched Peter swagger up to the bar, she began to relax. A good thing she'd explained the situation. No danger now of any misunderstanding. And it would be good to have someone to talk to about Fergal .

But Peter wanted to talk about himself. Over their

second drink she learned he was twenty-three, and had passed the preliminary accountancy exam. There were more years of study ahead of him, he said. But the beauty of it was you could train and work at the same time. It was an interesting job. He liked figures and enjoyed travelling the country, doing audits.

'You're good with people,' Cathy said. 'Not like your brother.'

'Oh, Jimmy can put on the charm.' Peter grimaced wryly. 'He and Da don't bother making the effort for the lower orders.'

'Minions like me? But you're his son.'

'You don't have to remind me. All I get is lectures about living up to the family name. He's convinced I'm going to let him down.'

She was surprised. 'What reason has he got to think that?'

Peter looked sheepish. 'I was a bit of a hard man at school. Got drunk after the Junior Cert, made a show of myself.'

'A lot of people do. It's part of growing up.'

'Try telling the old man that.' He shrugged. 'You'd think he was never young. He hit the roof. I was grounded for weeks. Most people would've learned from that. But not me. A group of us in fifth year started missing classes, skiving off to the pub during study periods. The teachers found out. Then the shit hit the fan. Some guys were expelled. Because it was my first time, I got away with a suspension.' His mouth twisted wryly. 'My mother managed to persuade the headmaster that I'd never get into trouble again.'

'And did you?'

Peter looked solemn. 'I was scared shitless. I could see my future in ruins, just as my old man prophesied. Looking back, getting caught was probably the best thing that could have happened. I turned over a new leaf. Kept my nose clean. Got stuck into the books. Did a good Leaving Cert.' He gave a rueful shrug. 'But I've never been able to live it down with my da.'

'In time, you will.'

'How much time does it take? No, Cathy, he's had a down on me ever since.' His face darkened. 'Sometimes I can do nothing to please him.'

'And you try so hard,' Cathy said. 'Is that why you cut your hair short?'

Peter laughed, spreading his hands in mock defeat. 'How did one so young get to be so cynical?' His face softened. 'Do you know something? You and I are going to be friends.'

'I hate the idea of you going out with someone else,' Fergal wrote from the seminary. 'But obviously I can't tell you what to do.'

'That's big of him,' Noreen said. 'But then Fergal was always a *good* little boy.'

'I wish you wouldn't talk about him like that,' Cathy said. Noreen was her eldest sister, and her approval meant a lot. Although she was five years older, the two had always been close. Cathy had never forgotten the way Noreen brought her into her bed during the first dreadful nights after their father died, holding her close and murmuring words of comfort till she fell asleep. She was more of a mother than Mum had ever been. She could still remember her sense of shock and abandonment a year later when Noreen left to go to Dublin to train as a nurse. She came home for Christmas and holidays after that. But it wasn't the same. And she'd changed too. Although she still looked like the old Noreen, with Mum's dark colouring and Dad's twinkling eyes, in other ways she'd become a stranger. A confident, self-reliant stranger, with that indefinable air of having grown up and moved on. That's what the big city does for you, Cathy told herself. As soon as she finished school, she'd go away too.

Since coming to Dublin, she'd got to know Noreen in a new way. She felt her sister's equal now, with a job and a place of her own. Yet she relied very much on her support. It came as a blow to Cathy that Noreen had no time for the romance with Fergal. 'You're out of your mind,' she said when she heard. 'Get sense, girl, and forget him.

But Cathy couldn't do that. Not even after she met Peter and started seeing him outside the office. 'You'd need to watch that fella too,' Noreen said. 'He sounds like a real city slicker. But anyone would be an improvement on that mother's boy, Fergal O'Reilly.'

'That's not fair,' Cathy said. 'You still think of him as a boy of twelve. He's grown into a fine man.'

'I met him at Christmas.' Noreen shrugged. 'If anything, he's too handsome.'

'You must be joking.'

'You can laugh, Cathy.' Her sister's round, rosy face was unusually serious. 'But I know what I'm talking about. It's not just his looks. There's something about him. And that mother of his . . . '

'You can't hold people responsible for their mothers. Look at Mum, she's not behaving rationally at the moment.'

Noreen frowned. 'Because she wants to sell the house and marry Uncle Vinnie? It's not the same thing. Look, Cathy, I know he's not exactly God's gift to women – '

'That's putting it mildly.'

' – but he *was* Dad's brother. He's family.'

'She could do better.'

'He's the one she wants. Mum's in her fifties. Old enough to know her own mind.'

'And I'm not?' Cathy was stung. 'I'll be nineteen in August. Look, Noreen, I've been in love with Fergal for years. And he feels the same.'

'What's he doing in the seminary, then?'

Cathy felt a sense of despair. Noreen just didn't want to listen. 'We've been through all this before.'

'And we'll go through it again before you're much older,' her sister said. 'Take my advice and forget him. He's bad news. That other fella sounds a much better bet.'

Cathy began to look forward to seeing Peter. Although he wasn't anxious to draw attention to their friendship, he usually managed to sneak a moment with her in the office. Then he'd be waiting outside her house that evening in his old Opel Kadett, jumping out eagerly to help her into the car, which had a dodgy handle on the passenger door. As they pulled away from the kerb, the exhaust pipe belching fumes, Cathy pretended not to notice the faces of kids in neighbouring front gardens, and adults out for a stroll. Let them stare. We have wheels and can go any place we want.

She found Peter a willing guide. As the old car wheezed around the city, he named streets and pointed out buildings of interest. Some evenings they went out to Howth, driving along the coast road, with its view of hills and mountains across the bay. They parked the car near the harbour and climbed Howth Head in the dusk to reach the summit, where they could admire the lights encircling the darkness like a dazzling necklace.

Other nights they crossed the river to see the bay from the far side. While Peter identified landmarks to her, Cathy tried to grasp the dimensions of the city which was now her home. She enjoyed the trip along the coast road and was enchanted with Dun Laoghaire, its long seafront and Georgian terraces. Although it was a bustling town, the west pier had a peaceful air, with people strolling in pairs or in families, the night air soft on their faces.

'Fergal would love this,' Cathy said one July evening. She felt Peter grow still at her side. But when she glanced at him, his face gave nothing away.

'Won't be long now.' His voice was flippant.

'Another few weeks and you'll be seeing Lover Boy again. I suppose he's home already?'

'I'm not sure.' Cathy frowned. 'Fergal said something about spending a few weeks in a parish in west Cork. Some kind of work experience,' she said doubtfully. 'Although what use a clerical student would be, I don't know.'

'Hearing confessions on the sly,' Peter said with a grin. 'Might try a bit of that myself. Think of the sins you'd hear . . . '

'Do you have to joke about everything?'

'A thing I don't understand,' he said, giving her a bland stare, 'is why he'd do something like that if he's packing it in.'

Cathy had wondered too. She looked at him stonily. 'So?'

'Sounds like he's hedging his bets. Or he could be stringing you along.'

She felt her face redden. 'Fergal's not like that. I've known him all my life. He probably doesn't want to let someone down.' She glared at Peter. 'You don't know what you're talking about.'

'OK, OK. You know him, I don't.'

'Yes, I do.' Cathy's voice was firm. Peter was a nice guy but it wasn't in his interest to make Fergal look good. Although he seemed content to accept the friendship on her terms, she suspected that he'd like it to be something more. But she couldn't worry about his feelings, not when she had Fergal to think about.

She couldn't wait to see him. Only another few weeks, and they'd be in each other's arms again. This was going to be the best holiday ever.

SEVEN

On the last Friday in July, James O'Donohue & Sons closed for its fortnight's annual holiday. The next morning Cathy took the train to Cork. Her aunt Helen met her at the station and drove her the twenty miles to the small town where her mother and Detta lived. On the way, she told Cathy that Louise had found a buyer for the family home.

'I don't believe it!' Although she'd known since Easter that the house was to be sold, she'd managed to convince herself that her mother would see sense and change her mind. A vain hope, she realised when they arrived at the neat white bungalow overlooking the main road at the edge of the town and found an auctioneer's sign sticking out of the front hedge. As she trudged up the hilly driveway, she still felt a sense of disbelief. Her family had always lived in the white, green-shuttered bungalow. She couldn't even imagine them living anywhere else. It was a mistake, she told herself. Or someone's idea of a joke.

Inside the bungalow, she found her mother at the kitchen table making lists, while Detta and the housekeeper, an elderly woman called Mary, went through cupboards, sorting and discarding their contents into black plastic sacks. As she tried to take in the scene, Cathy's eyes swam with tears. She stood unnoticed in the doorway until her aunt urged her forward. At the sound of their voices, her mother looked up and threw them a vague smile.

'Ah, there you are, child. And Helen too.'

'Good,' Detta said. 'We could do with more help.'

'I'll make us a pot of tea.' Helen, ever practical, moved to the electric kettle. 'Get some cups, Cathy.'

But Cathy ignored her. 'What's going on, Mum? Why all the rush?'

She saw her mother exchange a smile with Detta.

'We've had a change of plan.'

'You mean the wedding date's fixed?' Cathy was aghast. 'But I thought . . . '

'Now that we've got a buyer, why wait?' She heard the barely suppressed excitement in Detta's voice. Anyone would think she was getting married, Cathy thought sourly. She listened without enthusiasm as her mother and sister outlined their plans. The wedding would take place at the end of September. Everything was arranged – the church, the flowers, the hotel reception. The bride's outfit was at the second-fitting stage, the honeymoon booked. Because Noreen was so tied up at the hospital and didn't get home often, Detta was going to be bridesmaid, with two small Carmody cousins as flower girls. An older relative would be Vinnie's best man. The couple planned to fly out to Lanzarote the day after the wedding.

'Imagine Vinnie being away for the All-Ireland Final,'

Detta said. 'It must be love.'

Love? Difficult to connect gruff, stalwart Vinnie with that emotion. Besides, Cathy didn't like to think of him and her mother in that way. There was something incongruous about talk of weddings and honeymoons at their age. Maybe she was being unfair to Mum. Noreen had seemed to think she was. The last time she and her eldest sister had discussed it, Noreen said Cathy's attitude was immature. Maybe it was. But as she listened to Detta gushing on about the arrangements, she felt sickened. It would be easier to take if her sister was the one who was getting married. More normal somehow. Not that Detta was seeing anyone at the moment. Or if – Cathy caught her breath at the thought – it was herself and Fergal. Although that was years away. She wasn't interested in marriage yet; she had too many things she wanted to do first. But if she ever did think of getting married, he'd be the one.

'Is Fergal home?' She tried to keep her voice casual. 'Have you seen anything of him?'

'What?' Detta frowned at the change of subject. 'He was around yesterday, asking for you. Now, about the flower girls, Mum . . . '

'He looked well,' Louise said to Cathy. Her face had lit up at the mention of Fergal. Unlike Detta, she was remarkably serene about her wedding. The prospect of moving to the farm didn't provoke in her the same excitement it did in her second daughter. She put her lists down on the table, giving a sentimental smile. 'I never thought I'd say it, but the clerical clothes suit him, with that lovely fair hair of his.'

Cathy felt a pang of unease. 'Is he still wearing black?'

Louise nodded. 'Although apparently it's not mandatory in the holidays.'

'Maybe he likes being set apart from the common herd.' Detta's voice was caustic.

Cathy's chin went up. 'Fergal's not like that.'

'No?' Her sister looked sceptical. 'Well, here's your chance to find out.' A shadow had passed the kitchen window. As they heard an eager rap on the back door, she gave a sardonic chuckle. 'I do believe that's his reverence now.'

They were shy with each other at first. She felt embarrassed, greeting Fergal under her family's watchful gaze. But even after Louise had urged the pair of them into the sitting room, saying that she and the other women had to get on with the work, Cathy still felt awkward, unsure of what to say. The black clothes made him look like a stranger. But a handsome one. He'd filled out and seemed taller. What she'd told Noreen about him was true. He was turning into a fine-looking man.

'It's been a long time since Easter,' she said hesitantly.

A shadow crossed his face. 'Oh, Cathy!' She heard the break in his voice. 'I've missed you.'

'Me too.'

Then his arms were around her, his cheek pressed against hers. She felt his warmth and his nearness, her senses stirred by his own special smell. Their lips met, and they kissed long and lovingly.

'You've no idea how much I was looking forward to that,' Fergal sighed. As they sat down together on the sofa, Cathy recalled their first kiss. It had been the Christmas they were both in fifth year, on this very sofa. They'd come back to the bungalow after a party. The house was quiet; Louise was in bed and Detta was out with friends at a disco. They made coffee and drank it in the sitting room while the fire burned low in the grate and lights glittered on the tree in the corner of the shadowy room. She could still remember her surprise when Fergal put down his coffee mug and turned to her. It wasn't Cathy's first kiss – she'd gone out with other boys during the previous year and was seeing someone else over Christmas. But she and Fergal had just been friends, nothing more. As his lips sought hers, she'd felt her heart thump with excitement. And apprehension. Although there was a sense of inevitability about the kiss, she wondered what the future would hold for them.

Now, as they sat together holding hands, with the sun streaming in through the large picture window in the sitting room, her eyes examined him hungrily. After that first kiss, she'd known that she and Fergal were made for each other. And she still felt the same way. She was so content to be with him that at first she barely listened to what he was saying.

'Cathy, you mean so much to me. I don't want to lose you.'

'But why would you?' She was surprised. 'My feelings haven't changed.' She looked at him anxiously. 'Have yours?'

'No,' Fergal said in a low voice.

'You really mean that?'

'Of course I do.'

'Does that mean you've made up your mind?' She was overjoyed. 'But that's . . .'

'Hold on a moment. I didn't say . . . '

'But Fergal, you said you'd decide.'

'And I will, I will. But you must realise what a big decision this is for me.' His face grew serious. 'I've got to be sure it's what God wants.'

She hated when he spoke like that. 'But what about you? What do you want?'

'I want what God wants.' She remembered that solemn, blue-eyed look so well from when they were children. 'We can't rush Him.' His voice was gentle but firm. 'He's the one who matters in all this.'

But what about me? Her heart sank. *Don't I count?*

'Wouldn't you know he was just made for the priesthood?' Mrs O'Reilly looked eagerly at Cathy over the low hedge between the two back gardens and then at Mr O'Reilly nearby, who nodded his agreement. 'Ever since he was a child.' Fergal's mother was a solidly built woman in her fifties with wispy ash-blonde hair hanging lankly on either side of a podgy face. Her prominent blue eyes always reminded Cathy of a stuffed hawk in a glass case she'd seen on a school trip to the Natural

History Museum. As she peered over the hedge, her usual expression of vague disapproval gave way to a fond smile. 'Father Cassidy says Fergal's a natural on the altar.'

'The altar?' Cathy glanced at her uncertainly, then at Mr O'Reilly, a spare, poker-faced man with a greying moustache who was clipping the hedge with a kind of savage precision. 'But he's not ordained yet.'

'Oh, he's years of study ahead, no bother to him. But Father Cassidy says it's never too early to start.' Her voice took on a solemn note. 'From the moment they enter the seminary, Cathy, they're promised to God.'

A suspicion began to dawn on Cathy that Mrs O'Reilly hadn't sought her out that morning just for a chat. She smiled nervously at the older woman, and waited.

'You've been very good, dear, writing to Fergal with all the news, helping him settle in.' Although her neighbour's tone was amiable, the hawklike eyes were cold. 'But there's no need for it any more.' She glanced at her husband, who gave a grunt of assent, then went on clipping leaves and branches as if his life depended on it. Cathy wasn't taken in by his apparent lack of interest. Mr O'Reilly might be a man of few words but he was every bit as formidable as his wife. She recalled that when she was growing up, the neighbourhood kids had been terrified of him. It was rumoured that anyone caught crossing his vegetable patch or pilfering fruit would be locked in the garden shed. Not that she'd ever known this to happen. The threat had been enough.

She wasn't afraid of him now, Cathy told herself. But as she gazed at Fergal's parents, she felt a sense of betrayal.

'I didn't tell her about the letters.' To her surprise, Fergal seemed unperturbed. 'She probably found them.'

'She goes through your things?' Cathy was aghast.

'Ever since Anne and I were children,' he said half-laughingly, 'Ma's a bit like Our Heavenly Father in the Gospels. Not a sparrow falls but she has to know about it.'

'It's not funny. I don't know how you can stand it.'

'You get used to it.' He shrugged. 'You learn to keep things out of her way.'

'But she has no right.' She was baffled by his calm acceptance. A thought struck her. 'Your sister? Surely she didn't put up with that kind of thing.'

He laughed. 'They used to have run-ins all the time. Probably one of the reasons Anne left home. Of course, my sister wouldn't be one of the most tolerant people either.' He gave a resigned smile. 'A bit like Ma, I suppose. Look, Cathy, don't take it so personally.'

She felt her face flush. 'She read my letters!'

'Now, we don't know that.'

'Ah, come on, Fergal!'

'OK, I admit I was a bit careless.' He gave her a placating smile. 'Sorry.'

'Your mother reads my letters to you, and warns me off.' Her voice rose indignantly. 'And all you can say is "Sorry"?'

'What else can I do?' His voice was reasonable. 'Cathy, don't be too hard on Ma. Deep down, she means well.' He grinned suddenly. 'If it doesn't bother me, why should you mind?'

'I can think of several reasons.' But she knew it was no use arguing. Although she'd been the leader and instigator of adventures when they were growing up, in recent years she'd discovered a quiet stubbornness about him which, though exasperating at times, was still deserving of respect. 'OK, I'll try to ignore her. But Fergal . . . ' She felt a pang of alarm. 'I've only another week of my holidays left.'

'All the more reason not to be wasting time on silly arguments.' He smiled as he took her hand. 'What do you want to do? Head over to the tennis club for a game, or sit here in the sun?'

'I don't want to stay here if your mother is going to be looking at us over the fence.' She got up from the rug spread out on the grass under the maple in the back garden and said with a sigh, 'Tennis it is.'

The days went by much too quickly. And they had so little time together.

'I know it's your holiday, Cathy,' Louise said. 'But it's only six weeks to the wedding. We'll be moving out immediately after the honeymoon, so you'll need to get your room sorted before you go back to Dublin.' She left out a roll of black plastic bags and went back to making lists, sighing audibly to herself over which pieces of furniture would go to the auction rooms and which would go with them to the farm. 'Remember, anything you want to keep can be stored in boxes. Vinnie says there's a huge attic.' She'd already explained that Cathy wouldn't have her own bedroom in the farmhouse. When she came down for weekends, she'd be put in a guest room.

'OK,' Cathy said. But as she went into the pretty bedroom she'd had since childhood, her spirits were low. She glanced at the shelf which held her collection of soft toys. Each doll and stuffed animal had a memory attached to it. Parting from them was like giving away a piece of herself. But she couldn't bring them to Dublin with her. And there was no way she'd let them moulder in a dusty attic. She swept them into a black bag for Aunt Helen to take to the hospital, where they might give some child pleasure. The thought brought no consolation. All over the house, the familiar landmarks of her childhood were being dispersed, scattered between salesrooms and the Vincent de Paul, or packed away in boxes in the attic of an old farmhouse she would never, ever look upon as home.

Grow up, Cathy. Time to move on. But as she went through drawers and cupboards, she felt a growing sense of disbelief. This bedroom would no longer be hers. The house would belong to someone else. Strangers would eat their meals in the kitchen, watch television in the airy lounge and lie out on the back lawn under the shady maple tree. It wasn't fair. As her eyes filled with angry tears, she was gripped by the sharp pain of impending loss.

'I'll miss the old place, of course,' Detta said. 'But I don't think Mum felt the same way about it since Dad died. No harm for her to make a fresh start. Or for me, either.' Her face brightened. 'You've no idea how much I hated working in that office. Be reasonable, Cathy. You've left home. You can't expect us to hold on to this house so you can come for the odd holiday.'

'No,' Cathy said. 'But . . .'

There was no point in arguing. If they talked for a thousand years, Detta would never be made understand. Was there anyone who did? Even Fergal seemed to have no perception of how she was feeling. He was sympathetic whenever she mentioned losing her home, but she felt he was only going through the motions, his mind on other things. Of course it was an unsettling time for him too. But not for much longer. Once he made his decision, she consoled herself, everything would fall into place.

The night before she went back to Dublin, as they walked under the spreading elm trees on the path by the river, he broke the news to her. The sound of the water obscured his soft voice at times but the meaning of his words was unmistakable.

'You're going back?' Cathy was stunned. 'After everything you said?' Close to tears, she shook his hand away. 'It was all lies.'

'No!' Fergal looked distressed. But he didn't try to take her hand back. 'I do care for you. But I've always wanted to be a priest.' His face was determined. 'I can't give that up.'

'It's your parents. Your mother . . . '

'If I wanted to leave, no one could make me stay.'

She pictured his mother's smug face, the cold, hawklike eyes.

'I don't believe that.' But even as she said it, she knew he told the truth. As she watched his face, the realisation grew. Fergal had always suited himself. Their relationship had existed on his terms, not hers. Her shoulders slumped in defeat. 'Maybe I do.'

She saw his look of relief. 'That makes it so much easier.'

'For you, maybe.' She felt the first stirrings of anger. 'But what about me?'

'But, Cathy, this doesn't have to mean the end of us. We can still see each other.'

'What would be the point?' she asked bitterly.

'We can still be friends.' His voice was careful. 'Celibacy's just a church rule. It wasn't always there. It might only be a matter of time before they allow priests to marry.'

'You wish.' She turned away angrily. 'When we're both in Zimmer frames.'

'Cathy, wait.' He caught up with her and touched her arm. 'We can still write, meet during the holidays.' His voice grew persuasive. 'It doesn't have to mean the end of our friendship.' They rounded a bend in the river, and the weir came into view. He raised his voice to be heard above the sound of the water. 'I don't want to lose you,' he said urgently. 'Say you'll think about it.'

The river had a metallic sheen as it flowed over the

weir. Two boys stood near the water's edge, lobbing sticks into the eddying stream, calling sporadically to each other. Long fingers of pink streaked the sky above the trees on the opposite bank. Some of their leaves were already tinged with brown. The summer was nearly over. What a pity things had to end. She felt sadness crushing her.

'Cathy.' Fergal's voice seemed to come from a long way off. 'Say something, will you?' She turned to find him watching her, a tentative smile on his face.

She glanced in the direction of the boys scampering at the water's edge. 'I don't see any future for us.'

'Don't say that.'

A cold feeling came over her. 'You can't have it both ways, Fergal.'

She saw him wince. 'I don't want us to end things like this.'

'It was your choice.'

'At least think about it,' he said pleadingly.

She picked up a small leafy branch lying on the ground, tossed it into the river and watched as it was borne swiftly downstream. When she spoke, her voice was calm, indifferent almost.

'I don't need to think about it.' She turned on her heel and walked swiftly along the path, without looking back.

Peter, looking tanned and fit, met her off a packed train the following evening.

'You shouldn't have bothered.' She was too deep in

misery to be grateful. 'I could have got a taxi.'

'You'd be all night waiting for one. But not to worry.' He made a flourish. 'Esmerelda, my trusty banger, is at your service.' He picked up the heavier of her cases. 'Follow me.'

Despite her protests, she trailed after him through the crowds at the station entrance, out to the old Opel neatly parked among the cars lining the kerb. She left Peter to stow away the luggage and sank into the passenger seat. When he got in beside her, his face was eager.

'You look great. Good holiday?'

'OK. How about you?'

'Picture it for yourself.' He rolled his eyes. 'A fortnight with the family in Rosslare. The da being all sporty.' He grimaced. 'As for the kid sister from hell . . .'

'You got plenty of sun, anyway.'

'That's true.' He looked pleased. 'The sunny south-east lived up to its promise. About the only thing that did. But I'm definitely going to Spain with the lads next year.'

Cathy felt leaden inside. All her next years seemed to stretch endlessly ahead. How would she get through the next few hours, never mind the rest of her life? As they pulled out into the traffic, she tried to look interested in what Peter was saying, but images of the previous night kept running through her mind like a tape that wouldn't switch off.

'Why do I get the impression I'm talking to myself?' His voice brought her back to the present. 'Where were you, Cathy? Still in Cork?'

'Something like that.' She saw to her surprise that they were nearly there. From now on, her only home would be a bedsitter on the top floor of a grotty old house. Her misery deepened as the car drew up at the gate. In the dying light of the August evening, the house had a forlorn look. Just the way she felt inside.

'A bit Gothic horror, isn't it?' She tried to laugh. But it came out as a sob. 'I'm sorry.' She turned away to hide her face, fighting to regain control of herself. She felt his hand on her arm and shook it away angrily. 'I'll be OK in a minute.'

She heard Peter sigh. 'I'll get the luggage from the boot.' He came back almost immediately. 'If you open the front door, I'll bring the cases up.'

'If you want to.' Cathy got out of the car, wishing he'd leave them and drive away. She wanted to be alone, to crawl into a dark corner and die. But she knew she couldn't manage to bring the cases up two flights of stairs on her own.

'What's in them, anyway?' Peter panted as they stopped on a landing to rest. 'Gold bullion? Did you rob a bank?'

'Just a few things from home. Souvenirs of a previous existence.' Ignoring his puzzled look, she set off again. Only another flight of stairs, a few paces across the landing. But when they arrived at her doorway Peter insisted on bringing the cases inside.

The bedsitter was bathed in the evening sun; it was the time of the day when the room looked its best. The light turned walls and windows to gold, touching them with beauty. But it was an illusion, she knew, soon to vanish. As she glanced around, she felt none of her earlier pride of ownership. The odour of the last takeaway she'd eaten still lingered in the musty air. Dead flies lay feet-up on the windowsills and there was fluff on the dun-coloured carpet. After the bright, airy bungalow she'd left a few hours earlier, the bedsitter was cramped and squalid. She felt her guts tighten.

'Shit!' She sat down abruptly in a chair. 'Shit! Shit! Shit!'

'Cathy?' Peter turned from opening a window, surprise on his face. 'Are you OK?'

'No.' *What a stupid question.* 'I'm not.'

'Things didn't go well in Cork, I take it?'

'They're selling the bungalow. My mother's going ahead with the wedding.'

'That isn't what I meant.'

'I know.' She pressed her lips together. 'But I don't want to talk about that.'

His eyes examined her face. 'What you need is a drink.'

'There's a bottle of wine in the fridge.' She remembered putting it there, thinking she'd have something to celebrate when she got back from Cork. She had hoped Fergal might be drinking it with her. How could she have been so naive? As Peter clattered around with bottle opener and glasses, she sat slumped in her chair, studying the geometric designs on the wallpaper. How hideous they were. How could she have thought that somewhere like this could be home? It looked as if she'd been fooling herself about a lot of things. As the wallpaper began to blur before her eyes, she felt a hand on her arm.

'Here, you'll feel better after this.'

She took the glass and held it against her hot cheek. 'I doubt that.'

'Now don't start crying again. Will you drink the friggin' stuff, for God's sake. Sorry, Cathy, I didn't mean to shout.' He gave her a helpless look as he sat down opposite her. 'I hate to see you like this.'

'You're a good friend, Peter.' She sipped the wine, grateful for its sharp coolness. Suddenly she was glad he was there. Maybe it would be good to talk about it, after all.

'The nerve of the guy,' Peter said when she'd finished. He topped up her glass. 'If it's any consolation, you did the right thing.'

Despite the wine's warm glow, she felt a sense of anguish. 'Knowing that doesn't make it any easier.'

'It will, in time.'

'How do *you* know?' She felt irritated by the certainty in his voice. 'Are you an expert?'

He gave a wry smile. 'I know what it's like to be dumped.'

'It was my decision,' Cathy said indignantly. She saw his smile widen. 'Oh, God!' She gulped her wine. 'Who am I trying to fool? Of course I was dumped.' Her tone grew bitter. 'He was too pure and noble.' She mimicked

Fergal's reasonable tones. '"But remember, Cathy, God must be part of the equation." Whatever that means.' Her voice caught on a sob.

'Sounds more like a triangle,' Peter said. 'I know – the Eternal Triangle. Get it?'

'It's not funny. How would you like to be dumped in favour of the Almighty?'

'Oh, I don't know. A helluva lot better than seeing your girlfriend go zooming off on the back of a motorbike with Godzilla's first cousin. *And* you'd never have to worry if he was better than you in bed.'

'Who? God or Godzilla?' She gave a shriek of laughter. 'Oh, dear, I think the wine must be going to my head.' She looked around for more, but the bottle was empty. 'Pity. I liked it.'

'I have another bottle in the car.' Peter watched her, his head cocked to one side. With his bright, alert eyes he reminded her of a terrier her family used to own. 'Will I go down and get it?'

She thought for a moment, felt reckless suddenly. 'Why not?'

'Good girl,' Peter said. While she waited for him to come back, she kicked off her shoes and made herself more comfortable in her chair. There was a lot to be said for wine. The edge of her anguish had dulled. And, joy of joys, she could have a lie-in tomorrow. Because of the bank holiday earlier in the month, the office didn't reopen till Tuesday. Things could be worse, she told herself as she heard Peter's footsteps outside.

'The beauty of red wine is . . .' Peter sounded as if he'd discovered the secret of the universe '. . . it doesn't have to be chilled.' He grinned smugly. 'Saves time.'

Cathy felt suddenly argumentative. 'But aren't you supposed to let it stand after you open it?'

'Bit late for that. After you've guzzled half the bottle.'

'What do you mean, *I've* guzzled it?' She stared at him indignantly.

'OK, OK. *We.* Do you know something, Cathy, you've quite a temper at times.'

'No, I haven't . . .'

'It's OK, I like fiery women.' He moved his chair so that his face was only a few inches away. 'And I like you, Cathy Carmody. Right from the minute I first saw you.'

'I like you too, Peter O'Donoghue.' Daylight had long since faded from the room. Although a lamp in the corner was on, she could barely make out the outlines of his face. Maybe it was time he went home. But when his arms went around her, she found herself hugging him back. 'You're a good friend, Peter. Worth two of Fergal any day.'

'Forget him, Cathy, He's not worth it.' Peter's lips were warm against her face. His hand caressed her spine. 'The guy never cared for you . . .'

'You're right,' Cathy said sadly. But I'll never forget him.' She caught her breath on a sob. 'Never.'

'Of course you will.' His voice was a murmur, his hand kept up its stroking. 'He didn't deserve you. You're too good for him.'

'Oh, Peter!' She was touched by the affection in his voice. 'You're the only one who understands me.' Although she liked the feel of his arms around her, some instinct of caution made her pull away. 'Let's have another drink.' She reached for the wine bottle. 'One for the road?'

'Not a good idea.' He gently took the bottle from her. 'Too much wine makes you sleepy. Remember?'

'Did I say that?' It was hard to remember what she had or hadn't told him. 'But you're right.' She blinked at him in the dim light. The room swam around her, Peter's face seemed distorted and far away, then came back into focus. 'Mustn't fall asleep. Got to keep my wits about me. But I need to lie down for a minute.' As he helped her over to the divan, she found herself giggling foolishly. 'Towser . . . that was his name.'

'Who?' He sounded baffled.

'Not *who*, what.' Although the walls had started advancing and receding, as she sat down on the edge of the bed, Cathy felt it important to explain. 'That dog we had when I was little . . . the terrier . . . '

'You're a funny girl.' The mattress rushed up to meet her. When her head hit the pillow, she heard him say, 'Do you know, I've never met anyone like you.'

Cathy opened her eyes.

The bedside lamp was on.

The walls had stopped moving. Thank God for that. Her head was muzzy and her arms and legs were leaden. Yet she felt alert. A strange sort of alertness.

As if time was standing still. Someone moved just outside her line of vision.

'It's OK.' Peter's voice. She heard the divan creak under his weight. His body gleamed whitely above her. 'Only me.' She felt his nakedness as his skin brushed against hers.

Cathy was surprised to find she was naked too. She had a confused recollection of his hands helping her undress. 'But I thought I was dreaming.' Her words sounded indistinct, taking a long time to come out.

'What did you dream?' His voice was affectionate, teasing. Then became tinged with wonder. 'God, you're beautiful, Cathy.' His hands caressed her body, gently touching her breasts, tracing the mound of her stomach, the inside of her thighs. 'I think I'm dreaming too.'

Fergal never touched me there. She was sad at the thought. And now he never would. She felt weighted down by her sadness. At the same time, she was detached from her surroundings. Even when his tongue probed her mouth, his hands growing more urgent, his fingers touching places inside her where no one had touched before, she had the unreal feeling that her body belonged to someone else. Maybe she was dreaming after all. She let herself slip away into sleep.

She opened her eyes again. Then closed them quickly against the sharp light pouring in past the undrawn curtains. As she fell back against the pillows, every bone in her body ached, while sledgehammers pounded at her temples.

'Want some coffee?' She opened a cautious eye, to see Peter dressed only in boxers standing by the kitchen counter, grinning at her. As she sat up, Cathy realised with a shock that she was naked under the bedclothes.

'Oh God!' She covered her breasts hastily. 'We didn't . . . '

His grin faded. 'You don't remember?'

'No.' She winced at the pain in her head. 'What happened?'

'You really don't remember?' His smile was both smug and embarrassed. 'It was beautiful.'

'I don't believe you.' But she knew by the way he smiled it was true. As fragments of the previous night began to resurface in her memory, she became aware of a pungent, unfamiliar odour and felt a soreness, a sticky wetness between her legs. 'Oh, my God!' She stared at him in horror. 'How could you, Peter? I was drunk.'

His smile vanished. 'I'd had a few myself. But I thought you wanted it too.'

'Then it looks like we both made a mistake.' She stared at him bitterly. 'A great friend you turned out to be.'

A dull red colour spread over Peter's face. A note of truculence came into his voice. 'You didn't do anything to stop me.'

'How could I?' But her head hurt too much to argue. Besides, it was too late. No amount of talk would undo what had been done. 'I think you'd better go.' Turning her back to him, she lay facing the wall. There was silence for a moment. Then she heard rustling sounds as he put on his clothes. She heard more movements as he came and stood near the bed.

'Cathy . . . look.' The truculence had gone from his voice. He sounded unsure. 'If I'd known it was your first time . . . '

If she lay very still, it might ease the pain in her head. If he went away, she might be able to pretend that none of it had happened.

'Look, I'm sorry. If I can make it up to you . . . '

Please go away, Peter. But still she didn't speak. After a while, she heard him moving away.

As soon as the door clicked behind him, she turned her face into the pillow and wept.

She was a different person now, Cathy told herself six years later. As she sat in the train bringing her back from Cork to Dublin, she stared dry-eyed at the images of the carriage interior reflected against the blackness of the March night. She thought of the young girl weeping in loss and disappointment that August morning. What a pathetic fool that girl had been. When you thought about it, she probably deserved everything that was coming to her.

EIGHT

On the Sunday following his meeting with Cathy in the wine bar, Stephen rang his mother to say that he could make it for lunch that day, but he needed to be back in time to say the evening Mass. Although she sounded pleased, he sensed her disappointment that the visit would be so short. Not that she made a fuss. It wasn't her way. Mum was so understanding, he thought as he put down the phone. She hadn't said a word either when he'd cancelled Thursday night at such short notice. Yet he felt guilty about how little time he was managing to give her nowadays. Although she was an independent woman with a busy life of her own, he knew how much his visits meant to her. And not just to her. To himself too. For the first few years after he was ordained, before he managed to make a social life for himself, she'd been the only woman friend he had. And he'd always enjoyed her company. Lately, though, they seemed to be spending less and less time together.

It was mostly because of the demands of his work. Besides, life was more complicated nowadays. As he drove out along the coast road, although it was Sunday, traffic was brisk. A sign of the times. Dublin was a changing city in which people were constantly on the move. Everyone led busy lives there, and he was no different. His mother, of all people, would understand that. Still, he wondered what she'd say if she knew he'd cancelled Thursday night because of a girl. Would she be so understanding then?

But it was too nice an afternoon to indulge in self-recrimination. The air was mild for early March. The sun was glinting off the sea at Booterstown, and when he turned into the avenue where his parents lived, he saw that a number of flowering trees were in bloom. The houses in this avenue had an exclusive air to them. Large, prosperous-looking, set a little apart from their neighbours, in well-kept leafy gardens. Every time he came back to visit his family home, Stephen was struck by the contrast between his parents' lifestyle and that of the majority of his parishioners. Two cars of fairly recent vintage were parked in the driveway, while over the top of the fence separating the front garden from the back could be glimpsed a large, old-fashioned greenhouse, flanked by the upper branches of apple trees barely in bud. The house itself had a sturdy Virginia creeper climbing up the front walls and an ornate front porch with a gleaming tiled floor. Once he had taken all that for granted. Now, as he left his car in front of the double garage and crunched across the gravel, he felt as if he was entering a rarefied world light years away from the drab little dwelling, with its dingy paintwork and weed-infested garden, which was his home for the foreseeable future.

Not that he begrudged his parents their lifestyle. Just because he had chosen a more austere way of life, it didn't mean he expected them to do the same. If anything, he was glad that his mother, in particular, had never known the hardships and deprivation suffered by many of his parishioners. But as always, when he turned the key in the front door and stepped into the spacious, gleaming hallway of his parents' house, he wondered if they realised just how fortunate they were to live like this in a world that contained so much poverty.

Stephen found his sister, Gillian, and her husband Mike having a pre-lunch drink with his father in the big drawing room at the back of the house. Gillian was twenty-five, the youngest in the family. She and Mike had been married the previous summer. Her marriage had come as a bit of a shock to Stephen, who had taken for granted that Jack, three years his junior, would be the first to go. But Jack was having too good a time to want to settle down and Gillian had said she had no intention of waiting till he'd got a bit of sense. Although the wedding had been seven months ago and Stephen had performed the ceremony, he was still trying to come to terms with the idea that his little sister was no longer a child.

'You just made it in time, big brother.' Gillian gave him a quick hug. 'Mum's in the kitchen. And Dad's starting to fuss.' Her dark-brown hair, the same colour as his own, was tied back in a ponytail. Dressed in jeans and a casual sweater, and wearing oversized spectacles which made her little pointed face look even smaller, she looked about eighteen, he thought. As did her husband. Although Mike was a qualified computer engineer, he still had the gangling look of youth about him, with a scrawny Adam's apple and the air of having only recently started shaving. Looking at the pair of them, Stephen felt old suddenly.

'I had a sick call to make on the way. It took longer than I expected.'

'Far be it from us to keep you from your duty.' His father gave Stephen a sardonic smile, but made no move to get up from his seat near the fireplace. Henry Brown was an elegantly dressed man, with thinning hair, a handsome though gaunt face, and the spare build of someone who'd been an athlete in his youth. His bony fingers twirled the stem of a sherry glass containing about a centimetre of amber liquid. 'As you can see, we're almost ready to eat. But help yourself to one if you wish.' Although he could play the attentive host when he wanted, he never put himself out for his eldest son. 'Or you might prefer to wait for the wine. It's quite a decent Rioja.'

'Thanks,' Stephen said curtly. 'I'll go and say hello to Mum.'

He found his mother taking a roast out of the oven. A succulent aroma filled the kitchen. 'Just in time, Stephen.' Her face lit up when she saw him. 'You can help me make the gravy.'

'Sure thing.' He leaned against the edge of the table and watched as she moved around the kitchen. She was light on her feet for a big woman, he thought. Although Stephen took after both parents in looks, it was from his mother's family that he got his height. When he was a child, he remembered, she'd been slim and long-legged but she'd thickened over the years. Now, in her late fifties, Grainne Brown was heavily built. Her height could carry it, he told himself. And it suited her looks. With her strong, well-defined features and brown hair streaked with grey, she had a solid air to her. Not so much earth mother as Mother Courage. A woman you could depend on. 'How's life treating you, Mum?'

'Fine, Stephen, fine.' Although her face was flushed from the oven's heat, she wore her usual air of composure. 'Can't complain.' Even if the sky was falling, she'd still say that, he thought. She stirred a saucepan and shot him a shrewd glance. 'It sounds as if you're rushed off your feet.'

'Mustn't complain, mustn't complain,' he said teasingly, waiting till she laughed in return.' Actually, I feel I'm carrying the weight of the parish at the moment.' As soon as the words were out, he regretted them. Not because his mother wouldn't be interested. She was a good listener, often acting as a useful sounding board when he'd a specific problem. But he had long ago made a rule for himself never to involve her in the petty details of parish life, or to dwell on the personalities of the people he worked with. It was a good rule, and whenever he departed from it, it was usually a mistake. 'But I reckon it'll sort itself out once the new curate finds his feet.' Despite his rule, he couldn't help saying, 'He's like someone on a different planet.'

But mothers don't always play by the rules, either. 'What happened to that nice Father Hennessy?' She gave him an innocent glance as she handed him a wooden spoon, directing him towards a saucepan on the electric hob. 'Will he come back, do you think?'

'Well, as I understand it, he's still on leave, Mum.' Stephen tried to remember how much he'd told her about Brendan. Not that there'd been much to tell. He'd been unable to get any more information out of the parish priest the last time they'd spoken about it. 'Old man Mulvey keeps his cards close to his chest.' Which was an added pressure on Stephen, who was getting tired of having to stave off enquiries from interested parishioners. He saw her speculative look, and sighed inwardly. Discretion was one thing, but he hated being put in the position of having to lie to his own mother. 'It's kind of a delicate matter.'

'Aha!' Her dark eyebrows snapped together. 'Woman trouble.'

'Ah, Mum!' Stephen looked at her in dismay. 'Don't start jumping to conclusions.'

'And don't you take me for a fool.' She gave him an unsmiling look. Her eyes narrowed. 'It *is* a woman, isn't it? Not something worse?'

Stephen nodded reluctantly.

She nodded too, with grim satisfaction. 'As if I didn't know what men were like.' As he stared back at her, it occurred to him that when he was growing up, such a conversation would have been unthinkable with his mother. In those days she'd had the attitude, common enough then, that priests were some kind of higher beings, half-men, half-angels. As if the vow of celibacy were a magic cloak that protected the wearer from temptation of the sexual kind. It had hit her hard, he knew, in the last few years when all those stories of clerical abuse had started making the headlines.

As if she guessed his thoughts, Grainne Brown said bitterly, 'I used to think all priests were good men like my poor brother, Jimmy. But then there was a time when I thought that most men respected their marriage vows. And I was wrong about that too.'

'It's always a mistake to put people on pedestals,' Stephen said. 'Anyway, Brendan Hennessy isn't cheating on anyone . . .'

'He mightn't have a wife to betray.' His mother's voice was crisp. 'But he made vows to God. There's no great difference, in my book.'

'That's arguable . . .'

'It's what I think, anyway.' She headed for the door leading to the dining room. 'Listen, Stephen, don't let the gravy boil over. I'm going to check the table in case Gillian forgot something. Then we'll eat.'

'OK, Mum.' As he waited for her to return, he kept his eye on the gravy and his mind on the conversation they'd just had.

Stephen had been in his twenties when he first realised that his father was being unfaithful to his mother. He'd suspected since his early teens that something wasn't right about his parents' marriage, but he wasn't sure what. It wasn't because they spent a lot of time apart, although Dad's business took him away from home from time to time: it was more the way they behaved when they were together. It was hard to put his finger on it, but he sensed there was something missing. Not just physical intimacy, which in itself meant nothing – few of his friends' parents were demonstrative with each other in public – but something deeper. It was only years later that he put a name to it, but at the time all he saw was a distance that he hadn't noticed between other married couples. Which was strange, because he knew his mother as a loving woman always ready with a kiss for childish hurts, a hug of encouragement when you were feeling down.

His father, on the other hand, was more the stiff-upper-lip kind of parent, but even he'd been known to show moments of gruff affection when they were kids, particularly towards Gillian, on whom he doted. But Stephen told himself that his parents' marriage was none of his business. He had other things to think about. And maybe he'd misread the situation, anyway. So it came as a shock to him when, a couple of months after his ordination, his mother told him that his father was having an affair with a married woman, ten years his junior. She was separated from her husband, Grainne Brown said, and lived only a short distance away from them in Mount Merrion.

'How did you find out?' Stephen asked, more to give himself time to adjust to the news than from any real wish to be told. 'Is it someone you know?'

'Not this time,' his mother said grimly.

He looked at her in disbelief. 'You mean it's happened before?'

'Oh, yes.' She gave a tight little nod. 'The first time, that I *know* of, was after Jack was born.'

'As early as that?' Stephen was appalled.

'For all I know, he was deceiving me after the honeymoon. He said he wasn't. But maybe he was just good at covering his tracks. He said it was a one-off, begged me to take him back. Like a fool, I did. It took a long time to build up the trust again. After that, things seemed OK for a few years. But he got a bit careless. When Gillian was a toddler, I discovered he was having an affair with a friend of mine.' Her face darkened. 'A close friend. She was married too. When her husband found out about them, she wanted to run off with Henry. But your father dropped her like a hot potato and scuttled back to me. Her marriage broke up anyway.'

'And you forgave him? Again?' He stared at her, puzzled. 'But why?'

'Marriage is for life, Stephen.' He saw her lips press tightly together. 'As a priest, you should know that.'

'Yes, but . . . '

'I wanted to give the three of you a stable background. A child is entitled to two parents.' She gave a little shrug. 'He's been a good father, in his own way, and we've never wanted for anything.'

'Not materially, anyway,' Stephen said. 'But there's been a price for you.'

'Either way, I'd have paid.' He saw the pain in her eyes.

'Oh, Mum!'

'Look, Stephen.' She lifted her chin. 'There was no way I was going to let you children grow up in a broken home.'

He was profoundly touched. 'But you don't have to stay now. Gillian's finishing school.'

His mother shook her head. 'She still has college. You know how she feels about her father. It'd break her heart if we . . . '

'It would be hard on her, I know that, but it's not fair to you,' Stephen said. 'And I don't see how you can stay, now that you know about this other woman.'

She looked surprised. 'But it won't last. I've told you. They never do.'

'But, Mum, how can you?' He was baffled by her calm acceptance of the situation. He felt a murderous rage against his father. 'He's not going to get away with this.'

'He has before.' She gave a resigned little smile. 'Look, I don't want you to say anything about this. I know your father's not going to change. But I have a way of life too. One I enjoy. I won't break that up without a lot of thought. And as I said, there's Gillian to think about. Leave it, Stephen. It's going to take time.'

'Take all the time you want.' He reluctantly conceded defeat. 'It's a decision only you can make.'

That had been eight years before. Gillian was long finished college and had got married the previous year. There was nothing to keep his mother now. But she was still there, running the house with her usual calm efficiency. A woman came in to help, but he was aware that his mother worked hard at creating an atmosphere of comfort. Flower arrangements in the hall, beautifully cooked meals, well organised laundry cupboards, fluffy towels in all the bathrooms. As he watched her presiding over the family meal in the elegant dining room, he marvelled at the way she carried off the role of contented wife and mother. How had she kept it up for so many years? Pretending she'd a good marriage, when in reality it was an empty shell? Looking at her, he thought of the misery she must have suffered and could only guess at the reserves of strength needed to maintain this mask of normality.

As for Dad! Stephen had to hide his contempt as he glanced at him across the table. Just look at him, sitting there expounding on the shortcomings of the construction industry, with Gillian and Mike hanging on every word. He winced as he saw the affection with which his sister gazed at her father, the respect on the young man's face. My father, the solid family man, Stephen thought bitterly. My father, the hypocrite. He had a sudden image of the whited sepulchre in the Gospels and saw the worms swarming under the facade. With a spasm of nausea, he put down his knife and fork.

'Are you all right, Stephen?' His mother threw him a troubled look. 'Is the beef OK?'

'It's delicious, Mum.' He picked up the knife and fork again and forced himself to eat. But the food had lost its savour. As he chewed, he made a conscious effort to follow the conversation, despite the fact that it held little interest for him. It seemed to be centred mainly around work, his father's and his brother-in-law's. Both men were engineers, although from different disciplines. His father ran his own firm of civil engineering consultants, while Mike worked with computers. Gillian too had a degree in computer technology. The three of them seemed to talk the same language, Stephen noticed. And not just on technical matters. They all belonged to the world of commerce and industry, market forces and new discoveries. A world of which he knew nothing.

'Of course, this is all Greek to Stephen here,' Henry Brown said, and laughed at his own wit.

'If it was, I might have a better chance. Latin, anyway.'

'If you prefer, we'll talk about the Dead Sea Scrolls.' Henry gave a twisted smile. 'Or some other irrelevancy in this day and age.' He'd never forgiven his son for choosing the priesthood when he could have had a successful career as an engineer. Even though Jack, Stephen's younger brother, had followed in his father's footsteps and now worked in the family firm, Henry was obviously still bitter over what he saw as his elder son's defection. He seldom lost an opportunity to belittle Stephen's way of life and to emphasise what a mistake he'd made. I should be used to it by now, Stephen told himself. And anyway, Dad's opinion doesn't count for much. But his attitude still rankled.

Reminding himself that 'the soft answer turneth away wrath', he asked, 'Jack not here today? Can't see him missing one of Mum's Sunday roasts.'

'He's in Galway for the weekend.' Gillian looked impish suddenly. 'I don't think he went on his own.'

He saw his mother's face tighten. 'Jack has a lot of friends, dear.'

'Friends, yes. But I don't think he went with a crowd.' There was a wealth of meaning in Gillian's voice.

Stephen glanced at his mother again, but her face gave nothing away.

'Jack'll settle down one of these days, Mum,' he said with more assurance than he felt. 'He's just sowing his wild oats.' He'd been saying that since his brother had left school, he thought. At this stage, Jack should have several fields planted with the stuff.

'As long as it's just oats he sows,' his father said dryly.

Old hypocrite. Stephen kept his face blank as Gillian and Mike collapsed with laughter. He's a good one to talk. As he looked at his father, he felt his fists clenching. It was an ordeal to have to sit in the same room as him. If it weren't for Mum, he'd walk out that door and never set foot in the house again.

'When are you coming to visit us, Steve?' Gillian asked after lunch, when they got a moment alone together. 'The new house is brilliant, although we've only bare boards so far. But we do have furniture. A bed, of course.' She dimpled. 'A table and chairs. We'll be able to offer you a meal. Mike's quite a good cook.'

'I always knew you were spoiled rotten.' Stephen grinned at her. 'That poor guy doesn't know what he's let himself in for. But it's great to see you looking so happy. Married life suits you.'

'Can't complain,' she said in an unconscious parody of her mother earlier. But unlike her, Gillian radiated contentment. His sister had always been attractive, but today he noticed a glow about her he'd never seen before. 'I'd really recommend it, Stephen. You've no idea what it's like to wake up every morning with the person you love.'

'I can only guess about something like that.' He saw her look of surprise. 'Not that I do – dwell on it, I mean.'

'Well, I should hope not.' Gillian gave a hearty laugh. 'Priests are supposed to have a mind above all that. Aren't you meant to take cold showers and practise the lotus position?' Although she made a joke of it, he realised that she was embarrassed. When it came to something like that, there wasn't much difference between her and her mother's generation, he thought wryly. Taking his cue from her, he gave a light laugh.

'A low-protein diet helps too. And age.' He gave an exaggerated sigh. 'I'm getting too old for that kind of thing.'

'Poor old brud,' Gillian said 'One foot in the grave.' Her face lit up suddenly. 'Not too old to be an uncle, though.'

'A what?' He felt a jolt of surprise. He thought of his father's earlier comment about Jack. 'Don't tell me that brother of ours . . . '

'Not Jack, stupid.' Gillian's face was wreathed in smiles.

'But . . . ' He gave a sharp intake of breath. 'Not you?'

'Why not? I'm an old married woman.' She beamed at him. 'Why wouldn't I be pregnant?'

'But you can't be.' Stephen was stunned. 'You're too young.'

'I'll be twenty-six in May. We're not talking teen pregnancy here. Of course, it's early days. We've told very few people yet. Mum and Dad are thrilled. I thought you would be too.'

'Well, of course I am.' He made the response automatically. 'That explains the glow you have.' He felt a sudden misgiving. 'But how will you manage? From what I hear, babies don't come cheap.'

'We both have good salaries,' Gillian said. 'And the company I work for encourages women to stay in their jobs.' She gave him a look of tolerant exasperation. 'There's a labour shortage, or hadn't you heard? Their crèche should be up and running before September.'

'Is that when the baby's due?'

'Yes.' Her face lit up. 'Oh, Steve, wouldn't it be funny if it was born on your birthday?'

'Hilarious.'

'What's up?' Her smile faded. 'Do you think I'm too selfish to make a good mother?'

'Of course not,' Stephen said quickly. 'It just seems so soon. Most people wait a few years.'

'Mike and I want to have our family young. Look, I

know you think I'm a bit spoiled. The youngest usually is. And Mike often gives in to me when he shouldn't. But I've always loved kids. It's about time I started thinking about someone besides myself.' She looked at him earnestly. 'It's awesome, Steve, the thought of having a child.' Her eyes grew solemn behind her big spectacles. 'But a bit scary.'

'Oh, Gill.' He felt suddenly ashamed. 'I'm the one who's being selfish. I couldn't get my head around the idea of my baby sister turning into a parent. All of a sudden, it made me feel old. I remember I felt the same way when you were getting married. But each time I was thinking only of myself.' His face softened as he looked at her. 'Having a child is bound to be scary. In your place, I don't know how I'd feel. But I know you'll make a great mother.' He bent to kiss her cheek. 'My warmest congratulations to both yourself and Mike.'

'Thanks, Steve.' She hugged him affectionately. 'And I know you'll make a great uncle.'

Although they both laughed, Stephen had a sudden feeling of sadness. Having a child was a big responsibility. She and Mike were so young. So untried. God only knew what lay ahead of them. He thought of his mother's experience in her marriage and prayed his sister would never know a similar disillusionment.

It was only later, when he'd said his goodbyes and was driving back along the coast road, that he realised some of the sadness was for himself.

And there was envy, too, if he was honest.

He heard Gillian's confident young voice. *You've no*

idea what it's like to wake up every morning beside the person you love.

No idea, little sister. I haven't a bull's notion.

And he never would.

Try to think positively, he advised himself, almost running a red light in his preoccupation. Celibacy is not a negative thing. He reminded himself of the words of one of his professors in the seminary. Celibacy is one of the jewels in the crown of the priesthood. The royal priesthood, as it says in the Mass. Celibacy frees a man to serve God more fully. Without attachments, without a wife or children, there can be no hostages to fortune.

It made sense after all. He travels fastest who travels alone.

But where am I travelling to? The question seemed to resonate down through a deep well of loneliness. No immediate answer came to mind. After he parked his car on the cracked strip of concrete in front of his house, he let himself into the empty hallway. A red light blinked in the gathering dusk. Three messages were waiting on the answering machine. All to do with parish work, none of them urgent. As the machine went silent, his loneliness grew. Peering at his watch in the half-darkness, he felt a desperate need to compose himself before he said the Sunday evening Mass. There'd just be time to fit in some meditation before he left for the church. Prayer and meditation were the answer. They usually were. *Be still and know that I am Lord.*

Although he felt calmer half an hour later as he

mounted the altar steps in front of a crowded congregation, the question he'd asked himself earlier still troubled him. Later in the Mass, when he heard the epistle from the second letter of Paul to the Corinthians, he found himself praying along with the reader, 'Let there be light shining out of darkness.'

A few days later, Stephen came home to find a message waiting for him on his answering machine. 'Hi, Stephen. Cathy here.' Her voice sounded a little breathless, but it had a determined gaiety that brought an answering smile to his own face. 'I've decided to take you up on that offer. Why don't you give me a call?

'What made you decide?' Stephen asked.

Her eyes challenged him across the table. 'What made *you?*'

'Good question.' He glanced around the wine bar while he thought of an answer. 'Don't take this the wrong way, Cathy, but I think you need a friend.' As he said it, he wondered if it were the whole truth.

'Is there a right way to take that?' He saw her eyes flash. 'You see me as some kind of needy person?'

Too late, he saw the pit he'd dug for himself. 'I don't know how to answer that.'

'You might try the truth.'

'You don't pull your punches, do you?' He smiled wryly. 'OK, I'd like to be friends with you. Do I need another reason?'

'No.' He saw her face relax. 'But you're right, I do

need a friend. I realised that over the weekend.'

He liked the simple way she said it. Could he be as honest with another person? 'What happened over the weekend?'

She took a moment to answer. 'I went home to Cork. It stirred up a lot of memories.'

'Good or bad?'

Her face clouded over. 'Bad, mostly.'

'Want to talk about it?'

'No.'

He cocked a quizzical eyebrow. 'Never?'

She thought for a moment. 'Not tonight, anyway.'

He felt hopeful. 'If you ever do . . . '

'I know, Stephen.' Her eyes studied him thoughtfully. 'Maybe when we get to know each other better.'

Patience, he counselled himself. He couldn't help saying: 'I might hold you to that.' He grinned to take the sting out of his words. 'In the meantime, "The time has come, the walrus said, to talk of many things".'

'"Of shoes and ships and sealing wax and cabbages and kings".' Cathy's face lit up as she completed the quotation. 'My father was a real fan of Lewis Carroll's.'

'My mother,' Stephen said. 'I was practically weaned on *Alice in Wonderland*.'

She gave him a look of delighted complicity. 'Me too.'

They swapped favourite authors, discussed films they'd both seen, and discovered a common interest in foreign travel. After Stephen had described a trip to Pompeii he'd made while touring Italy a few years before, Cathy began telling him about her holiday in Crete the previous summer. 'The nightlife was hectic. We had a ball.'

'Obviously hasn't changed since my day.' Stephen gave a reminiscent chuckle. When he saw her surprise, he said unguardedly, 'I wasn't always celibate.' And immediately regretted the words. 'I'm sorry, I shouldn't have said that.' He wondered what impulse of male vanity had caused him to react the way he had.

'Why not? If it's true.' She gave him that clear-eyed look that always made him slightly uncomfortable. 'Is it?'

'Yes.' He hesitated. 'Maybe I shouldn't be telling you this, but I sowed a few wild oats before I entered.'

'I'm glad. Makes you more human, somehow.'

'More human?' Stephen was stung.

'Well, you never really show your feelings, do you.' She wrinkled her nose thoughtfully. 'I'm not saying you're heartless. You can be very kind. I'm sure you have people queuing up to go to Confession with you. But it's a professional kindness – a bit like a mask.'

He nodded. 'Jung called it a persona. It's the face we show to other people in our different roles. And, of course, in my job as a priest . . . '

'I get the impression you wear it all the time. But maybe it's just with me.' Cathy frowned. 'Why do I always get the feeling that you have on some kind of armour?'

'Not a bad description,' Stephen said dryly. But he was disconcerted by the acuteness of her observation.

To hide his discomfort, he took refuge in humour. 'I'll have to watch my step with you.' He grinned. 'It won't be easy to pull the wool over your eyes. You're . . . '

'Not just a pretty face?' She raised an ironic eyebrow. 'You're doing it again, Stephen. And you still haven't answered my question.'

'OK, OK.' He threw up his hands ruefully. 'You got me there.' She really was the most exasperating girl he'd ever met. But he felt a sense of exhilaration too. 'Even the best of armour has its chinks, and you know how to turn the knife.'

'You deserve it.'

'That's a bit cruel.' *God, she was lovely, sitting there, her face slightly flushed, a little smile playing around her lips. Would you blame a man for needing armour?* 'But seriously, Cathy.' With an effort he brought his attention back to the argument. 'I know what you're saying, but there are good reasons . . . Look, you've got to understand my position . . . '

'And you've got to understand mine.' She looked at him candidly. 'You want me to trust you, don't you?'

'Yes,' Stephen said. 'I do.'

'Well, it cuts both ways.' Still her gaze held his. 'You do realise that?'

'Yes,' he said again. But he turned away from her eyes, disturbed and challenged by what he saw there.

Stephen slept badly that night. After he'd dropped Cathy at her apartment, he drove home, his mind in a whirl. He felt slightly off balance, as if he was on an emotional see-saw. One moment he was laughing to himself, going back over the events of the evening with a sense of exhilaration, the next he found himself filled with apprehension. A half-hour of prayer and meditation before bed briefly restored his equilibrium, but once his head hit the pillow he was back on the see-saw again.

What had he let himself in for? Was he out of his mind? A young girl like that . . .

But all they were talking about was friendship. Nothing more.

Was friendship between the sexes possible?

Of course it was. Look at himself and Eileen.

That was a different kind of friendship. Anyone could see that. And Cathy was a very different kind of woman. As he tossed restlessly in the darkness, he found himself trying to think of words to describe her. Full of surprises? Maddening? Beautiful? Yes, she was beautiful. He wasn't going to deceive himself about that. But it wasn't just her beauty that appealed to him. It was her intelligence, her sense of humour, her honesty. Especially her honesty. It struck a chord in the centre of his being, calling for his respect, and demanding a similar truthfulness on his part.

Which made it all the more puzzling that she wouldn't confide in him, wouldn't tell him what had happened in the past to make her so sad. Because she was sad, Stephen knew. Under her gaiety, her sense of humour and her self-confident ways, she was deeply sad. All his instincts and training told him so. Poor little Cathy! He felt suddenly protective towards her. If only he could find out what was troubling her. Once he did, he felt sure he could help her, if only she would give him the chance. Earlier that evening he'd counselled himself to patience. Everything comes to the one who waits. But now, as he lay in bed staring into the blackness of the March night, he felt sudden doubt, felt a sense of inadequacy when he thought of Cathy. He found himself praying that he'd be equal to whatever was asked of him.

Still sleep eluded him. Switching on the bedside light, he reached for his breviary and tried to concentrate on the prayers. But he kept seeing her face, hearing her voice. He threw down the breviary and picked up a book of poems by an Eastern mystic that Sister Eileen had lent him. As he scanned the pages, he felt a surge of affection at the thought of the nun and her quiet, undemanding friendship. Compared to Cathy, Sister Eileen was like a limpid pool. No surprises there, thank God. In the year since they'd first met, he'd come to value her support and her wise counsel. Even when their views differed, she always had something useful to say, possessing the ability to put the opposing case without rancour, occasionally even causing him to reassess a previously entrenched opinion. She always gave him food for thought. He wondered if he should tell her about Cathy. He was seized by reluctance and dismissed the idea. Maybe some time. But not yet.

'I didn't see you at the parish centre AGM the other night, Stephen.' A slight frown creased Sister Eileen's brow when she called in to the sacristy one morning after the ten o'clock Mass. 'You said you'd be there.'

'Something came up.' A man was entitled to some private life, he thought, as he folded the Mass vestments and gave them to the sacristan to put away. That was the night he'd met Cathy, he remembered. Ridiculous to feel guilty at missing an unimportant meeting in order to see a friend. 'I'm sure they managed fine without me.' Because of the guilt, his tone was crisper than he'd intended. He saw Sister Eileen's eyes widen but she said nothing. As Stephen took his jacket down from a peg near the door, he turned to find the two women watching him.

'Was there something else, Breeda?'

'Mary wants a word with you in the office, Father. She said to be sure to call in after Mass.' The sacristan gave him a shrewd look. 'I'd say she has a job for you.'

'So what else is new? What about young Father McMahon?' It was time the new curate started pulling his weight, he thought. 'Is he still working in the parish?' His voice was heavy with sarcasm.

Sister Eileen gave a playful laugh. 'You know what Pope John the twenty-third said when asked how many people worked in the Vatican?'

'Yes, I know,' Stephen sighed. 'About half of them. With the clergy in this parish, it's not even that many.' He was surprised to see Breeda Cullen's mouth twitch as she padded away on rubber soles. He would never have suspected her of having a sense of humour. Probably having a laugh at his expense, Stephen decided gloomily. He'd long suspected he wasn't one of Breeda's favourite people.

'Oh, come on,' Sister Eileen said. 'It's not that bad. Anyway, I suspect Mary has a bit of a crush on you. That's why you get all the jobs.'

Stephen looked at her in surprise. It was so unlike her to make a remark like that. 'Careful, Sister. You should watch the company you keep. Dolores's sense of humour must be catching.'

Eileen's face went pink. But instead of rushing to the other nun's defence, she gave him a thoughtful look. As they left the sacristy and went into the churchyard she asked, 'What's wrong, Stephen? Not like you to be so edgy.'

'Nothing's wrong.' Nothing he wanted to share. He shrugged. 'Lent, Sister. A time of gloom and doom. Could be my batteries are low after the winter.' Without waiting for a response, he headed to his car, parked a few feet away. 'That's me finished for the day. I'm off to the gym.'

'But what about Mary,' Sister Eileen called after him. 'She wanted to see you.'

'It'll have to wait till tomorrow,' Stephen said shortly. 'Wednesday's my day off, remember.'

After an hour in the gym, working up a sweat on the treadmill and using the weights, Stephen felt his mood begin to lighten. He found himself singing in the shower afterwards. It was good to have a day off. When you worked on Sundays you needed that time to yourself during the week. He wished he could work out in the gym more often but once a week was better than nothing. It kept him toned. As he towelled himself dry he patted his flat stomach for reassurance. No sign of a paunch, thank God. Then he laughed ruefully at what he saw as his own vanity. But there was nothing wrong in keeping fit, was there? Just because you weren't out chasing women didn't mean you had to let yourself turn into a slob. Having satisfied himself on that point, Stephen finished dressing and walked back to his house with a renewed sense of vigour.

As he strode along he thought of Sister Eileen's comment about Mary Grimes, the secretary. He'd been embarrassed, rather than flattered, by what the nun had said. Normally he'd have dismissed a remark like that straightaway with a laugh. But today he found himself dwelling on it. Not on Mary and her feelings for him. That had just been Eileen trying to wind him up. He knew the secretary was in a steady relationship and was planning to marry. Stephen had been asked to perform the ceremony. But he found himself wondering about young women in general. He'd heard enough over the years from his sister, Gillian, to know that most girls in their early twenties were not interested in older men. Unless they were looking for a father figure.

How old did you have to be to qualify as a father figure? Stephen frowned to himself, not sure if he liked the direction his thoughts were taking. He was eight years older than Cathy. His frown deepened as he realised that lately he seemed to be spending a lot of time thinking about her. Far too much, probably. She wasn't the only person who needed his help. But none of them intrigued him as much as she did, he had to admit that. He was determined to get to the bottom of what was troubling her, and the sooner the better.

That was why he'd tried ringing her last night. And that was why he'd been a bit short with Eileen in the sacristy. It wasn't Lent and its penitential aspect that had caused his sombre mood this morning. It was because every time he'd rung Cathy's apartment he'd got the answering machine. And it hadn't even been her voice on the tape but a sharper, less melodious one. *Too busy having a ball to talk to you,* the voice had said with blithe indifference. *Leave your name and number and we might get back to you. But don't count on it, ha ha!* Stephen had not shared her amusement. And hadn't left a message either. He began to wish now he had, but it had probably been the wisest course. There was no point in advertising their friendship. Besides, it was better not to rush things. Sooner or later, Cathy would trust him enough to tell him her secret. Let her come to him. In the meantime, the best thing to do was to put her out of his mind. He'd head into town, have a leisurely lunch, browse the bookshops and enjoy his day off.

But this proved to be harder than Stephen antici-pated. As he went about his day, Cathy was never far from his thoughts. A poster in a travel agent's window reminded him of their conversation about his last holiday in Italy. A couple of ragged urchins singing discordantly under a lamp-post in Grafton Street conjured up the first night he'd met her, vividly reminding him of her indignation at the plight of the homeless beggar. And everywhere he went his eye was caught by young women. At the glimpse of a shining bell of brown hair, a confident stride, a slim figure moving away through the crowds, his heart would give a leap, to be quickly replaced by a flat sense of disappointment. And then into his mind would flash the image of Cathy as she'd looked that night across the table in the wine bar, and his heart would leap again. And he'd have to stop himself from smiling foolishly at passers by.

Get a grip. Stephen stared unseeingly into a shop window and tried to control his wayward thoughts, forcing himself to focus on his plans for the evening. He liked to relax on a Wednesday night. Have a meal out, maybe go to a film or a play. Sometimes he met a fellow priest, one of several friends he'd made during his time in the seminary; occasionally he took his mother or Sister Eileen to the theatre, although more often than not he went alone. If he'd nothing planned he might spend the evening at home, reading and listening to music. It looked as if tonight was going to be like that. But for once the prospect of being on his own didn't appeal. On a sudden impulse, he took out his mobile phone and switched it on. Cathy's work number was entered in the address book. It wouldn't take a moment to get through to her. He hesitated. It was very short notice. But even if she wasn't free to meet him tonight, it would be nice to say hello. After all, it was nearly a week since they'd seen each other. But still he hesitated, gazing irresolutely at the keypad while her number flashed up on the screen.

Friends don't need a reason to call each other, he argued while the crowds jostled around him on the cobbled street, and the same pair of urchins he'd seen earlier stood under the lamp-post, still singing the same street ballad raucously and out of tune. Friendship was one thing. But a man of his calling shouldn't be ringing women to ask them out on dates. Stephen sighed to himself and switched off his phone. As he moved away, he passed the street singers and saw without surprise that there were very few coins in the cardboard box at their feet. Most people were hurrying past them, smiling in contempt.

Good enough for them. He couldn't help smiling himself. Pair of chancers. Not a note between them. Why weren't they at school? But something made him slow his footsteps and drop some money in the box. Another image of Cathy flashed into his mind, Stephen sighed to himself again. With a little shrug of defeat, he switched his mobile phone back on. And dialled her office number.

NINE

'And so you see,' Paul Kinsella said, 'if you take last month's figures, and project this month's, based on the first fortnight . . . '

With his sparse hair and bony face, he had the look of a medieval monk, Cathy thought. Which was funny, because Paul wasn't a bit religious. The gospel of profit and loss was the only one he was interested in. He and Stephen would have nothing in common. Paul was out to save money, not souls. As she looked pensively at her boss, she became aware that he'd broken off his explanations to give her a quick glance.

'Cathy, you're not with me.' His eyes narrowed suddenly. 'What exactly don't you follow?'

'I'm sorry, Paul. It's not the figures. It's me.' Cathy gave a heavy sigh. She just hadn't been on top of the job all morning, had kept making simple mistakes and forgetting things. It even had slipped her mind earlier that it was Wednesday and that Paul was due in for his weekly pep talk and brainstorming session. She'd let Martina, her assistant, leave for an early lunch just before he breezed in the door. Not that Paul had been unduly upset; the less contact he had with Martina the better, he said. But Cathy was annoyed at herself. It meant that, afterwards, she'd have to go over everything a second time. And she found herself exhausted at the prospect. 'I'm just not with it today, can't seem to concentrate.'

'A hard night last night?' He nodded understandingly.

'Why do non-drinkers always assume that the rest of the population goes around with a perpetual hangover?' Cathy asked irritably. 'Actually I went to bed early. Much good it did me.' She gave him a rueful look. 'But I do have a headache. I think I'm coming down with a bug. Either that or I'm losing my mind. Martina's been in seventh heaven, of course, pointing out all the things I've done wrong this morning.'

'If I had to work with that woman, I'd have lost my mind years ago.' Paul grinned. 'Why do you think I opened the second shop? But seriously, Cathy, you don't look the best.' His eyes studied her with concern. 'You're as white as a sheet. Listen, why don't you go home, take a couple of paracetamol and get your head down for a few hours. I'll hold the fort till Martina gets back.'

'Are you sure?' Cathy felt a twinge of guilt about having misjudged Paul. He had decent instincts, she told herself. Even if it sometimes seemed as if making money was the most important thing in his life. 'What about that software order?'

'You can sort it out tomorrow.' He gave her an anxious look. 'You'll be OK by then?'

'Of course. It's probably one of those twenty-four-hour things.' But, as she got ready to leave the office,

Cathy knew she sounded more confident than she really was. All she knew was that she was so tired she just wanted to go home and fall into bed. And never get out again.

It was a relief to get under the covers. To lay her burning face against the cool pillow and lie in a darkened room. There was only a faint hum of traffic in the distance; the mews itself was hushed and peaceful. None of the tenants of the other apartments seemed to be at home, and everywhere was quiet. Everywhere. Except inside Cathy's head. Inside there was turmoil, her thoughts grinding on relentlessly, never letting up.

Life didn't feel worth living any more. Her days seemed to stretch endlessly ahead. Was there nothing she could do to make herself feel better? Maybe it was time to look for a new job. The idea had occurred to her earlier that day as she listened to Martina gleefully pointing out another error she'd discovered. As Cathy resisted the temptation to stuff a load of invoices down her assistant's throat and cut short her stream of self-righteousness, the claustrophobic feeling of being cooped up in a small office behind a not-very-large shop suddenly descended on her. Every day you found yourself encountering the same problems, seeing the same faces, having the same conversations.

What about her original ambition of working for a bigger organisation with a larger workforce and better opportunities? Maybe now was the time to resurrect it, to take stock and examine her options. There were plenty of positions on offer for someone with her ability and experience. Maybe now was a good time to change. To move on.

Maybe. But move on from what?

From the job? Or from herself?

Oh, if only one could. A tight knot began to form in her stomach and she felt a sense of despair. Changing her job wasn't the answer. There was no use pretending. She might as well face the truth. She was only fooling herself if she thought that PK Computers was the reason for her headaches, her exhaustion and her sleepless nights. The trouble lay much deeper than that.

Ever since she'd come back from that weekend in Cork she'd been plagued by memories. The trouble with opening a door to the past was that once you stepped through, it was almost impossible to turn back. God knows, she'd tried. In the ten days since her trip home, she had *really* tried. But she knew she was losing the battle. Even when she cut one memory short, putting on the brake as soon as she saw where it was heading, another one would rear up. And another. Until her head had ached with the effort of trying to avoid them. When she was in the office, she'd been able to blame the headache on other things. Pressure of work, a flu bug doing the rounds, Martina. But lying here alone, she could no longer deceive herself.

Oh, God! She felt the knot in her stomach tighten. Felt the weight of the past press down on her. Felt her whole being trying to escape from it. *Whatever I do, I never want to go down that road again!*

A bell sounded shrilly, pealing through the apartment. Someone was at the door. Darkness had fallen. She could see the faint glow of the street lamp against the curtain. Cathy lay still, a confused memory of fragmentary dreams overlaying her mind. She'd no idea of how long she'd slept, or of who might be ringing at her apartment door. Maybe whoever it was would give up and go away. But the bell rang again. She sat up and turned on the light. The numerals on the bedside clock said six-thirty. She sighed, and groped for something to put on over her short nightgown. It was probably Liz. She must have forgotten her key. Cathy had switched on the hall light and was about to open the front door when she remembered that Liz had told her she was meeting someone straight from work and wouldn't be back till later that night. Anyway, Liz had her keys; she'd seen her snatch them up this morning and put them into her bag.

Shit! Probably some kid selling tickets or collecting for something. She peered through the spyhole in the door. Although it was dark outside, the lamp above cast enough light for her to make out the features of the man waiting on the doorstep. To her astonishment, it was someone she knew.

'Stephen! What are you doing here?' she asked, opening the door.

Just about to leave, he moved back into the light at the sound of Cathy's voice. 'They told me you left work early.' She saw his look of concern. 'Are you OK?'

'Some kind of bug.' She smoothed back her tousled

hair, suddenly conscious of her bare feet under the loose kimono. 'But I'm fine.'

'You don't look it.' He studied her face for a moment. 'And standing out here in the cold won't help.' Before she'd time to say anything, he ushered her back into the hallway and quickly stepped in after her. 'OK if I come in?'

'Looks like you already have.' Cathy gave a reluctant smile. Then, half-repenting her ungraciousness, she led the way into the living room. When she switched on the light, she noticed that the long curtains beside the patio doors needed to be drawn. Anxious to block out the blackness pressing against the glass, she hurried to draw the heavy velvet across them. 'You should have told me you were coming.'

'It was a spur-of-the-moment decision.' She saw his gaze sweep over the furniture, the photographs, lingering for a moment on the Monet prints. 'You're right.' His eyes came back to meet hers. 'I should have rung first. I'm sorry.'

'Well, OK.' Disarmed by the apology, she stared at him, clutching her kimono around her. 'I probably wouldn't have answered the phone. I was asleep.'

'And I woke you?' She saw the regret on his face. 'Look, I shouldn't have come.' He stared at her irresolutely. 'Maybe I should go.'

'No, I'm feeling better. I'll make us some coffee.' She glanced down at her bare feet. 'If you don't mind waiting while I go and put some clothes on.'

'As long as I'm not in the way,' Stephen said. 'Is that

the kitchen through there? While you're changing, I'll make the coffee.'

'Only instant, I'm afraid. I know you like the real thing.'

'I'll convert you to my ways yet.' He grinned. 'I hope it's a good brand.'

'Don't be such a snob.' Suddenly she was glad he'd come.

'You look much happier now,' Stephen said when she came back into the room about ten minutes later wearing a casual sweater and jeans, her hair brushed into its customary shining bell. He put down a laden tray on a low table near the couch, and handed her a steaming mug. 'Although what you were wearing was very nice. The Japanese design was so pretty, so graceful.'

'Yes. But I didn't think it was quite . . . '

' . . . appropriate?' She saw his smile of approval.

'You have good instincts, Cathy. Follow them and you'll never go wrong.'

'Do you talk like that to everybody?' She looked at him morosely. 'Or is it just me?' She saw the surprise on his face. 'Maybe you don't realise it, but you can be really patronising sometimes.'

An awkward silence fell. But he didn't take up the challenge. 'Here, have a biscuit.' He held out the plate. 'I poked around in your cupboards. I hope you don't mind.'

'Why should I?' She sipped her coffee, suddenly

grateful that the awkwardness had passed. 'Nice to meet a man who knows his way around a kitchen. But I didn't think priests . . . '

'When you live alone, you need to.' He smiled wryly. 'I had to get my mother to give me a few cookery lessons. Basic stuff, nothing fancy.'

'You live by yourself? But I thought . . . '

Stephen looked rueful. 'Not too many priests have housekeepers nowadays. Although my parish priest does all right for himself.' He gave a resigned shrug. 'But that's par for the course. The rest of us have to fend for ourselves.' He chewed a piece of biscuit and grinned. 'Somehow we muddle through. And at least there's the privacy aspect.'

'For someone who likes their privacy, you don't care much for mine,' Cathy said. As soon as the words were out, she regretted them. 'God, I'm sorry!' She gave Stephen a horrified look, only to see that he'd put down his coffee and was getting up from his chair. She put her hand out pleadingly. 'I don't know why I said that. I didn't mean it.'

'It's OK if you want me to go.' Stephen's voice was gentle. 'I'll come back another time when you're feeling better.'

'I don't think I'm ever going to feel better.' Cathy stared at him miserably. 'Please don't go. I don't want to be on my own.'

She saw Stephen's face soften. To her relief, he sat down again. 'What's wrong, Cathy?' he asked. 'Why are you angry with me?'

'I'm not angry with you. I'm not angry with anyone.'

'I think you are.' Stephen's gaze held hers. 'Are you angry with yourself, perhaps?'

She felt a knot forming in her stomach. 'Why should I be angry with myself?'

'It was just a thought,' he said evenly. 'If not yourself, then who?'

She tried to look away. But still his gaze held hers. Grey eyes could be cold, she thought. But his were warm. And kind. 'I think I'm angry with God.'

He showed no surprise, just nodded.

'Well, maybe not God. I'm not even sure there is one. But . . . '

'Sometimes people get angry at life.'

'Well, maybe. But I've no reason to be. I mean, I've a great job. I love this apartment. Things are going well . . .'

'You had your bag stolen a few weeks ago. Today you left work because you were sick.' He raised an enquiring eyebrow. 'Maybe things aren't going that well.'

'I was upset after the mugging. But I got over it. As for being sick today . . . it's nothing.' She gave a light laugh. 'Probably too many late nights.' When he didn't laugh with her, Cathy's smile faded. She stared at him resentfully. 'You're asking a lot of questions.'

'I won't if you don't want me to.' Stephen's voice was gentle. 'We can talk about something else, if you like.'

'No!' The knot in her stomach was becoming more painful. She didn't want to fight it any more. She stared helplessly at him. 'It probably sounds mad . . . '

He said nothing but gave her an enquiring look.

' . . . but I feel that maybe . . . you were sent.'

She saw his face grow alert. 'To do what?'

'I don't know.' She found it hard to speak. She crossed her arms protectively across her stomach, gritted her teeth and forced the words out. 'I think . . . maybe . . . to listen.'

Stephen's eyes were bright as he looked at her. 'Go on,' he said gently.

Despite the encouragement in his voice, Cathy felt her resolve falter. 'I want to. But I'm afraid.'

The room had gone quiet. Stephen saw the frightened misery in her eyes, noticed the way her body was braced, holding on to its pain. He was filled with compassion and was seized with an almost over-whelming desire to take her in his arms, to pour out words of comfort. An impulse he knew he had to resist. The time wasn't right. If he wanted to help Cathy, it was essential to make himself as unobtrusive as possible. And that meant putting his own feelings on hold. As he gazed at her, he kept his voice to a soothing murmur.

'Why don't you tell me what's troubling you? And no matter what it's about, I promise I won't judge.'

'Can I hold you to that?' He saw her eyes lose their fear, saw the quick gleam of hope. 'Whatever I tell you?'

Stephen nodded. 'You have my word on it.'

'OK.' He saw her brace herself again. 'Maybe I will.'

She stumbled over the words at first, the sentences halting and disjointed, their meaning not always clear even to herself. 'It was my first year in Dublin.' As she spoke, she felt she was going back over forbidden ground, breaking a taboo she'd placed on herself. Although the events had happened six years before, she'd never allowed herself to talk about them to anyone, not even Liz, her closest friend. Yet here she was, opening up to a virtual stranger. She had a sudden sense of unreality and doubt. But even though she hesitated, some urgent need drove her on. And there was something about the man sitting quietly opposite which invited her trust. As it became obvious that he wasn't going to interrupt or make comments, that all he would do was listen, her words became more fluent. After a while, as her confidence in her narrative grew, she began to forget his presence and become more and more immersed in the past.

It was 1994. So much had happened that year, it was difficult to know where to begin. That was the year she'd first come to Dublin, the year the bungalow was sold, the year Louise, her mother, had got married again. And, as if that wasn't bad enough, it was the same year that her eldest sister had gone away. Noreen broke the news in August, not long after Cathy got back from her holiday in Cork, that she'd accepted a nursing job in Saudi Arabia and was flying out ten days after Louise and Vinnie's wedding.

'You can't mean it?' Cathy was stunned. Coming so

soon after the break-up with Fergal, she viewed Noreen's departure as another one in a series of betrayals. 'Didn't you tell me that no man was worth running after?' Because it seemed that Gavin, a man Noreen had been seeing for some time, was the one dictating the move. He was leaving shortly for London and then on to Dubai, where he was taking up a surgical post in the same hospital in which Noreen was planning to work.

'I'm not running after anyone. I'm going for the money. Just as Gavin is.' Noreen grinned suddenly. 'But you don't think I'd be mad enough to leave him out there on his own for two years with all those expat nurses, do you?' Her expression grew softer as she looked at Cathy. 'I feel bad about leaving you, dote. I'd bring you with me if I could. But you're going to have to stand on your own two feet sometime. Look, you'll be fine. You've got everything going for you. You've a job, somewhere to live, and let's face it, you're a lot wiser about men than you were when you came to Dublin first. It was an awful pity, what happened with Peter.' Cathy saw the sympathy in her eyes. 'But you'll just have to put it behind you, put it down to experience. You'll never make that mistake again, believe me. And don't worry.' She gave her a quick hug. 'I've asked my mates to look out for you until you get more settled in. Look, I'm telling you, you'll be fine.'

Cathy didn't share Noreen's confidence but she knew she'd just have to get on with things and hope that it would all work out for the best. Anything could happen in six weeks, she told herself. There was still time for her sister to realise what a mistake she was making, and to change her mind. In the meantime, there was Mum's wedding to be got through.

If ever there was an occasion for putting on a brave face and hiding her true feelings, this was it. When the day arrived, Cathy didn't know how she was going to get through it without breaking down, but she found the courage from somewhere. Everyone else seemed to be having a wonderful time. Especially Noreen, who kept saying that it was her last chance to meet all the relatives and old friends before she went away, and had every intention of making the most of the occasion.

'You've been a real wet blanket all day,' she said to Cathy as soon as the meal and the speeches were over and the dancing was about to begin. 'OK, I'm not crazy about Uncle Vinnie either, but he's Mum's choice. She's the one who's got to live with him, not you. Lighten up, Cathy. Get out there and enjoy yourself. You're only young once.'

She didn't feel young. She felt old and tired, with all the cares of the world on her shoulders. It wasn't only the thought of losing Mum to Uncle Vinnie that troubled her, she knew. Nothing had gone right in her life lately. What was there to lighten up about? The thought of Fergal lay heavily on her. Seeing his parents earlier that day at the ceremony in the little country church had helped to remind her of her loss. She recalled the smug way Mrs O' Reilly had told her that he was back in the seminary and wouldn't be home again until Christmas.

Although Cathy was thankful he hadn't come to the wedding – meeting him would have been too painful to bear – she found herself dreading the thought of a future that didn't hold him. The old relationship was over. That knowledge had begun to sink in. Even though he had written to her after that evening by the river, promising always to be her friend, and she'd written a polite note back, she knew there would be no more letters between them, and once the bungalow was gone and their families were no longer neighbours, there would be few opportunities to meet. It was probably for the best, under the circumstances. A clean break was better in the long run. But knowing this was no consolation; the loss still felt raw, like a gaping wound. As Cathy gazed around the wedding reception, watching the other happy revellers, she wondered if the hurt would ever heal.

It might have been easier to bear if she'd had someone to confide in, if she still had her friendship with Peter. But that was out of the question after what had happened the time they'd got drunk together. Cathy didn't like to dwell on the details of that night. She had decided to take Noreen's advice and put the whole thing behind her, which wasn't difficult, as she had only the vaguest recollection of what had taken place. But she still felt angry and betrayed by the way Peter had taken advantage of her. On her first morning back in the office after the holidays, he'd awkwardly tried to have a conversation with her, behaving as if nothing had happened. Cathy had been polite but distant, and Peter had never made the attempt again. It was probably the best way, she told herself. Another clean break. But she missed the old easy relationship, and her evenings were lonely without his cheerful company.

Mum was probably lonely too. She had a sudden flash of insight as she stood with the other guests on the edge of the dance floor and watched Louise, radiant in sapphire-blue silk which brought out the silvery sheen of her hair, as she took to the floor with her new husband for the first dance of the night. Loneliness could make people do foolish things. I ought to know, Cathy thought. It might explain why an elegant, educated woman like her mother had settled for a slow-moving, portly farmer whose only interests seemed to be in milk yields and cattle quotas. Although Vinnie had acquitted himself well enough during the speeches, she admitted grudgingly, even if his humour had tended to be heavy-handed and laden with bucolic wit. Of course, he was at his best today, all spruced up, with a new haircut, his neck closely shaved under the collar of his formal dark suit. But give him time, she told herself. It wouldn't be long before he was back in his old corduroys and plaid shirts, with two-day-old stubble and dirt under his nicotine-stained fingernails.

Still, as Noreen had said, he was Mum's choice, and she was old enough to know her own mind. And Cathy was a grown-up too, she reminded herself – much too old to be wearing her heart on her sleeve. She pinned a smile on her face, held her head high and joined the others on the floor, dancing with anyone who asked her. She had no shortage of partners and the next few hours passed quickly. Even though she told everyone she was having a great time, she felt nothing but relief when the night was over.

The next day was Saturday. Although Noreen planned to stay on for a few more days with Detta in the bungalow, Cathy packed the last of her things to be included in the move to the farm, said a final goodbye to her old home and got a lift back to the railway station in Cork with Aunt Helen, who had stayed with them overnight. As the ticket-checker waved her through the barrier and she went slowly down the tunnel that led to the platform where the Dublin train was waiting, Cathy had the feeling that a chapter in her life had closed. There was no turning back. No way of knowing, either, what lay ahead.

She went with some of Noreen's friends to see her and two other nurses off at the airport. They were heading to London, for the next leg of their flight to Saudi Arabia. Amid all the laughter and the good wishes, Cathy felt a sense of disbelief. Right up to the last minute, she had hoped that her sister would change her mind. She tried to hold back the tears as she hugged her goodbye.

'Don't forget to come back, Noreen.'

'As if I would, dote. And don't you forget to write.'

'As if I would.' Cathy's voice was equally matter-of-fact.

One of the other nurses had her parents seeing her

off. Cathy heard a keening note in the mother's voice as she threw her arms around her daughter. 'It's only for two years,' the woman's husband kept saying. 'We won't feel the time go.' But his wife's heaving shoulders gave the lie to this. Cathy began wishing that Noreen would go before they all broke down and made shows of themselves, like the other nurse's mother.

Suddenly they were gone, the three of them, striding jauntily through the gate, going all too quickly past the security barrier, with Noreen looking back to wave to Cathy. Then she was lost to view among the other passengers.

'I just can't believe it,' said Declan, one of Noreen's friends. He had been in the running before Gavin, Cathy remembered. She saw him bite his lip and wipe away a furtive tear. 'I just can't take it in.'

'Me neither.' Moya, a small, dark-haired, vivacious nurse who had lived with Noreen, shook her head regretfully. 'She was a good friend. We'll not see her like again.'

'She's not gone forever,' Cathy said. But the two years seemed to stretch ahead to infinity. She fought down a feeling of panic. 'She'll be back before we know it.'

'Of course she will.' Moya gave Cathy's arm a friendly squeeze. 'Why don't we all go and have a drink?'

'Good idea,' said Declan, and two other nurses whom Cathy hadn't met before agreed. They all piled into Declan's car and drove out of the airport. When they got to Drumcondra, Cathy decided not to go to the pub with them. She asked Declan to drop her at the end of her road, saying she was tired and needed an early night. When the others protested, saying a few drinks would cheer her up, she refused to change her mind. She wasn't in drinking form, she explained. She had an upset stomach.

'A drop of warm milk before you go to bed,' Moya advised. Declan, equally concerned, insisted on seeing Cathy up the front path of the old house, waiting at the foot of the steps until she'd opened the heavy front door. 'Stay in touch,' he said before he left her. 'You have my phone number, and Moya's not far away. Remember, if there's anything you need . . . '

'Thanks. I won't forget.' Why couldn't her sister have been content to settle down with a nice man like Declan, instead of having to trek off over half the world after Gavin, the snooty doctor who'd always behaved as if he was one of God's gifts to women? But then, when it came to falling in love, there was no rhyme or reason to it. There was no point in blaming Noreen, Cathy told herself, trudging up the two flights to her solitary bedsitter. If logic had anything to do with it, she would have lost interest in Fergal once he'd gone away to be a priest. She'd never have let him hurt her the way he had. And that night with Peter would probably never have happened. There was no use crying over spilt milk. Cathy sighed as she turned the key in the door of the dark, silent bedsitter. From now on she would let logic rule her life.

Cathy was having a dream. She was telling Noreen that she and Fergal had made love.

'It was beautiful.' Although she felt wistful that she couldn't remember it happening. She just knew that it had. 'We're going to be married some day.'

Noreen looked unimpressed. 'But you *were* careful?' she asked. 'He *did* use something?' When Cathy didn't answer, she said, 'You're probably OK. Fergal O'Reilly never did anything foolish in his life.' There was scorn in her voice. 'He still has his Communion money.'

Cathy found herself laughing. What had that got to do with anything?

And then she was awake, lying in the darkness, her heart thumping.

Dreams were funny things. Cathy remembered reading in a magazine article that they were messages sent by the subconscious to the conscious mind, drawing attention to things that people had forgotten about, or wanted to ignore. According to this article, some famous Swiss psychologist – she couldn't remember his name offhand – had said: 'You ignore these messages at your peril.'

At your peril. Cathy had scoffed to herself at the time. The phrase was so dramatic, it had stuck in her mind. But now, as she lay in the dark, trying to get back to sleep, hearing the usual sounds the old house made at night – creaking floorboards, water pipes gurgling in the attic overhead – she found herself thinking that maybe there was some truth in all that dream stuff. After all, what about those times you dreamed you were having your period and woke up in the morning to find it had come? Sometimes when you were least expecting it. And what about . . . ?

A door slammed down below. Footfalls on the stairs. Then silence. A complete silence. The old house seemed to be holding its breath. No shifting boards, no gurgling water. Silence. A blankness in her head. And a tightness in her chest, as if two hands were squeezing her heart.

Then the motor of the bedsitter's ancient fridge kicked in, its bronchial wheeze setting off all the other noises. And Cathy's brain began to work again. She did a quick calculation and breathed a sigh of relief. It was OK. Her period wasn't due for another two weeks. Besides, what was the problem? What had happened with Peter had only happened once. There was nothing to worry about. She forced herself to go to sleep. She would laugh about it in the morning, she assured herself.

Next day was Tuesday. Because of her disturbed night, Cathy overslept and had to dash for the bus. No time for breakfast. She'd buy a bun in the shop and eat it at her break. Not that she felt hungry. The air in the bus was stuffy enough to take your appetite away. The petrol fumes from the engine had made her want to get sick as she passed it. And now there was a really strong stink of tobacco coming from the man sitting beside her. It was enough to make your stomach turn. What a smelly city, Cathy thought, as she tried to concentrate on the paperback she was reading. It was a wonder she hadn't noticed before.

The rest of the week went by in a blur. They seemed to be busier than usual in the office. Most evenings she felt so tired after her day's work that as soon as she'd eaten and tidied up the bedsitter, she'd only enough energy to climb into bed and watch a couple of programmes on the rented television set before she fell asleep. *This can't go on. I'm turning into a wage slave.* But all that was going to stop. Moya and a couple of other nurses were going drinking and clubbing on Friday night and they'd asked Cathy to go with them. It was time she started living a bit.

'You're a slow drinker, Cathy,' one of the nurses called across the pub. 'You'll never catch up with us at this rate.' The bar around them was crowded with jovial Friday-night drinkers, the air heavy with cigarette smoke and the smell of beer. 'Sure, you're no *craic* at all.'

'Don't mind her,' Moya said to Cathy. 'I hope you're not pining for Noreen?' She touched Cathy's arm, her face sympathetic in the dim light. 'Or is the tummy still bothering you?'

'No, that's fine now,' Cathy lied. She took a swallow from her glass and noticed that the beer had a metallic taste to it. 'I'm just tired. It's been murder at work all week.'

'It'll be easier when you get a bit more experience.' Moya nodded wisely. 'I'll never forget my first year away from home. I was tired all the time. My periods went haywire – of course, that sometimes happens.'

'Oh, really?' Cathy looked at her with interest. 'I didn't know that.'

'Oh, yes. Didn't have one for months. It didn't bother me, but my poor mother was worried.' She laughed. 'The minute I went home for the holidays, she brought me to the doctor.'

'And?'

Moya's reply was lost in the sudden burst of laughter that rose from the group around them. She shrugged, smiled apologetically at Cathy and was about to turn away.

'What happened?' Cathy tried to shout above the din. 'With the doctor?'

'Nothing.' Moya turned to face her. 'He said they'd come back in their own good time. And they did. Of course, I didn't know what the fuss was about. But then, I hadn't been up to anything, had I?'

Cathy's throat was dry. 'No, of course not.'

Someone pulled at Moya's arm. Before she turned away, she said kindly to Cathy, 'You could probably do with a tonic. Get something from the chemist.'

It was a flat, oblong piece of plastic, a bit like those thermometers people put inside a fridge to check its temperature. Instead of numerals, this one had three little windows in it. The first window showed a mark to say that the test had worked. The other two had matching blue lines.

'It can't be.' Cathy looked at it despairingly. Maybe she should go out and buy another one. It was Saturday afternoon; there was still time before the shops closed. But she knew there'd be no point. It was the second test kit she'd bought that day. And both had said the same thing.

Maybe she should have waited till the morning to repeat the second one. It worked better with a fasting specimen. But as she hadn't eaten all day it would hardly have made much difference, would it? She might as well accept it: the test was positive. And she knew anyway. The signs had all been there.

There was no use in clutching at straws by telling herself that Moya was probably right, that she was irregular at the best of times, that her nausea was caused by stress and her breasts felt heavy because she was premenstrual. Last night, when she'd checked her diary and found that although there was a little tick against 6 August, there was no corresponding one for September, or for October, she'd known straight-away. There was no use in telling herself that she'd probably forgotten to record it, that she'd been so caught up with the worry over Noreen going to Saudi, not to mention the whole business of Mum's wedding, that she'd just been too busy to notice if she'd had a period or not. To be honest, she'd probably known all week, and just hadn't wanted to face up to it. But ignoring something never made it go away.

And it won't go away now, Cathy told herself. She sat down on the edge of the bed and tried to control her mounting panic. She found it difficult to breathe and it felt like there was a tight band around her head.

This isn't happening. It's a bad dream. A nightmare. What am I going to do? She tried to think but her thoughts began colliding madly with each other. *I can't have this baby.* She glanced around the cramped little room with its shabby carpet and ancient cooker. Her eye fell on the black mould on the ceiling over the sink. *You couldn't rear a child here. What chance would the poor little thing have? Imagine trying to bring a buggy up all those stairs. They probably wouldn't let you, anyway.* All the other tenants were single people like herself, or young working couples. *I could get somewhere else.* What else would she find, on the money she earned? And she probably wouldn't have a job once they found out.

Could they fire you for being pregnant? But would she want to stay on, with everyone knowing? She'd have to leave work, go back home. But where was home now? She didn't even have her own room in the farmhouse. Everyone would want to know who the father was. And how it had happened. She felt her cheeks burn with shame at the thought of trying to explain. She pictured the disgust on Detta's face, heard her biting, sarcastic voice.

There's no way I can tell Mum. I've already disappointed her by not going to college. She thought back to the time of the Leaving Cert results, recalling the horror with which her mother had reacted when she heard Cathy was turning down her offer of a university place ' . . . in favour of some tuppenny-ha'penny commercial course. Your grandfather would turn in his grave.' Louise had kept up a storm of protest for weeks. How much worse it would be this time. It didn't bear thinking about. No, I can't face her, Cathy thought.

And what about Vinnie and all the relatives? She felt she would rather die than shame her mother in front of them. She pictured the reaction of the O'Reillys and the other neighbours, the whispers, the condemnation. And what about Fergal? What could she say to him? Was there any way he would understand? With a sob, Cathy buried her face in her hands. Oh, God! if there is a God, tell me what to do. If only Noreen was here.

Around and around her thoughts went, like tiny animals trapped on a wheel. All that night. And most of Sunday. Again and again she went over the arguments. As with the test, she kept coming up with the same answer. When the solution first suggested itself, she shrank back in horror.

I couldn't do it. I've always wanted children.

Some day, yes. But not like this. Some day when you're properly grown-up and can afford to give the baby all it needs.

But.

This is the wrong time, Cathy. Face up to it. There's no other way.

Once the decision was made, she tried to calculate her finances. Although she was careful with her money, buying a new outfit for Mum's wedding had put a hole in her savings. She wasn't sure exactly how much cash she'd need but she knew she didn't have enough. It would be too late by the time she'd saved it up. And there was no one she could borrow from. She pressed her hands against her forehead. There had to be someone who could help her. Think, Cathy, think! And then the answer came to her.

'Hi Peter.' She kept her voice cheerful as she plonked a thick folder down on the desk beside him. 'A little something to brighten your Monday morning.'

'Oh, hello, Cathy.' There was surprise on Peter's face as he looked up at her. Relief too. 'Does this mean the cold war is over?'

'Why not?' There was no one else in the office; she'd picked a time when she knew Jimmy, the older brother, would not be there. She'd spent most of the previous night planning her strategy. Although her courage faltered for a moment, she kept her resolve steely and her voice light. 'There's no reason, I suppose, why we can't still be friends.'

'No reason at all.' Peter looked at her eagerly. 'I knew if I kept away from you, you'd come round. You're a great girl, Cathy. I knew you wouldn't hold a grudge.'

She winced inwardly at the triumph in his voice. 'Life's too short.'

'You're so right. Listen, how about meeting tonight for a few scoops?'

'Tonight?' She looked doubtful, pretended to consider.

'Ah, come on,' Peter urged. 'We've a lot of catching up to do.'

'Yes,' Cathy said quietly. 'We have, haven't we?'

'It's not mine!' Peter put down his pint and half-rose from his seat. A belligerent look came over his face. 'You're not pinning this one on me.'

'The way you did on me?' Her heart was knocking against her ribs, her knees trembling under cover of the bar table, but she managed to keep her voice calm. 'It was my first time.'

'I don't believe it. Didn't you and Lover Boy . . . ?'

'Say what you like about Fergal, he was a decent man.' She couldn't keep the scorn from her voice. 'He'd never have done something like that.'

'Come on,' Peter said. But a lot of the bluster had gone out of him. He looked at Cathy's face and his own turned white. 'I thought you were on the pill.'

'No.' Cathy's voice was bitter. 'But you never bothered to ask, did you?'

'So it's true?' Peter sank down on to the cushioned seat as if his legs had lost the ability to support him. He put his hand to his head. 'Oh, Christ! Oh, Christ!'

She watched him, saying nothing. She saw him trying to take in the meaning of what she'd told him. After a moment he looked up and said in a small voice, 'What are you going to do?'

Cathy glanced around the bar. It was early, and a slack night. An elderly man sat up at the counter watching the sports channel with the barman. Although she and Peter were the only other drinkers, and could talk without fear of being overhead, she kept her voice flat and unemotional.

'I can't have this baby, Peter. I've only just turned nineteen. I have a crap job. I couldn't support a flea on what I earn. But even if I could, I wouldn't. It would kill my mother.'

'Mine too.' Peter's face twisted for a moment. 'Oh, Christ, Cathy, what have I done? How could I have been such a shit? A selfish shit!' He groaned suddenly and thumped his forehead with his fist. 'My father was right. I'm no bloody good. I should be shot.'

'You're probably right.' Cathy looked at him coldly. If she had had a gun in her hand, she'd have done the job herself. She wondered how they could ever have been friends. But there was no point in alienating him if she wanted his help. 'Look, I know you're sorry but it's too late for that now. Wringing your hands won't solve anything.'

'What will?' Peter groaned.

'I have a suggestion.'

Peter glanced at her alertly. He had that terrier look to him again.

'Tell me about it,' he said.

It turned out to be even easier than she had hoped.

'I've a friend over in London,' Peter's brother said. It was a different bar this time. One Cathy had never been to before, out the country a bit, where Jimmy had driven the three of them in his car. 'You can stay with him.' He gave her an unsmiling look. 'Did you ring that number Peter gave you?'

'I've an appointment for Saturday morning.' Cathy was amazed at the speed with which everything was happening. 'I'll have to fly out on Friday evening.'

'I'll organise that,' Jimmy said crisply. 'You can pick up the tickets at the airport.' He handed her an envelope. 'The money for the clinic. You'll have to pay for any other expenses.' In a few years' time, she thought, he would be a carbon copy of his father. Ever since he'd met her that evening, he'd made her feel like a piece of shit he'd wiped from his shoe. Yet she felt grateful to him.

'Thanks,' she said awkwardly.

'I'm not doing it for you.' Jimmy glanced at Peter, who sat nursing his pint with a hangdog look on his face. 'Get in another round.' As if glad to be given something to do, Peter jumped up and headed for the counter. Jimmy's eyes followed his younger brother for a moment, then turned to look coldly at Cathy. 'Who else knows about this?'

'Nobody,' she stammered. 'Just the three of us.'

'Good,' he grunted. His eyes narrowed. 'But if my father ever hears . . . '

'He won't hear it from me,' Cathy said fervently.

'See you keep it that way.' She saw his face relax. His manner became almost cordial. 'It's not up to me, of course,' Jimmy said pleasantly, as Peter came back with the drinks. 'But if you take my advice, as soon as you come back you should think about looking for another job.'

Her plane landed at City Airport, a small terminal on the outskirts of London's East End. As Cathy came through the arrivals area, she saw a stocky, dark-haired young man with a gentle face standing behind the barrier, holding up a piece of card with her name on it. She went over to him.

'Hi, I'm Cathy.'

He had a pleasant smile. 'How's it going? I'm Damien.'

Cathy was surprised. She'd been expecting someone more businesslike. But what a relief not to be met by another Jimmy.

'We were at school together,' Damien said as he took her bag from her and led the way out of the building. 'We move in different worlds nowadays. But . . . ' – he gave an embarrassed grin – ' . . . he did me a couple of favours once.'

The Jimmys of this world would always collect, Cathy thought. But she was in no position to be critical. 'Lucky for me,' she said, and followed Damien out to the row of waiting taxis.

The air felt crisp and autumnal, and the city lights were dazzling against the night sky. Cathy had flown before – she'd been to Lourdes a few years earlier with her mother and Detta – but it was her first visit to London. Normally she'd have felt excited at visiting a new city and would have been gazing eagerly around her, trying to take everything in, but tonight she felt no great interest in her surroundings. Not that there was much to see, just the arc lamps lining the curving motorway and some tall, lighted buildings in the distance. As the taxi sped towards the city, she was grateful that Damien had chosen to sit in front beside the driver so she didn't have to make conversation with him. She leaned back in her seat and closed her eyes, breathing a prayer of thankfulness that she'd got this far.

What a nightmare the past week had been. She hoped she'd never have to go through another one like it. Having to hide her feelings from everyone, having to lie and pretend and act normally, while all the while the fear of being found out had been like a rat gnawing away at the pit of her stomach. And then the rush to catch the flight out. As the taxi battled its way through the Friday-evening traffic, she'd prayed they would make it to the airport in time. When she got to the busy terminal, she was terrified she'd see a face she knew. Someone from the office, meeting a plane. Or one of Noreen's friends, maybe. Or, horror of horrors, someone from down home, flying out on holiday. In the departures area, she was reluctant to meet the eye of the clerk at the check-in counter as he took her boarding card, convinced that he suspected the purpose of her trip. There had been a slight delay at the boarding gate. She was afraid for a while the plane wouldn't take off, but eventually it had. And she was here. At last. Now there was the thought of the following day to face. But not just yet.

Cathy felt the taxi slowing down. She opened her eyes to find that the driver was carefully nosing his way through narrow, cobbled streets with grey buildings on either side – small houses, a greengrocer's shop, a pub on the corner. Then she saw a huge, Victorian-looking building with many gabled roofs and tall windows. A number of ambulances were parked at its front, while another ambulance raced, its siren screeching, through a large red-bricked archway. The taxi went slowly down the narrow street past the archway and pulled up at a small apartment block which was obviously part of the hospital complex. Damien must work there, Cathy told herself. And her heart began thumping as she asked herself just how much Jimmy had told him.

As it turned out, it was not Damien, but his wife, Jen, an attractive redhead with a Cockney accent who was working as a receptionist in the hospital. Damien was a commercial artist who designed paper bags for a living and painted portraits on the side. 'He can do anything from a photograph,' Jen told her. 'He's gifted.' She gazed at her husband fondly. 'He'd love to do it full-time, but there's no money in it.'

Damien said nothing, just grinned. In his own way he was as taciturn as Peter's brother, Cathy thought. But much nicer. When she'd tried to pay for the taxi, he'd waved her money away. 'Any friend of Jimmy's . . . ' he'd said.

But if Damien was quiet, Jen made up for it. She had a warm, bubbly personality. It was impossible not to like her. After they cleared away the remains of the Indian takeaway they had for their supper, she showed

Cathy around the small flat, which was clean and tidy, with the featureless furnishings that come with rented accommodation. But Jen had added some colourful touches: a few pieces of lustrous pottery, an eye-catching Picasso print, a bright, handwoven blanket, a souvenir of a Mexican holiday, draped over the back of the couch. Between them, they managed to give the place a personal look.

'It's all right, but it's a bit small,' she said when Cathy admired the apartment. 'We've our names down for a two-bed.' She patted her stomach and grinned at Damien. 'We're going to need the extra room when the baby comes.'

Cathy was taken aback. 'You're pregnant?' The idea was somehow unsettling. 'I'd never have guessed.'

'I haven't begun to show,' Jen giggled, 'but you should see my boobs. They're enormous.'

'That's enough of that, woman,' Damien said, his face a mixture of pride and embarrassment.

'Silly thing!' Jen grinned back at him, squeezing his arm. As Cathy watched them, it occurred to her that if either of them had any idea of the truth about her, they were very good at hiding it. Both seemed to have accepted without question her cover story of having come to London for a job interview. No, Jimmy hadn't told them, she decided. Which was a relief. The fewer people that knew, the better. Despite this, when she saw Damien put his arm around Jen, she found herself wishing that she had the courage to tell them. She wished too that she had someone to hold her like that.

She spent the night on the living-room couch. Towards morning, an ambulance siren woke her from an uneasy sleep. For a moment she thought she was back in Dublin, in Noreen's little house, where she'd stayed when she went there first. Then she remembered where she was. And why. And the rat began gnawing at her stomach again.

'I suppose you're nervous,' Damien said the following morning as he walked to the Tube station with her. 'It must be a bit of an ordeal.'

Cathy looked quickly at him. Did he know something, after all? But his face showed nothing but friendly interest. 'I'll be fine,' she said. Despite her apprehension, she couldn't help glancing around curiously as they walked along the busy street. She'd expected that London would be different to Dublin, but not as different as it seemed at first glance. Many of the people they passed had dark skins and a lot of the men wore turbans. High up on the gable walls on street corners the name plaques were in English and in a curling script that Damien told her was Urdu. They turned a corner and saw a street market that could have been in Calcutta or Bombay: the stalls were hung with bright clothes and scarves and the vendors and shoppers alike wore flowing garments. Nobody seemed to be talking English. How could Damien live here without feeling homesick?

As if he guessed what she was thinking, he grinned at her. 'Bit of a culture shock, eh? A far cry from Grafton

Street and good old Neary's. But it's the mixture of ethnic groups that I like, and the different types of faces. Makes life more exciting.' He gestured. 'The Tube station's this way.' They crossed the street and went in through a shabby entrance hall with peeling paintwork and graffiti on the walls. Damien pointed her in the direction of the ticket office. 'Now, remember to change at King's Cross and take the Northern Line.'

Cathy nodded. She had the little map of the Underground he'd given her, knew what the coloured lines stood for and had worked out her route. 'I'll be fine.'

'Of course you will,' Damien said. He waited till she'd bought her ticket. As she went through the turnstile, she looked back to see him giving her the thumbs-up sign. A nice guy, she thought. Jen was a lucky woman. It was a shame to have to deceive him.

When she came up from the Underground into the sunlight, she felt the sharpness of autumn against her face, and saw straightaway that she was in a more prosperous part of London than the one she'd left behind. She found herself walking down a narrow, bustling high street lined with trendy boutiques, bistros and specialist food shops. Following the directions she'd been given over the phone earlier in the week, she turned the corner at a mullioned pub, leaving the shops behind. Ten minutes' walk through a quiet residential area brought her to the clinic, a large, ivy-covered house with a neat gravelled space in front.

Except for a discreet brass plate beside the front door, the building had very little to distinguish it from its well-kept neighbours. Inside, the decor was tasteful, with pastel colours and potted plants in the reception area. Classical music played gently in the background. An efficient woman with short, greying hair looked up from the desk as Cathy approached it.

'Cathy . . . Carmody?' The English voice stumbled over the unfamiliar surname. 'Please take a seat for a moment.' She waved Cathy past a potted palm tree to a waiting area, where a woman sat flicking through a magazine with a young girl beside her. As she took a seat, Cathy glanced at them but the woman's gaze went back to the pages in front of her, while the girl's eyes were already fixed on a point on the carpet between her heavy Doc Martens. She had long, skinny legs in coloured tights and wore a fake-fur jacket over a pleated tartan miniskirt. Long drifts of hair, the colour of a sparrow's wings, fell from a central parting down either side of her narrow little face, half-obscuring it.

My God! Cathy was shocked. *She's only a child! She couldn't be more than thirteen or fourteen! What kind of man would do that to someone so young?* Not wanting to stare, she shifted her gaze to the woman. Probably the mother, she decided, or maybe an aunt. She wasn't as young as she'd first appeared, with her smart, straight hairstyle and long camel overcoat over polished leather boots. Her face showed lines of weariness, and the thin fingers restlessly turning the pages of the magazine had an old look to them. Maybe the girl was the youngest in the family, like herself, Cathy thought. She tried to picture her own mother sitting there but the image was so incongruous she banished it from her mind immediately. Even when she'd gone to the dentist as a child, Noreen had always been sent to accompany her. Just then, a stocky, middle-aged woman in a white dress appeared around the potted palm to usher the other two away. When the girl got up to clump across the floor in her heavy-soled boots – her long, thin legs making her look like an awkward stork – Cathy saw the older woman put her arm across the narrow shoulders and give her a gentle squeeze. Everyone has someone but me, she thought.

But it wasn't too long before the same white-uniformed woman came back to beckon to Cathy. She showed her into a tiny room, less attractive than the reception lobby, containing a small, tubular table strewn with several tattered copies of *Hello* magazine, flanked by some functional chairs. A print of West-minster Abbey hung crookedly on one wall.

'Be with you in a moment, dear,' the woman said. And Cathy was left alone again. She picked up one of the magazines but felt too restless to read and put it down unopened. Her mouth was dry. She felt a hollow sensation in her chest, and she began to think of her mother again. But this time, her image of Louise had an accusing look to it. As she heard footsteps outside in the passage, Cathy was visited by the wild fear that her mother had found out what she was about to do and had followed her to England to prevent it. When she saw the door opening, she gazed at it with her heart beating wildly. She managed to hide her relief when the stocky, white-uniformed figure came into view.

'Now, dear.' The nurse's voice had a pleasant burr to it. 'This won't take long.' She sat down opposite and opened a folder containing a couple of printed forms. 'Tell me now, what is your date of birth?'

Her heart still thumping, Cathy heard her own voice give hesitant answers to the questions she was asked. This is it, she told herself. No going back.

'It's not too late to change your mind.' The doctor, a graceful Indian woman with traces of grey in her smooth dark hair, looked enquiringly at Cathy. Although she had a livid caste mark on her forehead, she wore western clothes under her white coat. 'Would you like a little more time to think it over?'

'Can we just get it over with?' Cathy said. Not that she was looking forward to it. Her face still burned at the memory of the physical examination, even though the doctor's hands had been gentle. Thank God it hadn't been a man. But the sooner she was out of here, the sooner she could get on with her life. 'Look, I've already told you, my mother lives in the country. They're old-fashioned people. She'd never get over the disgrace.'

'And what about you?' the doctor asked gently. 'Are you sure you don't want the child?'

'No. I've already told you . . . ' Panic began to grip her; she heard her voice rise. 'I've made up my mind.'

'There's no need to upset yourself.' The older

woman's voice was soothing, her dark eyes full of compassion. 'I just want you to be absolutely sure.' She looked at her watch. 'It will be an hour before we're ready for you. It's such a beautiful day. There's a really nice walk near here.' She smiled at Cathy. 'Ask at the reception for directions.'

She walked halfway back towards the high street, turned right, and found herself at the bottom of a hilly road with shabby houses on one side and trees and open grassland on the other. The road was strewn with fallen leaves. As Cathy climbed the hill, the low autumn sun took the sharpness from the air and glinted off the red and gold foliage of the trees. Had the doctor told the truth when she'd said the theatre wasn't free? Or had it been a ploy to give her more time to think? What difference did an hour make? Her mind was made up. The path grew steeper. Away to her left, a woman pushed a baby buggy across the grass while a small child toddled eagerly beside it. As she stopped for a moment to watch them, she saw the baby's fat little legs faltering over a tussock and noticed the firm yet gentle way the mother reached down to steady him. Cathy sighed and walked on.

As she neared the top, a man came briskly down the path, avoiding her with a muttered apology. She was reminded of her father, remembering his quick, impatient stride. Dad had never wanted to waste a moment. It was as if he had known he had so little time. But how he'd loved life. 'It's a precious gift,' she recalled hearing him say once. 'Use it wisely, Cathy.' *That's what I'm trying to do, Dad.* But would he agree with her, if he knew?

When she reached the viewing area at the top of the hill, she saw that it was a flat circle, the ground levelled by many feet. From here, the receptionist in the clinic had told her, you could see landmarks all over the city. At the front of the viewing area, she noticed an upright piece of stone standing like a narrow altar, with a flat metal top. As she drew nearer, she saw etched in the metal an outline of the buildings, domes and spires that lay below, spread out in the distance. She examined it, mildly curious.

What am I doing here? Trying to decide if that's Saint Paul's down there, or maybe the dome of the Zoological Gardens, like a tourist with nothing else on my mind? 'You need to be sure,' the Indian doctor had said. She was suddenly struck by the unfairness of it all. What other choice was there? And why did she have to make it on her own? As she stared down the hill, she saw joggers on the lower slopes, people out for a stroll. She thought of her father again. If only he hadn't died. If only Noreen hadn't gone away.

But even if Dad was here standing beside her, she thought, the decision would still be hers to make. She recalled a conversation they'd had a few weeks before he died. They were discussing the subjects she needed to pick for secondary school. Despite his help, she was finding it difficult to decide between ones that clashed on the timetable. 'This is too difficult, Dad.' She gave a sigh of exasperation. 'It would be much simpler if I could do them all and not have to choose.'

'Cathy,' her father said, 'as you go through life you'll be faced with many choices, some of them a lot harder than whether you should do science or home economics. You might as well get into practice now.' He gave her a kindly look. 'But remember, you can only do the best you can. And once you've made the decision, don't agonise. Just go ahead and do it.'

Cathy glanced at her watch. She straightened her shoulders, taking one last look at the view, and started down the hilly path.

After it was over, they led her to the recovery room and told her to rest. As she lay there, she heard movements behind the curtain separating her bed from the next one. She wondered if it was the young girl in the Doc Martens, but her mind felt too blurred to hold on to this thought. Just before she drifted off to sleep, she heard muffled sounds, like someone crying. She wanted to go to the girl, but her limbs felt like lengths of piping she'd seen earlier in the Underground, piled up near the entrance to a tunnel. Pipes so heavy it would take two men to move them. There was no way she'd be able to lift them off the bed. She wished someone would come and comfort whoever was crying. When she opened her eyes again, it was late afternoon. The curtain was drawn back and the bed next to hers was empty. She wondered if the whole thing had been a dream.

'What kind of firm was it?' Jen asked. 'You never said.'

She thought quickly. 'Medical supplies.'

A gleam of interest sparked in the other woman's eyes. 'Maybe I'd know them.'

'You wouldn't,' Cathy said hastily. She'd forgotten Jen worked in the hospital. 'Look, I don't really want to talk about it. They gave the job to someone else.'

'That's too bad.' Jen was full of ready sympathy. 'And after you travelled all that way. You must be feeling as sick as a parrot.'

She had a dragging feeling at the base of her stomach and her head ached. 'I've felt better.'

'Never mind, we'll take you down the pub to cheer you up.'

'Good idea.' Damien grinned. 'We'll help you drown your sorrows.'

'Thanks, but I'm a bit tired,' Cathy said. 'You go on your own.' She forced a smile. 'Look, I'm not sorry I came.'

'Well, as long as you feel that,' Jen said doubtfully. Her face brightened. 'Jimmy will be pleased, anyway.'

Cathy's heart gave a frightened thud. 'Why should Jimmy care?'

'That he won't be losing you, after all.' Jen threw her a coy look.

'He's not my boyfriend.' When she saw her surprise, Cathy felt she should offer some explanation. 'Peter's the one . . . '

'Oh, well then,' Jen said comfortably. 'Same thing, really. All in the family.'

'Either way,' Damien agreed, 'they'll be glad to have you back.'

She kept her face blank. 'I'm sure you're right.'

'Well, you seem to have gained a lot of experience in your six months in James O'Donohue's.' Emma, the recruitment consultant, was an attractive, smartly dressed young woman only a few years older than Cathy. 'Some of these smaller offices can be a good place to start.' She smiled enquiringly. 'But I take it you'd like somewhere bigger?'

Cathy nodded. 'The bigger the better.'

'Some of the large organisations can be a bit impersonal.' Emma glanced around the cheerful interview room. 'I prefer smaller, more intimate places myself. But then, we all have different needs.'

'A bigger place would provide more opportunities for advancement,' Cathy said. 'And the money's bound to be better than I'm getting.'

'That wouldn't be hard.' Emma pushed back her shining hair with a well-manicured hand and smiled again. 'It looks like you know what you want.'

'I'm learning fast.' Cathy envied the other girl her smart hairstyle and her polished manner. She promised herself that in a few years' time she would be like that. 'As you say, the last six months was useful experience. But I want to move on.'

Mrs Dunne accepted her resignation with equanimity, expressing neither surprise nor regret. Her manner reminded Cathy of a poem she'd learned at school about a river. 'Men may come and men may go, but I go on for ever.' Sinéad, the senior typist, was more open about her feelings. 'That's two quid you owe me, Mrs D.' She gave a hoot of satisfaction. 'Told you she wouldn't last longer than six months.'

Cathy was taken aback. She felt tears prick at her eyelids. 'Thanks very much.'

'There's no call to take it like that.' Sinéad was unabashed. 'You lasted longer than anyone. The girl before you left after three months. The one before that only stayed a fortnight. I can't for the life of me see why.' She examined her nicotined fingers thoughtfully. 'We're like one happy family here, aren't we, Mrs D.?'

If so, I must be the black sheep of it, Cathy thought. Ever since she'd come back from London, Jimmy had ignored her most of the time, addressing her only when the work demanded it, his manner brusque and unfriendly. Peter kept out of her way, always managing to avoid her eye when he passed through the front office. What else could she expect, she told herself. She didn't want to talk to them either. But the strain of working in an unpleasant atmosphere was beginning to tell.

'Young ones nowadays have no staying power,' Mrs Dunne said. 'I was saying that to Mr O'Donohue only the other day.' She gave a complacent nod. 'And he agreed with me.'

But if her employer had anything to say about Cathy's departure from the firm, she never found out what it was. During the fortnight she worked out her notice, he gave no sign that he knew she was going, behaving with his usual lofty manner whenever he passed through the main office, with words only for Mrs Dunne. Cathy thought she noticed a gleam of satisfaction in Jimmy's eye any time his gaze encountered hers, which was seldom. Peter seemed to be out of the office a lot. The day she left, he was nowhere to be seen. Sinéad said he was sick, but the boss's secretary, pursing her lips, said he was away doing an audit. At the tea break, Mrs Dunne produced a jam sponge and Sinéad surprised her with a good-luck card, but none of the O'Donohues acknowledged Cathy's impending departure. When the evening came, she put the cover on her computer, gathered her belongings, said goodbye to the two other women and clattered down the noisy staircase into the raw November night. And freedom.

The new job was with a large insurance company. There was a decent increase in salary. The work was not demanding and the prospects were good. But she found herself thinking of what the woman in the employment agency had said. Large firms *were* more impersonal. There were six other women in the administration department. They were friendly in the office, but that was as far as it went. Attempts to get to know any of them better were smilingly ignored. Sometimes she despaired of making new friends.

'You've got to give it time,' Moya said one evening, a few weeks before Christmas, when Cathy called around to the little terraced house near the hospital. 'It won't happen overnight. But you know you've always got me and Karen.'

Cathy gave her a grateful smile. The two nurses who'd shared the house with her sister were kind, but they were Noreen's friends, not hers. It was important to remember that, and not take advantage of their generosity. 'But you wouldn't want me to be crying on your shoulder all the time,' Cathy said.

'The trouble is, you never cry on anyone's shoulder, Cathy.' There was a slight edge in the Donegal woman's voice, but her dark eyes were warm. 'If anything's worrying you . . .'

There was something solid about Moya. Of course, she was years older than Cathy – older than Noreen, even. The kind of person you could confide in. But there was no need now. What was done was done. There was a danger, too, that at her age, Moya mightn't understand.

'Everything's fine,' Cathy said.

But sometimes during the next few weeks she'd wake from sleep trembling and shaking, as if she'd had a bad dream she couldn't remember. Other times, she'd feel like someone who'd managed to jump out of the way of a double-decker bus – enormously relieved, yet shaking in horror at the thought of what had almost happened. She'd get over it in time, she told herself. It was a small price to pay for being able to move on with her life.

'And did you?' Stephen asked in the silence that followed.

He saw Cathy come back into the present with a jolt. She was looking at him in surprise. He'd been quiet for so long, he realised, just letting her talk, that she must have forgotten he was there. He watched her for a moment. 'Did you? Move on?'

'No.' She shook her head. 'In one way I did. But in another . . .' She broke off, twisting her hands together, staring into the distance. For a moment, he felt she'd forgotten him again.

'Cathy, look at me,' Stephen said softly. He saw the misery in her eyes. 'There's more to tell, isn't there? I've a funny feeling it's the hardest part.'

'Yes,' Cathy said. 'It is. '

'I was half dreading Christmas that year,' she said. 'Our first on the farm. Although I wanted to be back with my family, I hated that we couldn't spend it at the bungalow. There was another reason too. This might sound odd, but I felt I'd changed since I'd seen them last. That it would be written on my face for everyone to see.'

'That they'd know what had happened in London?'

'I was terrified they'd find out. But no one noticed. It wasn't the most exciting Christmas ever. Mum kept saying how dead the place was without Noreen. But she and Detta and Vinnie seemed to enjoy themselves in a quiet sort of way. At that time of the year, there wasn't much work to be done around the farm.

Everyone was relaxed, sitting over huge meals and lying in late in the mornings, which suited me because I felt exhausted most of the time. And very sad. It felt a bit like the first Christmas after Dad's death, only no one seemed to feel this but me. I kept telling myself that nobody had died. But it was no use. It was like I had this heavy burden all the time, draining my energy. I was home for over a week because I had the days off between Christmas and New Year. One day I felt I'd better do something useful instead of lying around the farm all the time, so I headed into Cork to have a look at the sales. I was walking down the South Mall' – her voice trembled suddenly – 'when who should I bump into but Fergal O'Reilly . . .'

'Cathy, it's great to see you!' His smiling face gave no sign that he remembered the way they had parted in August. He looked bigger, his shoulders bulked out by the heavy windcheater he was wearing. His fair hair was hidden under a black knitted cap. The girl walking beside him had a round, rosy face and curling brown hair. Attractive in an outdoor way, Cathy thought. 'This is Anne Marie.' Fergal drew her forward. 'She's in town for the sales.'

'Pleased to meet you,' Anne Marie said. But she didn't look it. Her small eyes swept over Cathy, taking in every detail, then went back to Fergal. 'I don't want to miss my bus.' There was a complaining note to her voice.

Two's company, Cathy thought. 'Well, it's been nice seeing you.'

'Wait, Cathy.' She saw Fergal rub his hands together, his breath puffing out in the chilly air. 'I'm just going to see Anne Marie off at the bus station. But why don't we go for a coffee after that? Catch up on the news.'

'I don't know . . .' She looked at him irresolutely. Despite the way things had ended between them, he was still one of her oldest friends. As she stared at his cheerful face, she realised she was glad to see him. 'OK. Why not?'

She saw Anne Marie scowl, but Fergal grinned. 'Great. See you in the lobby of the Imperial in twenty minutes, then.' As he turned away, Cathy saw him take the girl by the arm.

The big lounge bar was half empty; it was easy enough to find a secluded corner. Cathy asked for a glass of wine and heard him order a pint of lager. She glanced at him in surprise.

'Don't tell my mother.' Although he laughed, she knew he was being serious.

'Would I ever?' She laughed too. As he took off his windcheater, she noticed he was wearing a cable-knit sweater over jeans. There was no sign of a clerical collar. 'That girl – who was she?'

'Just a friend,' Fergal said quickly. He sat down beside her. 'Anne Marie works in the office in the seminary.'

She recalled the look on the girl's face and remembered the way he'd taken her arm. She was surprised not to feel jealous. So much had happened since that day by the river. Her feelings for Fergal seemed to belong to a previous existence, but even so, she was pleased to see him. Suddenly, without warning, her hands began to tremble and her voice quavered. 'Everyone needs a friend. They're hard to find.'

Fergal looked surprised. 'Is something wrong, Cathy?'

She shook her head. It was difficult to find the words. Better not to try. 'I'm OK, really I am.' She sipped her wine but her hand shook so much that she had to put the glass down.

'No you're not.' Fergal stared into her face. His voice was concerned. 'What's happened?'

'Nothing.'

'I know you too well to buy that.' He took her hand, smoothing out her trembling fingers. His own hands were firm and warm. 'Look, you've got to tell me.'

When she saw the sympathy in his face, she was suddenly able to find the words. 'Something did happen.' What a relief to tell someone. But as she spoke, after a few minutes she saw his face begin to change.

'Hold on a minute, Cathy.' There was shock and anger in Fergal's voice. He dropped her hand, moving hastily away from her. 'You say you slept with this guy? That night you went back to Dublin?'

'It was an accident. We had too much wine, and he . . . '

'You mean you were drunk?' She saw the incredulity in his eyes. 'And that's why you slept with him? Cathy, how could you?'

'I didn't mean to. You were the one I wanted.'

'And you could have had me. That's what I was trying to tell you last summer. But you wouldn't listen, would you?' She heard the bitterness in his voice. 'Oh, no, you were too busy passing judgement, telling me I'd no idea of morality. Morality, that's rich! The minute you dump me, you rush off and sleep with someone else.'

'I didn't dump you.'

'What else do you call it?' He looked at her bleakly. 'I offered you a caring relationship, and you turned me down.'

'But you weren't free . . . '

'Depends on what you mean by "free". But that's by the way.' He made a dismissive gesture. 'The important thing is, I cared.' His face twisted with sudden contempt. 'Not like that Peter. Your *boozing* partner.'

'I cared about you too. I still do. But you're not being fair . . . '

'*Fair?*' Fergal cried. 'Is what you did fair? Is it fair to be telling me this?' He looked vulnerable suddenly. 'Why are you telling me? Is it to hurt me?'

'I needed to tell someone. I thought you'd understand. It never occurred to me you'd be jealous . . . '

'You never thought about me at all, that's obvious.' His eyes narrowed. He looked at her closely. 'Understand what, Cathy? Come on, spit it out. '

Suddenly it was hard to meet his gaze. 'The thing is . . . a couple of months after that night, I discovered I was . . . ' – she glanced around, lowering her voice, although there was no one within earshot – ' . . . pregnant.'

'What?' He looked surprised. 'I don't understand.'

His gaze travelled over her slender body in its skinny-rib sweater and close-fitting jeans. 'You're obviously not pregnant now.' Unwilling sympathy crept into his voice. 'Did you lose the baby?'

Cathy sighed. 'I went to London for a termination. That's what I've been trying to tell you.'

'A termination?' She saw him recoil, horror on his face. All sympathy had vanished from his voice. 'You mean an abortion?'

'Termination, abortion,' she said defensively. 'What's the difference?'

'None.' Fergal's voice was cold. 'It's just another name for murder.'

'Don't say that.' She gazed at him pleadingly. 'I thought you'd understand.'

She saw his look of cold astonishment. 'You killed your child and you expect me to understand?'

'It wasn't a child, or even a baby. It was quite early on.'

'Do you really think that makes any difference?' He looked affronted. 'The soul is present from the moment of conception . . .'

'I don't believe that. Nobody really knows . . .'

'The Church does. That was a human being, Cathy. With a right to life. And you killed it.'

'Don't keep saying that.' She tried to fight back the tears. 'Anyway,' she challenged him, 'what about my right to choose?'

'It doesn't exist. That's something dreamed up by left-wing feminists and enemies of religion.' She heard the flat certainty in his voice. 'Church teaching is pretty clear on that.' He looked at her solemnly. 'Cathy, have you any idea of the number of babies destroyed every year? The thousands of Irish women like you who head over to the abortion mills in England, the millions in America? It's mind-boggling, Cathy. Think of having that on your conscience.'

She winced at the condemnation in his voice. 'But I'm not responsible for other people's decisions. I had to do what was right for me.'

'No, Cathy, I'm sorry,' Fergal said scornfully. 'If you thought you'd get me to condone murder, it's just not on. No one has a right to choose that.'

'And you've no right to pass judgement on me.' Cathy felt her anger rising. 'You, of all people!' She couldn't keep the contempt out of her voice. 'Planning to break your vows even before you'd taken them. What kind of priest will you make, I wonder?'

'Insult me if you want to.' If she'd hoped to put a dent in his certainty, she hadn't succeeded. Although Fergal's eyes had flickered at her taunt, his manner had lost none of its self-righteousness. 'I've done nothing wrong, Cathy. You know that. But if I should happen to stray, I'll get forgiveness. The Church has always been understanding of the weaknesses of the flesh. In your case, though . . . ' He shook his head gravely. 'I tremble for your soul. The taking of unborn life is the worst crime there is. A sin against the Almighty Himself.'

'I've heard enough,' Cathy cried, making a grab for her coat.

'You need to hear the truth . . .'

'I don't need to listen to this.' Jumping to her feet, she left the bar and hurried out of the hotel. But his voice pursued her all the way down the South Mall. Cathy told herself to ignore it as she stumbled blindly through the needle-sharp rain that began to fall. Religious rantings that only a fool would take seriously. But how had the gentle, law-abiding boy with the quiet sense of humour, the boy that she'd grown up with, have turned into a such a pompous zealot? Could a year and a half in a seminary do that to you? Or had the signs always been there, and she just hadn't noticed? He was jealous, she told herself. And that had made him go over the top. He didn't really mean all those things. But she knew that he did. She remembered the way he'd recoiled from her and the horror on his face. Pain gripped her then, twisting through her body, the way his voice was twisting through her head.

It had grown dark: the street lights were on, the shutters already down on some shop windows. She hurried along without purpose. In Patrick Street, the Christmas lights blazed gaily above the heads of the passers-by. For a moment it seemed as if the coloured lights were spelling out what she'd done, for all the world to see. And she read the accusation on the faces of everyone she saw. Women in bus queues, laden with shopping, babies in buggies, children trudging through the rain, clutching their mothers' hands. All had the one message in their eyes: *Murderer! Killer of the unborn!*

No! A sob rose in Cathy's throat. She abandoned her aimless wandering. Like a hurt child, whose only instinct is to get home, she pushed her way through the crowds and plunged down the quays towards the bus station, the rain stinging her eyes. As she hurried along the line of country buses waiting at the kerbside, engines idling, she spotted one that passed the end of the track leading up to the farm. Jumping on board, she paid the driver and sank with a sigh into a seat near the back of the crowded bus. Almost immediately there was a slamming of doors, the engine revved up and the bus pulled away, moving quickly through the traffic down the lighted quays, heading for the outskirts of the city.

But there was no escaping the scene in the hotel bar, or the voices in her head. As she avoided the eyes of her fellow passengers, staring fixedly at the raindrops running down the darkened window, she found that Fergal's voice had been joined by others. She heard them all. Her mother, Detta, Uncle Vinnie, too, the neighbours, the nuns at school. A chorus of condemnation. And in the background, the accusing voices of little children.

Cathy thought her cheeks were still wet from the rain. But as she gazed unseeingly out the bus window, she realised that it was her tears trickling silently down.

The trickle grew to a flood, and she found herself giving way to great, choking sobs. The bus and its passengers faded away. She was back in the living room of her apartment, its walls shrouded in shadow outside the circle of lamplight. Her chest heaving, she saw Stephen watching her with sympathy.

'That's right.' His voice was gentle. 'Cry, Cathy dear.' He moved swiftly to sit at her side. She felt his arm around her shoulders. 'That's right. Get it all out.' She saw the compassion on his face. With a sigh she leaned her head against his chest and finally surrendered to the sorrow that engulfed her.

'I never grieved,' Cathy whispered when the first paroxysms had died down. 'I never let myself be sad.'

'What are you sad about?'

'Everything.'

'Are you sorry for what you did?' His voice was barely above a murmur. His arm held her in a comforting embrace.

Cathy thought for a moment. 'No, I'm not.' She felt the tears starting again. 'But I'm so sad that was the way things had to be.'

TEN

'Visit his parish?' Liz was outraged. 'Are you out of your tiny mind?'

'Take it easy.' Cathy couldn't help laughing at the look on her friend's face. 'I didn't say I would.'

'But to even think about it.' Liz shook her head. 'Listen, Cathy, do you know what they call women who get involved with priests?'

'You're reading too much into this.'

'Voco-busters,' Liz said relentlessly. 'It's kind of a trophy thing. I knew a woman once who . . . '

'I'm not like that.'

'Well, *I* know you're not. But that's what everyone will think.'

'Since when did you worry about other people's opinions?

'Cathy, I'm a journalist. I know people. And they generally think the worst. It's what sells papers, after all.'

'Sounds like a nasty business. If it's that bad, why do you stay in it?'

'Because it's the most exciting business in the world,' Liz said. 'OK, it can be nasty at times. But that's not the fault of the journalists. We're just giving the public what they want. People nowadays feel they have a right to be told everything – '

'Even if it means someone getting hurt?' Cathy looked at her doubtfully.

Liz shrugged. 'You know what they say, kiddo: you can't make an omelette without breaking eggs. A good story is worth the ruffling of a few feathers. And, at the end of the day, if it keeps my editor happy . . .'

'It all sounds a bit ruthless.'

'It's no worse than any other business,' Liz said. 'And better than some. After all, we journalists perform a service to the country. Don't forget, a free press is the mark of a democratic society.'

Cathy grinned at her. 'And there I was, thinking you just liked poking your nose into other people's affairs. I never realised you had higher motives.'

'Laugh if you want to,' Liz said. 'But I do have higher motives, even if they're not the ones you mean.' Her dark eyes were suddenly serious. 'I intend to go right to the top. And no one's going to stop me. One of these days, Liz Dennehy will be a name to be reckoned with.'

'Of course it will,' Cathy said. 'You'll get your chance.'

'And I'll be ready for it.' She saw Liz's mouth tighten with determination. 'The secret of success is to grab your opportunity when it comes.'

'You're right, Liz.' Cathy looked at her thoughtfully. 'Do you know, I think I might take Stephen up on his invitation after all.'

'Me and my big mouth,' Liz said. Then she laughed and gave a resigned shrug. 'Oh well, you're a big girl now.'

'Yes I am. And don't you forget it.'

She saw Liz look sharply at her. 'What has you so bright-eyed and bushy-tailed of a Monday night? An easy day in the office?'

'No, it was busy actually. I'd a lot of work to catch up on after the couple of sick days I took last week. But I'm still feeling good after my weekend.'

'But you didn't go out anywhere.' Liz looked baffled. 'I'd be stir-crazy after a weekend like that. It seems to me that all you did was lie around reading and sleeping.'

'And thinking,' Cathy said. 'I've been doing a lot of that.'

'Sounds dangerous. You wouldn't want to strain your brain. Although it seems to have done you good.' She stared closely at Cathy. 'You look really rested.'

'I'm sleeping better than I have in years.'

'I've no bother getting off.' Liz yawned. 'It's waking up that's the difficulty. I think I'll have a bath and an early night. Look at you,' she said enviously as she saw Cathy take out some blouses for ironing. 'Bursting with energy. You'll have to tell me your secret sometime.'

'Maybe I will.' She kept her voice light.

'And don't be wasting it on that priest,' the other woman advised. 'Go out and find yourself a real man.'

Liz had it all wrong. Stephen and she were just friends, Cathy told herself as she thought about it the following day during a slack moment in the office. But what a friend he'd turned out to be. She'd never met anyone like him. She couldn't get over how she'd been able to tell him everything on Wednesday night and how sympathetically he'd listened. Not once had she felt judged or condemned.

'I think your boyfriend did enough of that six years ago,' Stephen said. 'No wonder you went into denial over it.'

Cathy nodded. 'It hurt so much, I tried to pretend it had never happened.'

'I've known people to carry hurts inside them for twenty, thirty, sometimes as many as forty years before seeking help. It's very damaging. I'm glad you didn't let that happen to you, Cathy.'

'But why was he so self-righteous?' she asked. 'You'd think he'd never done anything wrong himself.'

'Some people feel so strongly about abortion that they lose all sense of proportion.' Stephen said. 'I've seen it happen more than once. They become fanatical, demonise those who disagree with them. And then, in Fergal's case there was probably an element of covering up his own failings, like the people in the Gospel who stoned the woman taken in adultery. By blaming you, he didn't feel so badly about himself.'

'What about you? Do you feel strongly about it?'

'Cathy, I told you, I'm not here to judge. It's a matter for your conscience.'

'I appreciate that, but I need to know.' Her eyes met his. 'Where do you stand on abortion?'

'It's contrary to Church teaching. It's never lawful.'

'Yes, I know.' Cathy's gaze didn't waver. 'But what about you?'

'You mean, how do I feel?'

'Yes.'

He didn't move his eyes away.

'I abhor it.'

Cathy felt as if she'd been punched in the stomach. She gave him a horrified look. 'But I thought you understood?'

'And I do,' Stephen said. 'At least I think I do.' He shook his head. 'You can never really put yourself in another person's shoes. It would be so easy for me to make a judgement, knowing that I'll never be placed in the position you found yourself in.' His voice was earnest. 'But I'm not going to do that. I don't have the right.'

She stared back at him, saying nothing.

He smiled reassuringly. 'Despite my abhorrence of abortion, I feel there may be occasions when it's justified, when it could be the lesser of two evils. One thing I do know is that worse things have been done in the past in the name of religion, or in pursuit of a just war, and the Church has stood over them.' He gave a wry smile. 'I don't know how many of my fellow priests would agree with me, though.'

Cathy felt a rush of relief. She smiled shakily. 'I think you'd probably be kicked out on your ear if they knew.'

'Probably.' Stephen grinned back. 'But that's my worry. What you need to do now is to try to put the whole thing behind you. Try to forgive those who hurt you and forget them. There are plenty of better men to choose from.'

'Are you sure? I haven't had much luck so far.' She gave a despondent sigh. 'I don't think I'll ever love anyone again.'

'Yes, you will,' Stephen said confidently. 'Once the hurts have healed, you *will* love again. Believe me.'

'What you need is a new man in your life,' Liz said as Cathy relaxed after work. 'Why don't you come out to the pub with me and Justin tomorrow night?' Justin was another journalist on her newspaper. Cathy was never sure if he was just a drinking companion or something more. For someone as open as Liz, she could be extraordinarily reticent when it came to her love life. Men came and went, but Justin always seemed to be there in the background. 'You never know what you might pick up.'

'You make it sound like a disease,' Cathy hedged. She hadn't heard from Stephen in almost a week, but she wanted to keep Wednesday night free, just in case. She knew it was his day off. But even if he didn't ring, the prospect of spending the night in a pub with Liz and Justin held no appeal. 'I know you mean well, but right now I never want another boyfriend, as long as I live.'

'Never is a long time.' Liz made a face. 'Just as well longevity doesn't run in your family.' She could be appallingly insensitive at times, Cathy thought. She'd learned long ago that it brought out the worst in Liz when you wouldn't take her advice. But right now she didn't feel like humouring her.

'And tact doesn't run in yours.' Cathy stood up and headed for her bedroom. 'I think I'll go and have a nice long soak in the bath before you hog all the hot water.'

'If you're going to be like that,' Liz sniffed.

But a few moments later Cathy heard a knock on her bedroom door. A shamefaced Liz stood in the doorway. 'I shouldn't have said that about your family. I'm such a bitch. I don't know how you put up with me.'

'I don't either.' But when she saw the other woman's big, dark, mournful eyes, Cathy's resentment melted away. 'None of us is perfect.' As friends went, Liz was one of the best she'd ever known. 'I was a bit bitchy myself.'

'You don't know the meaning of the word.' Liz's voice grew emotional. 'You've a heart of gold. You're one of the softest people I know.'

'I'm not that soft,' Cathy protested, not liking the picture it conjured up. 'I can be tough at times.'

'Only when you're pushed.' Her face was penitent. 'Friends?'

'Friends, Liz.' She put out her arms and the two women hugged. It struck Cathy that they went through this performance at least once a month. Then all would be forgiven and forgotten. Till the next time. 'Now, I really must have that bath.'

'I'll run it for you,' Liz offered. 'Take all the hot water you want.' She waved her hands magnanimously. 'And you can use my Christian Dior bath salts.'

'Actually, Liz, they're *my* bath salts,' Cathy said with a resigned laugh.

She was drying her hair when she heard the

telephone ringing in the living room. Let the machine take it. Liz was probably in the bathroom. Whoever it was would ring again. But a moment later, Liz, still wearing her penitential air, put her head around the bedroom door. 'It's for you.' She gave her a meaningful look. 'He wouldn't give his name.'

'He?' Cathy raised her eyebrows. She looked distrustfully at Liz. 'Is this one of your wind-ups?'

'No, I swear to God.' Liz made a crossing movement with her hand. 'I haven't a clue who he is.'

Her heart missed a beat. She padded barefoot to the phone and spoke breathlessly into the receiver. 'Hello, Cathy here.'

'It's Stephen. How have you been?'

'Fine.' She'd wondered if she would feel awkward after the intensity of what had happened at their last meeting, but as soon as she heard his voice, her face broke into a smile. 'Never better. And you?'

'Great.' She knew he was smiling too. 'Do you remember what we were saying about you coming over to see the parish?' To her surprise, his voice grew hesitant. 'Well . . . '

'You're having second thoughts?' *I might have known.* Maybe, like Liz had said, he was worried what people might think. 'Never mind, I'll take a rain check.'

'No, I want you to come. That is, unless you . . . ?'

'I'd like to.' She made her mind up quickly. 'When?'

'You would?' He seemed taken aback at the speed of her decision. He hesitated. 'Daytime would be better, but . . . '

'I can take a half day.'

'In that case, how about tomorrow?'

If Paul found out, he'd have a fit, she told herself. But she didn't care. Martina could hold the fort. 'OK, tomorrow it is.'

'That's great.' She heard his surprised laugh. 'Now, I'd better give you a few directions.'

When Cathy got off the phone, Liz, who'd been listening unashamedly, gave an amused chuckle. 'Sounds like the poor man didn't know what hit him.' There was grudging respect in her eyes. 'You don't mess about.'

Cathy made a modest bow. 'Not when it's something I want.' As she went back to finish drying her hair, she realised that seeing Stephen Brown again was something she wanted very much.

'Who was it, anyway?' she heard Liz call.

'Oh, just someone I met.' She kept her tone vague. 'Tell you about it another time.'

'You sly bitch. And there was me trying to fix you up with someone. I might have known you could look after yourself.'

Cathy laughed. 'As you said yourself, Liz, I'm a big girl now.'

Despite this, she felt her heart thumping with nervous excitement the following day as she got ready to visit Stephen. After a hasty sandwich in the office, she walked the few streets to the stop to wait for the bus which he'd told her to take. The journey was a short one, through an unfamiliar part of the city. As the bus rattled through the streets, the shops and buildings grew progressively shabbier. It was obviously one of the poorer and rougher areas. Cathy remembered Liz's comments of a few weeks before about the residents of places like this. As her eyes strained to find the landmarks Stephen had told her to watch out for, she wondered what lay ahead. The whole thing was probably a huge mistake – something to laugh about later and put down to experience. But there was no time for second thoughts. Here was the bridge Stephen had mentioned. Then the petrol station, the laundrette and the pub with the large painted sign. Get off at the next stop. Walk back to the petrol station.

She didn't have to, Cathy told herself. She could stay where she was till the terminus and catch the next bus back to town, explaining afterwards that she hadn't been able to get the time off. That might be the best solution. As she dithered, she saw the bright canopy of the petrol station. There was a pinging sound as someone pressed the bell. As the bus drew to a shuddering halt, she made up her mind. When she jumped down onto the pavement and heard the bus doors hissing closed behind her, she wanted to turn back. But it was too late.

Walking slowly along the pavement, she felt like a traveller journeying into the unknown. *To boldly go where no one has gone before.* She told herself to get a grip. *You're not in* Star Trek. This wasn't outer space, peopled by aliens. This was a dingy suburban street with busy traffic, and perfectly normal pedestrians going about their business. All the same, it was a relief when she walked back to the petrol station and saw Stephen's car parked on one side of the forecourt. And at the wheel, Stephen, reading a book. When he glanced up and smiled, she felt her spirits lift. It was going to be OK, after all.

The parish centre was a two-storey building with a flat roof, surrounded by low walls, about fifty yards down the road from the big, green-domed church. Stephen pressed a bell at the entrance, and the door was opened electronically by a grey-haired woman sitting behind a counter inside the hallway. They exchanged nods but he didn't stop to introduce Cathy, leading her past the counter towards the back of the building. They passed a staircase with a poster on the wall. *Weight Watchers: Mondays and Thursdays, 10 am.* Other notices on a door in front of them said, *Senior Citizens. All welcome* and *St Patrick's Day Social: Please Enquire.*

Help, Cathy thought, what am I letting myself in for?

'We won't stay long.' Stephen smiled at her reassuringly. 'I just want to give you an idea of the place.'

'Meet Sister Dolores. She's the parish social worker.'

Sister? Cathy glanced in surprise at the older woman who came forward. Surely things hadn't changed that much in the few years since she'd done her Leaving Cert? Maybe it was different in Dublin, but the ginger-haired woman in the bilious tracksuit reminded her more of an overweight teacher who'd once taught her PE than of any of the nuns, with their short veils, knee-length black skirts and dowdy white crimplene tops who'd been a big part of her schooldays in County Cork. But then, priests hadn't gone in for black leather jackets much either when she was growing up, she reminded herself.

'Well, well, well. So you've brought your sister to see how the other half lives?' Sister Dolores had a deadpan way of speaking. Working-class Dublin overlaid with a slight American twang. 'I must say, we're honoured.'

'Cathy's not my sister.' She saw Stephen's flustered expression. 'I'm showing her around the parish.'

The nun looked at her. 'Are you a journalist?'

Cathy was surprised at the suspicion in the other woman's voice. 'No, of course not.'

'Can't be too careful, nowadays.' Sister Dolores's round, freckled face relaxed. She grasped Cathy's hand in a strong grip. 'You're welcome to the parish. Come and meet a few people.' She glanced around the large room, where six or seven old people, mostly women, wandered in an aimless way while about twenty others sat in a circle at one end of the room watching a smartly dressed woman in her forties make a flower arrangement involving daffodils. 'This is Alfred.' The nun pounced on a frail man with a hearing aid. She raised her voice to a shout. 'He doesn't come to see us as often as he should. Do you, Alfred?'

The man grinned and fixed his bright old eyes on Cathy. 'I'd come every day if she was here. She's a stunner.' He winked at her before shuffling away.

The nun grinned. 'I'll bet you would, you old villain. Great old character,' she said in a quieter tone. 'Eighty-six, and he still hasn't lost interest. May we all be so lucky.'

Cathy found herself warming to the other woman. 'Do you run this place?'

'There's a committee for that. But I'm around if they need me.'

'She sorts out everyone's problems,' Stephen said. 'Isn't that right, Sister?' To Cathy's surprise, there was a slight but unmistakable edge to his voice. 'Look, we won't hold you up any longer. I know you're busy.' He began moving away. 'I can show Cathy around.'

'It's no bother.' Sister Dolores looked at him blandly. She turned to Cathy with a smile. 'It's not often we get anyone as young and pretty as you in here.' She gripped her arm tightly. 'Come on and I'll tell you about my great plans for a drop-in centre for mothers and babies.' Still holding on to Cathy, she led the way across the room, talking as she went, while Stephen silently brought up the rear.

'Sorry about that,' he said when they'd finally escaped from Sister Dolores and were ensconced in the sitting room of his small house, drinking coffee. 'She can be a bit hard to take at times.'

Cathy looked at him curiously. 'You don't like her, do you?'

'I didn't think it showed.' He looked rueful. 'The truth is, she doesn't like me. She wasn't too bad today. Normally she has a go at me, every chance she gets. I don't know what I did to deserve it.'

'Maybe you just rub each other up the wrong way. I work with a woman like that. But I thought Sister Dolores was OK. Although I learned more about the parish centre than I really wanted to.'

Stephen grinned. 'That's why I suggested a break.' He glanced at the cup she'd placed on the hearth beside her. 'More coffee?'

'I shouldn't really. But yes, please. It's delicious.'

He looked pleased. 'A girl after my own heart.' He took their two cups and went out. She heard him whistling down the tiny hall towards the kitchen.

This room was small too. Cathy examined her surroundings with interest. It was so tidy – Spartan, almost. Against one wall stood a small bookcase filled with books. A couple of easy chairs were drawn up on either side of the brick fireplace, where a gas fire burned brightly. The only other furniture was a low table holding a leafy potted plant. It stood in front of the wide window, where the world outside was kept at bay behind anonymous net curtains. Very few ornaments, she noted. A couple of brass-framed photographs stood on the mantelpiece. Two pictures, an original watercolour of a mountain scene and a print of Albrecht Dürer's *Praying Hands*, similar to one they'd had at home in the bungalow in Cork, hung on the walls. The carpet and curtains, although of good quality, were a featureless brown.

The room didn't give much away about its owner's personality, Cathy thought. As her gaze ranged over his few possessions, she wondered if Stephen's bedroom was equally austere. When he returned with the coffee, she glanced up at one of the framed photographs, a picture of a dark-haired woman with strong features and Stephen's mouth.

'Is that your mother?'

Stephen nodded. 'Taken a few years ago. The other one's my sister.' He took that photograph from the mantelpiece and handed it to her. 'Her graduation day.' Cathy studied the self-assured smile, the ridiculous oversized glasses, the confident tilt to the chin. Although turning down university had been her own choice, she felt a pang when she saw the mortarboard on the girl's abundant curls. 'What does she do?'

'She's in computers.' He smiled, looking both fond and proud. 'A smart kid, Gillian.'

'Must be.' She wondered why there was no photograph of his father and tried to remember what he'd told her about his family. 'Haven't you a brother?'

'Jack. There should be a picture of him around somewhere.' He laughed. 'Not that he ever stays in one place long enough for anyone to take his photo. Actually, I'm meeting him tonight for a drink. We don't see much of each other nowadays, but he rang me last night.'

Cathy's interest was aroused. 'Is he like you?'

'Not a bit. We're like two sides of the same coin.'

'Like what you were saying that time about joy and sorrow.'

Stephen looked surprised. 'When did I say that?'

'The last time we were talking,' Cathy said, 'You quoted some poet . . . '

'So I did.' He glanced at her in amazement. 'Clever of you to remember.' He shook his head. 'Jack and I are more like chalk and cheese. A bit of a character, my brother.'

'You're quite a character yourself.'

'Do you think so?' He seemed surprised. 'Do you know something?' He gave her another amazed look. 'You're very easy to talk to. I could sit and chat with you all day.'

'So could I,' she said eagerly. 'And after last week, I could tell you anything.'

She saw his face light up. 'I'm glad.'

'You have no idea how much you helped me.'

'Any time.' His eyes met hers. 'I want you to know that.'

'Thanks.'

As they sat there, looking at each other, Cathy was the first to speak. It was time to change the subject. Lighten things up a bit. 'Haven't you work to do? Shouldn't you be "about your father's business"?' A thought struck her. 'I forgot. It's your day off.'

She saw a gleam in Stephen's eye. 'I didn't expect you to quote Scripture, Cathy.'

'I'm full of surprises.'

'I'm beginning to realise that.' He gave her a thoughtful look. 'I would have liked to show you the church back there, only I wanted to get away from Sister

Dolores. Maybe we could stroll over when you've finished your coffee. Or we could take the car.'

'I wouldn't mind a walk.'

'After that, I was wondering . . . '

The doorbell rang, shrilling peremptorily through the house.

Stephen's smile faded. He got up quickly. 'I'll get rid of them, whoever they are.'

She heard him go to the front door and exclaim in surprise. Instead of getting rid of the caller, he let the person into the hallway. Cathy looked up to see the sitting-room door being pushed open. A tall woman in a long, navy raincoat came into the room, bringing with her the chill of the March evening.

'I hope I'm not interrupting anything.' The newcomer had a smooth oval face and long black hair twisted into a graceful knot at the back of her neck. Although she wore matching trousers under the raincoat and there was not a hint of a veil or a white crimplene jumper in sight, Cathy knew at once that she was a nun. Feeling as if she'd been thrust back to her schooldays, she instinctively got to her feet. Grasping the shapely, long-fingered hand held out to her, she felt a slight unease, but hid it under a friendly smile.

'Hello, Sister, I'm Cathy.'

'Yes, I know,' the nun said serenely. 'I heard.'

'Nothing goes on in this parish that Sister Eileen doesn't know about.' Although Stephen sounded amused, Cathy guessed by the way he fussed over the nun that he was embarrassed as he helped her off with her raincoat and repeatedly offered to make coffee.

'Dolores told me.' The nun's voice was tranquil, yet there was an intense look in the dark eyes that studied Cathy. 'It's not often someone your age takes an interest in religious matters.' She gave a smiling shrug. 'I thought I'd have to pop in and see you for myself.'

As if I was some kind of curiosity, Cathy thought indignantly. The way the other woman was talking, it made her youth seem more of a liability than an asset. Hiding her annoyance, she tried to make a joke of it.

'Were you expecting someone with two heads?'

'Indeed, no,' Sister Eileen said smoothly. 'I'll make my own coffee, Stephen.' She deftly took her raincoat back from him. 'And I'll hang this up while I'm at it.' She bustled out of the room, obviously very much at home. 'You look after your guest.'

But the relaxed atmosphere had vanished. Cathy glanced at Stephen, who was hovering irresolutely in front of the fireplace. 'Maybe I should go,' she said.

'No, stay where you are.' He gave her a helpless look. 'She doesn't usually walk in like this.'

The hell she doesn't, Cathy thought. There had been something proprietorial in Sister Eileen's manner towards Stephen. What was going on between those two? She didn't want to wait and find out. She got up from her seat. 'I'll see the church another time.'

'Don't go,' Stephen said. 'Eileen's a colleague. We see a lot of each other: it's part of the job. But I was hoping to spend the evening with you. I know a little Italian restaurant not far away from here where they do a terrific pizza, and the atmosphere's good. I thought after I showed you Saint Mary's . . .'

'But aren't you meeting your brother?'

'That's not till later. And I might be able to put him off.' As Sister Eileen's footsteps sounded in the passage outside, he said urgently, 'How about it, Cathy? Say you'll come. Do.'

'Well, OK.' She gave him a reluctant look. She hadn't warmed to Sister Eileen the way she had to Dolores. 'But I'm not interested in a threesome.'

'Neither am I.' She saw his face relax into a grin. 'It's a deal, then.'

The restaurant was a cheerful, unpretentious place with red-and-white checked tablecloths, slightly rickety chairs and stumps of candles stuck to old saucers. But the staff were friendly, and the food was delicious. The restaurant soon began to fill up. By the time they'd finished their main course, the noise level had risen considerably.

'I see what you mean by "atmosphere".' Cathy looked across the table at Stephen. 'And you were right about the pizza.' She marvelled at how well they were getting on. The conversation was flowing at an easy pace. There were no awkward moments. There were times when she'd had to remind herself that he was a priest. She sipped her wine and smiled at him. 'I'm glad I came.'

'So am I.' His face was relaxed and boyish in the candlelight. Dressed in a sweater and casual trousers, his body was fit and rangy. If you didn't know the truth, she mused, there was no way you'd guess his calling. There was nothing to mark him out from any of the men at the other tables with their wives or girlfriends. Except that he was better looking than any of them. Yes, it would be very, very easy to forget that he was a priest.

Stephen's thoughts were obviously running on a different track. 'Now that you've seen the parish, what do you think of it?'

Cathy was taken aback. The parish and what went on in it had receded pleasantly into the background. She was reluctant to bring it back into focus. Stephen was looking at her, expecting a response. She tried to recall what Sister Dolores had talked about earlier. 'There's obviously a lot going on. A lot of problems. All that poverty, homelessness, people on drugs . . . '

'You don't know the half of it.' Stephen's voice was sombre.

'But it looks like you're all doing a good job.'

He shook his head. 'A drop in the ocean.'

'Maybe,' Cathy said robustly. 'But I always remember a saying of my father's, "Better to light a candle than to curse the darkness".'

'Thanks. I needed to be reminded.' She saw his face soften in the dim light. 'You really are something.' There was wonder in his voice. 'You care about people.'

Good old Mother Teresa, that's me. If this keeps up, he'll be recruiting me into the sisterhood. 'Not enough to devote my life to it. My dad was the do-gooder in the family. Like him, I hate the thought of injustice and cruelty. But like most people, I don't do anything about it. I admire anyone who does.'

'I don't think you're being fair to yourself.' Stephen's eyes met hers across the table. 'I think you have a strong social conscience.'

'No.' She shook her head. 'Compared to you and Dolores, and Sister Eileen . . . '

'You've plenty of time,' he said. 'Sometimes it takes a while for people to find out what they want to do with their lives.'

'I think I have a fair idea. Tell me, Stephen,' Cathy said, more to change the subject than because she really wanted to know, 'what exactly do parish sisters do?' To her relief, before he could answer, his mobile phone began to ring.

'That'll be Jack.' He held it to his ear and listened for a moment. 'We're at the coffee stage.'

But we haven't even ordered dessert, Cathy thought, watching him curiously. He frowned. 'Well, OK, if you want to.' Stephen said. 'Fair enough, see you soon.' He gave her a resigned look as he put away the phone. 'He's on his way.'

'Here?'

'Afraid so.' Stephen shrugged. 'I hope two Browns won't be too much for you in the one evening.'

'I'll do my best to survive.' As Cathy grinned at him, she felt her interest quicken.

'Guessed you'd be here,' Jack said cheerfully. He glanced at the gingham cloth, the greasy candle-stub flickering in its saucer. 'Bit rough and ready for my money. But . . . ' He let the word hang in the air as he summoned a waitress, who quickly brought another chair and an extra wineglass. 'All the same . . . ' – he sat down beside Stephen and gave Cathy a glance of frank appraisal – 'there's nothing wrong with your taste in women, big brother.'

Stephen's face darkened. 'Cathy's a friend. I was showing her around the parish.'

'Well, of course.' There was a derisive note in the other man's voice. 'Now, let me guess.' He studied Cathy's face mockingly. 'She belongs to the Little Sisters of Perpetual Virginity. A very exclusive order these days.' He eyed the wineglass in her hand. 'And for the last hour you've been putting her through a course of spiritual exercises. Come on, Stephen. You're not going to explain away this gorgeous creature.'

Cathy gave him an indignant look. 'Do you mind not talking about me as if I wasn't here?'

Jack gave an exaggerated start of surprise. Leaning across the table, he took her hand and pressed it to his lips. 'My apologies, Cathy. I didn't mean to hurt your feelings.'

'Cut it out, will you,' Stephen said. 'I'm sorry, Cathy. Jack has this twisted sense of humour. He was dropped on his head as a child.' Although his tone was light, she sensed his embarrassment. 'The best thing to do is ignore him.'

'You won't get rid of me that easily.' Jack poured the last of the wine and looked around for a waitress. 'Let's get another bottle.'

'Not for me,' Stephen said. 'I'm driving.'

'Never could hold his liquor.' Jack winked at Cathy. 'How about you, my beautiful one. You'll have a glass, won't you?' He had the kind of smile that was difficult to refuse. Although she'd meant to follow Stephen's example, she found herself smiling back.

'Just a small one.'

'Great.' He ordered more wine and steak and chips for himself. He got the waitress to bring some garlic bread while the food was being cooked. 'I'm famished. I've been in the office all day.' He gave an exaggerated sigh. 'Working on a big project. The old man is keeping our noses to the grindstone.'

'Jack works with Dad in the engineering business,' Stephen said. He seemed to have recovered from his earlier embarrassment and sat listening to his brother with a resigned smile on his face. 'The old man can be a bit of a perfectionist.'

'That's a nice way of putting it,' Jack said. The two brothers laughed.

They were so unlike, Cathy thought, watching them. What was it Stephen had said? Chalk and cheese? Yet you could see a fleeting resemblance. More in the tilt of the head, and the way they spoke. To look at them, you'd never guess they were so closely related. Stephen was attractive, she thought, well built, with regular features. But Jack, with his glossy dark hair, finely chiselled lips and straight nose, had the kind of looks that turned heads. She found it difficult to keep her eyes off him.

It was ridiculous to feel so drawn to someone she'd just met, she felt. OK, he was what she and her school friends in their brash, adolescent days would have called a ride. But she was no longer seventeen. She'd met handsome men before, and looks weren't everything. But it wasn't just the looks. He had the intelligence and the personality to match.

Better watch your step, she warned herself. This was the kind of man who breaks hearts.

'So the priest turned out useful, after all.' Liz was still up when she got home. 'And now you've got a new man.'

'We've only just met.'

'But he was interested, wasn't he? He asked you out?'

'He wanted us all to go clubbing afterwards. Stephen said no, of course. I told him I had an early start tomorrow.'

'As if one late night would kill you. Honestly, kiddo, you're growing old before your time.'

'It wasn't that,' Cathy said quickly. 'He was gorgeous, and he seemed really interested. But something tells me he's the kind that thinks women are a push-over . . . '

'I know, sweeps you off your feet. Swears undying love as he gets you into bed. Next morning, it's, "Thanks for a great night. See you around." We've all been there.'

'Even you, Liz?'

'Not any more.' She gave a wicked grin. 'Nowadays I do the loving and leaving.' She looked speculatively at Cathy. 'But maybe that's all you need at the moment. You said yourself you don't want to get into another relationship for a while.'

'The thing is . . . there could be more to Jack than that. I wouldn't want to waste him on a one-night stand. Maybe I shouldn't rush into this. On the other hand, I could be reading it all wrong and I won't see him again.'

'Aha!' Liz grinned. 'I can't wait to meet this guy.'

'No you don't. I saw him first.'

'So what was all that about never wanting another boyfriend?' Liz gave her a shrewd look. 'Changed our mind, have we?'

Cathy remembered something Stephen had said. *You're going to start healing. When you do, you'll be able to love again.* She stared thoughtfully at Liz.

'Yes, I have changed my mind. About a lot of things.'

She found it hard to get off to sleep. So much had happened that day. Images passed through her head of things she'd seen earlier: the green-domed church, the old people in the parish centre, the drab streets. She thought of Stephen's neat little house, and of how comfortable they'd been with each other, until Jack had burst so suddenly into her life. Every time she thought of him, she felt intrigued and exhilarated, yet somehow slightly overwhelmed.

Had he that effect on everyone? Probably only on women. She remembered the look on Stephen's face when his brother sat down at the table. She frowned to herself in the darkness. He was a lovely guy. He'd make a good friend. But Jack was an unknown quantity. How would you describe him? Several words suggested themselves, but they all seemed inadequate. You might as well try to pin down a sunbeam. Maybe it would be easier when she got to know him. *If* she got to know him. She found herself hoping that she would.

As her eyelids grew heavy with sleep, she had a sudden image of Sister Eileen's serene face. How did the nun fit into all this?

ELEVEN

Rain was drumming off the roof of Sister Eileen's little Fiat Uno as she swung in through the gateway of Saint Mary's, windscreen wipers working furiously. What a miserable morning! It looked as if it was down for the day. This was no spring shower, she told herself, slowing to avoid hitting a couple of elderly figures toiling ahead of her under bedraggled umbrellas. It was spilling down from the heavens mercilessly. On days like this she found herself regretting that she hadn't joined a missionary order. Think of what it would be like to look up at the sky and see the sun shining every day. But they have rainy seasons in Africa, she reminded herself. And very probably in South America too. Besides, she loved working in her own country and wouldn't really like to live anywhere else.

She waited till the old people had safely reached the steps of the church, then drove smartly around the side of the building to the small parking area reserved for the clergy and other religious working in the parish. As she rounded the corner, expecting to see Stephen's green Nissan parked in its usual spot near the sacristy door, she found the space empty. Which was odd, because she knew he was saying the ten o'clock Mass. The clock on her dashboard showed five minutes to the hour.

That's funny, she thought. Sister Eileen frowned to herself as she parked her car. It wasn't like Stephen to cut it so fine. She knew how much he hated arriving late to the altar. The thought struck her that he might have walked to the church and was already there. But the rain had been bucketing down for the past half hour, and he was far too sensible to have set out in such a downpour. He hadn't said the earlier Mass. She knew this for a fact because she'd attended it herself before going home for breakfast. The new curate, Father McMahon, had been the celebrant, racing through the Mass at top speed, for all the world as if he'd had a train to catch. Her lips tightened. She hoped she wasn't beginning to sound like Father Mulvey, but there was no getting away from it: some of the young men coming out of the seminary had very little respect.

Talking of the parish priest, she remembered he'd told her yesterday that he was taking the 6.30 pm Masses all this week, so it definitely had to be Stephen saying the ten o'clock. So why wasn't he here? She frowned to herself again as she locked the car and put up her umbrella. There was no getting away from it, Stephen had been acting a bit odd lately. What about that girl he'd had in his house yesterday? She'd known priests who always liked to have young women around them, but he wasn't like that; she'd stake her life on it. He was too good a priest. It was all a bit of a mystery. At the best of times, Sister Eileen didn't like mysteries. And certainly not ones that involved Father Stephen Brown.

'Did you not give him my message yesterday, Sister?'

The atmosphere in the parish office was oppressive after the cold air outside. Oppressive and steamy, Sister Eileen thought. A raincoat was drying on a radiator. The electric kettle in the corner was coming to the boil. Rain pounding off the flat roof, sounding like hundreds of golf balls, increased the claustrophobic effect. She carefully placed her dripping umbrella in the stand near the door and smiled blandly at the secretary.

'What message would that be, Mary?' Sister Eileen wondered if there was any truth in what she had said to Stephen before, about the younger woman having a crush on him.

Mary's normally cheerful face clouded with exasperation. 'Stephen was to give me the name of someone who'd look at that leaking radiator at the back of the church.'

'What about the maintenance man?' Sister Eileen pictured the gnarled creature she often saw pottering around the church and its environs. She gave the younger woman a puzzled look. 'What has it got to do with Stephen?'

'Old Sylvie's been down with flu for weeks now,' Mary said. 'A lot of jobs are piling up. Although, to be truthful, he's getting a bit past it. The one we really miss is Father Hennessy. Lovely man. Very good with his hands.' She sighed. 'And always ready to help out.' She looked closely at the nun. 'Any idea when he'll be back?'

'None, I'm afraid.' The less speculation in that

quarter the better, the parish priest had said. 'About Stephen – I did give him your message. I'm surprised he hasn't been back to you.' Loyalty to him made her add quickly, 'I do know he had a lot on his plate yesterday.'

'So I heard.' There was an unusual note of dryness in Mary's voice. She gave a meaningful smile. 'Showing visitors around the parish centre, no less.'

Sister Eileen smiled thinly. 'News travels fast.' How had Mary found out? Dolores, of course. She felt herself frown. It was one thing to have tipped Eileen off about Stephen's visitor to the centre, but quite another to have been gossiping with the secretary. Dolores could be indiscreet at times. She'd have to have a word with her. In the meantime, here was more speculation to discourage. 'Listen, Mary, I've brought those notes on the prayer meetings for Lent that I need you to type up.' She fished around in a folder she was carrying and handed over several sheets of paper, pausing to point out some details with the secretary. Then Sister Eileen turned to go. 'I expect Stephen will be over to you after he's finished Mass.' Always assuming he turned up, she thought to herself.

The green Nissan was outside the sacristy when she went back to her own car. Sister Eileen was filled with remorse. How could she have doubted him? In the year since he'd come to the parish, she'd known Stephen to be a conscientious priest. What had made her suspect that he would ever fail in his duty? Just because he had been acting a bit out of character recently, pulling her up short a few times and not contacting her when he'd said he would, there was no reason to withdraw her trust. It was obvious that he was under a great deal of pressure because of Brendan Hennessy's absence. He needed support, not criticism. If a friend couldn't show a bit of understanding, where was he going to get it?

The rain had eased off. Glancing at her watch, she debated with herself about popping into the sacristy and having a quick word with Stephen. Mass should be finished by now. But she had a busy morning ahead of her making home visits to elderly parishioners too feeble – or unwilling – to get out and about. Duty calls, Sister Eileen told herself sternly. She'd catch Stephen later. As she drove her small car out through the church gates, she banished him from her thoughts. Her mind began sorting through the list of old people she planned to see that morning. It wasn't just duty that drove her on, she knew. She was doing what God wanted her to do. And she loved the work.

Sister Eileen Moriarty always attributed her skill in dealing with old people to the good relationship she'd had with her grandmother as a child, growing up in a small town in County Tipperary. She would often add with a light laugh that she probably owed her religious vocation to her, too. Although Eileen's parents were townspeople, with several thriving businesses handed down to them by their parents, Granny Moriarty – her father's mother – had been brought up on a farm, only going to work in the town after she left school.

Despite living in a tall, narrow townhouse with no front garden for all of her married life and most of her widowhood, her grandmother had never forgotten her roots. She had the countrywoman's calm acceptance of the rhythms of nature: the inevitability of the seasons, the cycles of birth, growth and death. She had a deep-seated belief in the goodness of God and a real respect for all things spiritual and religious. Because Eileen's mother worked full-time in the family drapery business and her father ran the pub, it was inevitable that she and her two brothers would spend a lot of time with their grandmother. And because Eileen was the eldest, and her granny's favourite, it was also inevitable that she absorbed many of the old woman's attitudes.

Granny Moriarty died when Eileen was twelve, but by that time she'd already decided that she would enter the convent as soon as she was old enough. And she made no secret of her decision. Her parents, neither of them religious people, were totally against the idea, dismissing it as a childish fantasy. When Eileen brought the subject up again the year she sat her Leaving Cert exam, her mother had hysterics, declaring that she didn't want to hear another word about it. Ever. Her father, being more cool-headed, insisted that she take an arts degree at university first. That way, she would always have something to fall back on if things didn't work out in the convent. And if she still wanted to be a nun after she graduated, he wouldn't stand in her way. Eileen knew that her parents hoped that going to university would chase all thoughts of the religious life from her head, but she allowed herself to be persuaded. What did a few years matter in the general scheme of things? Besides, as her father had said, it would be a way of testing her vocation. Not that she had any fears on that score. It would be interesting to sample what the world had to offer before she turned her back on it. But turn her back on it she would. It was her destiny.

And so it came about. Although it grieved her to disappoint her parents, whom she loved but considered far too materialistic for their own good, at the age of twenty-two, with an honours degree in English and modern languages under her belt, Eileen Moriarty joined a religious community of women who had dedicated their lives to serving the needs of the poor. Even though as an adolescent she had pictured herself entering an enclosed order like the Carmelites or the Poor Clares, shut away from the public gaze, lost in a world of private adoration, she changed her mind after she went to university. A few years of voluntary charitable work convinced her that God would be better served if she did His work out in the community. In the world, but not of it. There were so few labourers in the vineyard, she told herself. Only five young women entered the noviciate together. By the time Eileen took her final vows, there was just another nun and herself. Undaunted, she took up the challenge. She worked for a time in an old folks' home run by the order and spent a short but demanding period in a centre dealing with recovering drug addicts. She took a diploma in Bible studies in her spare time. Although she put her heart into all these activities, she found them curiously unfulfilling. Never mind, she counselled herself, God will reveal all in His own good time.

Soon after that, she went to Saint Mary's as parish sister. She settled in quickly. The nun who had been in the post before her had shared a house with Sister Dolores. Eileen was given permission to take her place. Even though she and Dolores didn't belong to the same religious order and their backgrounds were totally different, the two women became close friends. It was a friendship that was mutually supportive and satisfying. After six months, she realised that she'd finally found her niche. This parish in the inner suburbs, cursed with all the problems associated with the downside of modern life and blessed with few of its advantages, was the place where God wanted her to be. She was sure of it.

For three years, Eileen lived and worked contentedly in the parish, convinced that she had everything in life she was ever likely to need. Until, just over twelve months ago, Stephen Brown had appeared on the scene. To her surprise, another kind of friendship was born. And she realised, with a sense of wonder, that fate had so much more to offer than she had ever demanded of it.

Eileen did her best to banish Stephen from her thoughts while she did her home visits that rainy March morning. But as she went through the dingy streets and the drab housing estates of the parish, the thought of him lay at the back of her mind, like a shining talisman.

'I didn't sleep too well last night.' At the other end of the line, Stephen's voice was stiff. He was obviously not pleased at being quizzed over his timekeeping earlier in the day, Sister Eileen realised. But it was too late to be sorry she'd brought the subject up.

'Not worrying about anything, I hope?' she asked gently.

'What gave you that idea?'

She sighed inwardly. The phone call wasn't going quite as planned. It had seemed a good idea to give him a quick ring while Dolores was taking her turn at cooking the evening meal. She could hear her friend humming tunelessly in the background as she tended lamb chops under the grill. They'd be ready soon. And Eileen still hadn't found out anything about the young woman Stephen had been entertaining the day before, or, even more importantly, what had happened after she, Eileen, had left. *If* anything had happened. Eileen wasn't sure what she meant by 'anything', but she was convinced they had spent the evening together. Afraid of sounding too inquisitive, she kept her voice casual.'Had you a late night?'

'Late enough,' Stephen said. As the silence lengthened between them, it was clear he had no intention of expanding further. Eileen felt frustrated suddenly, and puzzled. He wasn't always so tight-lipped. On the contrary, he usually treated her as a confidante, telling her things about himself that he knew she wouldn't pass on to anybody, not even Dolores. For the first time in the year she'd known him, she felt awkward with him, unsure. She glanced quickly at the stocky figure of her friend pottering away in the kitchen end of the room. The living space in the small house was open-plan, which worked well most of the time and made the place seem spacious. But it had its drawbacks at times. Dolores seemed absorbed in testing the potatoes that were boiling on top of the cooker but Eileen knew she was listening to every word. Not that there was anything to hear. With a sigh of defeat, she saw that the chops had been taken out, sizzling, from under the grill.

'Listen, I'll have to go or Dollo will have the dinner cremated.' Which was unfair: Dolores was the better cook of the two. But her treachery was rewarded when she heard Stephen laugh. He was still chuckling as he said goodbye. *What's happening to me?* she wondered. *She's the best friend I have.* She put down the phone, her feelings in a turmoil.

'Didn't go too well, huh?' She winced at the gruff sympathy in the other woman's voice. 'I don't know why you waste your time with him, Eileen.'

'He's a good man, Dolores.'

'"And Brutus is an honourable man",' Sister Dolores quoted derisively as she drained the potatoes and put them into a serving dish. '"So are they all, all honourable men".'

Stephen would have been surprised to hear her recite Shakespeare, Eileen thought. It was a side to her that Dolores let very few people see. Maybe if he got to know her better, she might open up to him. But Eileen doubted that would happen. The chemistry between them wasn't good.

'You don't like him much, do you?'

'As men go, he's not that bad,' Dolores said. 'But sometimes he gets on my wick with his la-di-da accent and that way he has of looking at you as if you'd just crawled out from under a stone.'

'Ah, come on,' Eileen protested, 'Stephen never looks at anyone like that.'

'Maybe not at you. But then, you're like him, born with a silver spoon in your mouth.' She saw Dolores's face tighten. 'You didn't grow up in the Liberties. Your da didn't come home every Friday night and beat the tar out of your ma.'

'Thank God.' Eileen shuddered. 'I don't know how I would have coped. '

'Ah, for God's sake. Water under the bridge,' the other woman said impatiently. 'While we're standing here chinwagging, the food's getting cold.'

They ate their meal sitting in front of the coal-effect gas fire. Eileen would have loved a real fire – logs crackling in the grate, flames shooting up the chimney, as they'd always had at home. But it would have meant a lot of work – cleaning out grates, that kind of thing. And remembering to stock up on fuel. Dolores never seemed to mind tackling domestic jobs like that, but Eileen hated any sort of housework. She remembered it was her turn to hoover the house this week and bitched gently about it to Dolores.

'There was a lot to be said for community life, all

the same, Dollo. I know those big old houses took a lot to keep up. But there was always plenty of help in the kitchen, and someone to keep all those floors polished.'

Her friend gave her a shrewd look. 'As long as that someone wasn't you?'

'Well . . . ' Eileen gave an embarrassed laugh.

'Some poor eejit of a lay sister recruited from the lower orders to do all the donkey work, while the nuns from the better families didn't have to soil their hands. Those were the days.' She saw Sister Dolores's lip curl. 'Someone like me would have been lucky to get inside the kitchen door.' She grimaced. 'I'd have been given the job of cleaning the jacks.'

'It was a question of education,' Eileen said uncomfortably. 'Besides, only some orders were like that. There were others, like the Benedictines and the Carmelites, who made a virtue out of manual labour. Still do.'

Dolores grinned. 'And guess which ones you wouldn't have joined.'

'There's no need to rub it in,' Eileen said hastily. 'You've made your point. I always do my share, don't I? To work is to pray, after all.'

But Dolores hadn't finished with the subject. 'Just imagine. There'd be no cosy little trips to the cinema with Father Stephen in the old days.' She gave a wicked smile. 'The best you could hope for would be the odd chat in the parlour, with him trying to hold your hand when the Reverend Mother wasn't looking.'

Eileen felt her face grow hot. 'He doesn't . . . ' She

looked helplessly at Dolores. 'You know it isn't like that.'

'Maybe it would be better if it was.'

'You're incorrigible, Dollo.' She hid her embarrassment under a light laugh. 'With your attitude, I don't know how you made it through the noviciate.'

Dolores's smile grew broader. 'That's because the assistant novice mistress had the hots for me. Of course, I was thin in those days. Still had my looks.' Her face softened as she looked at Eileen. 'You can't run away from sex,' she said gently.

'I'm not running away,' Eileen said. 'I made a choice.'

'I wonder.' The other woman's homely face was pensive. 'What did any of us know at that age about what we were giving up?'

'I did.' Eileen's voice was firm. This was an argument they'd had before, and no doubt would have again. 'I've absolutely no regrets.'

'Not now. But wait till you're like me – coming up to fifty.' In the harsh light of an overhead bulb, Dolores looked every bit her age, Eileen thought. There were lines around her eyes, and strands of grey in her ginger hair. 'It's not just sex you'll have missed. Companionship. Intimacy. Children.' The words came out like stones being lobbed into a pool. 'Have you ever wanted children, Eileen?'

'I can't say I have.' Eileen frowned. 'No, it's not something I miss.'

'You will.' There was an edge of certainty in the older woman's voice. 'Just wait till your biological clock starts ticking.'

When she was getting ready for bed that night, Eileen thought about what Dolores had said. Children? Somehow, she didn't think so. Both her brothers had got married in recent years. Neither of them had had children yet, but when they did, she presumed it wouldn't affect her life much. She didn't see a lot of her family. She went home for a week in the summer, and spent an occasional Christmas there. But that was as far as it went. She wasn't opposed to the idea of nieces and nephews. When they grew older they might turn out to be interesting, but she didn't care, one way or the other. Despite all that biological-clock nonsense, she knew she wasn't maternal. She suspected she took after her mother, who'd always got other people to mind her children while she worked in the family businesses. Not that she resembled her in any other way, she told herself hastily. Money was all her mother cared about. And work. There was very little of the spiritual about her. Dad wasn't much better. Since they'd spent so little time with their own kids when they were growing up, she wondered why they so often said they were looking forward to having grandchildren. People were sometimes difficult to figure out.

Like Stephen, and the odd way he was behaving at the moment. Or Dolores, who, like herself, had a vow of chastity, but saw nothing wrong in having conducted intimate, not to say passionate friendships with other women. And she would probably do so again, given the chance. But then, Dolores had a funny attitude to a lot of things. She could be quite unorthodox when it came to matters of the faith. Of course, it stemmed from her years in the States, where she mixed with radical feminists. It was bound to have an effect. Eileen thanked God that she had never been exposed to anything like that.

It depended what you meant by intimacy, she mused as she sat down at her dressing table. She believed it was possible to be intimate with another person without going to bed with them. A lot of the problems in today's relationships were caused by people sleeping together but with no real intimacy. She thought of the way she and Stephen had grown close in the last year, with never a hint of impropriety in their relationship. Which was how things should be between them, despite what Dolores might say.

But he was a man, after all. He must have the same urges as other men, even if he kept them strictly under control. Eileen saw her reflection stare enquiringly back at her as she released the chignon at the back of her neck and began brushing the black hair which just reached to her shoulders. She gave herself a faint, embarrassed smile. Her hair was her one vanity. Once it had rippled down her back like a gleaming cloak. Having to relinquish her long tresses when she was received into the order had been a sore blow. She could still remember her sense of shock at the snip of the novice mistress's scissors. But no sacrifice was too great, she had told herself, in the service of the Lord. After a while, she'd got used to her shorn locks, although she'd never quite accepted them.

It was only in the last year that Sister Eileen had started surreptitiously growing her hair. It was against regulations, of course, but she always made sure to keep it hidden under a veil when she visited her religious superior in the mother house. It was only a small thing, she told herself – barely a venial sin. Pretty small potatoes compared with what Dolores had got up to in her time. She stared at her reflection, fingering the ends of her hair. She was about to plait it into two tidy pigtails – something she did most nights without thinking – but tonight she found herself hesitating. On a sudden impulse, she pulled down the neck of her cotton nightdress to reveal the white column of her neck, the tops of her rounded breasts. She gazed at herself with slightly parted lips. If Stephen were to see her like this, she wondered, what effect would it have on him?

Oh, God! What am I thinking? Her startled face stared back at her from the glass. Her whole body was suffused with shame. *The devil makes work for idle hands.* Sister Eileen threw down the hairbrush and reached for her rosary beads, beginning to recite the first sorrowful mystery. But even though she prayed fervently not to be led into temptation, she couldn't subdue her treacherous thoughts – couldn't banish the sinful memories that crowded into her mind. Although she'd promised herself that before renouncing the world, she was going to sample what it had to offer, Eileen was not adventurous by nature and had lived very quietly during her time at university. During her first year, she stayed in a hostel run by nuns; after that she shared a house in Donnybrook with three other students – young women like herself from homes in the provinces. Her days were divided between lectures, tutorials, periods of study and attending meetings of the various college societies to which she belonged. Unlike the majority of her fellow students, she spent very little time in pubs and was not interested in going to discos, preferring instead to go to concerts or plays with like-minded friends. Despite this, she was often asked out on dates. Because of her beauty, she had no difficulty in attracting men, but even though she enjoyed their company, she never allowed any of them to get too close. Eileen knew that her body was promised to Christ, and she never let herself forget that – not that she was even tempted. Until she met Alex Jordan during her final year.

He was some years older, a graduate student from an American university, doing a doctoral thesis on the works of Maria Edgeworth. One day he asked permission to sit in on a tutorial on Anglo-Irish literature which Eileen happened to be attending. As her eyes met his across the small group, she felt a shudder go through her like the thrill of an electric shock. She heard not a word of the discussion that ranged around her as she sat there, her senses in a whirl, trying not to betray her awareness of the bearded man who sat opposite. When the session was over, she drifted out of the room in a daze. It seemed the most natural thing in the world when he caught up with her outside the door and introduced himself. With only a sketchy knowledge of

Americans, she'd always assumed they were loud-mouthed and brash. This burly young man was well-spoken, had nice manners and was obviously sincere. Any misgivings she had about chatting with a complete stranger vanished immediately.

The next few weeks were exciting ones. She liked everything about Alex: his intelligence, his sense of humour, his looks. Although she was not usually given to flights of fancy, when she gazed at his dark, luxuriant curls and bushy beard glinting red in the sunlight, she sometimes pictured him in the kilt of his Scottish Highlander forbears and saw him marching to the skirl of bagpipes, a gleam in his fox-brown eyes. Then she'd laugh at her own fantasy. There was nothing warlike about Alex. He was kind and gentle, content to take his time in getting to know her. Unlike some of the young men she'd gone out with, he never forced his attentions on her; their growing intimacy was a gradual process which just seemed to happen naturally. Soon she began to look forward to his lips, to welcome his caresses. A familiar voice in her head counselled caution, but for once in her life, Eileen didn't want to listen to that voice.

We're not doing anything wrong. Nothing's going to happen. Alex wasn't that kind of man. And she wasn't that kind of girl. How easily human beings deceive themselves, she was to think, looking back on it years later.

It was on a spring weekend that it happened. A Saturday afternoon. They'd spent the morning window-shopping in Grafton Street, browsing through the bookshops, having coffee in Bewley's. It was one of Eileen's favourite ways of spending a Saturday. What a joy to have someone who shared her tastes. Later that evening, they were going to the theatre. Because the other girls in the house had gone home for the weekend, Eileen brought him back for a late lunch, which Alex had offered to cook. Salad, followed by pasta, accompanied by crusty bread and a bottle of red wine.

'Food and drink for the gods,' Alex said, topping up her glass. 'Forget all that nonsense about nectar and ambrosia.'

'This is the life,' Eileen said dreamily. Who'd have thought drinking wine in the daytime could be so pleasant? But then, everything she and Alex did together was enjoyable. She felt warm and relaxed as she gazed across the table at him, and had a sudden impulse to reach out and touch his hand.

'Oh, Eileen.' He took her hand in his firm, warm grasp. He smiled at her. 'You're an absolute doll, do you know that?'

'You're pretty nice yourself.' As his hand closed around hers, she felt something inside her begin to melt. The wine must be going to her head, she thought. In an attempt to take some control, she asked, 'What was that trick you were saying you could do with spaghetti? Although . . . ' – she heard herself giggle – ' . . . when we were children, Mother always said that once you start playing with food, you're no longer hungry.'

She saw his eyes gleam. 'Somehow I don't think your

mother would have had this in mind. Let go of my hand for a moment, honey. This is really neat.' He picked up a long strand of spaghetti from Eileen's plate, put one end of it into her mouth and took the other end in his. She saw the laughter in his eyes as he began to suck in his end of the pasta. Leaning forward, she let her lips meet his. It should have been disgusting, she thought, with all that tomato sauce over their lips but, as they kissed, she felt her whole body reacting to him. 'I'm still hungry,' he whispered. 'But not for food.'

The living-room floor was hard beneath her body, although he placed a cushion under her head. She could smell the dust from the carpet and feel the warmth of the electric fire.

'There should be blazing logs. A bearskin on the floor.' She saw his eyes gleam in the fading light of the spring evening as he knelt beside her. 'Oh, Eileen, you've no idea how I've waited for this moment.'

Although she made no protest while he unbuttoned her cardigan, then her blouse, as soon as he fingered her bra, she pushed him away. She should get up, she told herself. But she didn't move.

'OK,' Alex said equably. 'There's no rush.' He began taking off his own clothes, tossing the sweater and shirt onto the floor behind him. His chest was covered with curling tendrils of russet hair lighter than his beard. It grew in a darker line that ran down under the waistband of his trousers. When he unbuckled his belt and reached for his zip, she felt she should say something to stop him. But no words came. She felt an unfamiliar excitement coursing through her body as she lay watching him. When the trousers came off, she didn't turn her head away. A pair of striped boxers was revealed. Despite her excitement and her curiosity, she was relieved when he kept them on.

Then he was down on the floor beside her again, kissing her throat, the hairs on his chest tickling her skin. After that, it didn't seem such a big thing to let him remove the bra. After a few moments of his hands gently and reverentially stroking her breasts until the nipples stood up proud, she felt herself gasping and shuddering, breathing so fast that she didn't really notice that the skirt had come off. Her tights had somehow disappeared without her realising it. She still had enough presence of mind to retain her panties. But not enough to pull her hand away when he gently guided it down the front of his boxers.

Years later, as she lay in bed, remembering, Sister Eileen found herself blushing at the memory, recalling her pain and confusion afterwards in the confession box as she tried to find words that would indicate the gravity of the sin without actually admitting that she'd lain almost naked with a member of the opposite sex, and had held his manhood in her hands. How could you put that into words? But the priest, who'd been hearing her Confessions ever since he'd been recommended to her as a saint by the hostel nuns she'd stayed with during her first year in college, had wanted chapter and verse. Fortunately, he hadn't been as shocked as she'd feared: less the stern confessor, more like a friend interested in hearing the details that he gradually drew from her.

'Well, it could have been worse,' he said when she'd finished. His tone sharpened suddenly. 'I take it no actual penetration took place?'

Eileen's face burned at the words. 'No, Father,' she whispered. Although Alex had seemed bitterly let down at the time, he'd been a perfect gentleman about it. 'I can wait,' he'd said.

'Oh, well . . . ' Behind the confessional grille the priest sounded almost disappointed. 'If you say it didn't happen . . . ' His tone grew brisker. 'In that case, if you have a firm purpose of amendment, you can still go ahead with your plans for entering the convent.'

Thank God! She gave a shudder of relief. Gratefully she received her penance: the Apostle's Creed and two Hail Holy Queens.

Alex had not been as understanding as the priest. 'Eileen, honey, if we love each other, how can it be wrong?' Although it had happened thirteen years before, she could still see the shock and bewilderment on his face.

'Love has nothing to do with it,' Eileen said. 'What we did the other day was wrong. But I don't expect a non-Catholic to understand.'

'Hell and damnation, and all that stuff? But that's just superstition.'

'To you, maybe.'

'Look, let's not fight over this,' Alex said. 'I can see it means a lot to you, and I respect your right to your beliefs. We can work around it. Eileen, you know I'm crazy about you. I want to marry you.' His voice was solemn. 'I want to have children with you.'

Marriage? Children? She thought of what the priest in Confession had said about Satan laying traps for the unwary. He had even tried to tempt Christ in the desert, but Our Blessed Lord had held firm. As she would too. She thought of Granny Moriarty and her unflinching belief in the will of God.

'It's no use, Alex.' She hardened her heart against the pleading in his eyes. 'My mind is made up.'

God had allowed her to be tempted all those years ago. Sister Eileen shuddered as she remembered how very near she'd come to giving in to temptation that day – how close she'd come to the fires of hell. But, as the priest had told her in that long-ago Confession, it had been one way of finding out the strength of her vocation. And since then, her commitment had never wavered. If a new temptation came, she knew God would give her the strength to resist it. Having come to that conclusion, she fell asleep.Twelve

When his brother Jack rang looking for Cathy's phone number, Stephen's immediate reaction was to refuse.

'Come on, Steve, don't be such a dog in the manger . . . '

'Watch it.' Stephen's voice was curt.

'Well, it's either that or you want to keep her for yourself,' Jack said with a tiresome kind of logic. 'Which one is it?'

'Neither.' He was like an animal permanently in heat,

Stephen thought – always on the lookout for a conquest. 'Look, I'm not running a dating agency.'

'Never thought you were, dear brother.' Jack was suddenly all sweet reasonableness. 'But I want to give her a tinkle, see how she is.'

'All the better for keeping out of your clutches. Cathy's a nice girl, Jack. Not your type.'

'And what type would that be?'

'You know damn well.'

'Anger is one of the seven deadly sins,' Jack said in mild reproof. 'You ought to watch that temper of yours.'

'That's rich, coming from you.' The years dropped away, and they were boys again. Jack was being a pest as usual. Stephen felt his fists clench. 'Look, if that's all you want, I'm very busy . . . '

' . . . turning the other cheek?' He heard Jack laugh. 'Not to worry. I'll find out for myself.'

'Good luck to you, then,' Stephen said curtly.

Cathy was the next to ring.

'Just to say thank-you for the other day, and the dinner that night.'

Stephen's heart lifted at the sound of her voice. 'Maybe we could do it again some time?'

'Maybe.' He heard her hesitate, as if choosing her words. 'Your brother Jack . . . he's not a bit like you, is he?'

'You can say that again.' He wondered what exactly she was getting at. He put out a cautious feeler. 'Women seem to like him.'

'Well, of course. He has a great personality.'

'You mean he's handsome.'

'That too.' She laughed, as if startled by his bluntness. He heard her sigh. 'Like a Greek god,' she said.

Here we go again. He felt a stab of dismay. He'd seen too many women over the years fall victim to his brother's looks. With his ebullient personality, it added up to a winning combination. For Jack, Stephen told himself. The woman wasn't always so lucky. Despite this, some demon of honesty made him say, 'He was looking for your phone number.'

He heard her sharp intake of breath. 'You didn't give it to him, did you?'

'No. Do you want me to?'

A short silence. He felt his hopes rise. To have them come crashing down.

'Only if he asks again,' Cathy said.

It's your own fault, Stephen told himself, after he put down the phone. If he hadn't brought her out to dinner she'd never have met him. But he couldn't be sorry for that. Until his brother showed up, he'd been having a wonderful night. *Well, then, you should have put Jack off.* He couldn't think why he hadn't. Anyone with an ounce of common sense would have. *You know what he's like around attractive women.* The truth was, Stephen admitted, he'd been so caught up with Cathy's company that he'd forgotten about the arrangement with his brother till the phone call near the end of the meal. It was too late for regrets now. As Jack himself would say, hindsight was twenty/twenty vision. Stephen had never been possessed of that, he told himself, even at the best of times. And certainly not where Jack was concerned.

What was he going to do about him now? What *could* he do? If Jack wanted to see Cathy again, no argument of Stephen's would dissuade him. On the contrary, opposition would probably make him all the more determined. Particularly if it came from an older brother with whom he insisted on keeping up a friendly rivalry. If Jack got hold of the ridiculous notion that Stephen wanted to keep Cathy for himself, his determination would be all the stronger.

And it was a ridiculous notion, he thought. Offensive too. Although he should be used to Jack by now. When it came to women, he had a one-track mind. It would never occur to him that there might be another reason why Stephen didn't want him to ask Cathy out. And even if he knew, would he care?

But Stephen cared. There was no way he wanted Cathy hurt. He knew how vulnerable she was. After what she'd told him the previous week, it was going to take some time for the wounds to heal. The last thing she needed was to meet someone like Jack.

No, the person Cathy needed, Stephen told himself, was someone who would truly care for her, someone she could love in return. He would need to possess a lot of patience, though. And good sense. Cathy was a young woman searching to find her true self. The right man for her would have to be someone who'd want a close, loving relationship, yet be wise and unselfish enough to give her the space to develop into the person she wanted to be, not use her for his own purposes, as Jack would. The right man was a lucky devil, whoever he was. Stephen fought down a pang of envy as he realised that he could never be that man. His choices were already made.

Maybe now was the time to bow out and leave the way clear. He had done all he could for Cathy, hadn't he? He'd helped her unburden herself, helped her to grieve. Now it was up to her to take charge of her own life and go looking for the right person with whom she might fulfil her dreams. But there was one thing of which he was absolutely sure. That person was not Jack.

Maybe his own job wasn't over. As this struck Stephen, he felt his spirits lift. He didn't have to make any decision just yet. Until Cathy met the right man, she'd need a good friend to watch out for her. And if he couldn't keep her out of Jack's clutches, maybe he could warn her of what he was like. But when he recalled the eager note he'd heard in her voice earlier, he was afraid it might already be too late. He'd noticed a stubborn streak in her. Once she set her heart on something – or someone – Stephen suspected she'd be difficult to talk around. His spirits drooped again. It seemed an insoluble problem.

What will be, will be. He felt fatalistic as he went to make himself his third cup of coffee of the day. If the worst came to the worst, and Jack broke her heart, she would need someone to help her pick up the pieces. It wouldn't be the first time Stephen had been called upon to do just that where his brother was concerned.

Although it was six or seven years since he'd last set eyes on Fiona, Stephen could still picture the distraught expression she'd worn that day she called to see him. He'd met her several times before with Jack, but it was still a surprise to have her show up on her own at the parochial house. It was Stephen's first parish and he wasn't yet used to the niceties of entertaining women. As he showed Fiona into the bleak, draughty sitting room which the parish priest had set aside for the use of his curates, he enquired awkwardly if her visit was of a social or a pastoral nature.

'Neither,' Fiona said. 'Or maybe I mean both. I don't really know.' She twisted her fingers and gave him a distracted look. 'But he *is* your brother. Maybe you could talk to him.'

'What's the rascal been up to now?' Although he kept his voice light, he felt slightly apprehensive. From the little he knew of Fiona, she'd struck him as being a down-to-earth person. Not the kind to kick up a fuss over some trivial matter. 'Have you had a falling-out?'

She shook her head dumbly.

Stephen's eyes narrowed. He cast his mind back a few hours earlier to an emotional interview he'd had with both sets of parents of a teenaged boy and his pregnant fifteen-year-old girlfriend. The girl's father wanted to have the young fellow charged with rape;

the boy's parents said their son had been led astray. But wherever the fault lay, it had been clear to Stephen that a new life would shortly be coming into the world, and that someone would have to take responsibility for it.

Was that the problem here? Surely not. Jack was far too clever to make a mistake like that. Although, after almost a year of delving into the intricacies of other people's lives in the confessional, Stephen was no longer surprised at the kind of mistakes that apparently intelligent human beings made. Unless, of course, it wasn't a mistake. He shot a speculative glance at Fiona.

'Whatever it is, it can't be all that bad.'

'You think so?' She stared at him, dry-eyed. 'He's dumped me for another woman.'

'I see.' So she wasn't pregnant then. Stephen felt relieved. Even though she and Jack were adults, they were still very young. They were only a few months out of college, just starting in jobs, with not a penny between them. Whatever Fiona's parents might have said, he knew that his mother would never have understood. Like the mother he had seen earlier that day, she would probably have blamed the girl for ruining her son's life. His relief faded when he saw the anguish in Fiona's eyes.

'I'm sorry,' he said awkwardly. 'He doesn't deserve you.'

'Four years!' Her voice was bitter. 'That's how long we've known each other. Since our first week in college.' She looked indignantly at Stephen. 'Yesterday he told me he's been seeing someone else behind my back.'

Like father, like son. He bit back the words. It was only a couple of months since his mother had told him about her own marital problems. It occurred to him that Mum might have taken the young woman's side, after all. As he gazed at Fiona, the knowledge of his father's infidelities still rankled with Stephen. He couldn't keep the scorn out of his voice.

'You're probably well rid of him.' As soon as the words were out, he knew they weren't what she wanted to hear. That is, if she had even heard them. Fiona seemed to be lost in her thoughts, her gaze fixed broodingly on a spot on the faded wallpaper just behind Stephen's ear.

'Just let me get my hands on her, the bitch!' Her tone was savage. 'The nerve of her! I'm the one he loves.'

'But – '

'Four years!' She shook her head in disbelief. 'All gone, for nothing.' Her tone sharpened, grew decisive. 'No. No, it can't be! I won't accept it!' All at once she turned and focussed intently on his face. 'You've got to talk to him, Stephen.' He saw hope leap in her eyes. 'He'll listen to you.'

Stephen looked at her in dismay. Why did some people think the clerical collar conferred a kind of power on its wearer? Maybe he would get used to this in time, or eventually grow into their expectations of him. Somehow he didn't think so. He stared at Fiona, slightly unnerved by the intensity of her gaze. His dismay grew as he realised that she wasn't going to be fobbed off with a few placating words. At the same time, he felt pity for her. And anger at his brother. Jack shouldn't be allowed to get away with hurting people – although Stephen couldn't for the life of him see what he could do about it.

'I'll try,' he said reluctantly. 'But don't get your hopes up.'

'I don't love her.' Jack's voice showed no emotion. He could have been talking about the weather report. He looked mildly surprised. 'You're not saying I should marry her, just because that's what she wants?'

Put like that, it made nonsense of Stephen's argument. But he tried anyway. 'You told her you loved her.'

Jack grinned at him. 'You'd be amazed at the things people say in the heat of passion. But you wouldn't know anything about that, would you?' He gave a little shrug. 'Listen, Steve, if you were to marry every woman you slept with – '

'For God's sake, Jack, you've known her for four years!'

'I went out with other girls, too.'

'But you told her she was the only one.'

Jack shrugged again.

'Won't you even talk to her?' He remembered the look on Fiona's face. 'Jack, I think she's on the verge of a breakdown.'

'That's hardly my fault.'

Stephen stared at him, frustrated. 'You're a cold bastard!'

'Easy for you to talk, big brother. That vow of celibacy must come in handy sometimes.' Jack smiled at him, his voice still reasonable. 'Look, I don't poke my nose into your business. Why don't you keep out of mine?'

Maybe he had a point there, Stephen thought, looking back. And anyway, he hadn't wanted to intervene. But this time it was different. This time the shoe was on the other foot. It was his own territory that was being invaded now. It was Jack who was pushing in where he wasn't wanted. *Territory?* The word pulled Stephen up short. He found himself disturbed by the image it portrayed. For a moment his own attitude surprised him, offending his sense of fair play. 'Territory' was the language Jack would have used; it should have no place in his own vocabulary.

Cathy was not his property, he told himself. She had a right to go out with anyone she chose and he had no right to stop her. The wise thing to do was to stay out of it. And yet . . .

He had a sudden memory of Jack as a small boy, cheerfully pulling the limbs off one of Gillian's dolls, unmoved by his small sister's protests. Kids do that, Stephen argued with himself. It meant nothing. But Fiona wasn't nothing, was she? Even if Jack had thought so. And how many other women had there been since then? No, he'd have to warn Cathy. She needed to know what she'd be letting herself in for.

But how? And when? It wasn't something you could

[336]

say over the phone. They'd have to meet again, and he'd have to give some thought to what he was going to tell her. Handled badly, it might do more harm than good. But it would have to wait till later. Stephen sighed to himself, glancing at his watch. There was a parish to run and he seemed to be the only one prepared to do it. He drained his coffee cup, pushing the problem to the back of his mind. Right now, he was expected in the parish office.

He met Sister Eileen on her way out of the one-storey building. Her face lit up. 'Glad I caught you, Stephen.'

'I'm in a bit of a hurry.' Although he usually enjoyed their chats, he suspected she was going to bring up the subject of Cathy. Apart from a couple of brief telephone calls, he and Eileen hadn't had a proper conversation since the day the three of them had met in his house. Stephen knew it was only a matter of time before he'd have to satisfy her curiosity. But not just yet.

More with the idea of deflecting her attention than from any hope of gaining information, he asked quickly, 'Any idea of what's happening to Brendan?' The senior curate had been gone for nearly three weeks and there had been no word of him. 'I can't get anything out of the boss. I was wondering if you'd had better luck.' He gave an exasperated laugh. 'Old man Mulvey is being unusually tight-lipped.'

To his relief, his ploy worked.

'I was talking to *Father* Mulvey, yes.'

Stephen grinned at the slight note of reproof in Sister Eileen's voice. He always enjoyed ruffling her feathers with the flippant way he referred to the parish priest. 'And?'

'We did mention Brendan's situation.' She lowered her voice. 'But there's not a lot to tell.' He saw her glance back through the open door of the office, where Mary Grimes was reading some papers at her desk. 'It's a bit delicate.'

The same words, Stephen noticed, that he had used when discussing the matter with his mother a few days earlier. 'I understand.' He, too, glanced at the secretary. When he saw her look up from her work, he gave her a cheerful wave. 'Be with you in a minute, Mary.' Instinctively, both he and Sister Eileen moved out of earshot. 'OK, what's up?' he murmured.

Sister Eileen giggled almost girlishly and cast a nervous glance around, as if afraid that the parish priest might suddenly materialise out of nowhere. 'I don't even know if I should be saying this . . . '

'For God's sake!' He felt impatient suddenly. 'Brendan's my colleague. What's the boss playing at?'

'Who has a better right than you to know?' she said placatingly. 'I don't think he meant me to hear, but I think the poor man had to tell someone.' And Eileen had a way about her that invited confidences, he thought. 'He's worried, Stephen. Terrified that the newspapers might get wind of it.'

'I can understand that.' He felt his face flush with annoyance. 'But he surely doesn't think I would let anything slip.'

'No, of course not. Anyway, as far as he's concerned,

you already know most of it. He told you, didn't he, that Brendan has agreed to go to England for special counselling?'

'I thought he'd already gone. I assumed that's where he's been for the past couple of weeks.'

'That's just it.' Sister Eileen gave him a troubled look. 'He's still with his friend.'

'Staying with friends?' He felt a rush of relief. 'Well, maybe that's not such a bad idea. Give him a chance to think.'

'You're not listening to me, Stephen.' There was an unusual note of impatience in Sister Eileen's voice. 'I said *"friend"*. She gave him a meaningful look.

'Oh!' Light dawned suddenly. 'You mean his . . .?' He groped for a suitable word. 'Girlfriend' didn't sound quite right. Brendan was a bit long in the tooth for that. 'Lady friend' had an old-fashioned ring to it. 'Lover?' he hazarded.

'We don't know that they are,' Sister Eileen said reproachfully. But she didn't seem shocked at the word. 'Mind you, it would explain a lot of things.'

The matter-of-fact way she said this took Stephen aback. And then he wondered why he was surprised. Eileen, for all her Madonna-like looks, had a down-to-earth streak in her at times. 'What kind of things?'

She pursed her lips. 'It would explain why it took them so long to get him to agree to go to this place in England.'

'Took who so long?'

'The people the bishop sent, from the diocese. I get

the impression Brendan wouldn't meet anyone at first.' She shook her head. 'Father Mulvey thinks they really had to pressure him to agree.'

'What kind of pressure?'

When she said nothing, Stephen had a sudden image of the bishop's envoys descending on the errant couple. He found himself picturing a medieval situation where the weight of the magisterium of the Catholic Church was brought to bear on the mild, inoffensive curate. He wondered what arguments they had used. And what kind of woman was this widow who could inspire such intransigence in someone like Brendan? He gave Sister Eileen a surprised look. 'I'd never have believed he had it in him.'

'How little we know about our fellow human beings,' she said thoughtfully.

'Still, you say he gave in. So what happens next?'

'I don't know.' Her troubled look was back. 'Poor Brendan. I think he must be going through a crisis of faith.' Her face brightened suddenly. 'But with God's help and proper counselling, I'm sure he'll find his way back on the right path.'

'Do you think so?' A few weeks earlier Stephen might have agreed with her. Now he felt less sure.

'Brendan knows where his duty lies,' Sister Eileen said.

There were times when her unshakeable certainty was a consolation to Stephen. But this wasn't one of those times. All he knew was that he wanted to stop talking about Brendan Hennessy. He'd enough worries of his own. 'Look, Eileen, I hope you're right.' He was aware that he was being brusque but he couldn't stop himself. 'I have to get on. I'm running late as it is.' He glanced over at the parish office. 'Talk to you again.'

As he turned away, he saw her look of surprise. But there was no time to dwell on his own rudeness. He knew Mary Grimes was waiting with a stack of correspondence which the parish priest was supposed to have dealt with but which would be passed on to him. Stephen sighed to himself. Another legacy of the senior curate's absence. The sooner he made a start on it, the better. He wished all the same that he hadn't been so short with Eileen. As he went in, he heard her call after him, 'Will I see you later, Stephen?'

Good old Eileen. Thank God, she hadn't taken offence. Anxious to make it up to her, he turned back with a grin. 'I'll see how I'm fixed. Give you a buzz when I get home.'

But when he arrived back at his house a couple of hours later, all thoughts of ringing Sister Eileen were driven from his head. As he parked the car in his little driveway, he was astonished to see the spare figure of a grey-haired man dressed in casual, sporty clothes waiting for him on the doorstep.

'Well, talk of the devil!' The words burst from his lips.

'Hardly that, Stephen,' Brendan Hennessy said, looking at him in mild reproach. 'Just a poor sinner like yourself.'

'I was over at the house picking up the last of my things.' The older man carefully hung his windcheater over the back of a chair before sitting down at the kitchen table. As he leaned back in his seat, looking relaxed and fit in his golf sweater and faded cords, he smiled at Stephen, who was busying himself at the coffee machine. 'I'm glad I got the chance to say goodbye.'

'So you won't be coming back to us after you get back from England?' Stephen felt a pang of disappointment. 'Has the parish priest agreed to this?' Typical of old man Mulvey not to let anyone know, he thought.

Brendan Hennessy sat up straighter in his chair. His relaxed air vanished. 'What has Father Mulvey got to do with it?' There was an uncharacteristic belligerence in his manner. 'And who said anything about England?'

Stephen stared at him open-mouthed. 'But . . . ' Despite the shock he was feeling, his hands went on measuring out the water for the coffee. 'I thought . . . '

'The bishop sent the big guns to see me.' Brendan's face grew embarrassed. He avoided Stephen's eye. 'You'd say anything to get those fellas off your back. Listen, don't bother making coffee, there's a good man. Too much caffeine's bad for you.'

'Tea, then.' Stephen abandoned the machine reluctantly. If ever there was a time for a good belt of caffeine, it was now. But good manners propelled him towards the electric kettle. As he switched it on, he said cautiously, 'If you're not going to England for counselling, and you're not coming back to the parish, what *are* you going to do?'

'Counselling's a bit of a con, Stephen.' The older man looked at him frankly. 'Where the Church is concerned, it's just another name for brainwashing. You know that.'

Stephen was taken aback. 'No, no.'

'Maybe you haven't copped on to that one. But then you haven't got someone like Stella to keep you straight, have you?' Brendan looked suddenly boyish. 'God, Stephen! You've no idea.' The younger man heard the awe in his voice. 'She's a wonderful woman. I don't know how I ever coped without her.'

Stephen kept his own voice even. 'You haven't answered my question, Brendan.'

'I'm getting to it, don't rush me.' Brendan sighed. The boyish look vanished. 'There's no easy way to say this, Stephen. It's not just the parish. I'm leaving the priesthood.'

Stephen sank heavily into a chair and looked across the table at the older priest. For a moment he couldn't speak. When he did, he heard his own distress. 'In the name of God, why?'

Brendan gazed down at the table for a moment. When he looked back at Stephen, his face had lit up. 'Because I've found the person I've been waiting for all my life.'

'But what about your vocation?' Stephen's anguish grew. 'What about Jesus Christ?'

Something akin to compassion stirred in the other

man's eyes. 'If you knew what it was like to truly love a woman, you wouldn't have to ask that.'

'My mother passed away five years ago,' Brendan said. 'I suppose things came to a head then. We were pretty close. I was the youngest in the family. The others got married and went to live in different parts of the country, but I was always there for her. After my father died, my sister in Cork wanted Mam to go to her, but she didn't want to leave her friends and the town she'd lived in all her life, so she stayed put. She was only about forty minutes' drive from here on the motorway. It was easier to get to than some parts of the city, so I managed to see her pretty often. She was a warm, loving woman. And a great friend.' His face clouded over. 'Her death hit me pretty hard.'

'That's understandable,' Stephen said uneasily. 'I'd miss my own mother too, but – '

'It's not as simple as that.' The other man's quiet voice sharpened with slight exasperation. 'I didn't fall in love just to fill the gap my mother left in my life. Besides, I only met Stella about eighteen months ago.'

'But you said things came to a head when your mother died.'

'She had cancer. A slow death.' Brendan looked bleakly at him. 'When I was giving the homily at her funeral Mass, I remember saying how hard it was to accept that someone who'd always put her family first should be made to suffer like that. It didn't seem fair. I'm told it struck a chord with a lot of people in the congregation, especially among those with children. But afterwards I got to thinking. You do a lot of that when someone close to you dies.' He smiled ruefully. 'At night, mostly. And I came to the conclusion that, sad and all as my mother's death was, it was no tragedy. Death comes to us all eventually.'

'That's true.'

'And she'd had a full life,' Brendan said. 'She knew what it was like to love someone, to have children. She even saw her grandchildren. My father hadn't a great job – money was tight sometimes – but she always said they managed to have a laugh together. I knew nobody could ever take his place, but after he went I did my best to look out for her. At least she knew I was never far away.'

'She was lucky.'

He nodded. As he gazed at Stephen, his expression was bleak. 'But what about me? What had I got? That's what I kept asking myself as I lay awake at night. There I was, just coming up to fifty. I had nothing to show for my life. And never would. When I died, no son of mine would carry my coffin. No grandchildren would ever put flowers on my grave.'

In the silence that followed, Stephen found it hard to meet the other man's eye. When he heard the kettle come to the boil, he was glad to get up and attend to it. While he was busying himself making tea, Brendan sat at the table behind him, his head bowed. He didn't look up until the tea had been poured out and a cup placed in front of him.

'I tried to remind myself of why I'd become a priest,' he said. 'Tried to picture the people whose lives must have been enriched because of my ministry.' He shook his head. 'But I couldn't think of a single one.' The bleak look was back on his face. 'Anything I'd done could have been done just as well, if not better, by any competent cleric. I didn't matter in anyone's life the way my parents had mattered to each other, and to their children.'

'Sounds to me like you were a bit depressed,' Stephen ventured. 'Only natural after a bereavement. '

'After a bereavement you become public property. Everyone feels the need to tell you what you should do with yourself.' Brendan shook his head, giving a disbelieving laugh. 'The advice parishioners came up with! Go on holiday, get yourself a pet, learn a musical instrument – you name it.'

'People mean well.'

'I wonder.' He gave a harsh laugh. 'Colleagues were less kind. One suggested I renew my priestly vows, another that I go on a pilgrimage to Knock Shrine. My parish priest didn't put a tooth in it. "Snap out of it. There's worse off than you", he said. The doctor I went to for something to help me sleep was nearly as bad. He was a young, fit, sporty man. "You're too old for tennis," he told me. "Get out and play golf." By now I was at the end of my tether. I'd have tried anything. And something about swinging a golf club appealed to me. I'd played a lot of hurling as a boy. So I took his advice. It was impossible to get into a city club but I managed to find one about forty miles from Dublin.'

'And that's where you met . . . ?'

'Stella? Not straightaway. But as I got better at the game, I began entering competitions and going to some of the social functions. The doctor was right about golf. It helped to distract me from my misgivings about the priestly life, while I gradually came to terms with my mother's death. And I made some new friends. I'd come here, to St Mary's, by then.' He smiled faintly. 'Father Mulvey's a bit of a stick-in-the-mud, compared to the last man I worked with, but as long as you don't cross him, he lets you get on with things.'

'Lets you do all the work, you mean.'

The older man shrugged. 'To be honest, I was only going through the motions as a priest. I tried to be as conscientious as I could in carrying out my duties. But for the next few years, I lived for my weekly game at the club and any holidays or outings I could manage with my golfing partners.'

'Was Stella one of them?'

'She doesn't play golf.' Brendan laughed at the surprise on Stephen's face. 'Stella's brother has the catering franchise for the club. I used to see her helping out at functions after competitions, that kind of thing. We really only knew each other to say hello. But she always struck me as a very pleasant person.'

Stephen nodded. 'A motherly kind of woman?'

'Not exactly.' Brendan seemed amused by this. 'Although she does have a teenage son. Anyway, about a year and a half ago, someone told me her husband had died, so I went to offer my condolences. But it wasn't the unhappy occasion I'd expected. Apparently, they hadn't been living together for years. She was sad for her son's sake – although, between ourselves, it doesn't sound as if he was much of a father – but I think it was more of a relief to her than anything else. Not that she bad-mouthed her late husband. That wouldn't be Stella's style.' His face lit up again. 'She's a wonderful woman, Stephen. I knew that from the start. But don't just take my word for it.' He reached for his wallet and handed Stephen a snapshot. 'Isn't she beautiful?'

Pleasant-looking might be a better description, Stephen thought, as he studied the photograph. Stella's blue eyes were slightly prominent and her chin was a little too determined for conventional beauty. But she had an attractive smile and clear, unlined skin. She was probably still in her thirties. Early forties, at the most. He hid his surprise as he returned the photograph.

'This taken recently?'

Brendan gave a resigned smile, obviously not deceived by Stephen's casual tone. 'Why don't you come right out and say it?' His voice was defensive. 'You think she's a bit young for me.'

'Well . . . ' Stephen hedged. His gaze skated over the other man's thinning hair, the wrinkles beginning to form around his neck. 'Age is all in the mind,' he said smoothly. 'And I have to admit, I've never seen you looking as fit as you do today.' That bit was true, anyway, he told himself.

'It's not just her looks.' Brendan's eyes met his frankly. 'It's everything about her. Have you ever met someone that you immediately felt you'd known all your life? Someone you could sit talking to forever and tell them anything?'

'Yes,' Stephen said slowly. He kept his face blank. 'I think I know what you mean.'

'Well, if you ever meet anyone like that,' – the other man's voice was earnest – 'take my advice, do just what it says in the song. Once you have found her, never let her go.'

Sadness pressed down on Stephen suddenly. 'But Brendan, what about our vow of celibacy?'

'I kept mine for nearly thirty-five years, man and boy.' Brendan's gentle features hardened. 'I've done my bit.'

'But it was for life. You knew that.'

'What does a boy of eighteen know?' Brendan smiled faintly. 'Stephen, we were conned. And it wasn't just sex we were being asked to give up. Although that was bad enough. But what the Church made us do was turn our backs on the most meaningful part of life itself.' He shook his head, almost in disbelief. 'What they made us do was obscene.'

'No!' Stephen suddenly found his voice. 'I can't accept that.'

He and Brendan stared at each other for a moment.

'OK, Stephen, have it your way.' The older man shrugged. 'I suspect I was never as dedicated a priest as you. Stick with it, if that's what you want. As for me,

I've been given a second chance.' There was barely suppressed excitement in his voice. 'Marriage, father-hood, the lot.'

'Fatherhood?' Stephen frowned. 'You mean the teenage son?'

'Johnny's a grand lad, of course.' The other man beamed suddenly. 'But I wasn't just talking about him.'

'You're planning to have a family?'

Brendan's beam grew wider. 'It's gone past the planning stage, if you know what I mean.'

'I don't believe this,' Stephen burst out. 'You're not telling me she's pregnant?'

'Stella will be forty next year,' Brendan said, half-apologetically. 'We haven't much time. And we both want kids. Besides . . . ' – his eyes slid away from Stephen's – ' . . . it might help speed up the laicisation process.'

'Oh, my God!' Stephen got up from the table and began searching in the kitchen drawers for a cigarette. He sat down again, empty-handed. 'Does the bishop know?'

Brendan gave a sheepish grin. 'I think I'll leave that job to Father Mulvey. Once I tell him.'

'You mean he doesn't know?'

'I wanted to talk to you first.' The other man looked apologetic. 'I feel I dropped you in it, going off so suddenly. But under the circumstances, what could I do?'

'We've managed to muddle along without you.' Stephen tried to smile. 'So I don't suppose anything I could say would tempt you to change your mind?' He kept his tone flippant. 'Word on the grapevine had it that you were going to get the next parish that came up.'

'Thanks for nothing.' Brendan shook his head decisively. 'When I go to meet my Maker I want to leave more behind me than a set of golf clubs and a well-thumbed breviary.'

'It looks like you've already made sure of that,' Stephen said drily.

They talked for a bit longer before Brendan left for his meeting with the parish priest. 'I'm not looking forward to it.' He gave a wry grin. 'But the sooner it's over, the sooner I can get back to Stella.'

Stephen found himself wondering what it would be like to have someone waiting for you at home. 'Are you not afraid people will talk?'

The other man nodded. 'I don't know how much longer we can keep up the pretence that I'm Stella's lodger.' Anxiety coloured his voice as he got up from the table. 'And there's young Johnny to think of. We haven't told him about the baby yet.'

'I wouldn't care to be in your shoes.' As soon as the words were out, Stephen found himself regretting them. He looked slightly shamefacedly at Brendan and softened his tone. 'You've a hard road ahead of you.'

'Save your pity for yourself.' The other man returned his look with unexpected firmness. 'Stella and I have each other; we'll work something out.'

Stephen nodded, accepting the rebuke. 'I hope you

get a speedy resolution to your case.' He touched Brendan's arm gently. 'I'll remember you in my Mass tomorrow.'

'Great stuff.' The boyish look was back on Brendan's face. 'I knew I could rely on you to understand.'

'Did you?' Stephen stared at him bleakly. As he watched Brendan's agile figure dodging around the Nissan in the tiny drive before turning at the gateway to give him a cheerful wave, his sense of bleakness grew. When he heard the other man's car start up, he closed the door and went back to the kitchen, to search the kitchen cupboards again. This time, he found a book of matches and three cigarettes in a crumpled pack behind the box of candles he kept for emergencies. He stood and weighed them in his hand. *Probably stale by now. Better dump them in the bin.* Instead he placed them with the matchbook on the table, and went to another cupboard to take down the coffee jar.

Brendan's voice sounded in his head; the phrases from the old song hummed through his brain. *Once you have found her, never let her go.* As he measured out the coffee grounds, he found himself trying to remember the rest of the words. How did it go? It was from a well-known musical – it shouldn't be that difficult to remember. Suddenly his hand shook and a spoonful of coffee scattered all over the worktop. *Damn! That's what happens when you don't pay attention to what you're doing. Take it easy.* He carefully scooped up the precious grounds. That was the last of the jar. There'd be no more till the next time he could go shopping for it in town. He had better make a list. He glanced around the austere little kitchen, trying to think of what else he needed. He was getting low on other essentials, although they could be picked up in a local shop. Stephen smiled wryly to himself. The Lord might have said, 'I will make you fishers of men' but He'd never said anything about having to go down to the food market to stock up on cornflakes and toilet rolls.

Sister Eileen never seemed to have any trouble combining her ministry with running a house, he reminded himself. But women seemed to be better at that kind of thing, and anyway, there were two of them to share the chores. Was that why Brendan was abandoning the priestly life? Had he just got fed up with living alone? While he waited for the coffee to be ready, Stephen sat down at the table. He felt too agitated to sit still, and almost immediately got up again. His eye fell on the cigarettes and matches lying on the table top. It must have been about four weeks since he'd smoked the others in that pack. A miracle to have lasted that long. It would be a shame to go back to smoking now, especially during Lent. Think of the bad example, Father.

Father! What did the word mean, anyhow? He had a sudden image of Brendan Hennessy's lean, weather-beaten face. *We were conned, Stephen. It's the most meaningful part of life itself.*

The satisfying aroma of freshly brewed coffee began to fill the kitchen. Thank God for that. He inhaled luxuriously and poured himself a steaming cup. But the cigarettes were still there, tantalising him. Be sensible, he told himself. Dump them in the bin. But what was the point of behaving sensibly when nobody else was? And anyway, it was only a short walk down the road to the newsagent's, where he could buy a fresh pack.

It's either this or a stiff drink, he told himself. And drink was out. He had a couple of counselling appointments later that evening. Anyway, he didn't keep alcohol in the house. He shook his head, wondering what had got into him. If he wasn't careful, he'd be at the communion wine next. Suddenly that thought didn't seem very funny. Had Brendan stopped saying Mass? The thought struck him like a fresh blow. Did he miss it? He had been a priest for thirty years. How could he give it all up? Stephen felt anger searing his chest. How could he walk away just like that? He picked up the crumpled pack, shook out a cigarette and lit it. As the acrid fumes hit the back of his throat, he gave a sigh that was part guilt, part pleasure.

God, I needed that.

But the anger in his chest didn't go away. It gnawed at him and spread to his stomach. *How could he do it?* He found himself squinting through the cigarette smoke, staring unseeingly into the distance. *Get a grip, Stephen.* He went over to the grimy kitchen window and looked out at the untidy patch of grass and the few leafless shrubs that made up his back garden. He thought of the Gospel words: 'Many are called, but few are chosen.' The thought brought him no consolation. Although he and Brendan had never been close – at least, not till today – he felt as if he'd lost a brother. As Stephen stared out into the fading light of the windswept March evening, his eyes were heavy with unshed tears.

'It's always the quiet ones.' Father Mulvey's voice was bitter.

Stephen said nothing.

'I argued with him. I did everything I could to make him see sense.' Stephen noticed that the parish priest's ruddy complexion had a blue tinge to it. Although a vase of golden daffodils reflected the morning sunshine shafting in through the study window, the weather was cold for the end of March, and a fire still burned in the grate. His joints creaking, Father Mulvey knelt down beside it and poked the coals savagely. 'The poor sap wouldn't listen to me.' As he got up, dusting the ashes from the knees of his black trousers, he shook his head and gave a decisive grunt. 'Well, let there be an end to it.' He glared at Stephen. 'I never want to hear that man's name again.'

'Maybe you'd like me to remove all traces of him from the parish.' Stephen said.

His irony seemed to be wasted on the parish priest. 'No, no, you haven't time.' Father Mulvey made an impatient gesture. 'Let someone else sort all that out. Now, what about the date for the First Communions.'

'Let's see.' Stephen pondered, refusing to be

deflected. 'For a start, we can remove his name from the confessional . . . '

'Of course, of course.'

'And I believe Brendan often had a cup of tea in the office. Mary kept a special mug for him.' He shook his head judiciously. 'That'll have to go. Maybe we should smash it, in case it might contaminate others.'

'All right, Stephen, that's enough,' the older man said testily. 'Point taken.'

He ignored the ominous darkening of Father Mulvey's already ruddy complexion. 'I know, Dan! Have you thought about getting in contract cleaners to scour out his house?'

'Look, Stephen . . . ' To his surprise, he saw the older man making a real effort to control himself. 'Brendan's out of here. It was his own decision.' His voice, though brisk, was not unkind. 'He's gone, Stephen.'

'I know.'

'It's a great pity, but . . . ' He gave a little shrug. 'Life must go on. Look.' Again, Stephen was surprised at the conciliatory note in the older priest's voice. 'I know it hasn't been easy for you over the last few weeks.' He frowned suddenly. 'And that young waster they sent us hasn't been much help.'

Stephen gave a short laugh and looked at him bitterly. 'I'm surprised you noticed.'

Father Mulvey nodded. 'They tell me young Father McMahon is bit of a Scarlet Pimpernel.' He said the words with relish. '"They seek him here, they seek him there . . . "' He chuckled suddenly. 'Although whether he's in heaven or in hell, like in the poem, who can say.'

Stephen resisted the older man's attempt to win him over with humour. 'I've been run off my feet these past few weeks. You've got to do something about him.'

'Young Pimpernel's only a stopgap,' the parish priest said suavely. He smiled at Stephen, showing the dark tops of his dentures. 'I thought I'd explained that.'

Stephen marvelled at how smooth the boss could be when it suited him. He didn't trust him in this new, conciliatory mood. He kept his own voice hard.

'So?'

'I've had a word with the bishop. He's agreed to a replacement for Father Hennessy. No, Stephen . . . ' He held up his hand. 'Not another rookie, I promise you.' He smiled placatingly. 'Someone with more of a track record.'

'Someone who'll pull his weight?' Recalling another parish he'd worked in, Stephen was still suspicious. 'Not some dried-out alcoholic being put out to grass?'

'There's no doubt about it, Stephen, but you're a real doubting Thomas.' To his astonishment, he heard a note of tolerance in the older priest's voice. He was even more astonished to see the other man's bluff, ruddy features soften. 'But you're a good lad, even if you're a bit impatient at times.'

Wily old bird. Wonder what he's up to? 'I suppose this means there's some delay about getting a replacement?'

'A doubting Thomas,' Father Mulvey repeated, still tolerant. With a smile as if he was about to pull a rabbit out of a hat, he said, 'He'll be here in a couple of weeks. In plenty of time for Easter.' As his smile broadened, he looked expectantly at Stephen. 'Well?'

Although it was what he had wanted to hear, Stephen was surprised to hear his own lack of enthusiasm. 'That's OK,' he said dully.

'Only OK?' Father Mulvey raised an affronted eyebrow. He sighed to himself, obviously wondering whether to take offence. He decided against it. 'Well, that's settled, Stephen.' Glancing at his desk, which was, as usual, bare except for his leather-covered breviary, he reached into a drawer and took out a large diary. 'Now, maybe we could talk about those First Communion days.'

'Fine,' Stephen said. But his heart wasn't in the discussion that followed. As soon as he decently could, he brought the conversation to a conclusion, made his goodbyes and headed for the door.

'By the way, Stephen . . . ' He turned to see that Father Mulvey had followed him into the hallway. 'Remember that suggestion you made about letting girls serve on the altar?'

'Which you shot down.' The memory still rankled. As Stephen threw an impatient glance around the hall, it occurred to him that Father Mulvey's views on the liturgy belonged to the same era as the antique mahogany hallstand and the Malton prints climbing the staircase wall. Their last discussion on the subject had been futile and acrimonious. 'Why bring it up now?'

The parish priest cleared his throat behind him. 'I'm

not quite the dinosaur you take me for, Stephen.' There was mild reproach in his voice. 'I think maybe the time might be right – '

Stephen swung round in astonishment. 'Don't tell me you're having second thoughts.'

' – for discussion,' Father Mulvey said cautiously. 'I'm not promising anything, mind you.'

Still, it was a major concession. Before the events of the previous day, Stephen would have been overjoyed. But now he felt no sense of victory. He was baffled by his own feeling of indifference. What had happened to all his enthusiasm?

Father Mulvey must have been asking himself the same question. He peered anxiously into the younger man's face. 'Are you OK?'

'Never better,' Stephen said curtly. As he put his hand out to the front-door catch, he felt a hand on his arm. The parish priest cleared his throat again. When he spoke, Dan Mulvey's voice sounded troubled, hesitant – so unlike his usual hearty tones.

'All we can do is put it behind us. Close the ranks. And pray, of course.'

'I forgot.' Stephen's voice was suddenly bitter. 'Prayer solves everything.'

He couldn't settle to anything all evening. He was on call, but things were quiet. Nobody seemed to be in need of spiritual comfort that night. Which was just as well, Stephen thought savagely, because he had none to give. He tried to read, but the words kept dancing in front of him. His favourite piece of opera had no power to soothe him tonight. He thought of going for a walk, but when he put his head out his front door into the darkness, a strong wind beat against his face. He could hear it moaning around the rooftops, stirring the few stunted trees in neighbouring gardens. March going out like a lion, he told himself. When he closed the front door, his gaze fell on the telephone. Sister Eileen? She was the obvious person. He felt a sudden reluctance. Hers was not the voice he wanted to hear. Something Brendan Hennessy had said the previous day flashed into his mind. *Have you ever met someone you could sit talking to forever?*

When he punched in the number, the phone rang for a bit, then the answering machine clicked in. The voice on the tape was the one he'd heard on previous occasions, but the message had been changed slightly.

'Too busy having fun,' Cathy's flatmate said. For Stephen, in his impatience, her laconic voice betrayed a cool disregard for her listeners. He heard a provocative laugh. 'But if you leave your name and number . . . '

'Thanks for nothing, Kay, or Peg, or whatever your name is.' There was no point in getting angry, he told himself as he put down the phone. He'd catch Cathy later. But whatever fun she was having, it seemed to go on quite late. After another fruitless call, he took himself off to bed, where he slept fitfully for the rest of the night.

THIRTEEN

'That lemon cheesecake was to die for.' Cathy chased the last little piece around her plate before she put down her dessert fork with a sigh. 'The whole meal was beautiful.' And the restaurant, with its elegant yet modern decor, attentive staff and comfortable atmosphere, was one of the best she'd ever eaten in.

'A step up from that trattoria Steve brought you to.' She saw Jack smile in the lamplight. Both of the brothers had good teeth, she thought, but his seemed whiter. Maybe that was because his face was still tanned from a recent skiing holiday in the French Alps. 'I don't know where he found such a seedy little place.' His smile invited her complicity.

'The company was good that night.' Cathy was anxious not to be drawn into making comparisons. 'And that's the important thing.' She frowned slightly. 'Jack, not everyone can afford to eat in places like this.'

'You don't have to fly to his defence.' A little smile played around Jack's lips. 'Steve's more than capable of looking out for himself.' His eyes held hers for a moment. 'How about a brandy?'

She smiled. 'Not for me, thanks.'

'What's this? What's this?' She saw his look of glee. 'Afraid I'll get you drunk?'

She felt her face flush, then was annoyed at her embarrassment. 'You'll be lucky. I haven't been drunk in years.'

'Is that a challenge?' This time he held her gaze longer. Cathy stared back, unable to look away. She felt at a loss, embarrassed, yet oddly excited. His eyes were like Stephen's. A bit darker, maybe. It was difficult to tell in the soft lighting. No, they were very different. Something about them caused a tremor to go through her. She heard her heartbeat quicken, felt her lips part involuntarily. She pulled her gaze away with an effort. *Oh, God!* For a moment she'd been acting like a schoolgirl. *Pull yourself together.* When she saw a waitress heading towards their table, she hid her relief. 'Coffee! Mmm, that smells good.'

As Jack ordered a brandy, bantering good-humouredly with the waitress, Cathy studied the tilt of his dark head, his well-chiselled mouth. As her eyes travelled over the clean lines of his body, she sighed inwardly. God, he was handsome! Maybe not as tall as Stephen, but just as fit. And much better dressed. Well, he did have a more lucrative job. Which he'd need in order to pay for an outfit like that. The tie alone probably cost more than the waitress took home in tips that night. And what he must have paid for the cashmere jacket would have fed a family of four for a week.

But it wasn't the clothes, was it? Put him in a chain-store sweater and trousers, and he'd look equally attractive. Better still, take them off. *Oh no, Cathy. Not that again.* There was something about him that sent her hormones racing. As she met his eye across the table, she was glad he couldn't read her thoughts.

'My friend has just come out of a convent,' Jack said to the waitress, a prim-looking woman in her fifties. 'Very strict order. No alcohol after 10 pm. And men only once a month.' He shook his head sadly. 'She's finding it very difficult to adjust.'

She gave him a withering look. 'Will there be anything else, sir?'

'Don't answer that,' Cathy said. 'You'll have us thrown out.'

'Don't you believe it. The customer is always right.' As the waitress went away, he turned back to Cathy. 'You'd better finish this wine. A crime to waste a decent Cabernet.' Before she could protest, he filled her glass to the brim.

'I think you *are* trying to get me drunk.'

'Let's face it.' Jack's smile was sweet. 'I'm a bad influence. But no doubt my brother has already warned you about that.' He gave her a quick interrogative glance, then, seeing her surprise, smiled. 'Don't worry, he will.'

'I can't believe that. His own brother?'

Jack smiled thinly. 'Steve's not a great family man.'

'But . . . '

'It probably has something to do with that crap about "Leaving all others to follow Me". Whatever. Anyway, he hasn't much time for any of us. But the one he disapproves of most is our father.' He pursed his lips and shook his head. 'Oh, no! *Mein papa* would definitely not be his favourite person.'

'Well, I couldn't comment on that.' Cathy recalled an earlier conversation with Stephen. 'But why? What has your father done?'

'To my brother?' Jack looked surprised. 'The boot's on the other foot. Seems to me, Dad's the one who's been turning the other cheek.'

'That's not what I heard.'

'OK, so Dad was strict when we were growing up. But no worse than most fathers.'

Cathy nodded. 'Mine never let us away with anything. But he was fair. Kids need some discipline.'

'Steve couldn't see it like that.' Jack shook his head. 'He was always a bit of a rebel. Eldest son and all that.'

'The youngest can be too. I know my mother finds me hard to take sometimes.'

'Nothing wrong with a bit of independence.' She saw his teeth flash. 'I like feisty women, Cathy. But that's not what we're talking about.' His expression changed. He glowered suddenly. 'Steve always had to have his own way. When we were kids, he used to beat the crap out of me if I didn't do what he said.'

'Most boys do that.' She looked at him doubtfully. 'Although, not having brothers myself . . . '

'You don't know the half of it.' He fell silent as the waitress placed a brandy in front of him. Watching him, Cathy sipped her wine, but it lay sourly on her tongue. She grimaced and saw Jack dart her a look.

'It's a side to him you hadn't known about,' he said. 'Are you shocked?

'Well, maybe I am a bit. But that's all in the past, Jack. You were kids. What I don't understand is why he and your father still don't get on.'

He gave her a brooding look. 'Dad's a Protestant, you know.'

Cathy nodded. 'But that wouldn't explain it, surely.'

'Steve's very religious.'

'But . . .'

'I know, I know. It comes with the territory.' He gave her a meaningful look. 'But I mean *really* religious. He gets that from Mum. Real dyed-in-the-wool Catholic.' He smiled wryly. 'Error has no rights. I don't think she and Steve have ever forgiven Dad for not changing his religion when he got married.'

'I can't believe that! Stephen's not a bigot.'

Jack shrugged. 'He doesn't come across as one. But I know my brother. You know what really gets me? You'd think the Browns were a bunch of pagans till he came along. I bet Steve hasn't told you that Dad's uncle was a clergyman.' He glanced at Cathy's surprised face and gave a satisfied nod. 'That figures. Oh yes, Great-Uncle William rose quite high. If he hadn't been thrown from his horse when he was out hunting, he'd have been made a bishop. If you don't believe me, ask Steve.'

'I don't need to.'

She saw Jack's face soften. 'That's enough about my family. Boring sods at the best of times.' His smile lit up his face. 'The night is young, and so are we.' He clinked his glass against hers. 'Here's to the start of a beautiful friendship.'

'I've just come out of a relationship.' Cathy frowned slightly when Jack pulled into the kerb a couple of streets from her apartment. As he tried to take her in his arms, she said, 'I'm not sure I want to get involved again so soon.'

'We're talking goodnight kiss here.' He moved back into his own seat, amusement in his voice. 'Not a proposal of marriage.'

She laughed reluctantly. 'Yes, but . . .'

'OK, OK.' He held his hands up, palms facing her. She saw his eyes glint in the light of a nearby street lamp. 'Why don't we sit and talk for a bit?'

Cathy hesitated. She thought back to when they'd left the restaurant, dashing through the rain to reach his car which he'd parked illegally in a narrow side street. Most people would have been afraid of being clamped. But not Jack. 'Hasn't happened yet.' He'd whipped the steering wheel around, almost levitating the car to bring it down from the pavement, and grinned at Cathy. 'My old man says I've the luck of the devil.'

'The devil looks after his own.' Cathy thought of her father's saying. She found herself hoping it was true. You needed cool nerves to get into a car with Jack. He was a skilful driver but a fast one. Sometimes too fast for comfort.

'Do you approach everything the same way you drive?' she asked now. When she saw Jack's teeth gleam, she regretted the question. She felt her heartbeat quicken. 'On second thoughts, don't answer that.' She turned hastily, fumbling with the door handle beside her. 'It's been a lovely evening . . . '

The passenger door opened easily but a powerful gust of rain drove in against her. She recoiled back into the car, felt drops of water running down her face. At the same time, she was aware of Jack's body brushing past her as he pulled the door closed. She caught a whiff of spicy aftershave, then felt his finger gently trace the curve of her wet cheek.

'Better wait till it eases off.' His finger went on stroking. 'You don't want to get soaked to the skin.'

She had a sudden picture of his hands stroking her body and gave a shaky laugh.

'I thought we were just going to talk?'

'We are talking.' But his finger went on stroking her face, tracing the outline of her chin, her throat, the tops of her breasts under the neckline of her blouse, his touch as light as gossamer. 'What would you like to discuss? Global warming? The rate of inflation?'

She felt a tug of desire, suddenly aware of her body, tingling under the thin blouse. Jack's face was close to hers, but not touching. She could smell his spicy aroma, could feel the warmth of his breath against her cheek. She heard rain pounding on the car roof. Rivulets of water ran down the windows, shutting out the night, giving the illusion of a closed, secret world which only she and Jack inhabited. For a moment, common sense seemed far away. Cathy took a deep breath and lifted his hand from her breast.

'I think I'd better go.'

'The cost of sterling at the moment? Now that's a

good topic.' Jack took her hand and held it lightly to his lips. 'I'm not going to do anything. Don't worry.'

'I'm not,' Cathy said shortly. She felt shaken by her own response. She wasn't some pushover. It was only their first date. 'Jack, I really have to go.'

'In a minute.' His finger had started stroking again. This time on the soft skin of her arm under the sleeve of her jacket. 'It's hard to let you go. I really enjoyed tonight.'

'Me too.' As his fingers caressed her arm, she felt her defences begin to crumble. Her desire grew stronger. She knew that she wanted him to touch her all over. *Shit! I don't think I want to wait till the second date.* She turned her face towards his and felt his lips seek hers. To her surprise, the kiss he gave her was tender, but fleeting. Most definitely a goodnight kiss. She hid her disappointment with a light laugh. 'That was short and sweet.'

'I'm not always a bad influence.' Jack started up the car. 'This is what you wanted, isn't it?'

'Yes.' But she felt frustrated, outmanoeuvred. They turned the corner of the mews and pulled up at the front door of her apartment. 'Thanks for a nice evening. See you around.'

Jack smiled. He stretched out his hand and touched her face.

'Pick you up on Saturday,' he said.

'So you're going out with him again?' Stephen's voice was stiff.

'Don't you want me to?' Cathy asked.

'It's not up to me.'

His dismissive tone irritated her. 'Why bring it up?'

The line was silent. She waited for a moment but Stephen said nothing.

With an effort, she held on to her patience. 'But you don't think I should.'

Another silence.

Cathy sighed. 'Well?'

At last he spoke. 'I don't think he's right for you, Cathy.'

She felt angry suddenly. 'Look, Stephen, you might be a marriage-guidance counsellor but you don't know everything.'

'I know Jack.'

'He said this would happen. Now I know what he was talking about.'

'I'm not telling you how to run your life.' There was a dogged note in Stephen's voice. 'I just don't think he's the kind of person you should be with.'

'You're being unfair.' Cathy felt her anger mount. 'Just what gives you the right to pass judgement on other people? Oh, I forgot. Priests do that, don't they.'

'Now you're being unfair.'

'And it's not just Jack, is it? You disapprove of your father, too.'

The line was silent for a moment. Then Stephen asked quietly, 'Just what did he tell you about my father?'

The coldness in his voice struck her like a blow.

'Nothing, really,' she stammered. 'But I know you don't get on. If I knew why you had so little time for him – '

'You'll just have to take my word for it,' he said. 'I'm not prepared to discuss my family.'

He had never spoken to her in that way before. 'Are you telling me it's none of my business?' she asked.

She heard him hesitate. 'I wouldn't have put it quite like that.'

'But it's what you meant?'

'Since you ask, yes.'

Cathy gasped. She felt her face burn and heard the sudden thumping of her heart. *I don't believe this!* Tears filled her eyes. There was a tightness in her chest. For a moment, she couldn't speak. There was an answering silence at the other end of the line.

At last she found her voice – a high, angry voice she barely recognised as her own. 'Your brother was right about you. You *are* a self-righteous sod.'

How *could* he? How could he talk to her like that? Cathy put down the receiver in stunned disbelief. She blinked back the angry tears and glanced distractedly around the living room of the apartment. Normally the pretty room, with its familiar possessions, had a soothing effect on her, but tonight the sight brought no comfort. If only Liz was home. If ever there was a moment for a shoulder to cry on, this was it. But she was out on the town and wouldn't be back till late, Cathy knew. On second thoughts, maybe that was just as well. Knowing Liz's opinion of her friendship with Stephen, it struck Cathy that she might not be so ready with her sympathy. The last thing she wanted right now was to hear someone say, 'I told you so'. Even if it was justified. She'd just have to deal with this on her own. If she couldn't have the sympathy, she told herself, she could at least have the tea. But as she waited for the kettle to boil, her heart was sore.

Well at least she'd had the satisfaction of hanging up on him, Cathy told herself as she drank her tea. What satisfaction? Although she wasn't sorry for what she'd said, it had been a hollow victory. Some people might even say it had been a cheap shot. Maybe it was. But he deserved it. What kind of man would treat a friend like that? Especially one who'd opened up her heart to him. There were a lot of worse things she could have said, she thought grimly. She'd been much too nice to him. Her gaze fell on the phone. No, there was no point in having another slanging match. What good would it do? Besides, there was no way she would give him the opportunity of slamming the phone down on her.

He wouldn't do that. Would he? *Want to bet?* She heard her own snort of derision. What did she know about Stephen, after all? They'd met less than six weeks ago and had been out a few times together. OK, so he'd told her stuff about himself. But most of it had been superficial, she realised now. She was the one who'd confided in him, the one who'd taken all the risks.

Cathy sat down suddenly and stared blindly at the nearest wall. God, what a fool she'd been! What a stupid, stupid fool! How could she have allowed herself to trust him? After all she'd been through, surely she should have known better? Over the years, she'd been so careful. She'd let herself have a good time, but had never became involved, never allowed anyone come too close. Even after she'd fallen in love with that two-timer Alan, she'd remembered to be cautious. The past was none of his business, she had told herself. Looking back, she realised how right her instincts had been. It was safer not to trust anyone. And she never had. Until that day, a couple of weeks ago, when Stephen had come to the apartment, and against all the odds, she'd let down her guard. How had she let that happen?

It wasn't her fault. He'd kept after her. Worn down her resistance. And he could be very persuasive when he wanted to be. But maybe that wasn't being fair to Stephen. He hadn't forced it out of her, after all. Recalling the state she'd been in that day, she realised that she had needed to tell someone. And he had been the right person to tell. She remembered the sympathetic way he'd listened to her, the comfort he'd offered, the relief she had felt afterwards. Why regret it now? It wasn't as if he would tell anyone. 'Believe me, I regard it as under the seal of the confessional,' he'd said. And she'd believed him. Whatever else she might think about him, she knew he'd never betray her confidence.

But there were other betrayals, Cathy thought. She shuddered as she went back over the phone call yet another time. His coldness when he'd spoken to her, the brutal way he'd shut her out, making a nonsense of the closeness between them. That was gone now, the friendship over. Every time she thought of what he'd done, it was like ripping again at a fresh wound.

Don't do this to yourself, Cathy. He isn't worth it. And it's not like he was your lover. It's not like you went to bed with him.

If that was all he'd been, she told herself, it wouldn't hurt so much. But a good friend could be harder to find than a lover. Sex wasn't always the most important thing. What she'd felt for Stephen had gone deeper than that. As well as being a friend, he'd been the father she'd lost, the brother she'd never had. She'd known him such a short time, and now she was going to lose him. How could she face that loss?

You can't lose what you never had, Cathy. A true friend wouldn't have spoken to you like that. But that was no consolation. Hindsight never was. She recalled what Jack had told her about Stephen as a youngster. He hadn't changed since then. Look at how angry he'd been when she'd refused to take his advice. She shuddered to herself again. What a pity she hadn't paid more attention to what his brother had said. She'd have saved herself a lot of pain.

But even without Jack's warning, she should have seen it coming. The signs were all there. She recalled what she'd said to Liz after she'd first met Stephen: 'He's the kind of person who thinks he can solve everyone else's problems.' She should have remembered that, been on her guard. Because sometimes when you confide in someone, they think it gives them the right to tell you how to run your life. She felt her spine stiffen at the notion. There was no way she was going to let that happen.

Oh, well, it was a pity the way things had turned out. But it couldn't be helped. And everything would be different from now on. She was determined about that. Cathy dried her tears and made another cup of tea. If Stephen Brown thought he was going to dictate her choice of boyfriends, he was in for a sad disappointment.

Later, as she was thinking of going to bed, the telephone rang. Her heart gave a little leap. But she hesitated. If he was ringing to apologise, she didn't want to know. Let him wait. But just as the answering machine clicked in, she changed her mind and snatched up the receiver. It was Liz ringing on her mobile.

'Some of us are going on to a club.' In the background Cathy could hear the roar of voices, the clink of glasses. 'I won't bother coming home. It'll be easier to bunk in with someone.' The casual note in her friend's voice told Cathy she was going to spend the night with a man. Justin was the most likely candidate. But you couldn't be sure with Liz. It might be someone she'd met in the pub. One thing was certain. Whoever he was, she wouldn't be telling Cathy about him tomorrow. She never did.

'It was nice of you to ring, Liz.'

'Didn't want you to worry. Sleep tight, kiddo.' As the line began to break up she heard Liz give a low chuckle. 'Don't answer the door to any strange men.' Her words conjured up a memory of the night Stephen had come to the apartment. As Cathy put down the phone she recalled her surprise at seeing him on the doorstep and remembered vividly the way his face had looked under the porch light. She heard his voice in her head again.

Forget him. Forget that night. It was important at the time. But it's in the past. She closed the living-room door behind her and went into the bedroom. The phone began to ring again. Another slight leap of the heart. But this time she let the machine take it. After a few minutes, she went back into the living room. The red light on the answering machine blinked in the darkness. But the caller hadn't left a message.

They'll ring again. She stifled her disappointment. In the meantime, she decided to have a look through her wardrobe and consider what she was going to wear on Saturday for her date with Jack.

On Friday evening, Liz came home with bad news. 'My father's gone into hospital. I need to go home for the weekend.'

'Oh, Liz!' Cathy felt a rush of sympathy. 'I hope it's nothing serious.'

'Just tests. He'll be OK.' But her voice was terse. 'Ma's the one I'm worried about. She takes these things hard.'

'Well, of course.' Her heart went out to Liz. She remembered her own mother's distress at the time of her father's accident. 'But if it's just for tests . . .'

When she saw Liz bite her lip and say nothing, Cathy felt her sympathy grow. It occurred to her that she knew very little about her friend's family, except that she had brothers and sisters and she was the eldest. She seldom spoke about her father, and had always given the impression that she didn't get on well with her mother. Although her parents lived only a short distance from Dublin, she made fewer visits home than Cathy did, and the odd time she mentioned her siblings, it was always in a humorous, disparaging way. But then, Liz always acted hard-boiled. It was part of her image. And family was family, after all. Even though she didn't always see eye to eye with her own, Cathy knew if anything were to happen to any of them, she'd want to get on the first train home.

'When are you going?' she asked.

'That's the trouble.' Liz's face darkened. 'I've to cover this alternative-therapies seminar tomorrow. It'll be afternoon before I can get away. It'll be too late for the bus. And with the train drivers' dispute, I've no guarantee of getting a train.'

'What about Justin? Hasn't he a car?'

Liz gave a resigned shrug. 'It spends more time in the garage than on the road. This time it's in for a new fan belt.'

'Could someone else cover the seminar?'

Liz shook her head. 'It's too late. Besides, my editor would have a fit. It's an important assignment for me, Cathy. I can't afford to miss it.' She measured a centimetre in the air between finger and thumb. 'I'm this much away from getting a permanent contract. I managed to wangle an interview with this guru type who's come over from the States. If I do a good job on it, it could mean big things for me.'

'If there was only some way we could get you a lift afterwards.'

'What about that priest friend of yours.' Liz looked at her hopefully. 'Any chance he might oblige?'

'He probably wouldn't be free,' Cathy said. Stephen hadn't been in touch since their quarrel on Tuesday night. There was no way she'd contact him. Not even for Liz. As she looked at her friend's disappointed face, an idea struck her. It was a long shot but it was worth a try. 'Listen, don't get your hopes up. But I've thought of someone who might do it for us.'

'No problem,' Jack said, the moment Cathy asked him. 'Glad to be of service, darling. Although . . . ' – there was a bantering note in his voice – 'I *had* hoped you were ringing me for my own sweet self.'

'It's just an elaborate ruse to talk to you.' She felt her face break into a smile. She was glad she had rung him. And not just for Liz's sake. He really was a sweet guy. 'I'm amazed, though, to catch you in on a Friday night.'

'The night's young yet.' She heard the answering laughter in Jack's voice. 'But I was seriously thinking of saving my strength for tomorrow night.'

'Do you really expect me to believe that?'

'Now, would I lie to you?' Jack said. 'I'll call for you and your friend around four.'

Cathy turned around and beamed at her friend. 'It's all sorted.'

Liz said, 'You didn't have to do that, Cathy. I'd have found someone.'

'I thought you'd be glad.'

'You hardly know this guy.' Liz frowned. 'You don't want to be asking for favours so soon. It gives the wrong impression.'

'You don't have to worry about me.' Cathy was touched by her friend's concern for her when she had so many other things on her mind. 'Anyway, he was really nice about it. Just wait till you meet Jack. I know you're going to love him.'

'What has that got to do with anything?' Liz asked.

Cathy couldn't help noticing the look of surprise that passed between Jack and Liz when Jack came into the apartment. 'Do you two know each other?'

She saw Jack smile doubtfully. 'I've a feeling we've met.'

'I never forget a face,' Liz said. She frowned as she studied him. 'I know I didn't interview you, but . . .'

'My father.' His expression cleared. 'You did a piece on the engineers' annual conference a couple of months back. Dad's president this year. Don't you remember, you came to the office.'

'It rings a bell.' Liz gave him an unsmiling look. 'Small world.'

'Sure is.' Jack's voice was non-committal. He turned to Cathy and smiled at her. 'Well, what are we waiting for?'

'I'll just get my bag,' she said. 'Won't be a moment.'

As she hurried from the room, she felt a sense of puzzlement. Had she imagined a slight awkwardness there? Maybe they hadn't hit it off the last time they met. Liz could be abrasive sometimes – although not usually with men. And certainly not with men as attractive as Jack. Of course, it had been his father she'd interviewed that time. But still it was puzzling. She'd have to ask Liz about it sometime. Meanwhile, she hoped it wouldn't spoil the journey for them.

To Cathy's relief, once they got through the suburbs and reached the motorway, the other two were chatting away easily with no sign of awkwardness between them. Thank God for that! She'd been dreading the thought of a bad atmosphere in the car. Now that her two companions were comfortable with each other, she decided to sit back and enjoy the journey. She was getting used to Jack's driving style, although she felt it was more suited to the open road than the confines of city traffic. Liz, she noticed, had no qualms about the speed with which he drove. As the powerful car ate up the miles in the outside lane, Liz was poking her head forward to join in the conversation, her hands gripping the backs of the front seats. It was an awkward position, dangerous even. She remembered her sister, Detta, as a child being reprimanded for behaving in that way. As she felt Liz's hand brush her arm and smelt her perfume, Cathy felt irritated suddenly. She glanced at Jack, wondering if he was feeling equally crowded, but it didn't seem to bother him. As he drove, he kept his eyes on the motorway, but it was obvious that he gave the rest of his attention to what Liz was saying.

'But why don't you want to stay on the features page?' he interrupted her to ask. 'Seems to me to be an interesting kind of job.'

'Suitable for a woman, you mean?' There was an edge to Liz's voice. 'You think men are better at handling hard news?'

'I think you could handle anything, Liz.' Cathy saw Jack grin. 'I just thought it must be more pleasant interviewing celebrities, that's all.'

'It's not all celebrities,' Liz said curtly. 'And a lot of them, like the self-styled guru I met today, are a pain in the arse. Exploiting people's insecurities and laughing all the way to the bank. '

'But you've done some good articles on ordinary people,' Cathy said. 'How they managed to change their lives . . .'

'. . . winning through, despite impoverished backgrounds or early abuse.' Liz nodded. 'I've heard enough stories like that to last me a lifetime. News is more exciting, more immediate.'

'Scooping your rivals?' Jack said. 'Exposing political corruption? I can just see the headlines: Demon Reporter Liz Does It Again!'

'You can mock,' Liz said. 'But I'll get there, just the same.' To Cathy's relief, Liz sat back in her seat and gazed silently out her window for the next few miles. Not that there was much to see. The motorway lights had come on; the fields beyond them had grown vague and shadowy. Ahead of them were the moving tail lights of other traffic.

'I do believe ours is the next exit,' Jack said cheerfully. 'Once we leave the motorway, you'll have to direct me, Liz.'

'That'll be easy enough.' Her voice sounded gloomily from the back seat. 'Keep straight on till you hit the deadest town in Ireland.'

'Bar one,' Cathy said. She forgot her earlier irritation and glanced back at Liz in fellow feeling. 'Can't be worse than where I come from.'

'You girls must have had great childhoods,' Jack said as he slowed down for a roundabout on the outskirts of the town. 'Now, Liz, I can see you're dying to revisit the scene of yours.'

'This is it,' Liz said when they entered a housing estate, its roads lined on both sides with pleasant bungalows, each in its own garden. She got Jack to stop in front of a house with a wrought-iron front gate and a neatly trimmed hedge. In the failing light, a glowing porch lamp gave the place a welcoming look. Jack waited until she'd gone through the gate before he drove away.

'Alone at last.' He threw Cathy a smile. 'Thank God she didn't ask us in.'

'We wouldn't have gone.' She looked at her watch. 'They'd probably be sitting down to their meal.'

'Talking of which, after what Liz said about the backwardness of this place, I'd be afraid to chance any of the restaurants, but I know a pub on the way back that does a great steak sandwich.' Jack looked at her enquiringly. 'OK with you?'

'I've a feeling you're a man who always knows a good place,' Cathy said.

'Oh, you'd be surprised at the things I know.' He took one hand from the steering wheel, reached sideways and began stroking her thigh.

Cathy didn't move away. His touch was gentle but insistent, stroking her skin through the light material of her trousers.

'But we've the whole night ahead of us to find that out, haven't we?' Jack said. When they reached the roundabout leaving the town, he took his hand away, but his caress still seemed to linger on her leg. He threw her a smiling glance. 'Isn't that right, my love?'

Cathy felt a thrill of anticipation. She knew that tonight they wouldn't stop at a goodnight kiss. Before she gave herself up to the enjoyment of the evening, she found herself thinking about Liz. Remembering Jack's strained manner when he first came to the apartment, she said, 'You did like Liz, didn't you?'

'Is that important?' His voice was light. 'She's your friend.'

'And a good one.' Cathy was anxious for him to appreciate Liz. 'I don't know what I'd do without her.'

'She seems like a nice girl.' His attention was taken up with the road. 'Talks rather a lot.'

'You're not exactly the silent type yourself.' As she grinned at him, Cathy found herself hoping the weekend would go well for Liz and her family.

When she heard Jack's car taking off, Liz stopped halfway up the path of the bungalow. She waited until his tail lights disappeared around the corner of the road before she headed back towards the gate. She went through, closing it quietly behind her, and stood for a moment to rearrange the straps of her tote bag, so that both of her shoulders could take its weight. Then she walked quickly away down the quiet road.

FOURTEEN

' . . . and for your penance say the Hail Holy Queen. Now make a good Act of Contrition.' Stephen listened while the last penitent of the evening went through the prayer, and added in his own responses at the end. He gave his final blessing. 'Go in peace.' He slid the shutter across the grille with a sigh of relief. It had been a long day. A funeral in the morning, a wedding in the afternoon, and over two hours of this. He'd be glad to stretch his legs. Before leaving the confession box, he peered out through the curtains, checking for late-comers. But the benches were empty, his part of the aisle deserted. Thank God for that! He reached for his jacket and emerged into the dimly lit church.

Dan Mulvey was still at it. As he went down the aisle, he noticed two women and an elderly man waiting outside the parish priest's box. Strange character, Dan. He was sometimes hard to figure out. Although he could be brusque and dictatorial in his daily life, he had a reputation for being kind in the confessional; some of the older parishioners would go to no one else. Stephen smiled to himself as he went past the patient figures. Dan had another twenty minutes' work ahead of him, maybe longer. But then, he probably wasn't going anywhere else on a Saturday night. As he crossed over to the nave of the church, his footsteps echoing under the high, vaulted ceiling, Stephen found himself thinking about the older man.

What interests had Dan, anyway, apart from his ministry? A passion for watching Gaelic football on television, a trip to Croke Park once a year for the All-Ireland Final, a holiday every summer with his sister in Kerry. That about summed it up. He seemed to have few people in his life. Both his parents were dead. Apart from Dan himself, there were two others in his family: the sister in Kerry and a brother over in America. He lived quietly. Few of his parishioners would be in a position to entertain the clergy, and if he had friends outside the parish, Stephen was sure he'd have heard about them by now. Dan was not a secretive man. Except for his daily walks around the parish, he didn't go out much, seeming to be content to live in that old-fashioned house of his, with his housekeeper coming in every morning and departing every evening, leaving him to eat his meal alone on a tray in his study, without even a dog for company.

Not much of a life, Stephen thought. He dipped his finger in the big stone holy-water font at the back of the church and made a perfunctory sign of the cross before going briskly through the vestibule and out the main door. On the top step, he almost collided with Sylvie, the white-haired janitor, who was gazing up at the stars while puffing at a cigarette in that furtive way he had, its butt concealed in the palm of a work-stained hand. Stephen nodded to him.

'The parish priest's still there.' Not that the janitor was in any hurry to get away, he suspected. The church seemed to be the nearest thing to a home that old Sylvie had. His every waking hour seemed to be spent pottering around the building or the grounds, or drinking tea in his own private bolt-hole – a dark little shed behind the parish office. Stephen grinned at him. 'Don't go locking him in.'

The old man gave him a cynical look. He and Father Mulvey had been sparring partners for years. 'That'd be a hanging offence all right.'

Stephen laughed. 'How's the form, Sylvie?'

'No use in complaining, Father.' Although his bristly face was a network of wrinkles, the old man's eyes were surprisingly alert. He drew heavily on the cigarette butt, then flicked it down the steps into the darkness and gave a rheumy cough, phlegm rattling in his throat. 'But I'm not the better of that flu. Hard to shake, at my age.'

'That damp basement you live in doesn't help either.' Stephen looked at him in concern. 'Why didn't you take that room Sister Dolores found you?'

'And spend a fortune in bus fares?' The old man grimaced. 'Ah, no. Where I am is grand and handy for the church.' He lifted his face to the mild April night. 'I'll be fighting fit once we get a bit of sun.'

'At least ask the doctor for a tonic.'

'A good woman, Father. That's all the tonic I need.' Sylvie grinned, showing a mouthful of yellowing stumps. 'If you hear of one . . . '

' . . . I'll put you in touch.' Although he chuckled as

he went down the steps, Stephen felt a pang of revulsion. What woman in her right mind would have anything to do with him? Yet he felt saddened too. The need never went away, did it? God, I'm surrounded by lonely old celibates, he thought as he reached the car. Was there no escape from them?

As he took out his keys the realisation hit him. It was easy to pity poor old Sylvie. Easier still to feel superior to him. Dirty old man. Who'd have him? There was no way Stephen Brown was going to end up like him, was there? A gnarled old bachelor who spent his days pottering around a church building, the only real home he had. No, the hand Stephen had been dealt would protect him from a fate like that. Life had been kinder to him than to old Sylvie. Stephen would have his books, his CDs, a few quid in the bank, the odd visit to the theatre. He might even end up getting his own parish, and become another Dan Mulvey, rattling around in some parochial house, grateful for callers, fussing about the strength of his tea. Or, in his own case, his coffee. Stephen drew in his breath sharply. What was it Brendan Hennessy had said the previous week? Something about having nothing to leave behind but a set of golf clubs and a breviary. *And I don't even play golf.* Very funny. But no one was laughing, were they? All at once, a part of him wanted to weep.

Get a grip, Stephen. That sort of thinking doesn't help. As he drove out through the church gates, he slipped a cassette into the deck. The joyous strains of Handel's *Water Music* filled the car. But he couldn't change the tape in his mind.

What did it matter if he had little to leave behind, when his time came? He wasn't interested in worldly goods. If he was, he would never have become a priest. But Brendan wasn't just talking about possessions, was he? Stephen thought of what the other man had said about babies and having someone to come home to at night. Someone to have a laugh with, like his parents had laughed.

Curse Brendan Hennessy! All at once, the music seemed to mock him. He ejected the tape abruptly. If only he hadn't come back, stirring things up. Nothing had gone right since then.

But it wasn't Brendan's fault that you had the row with Cathy, was it? You made that mess all by yourself. Oh God, Cathy! She'd been at the back of his mind all day. All week. Ever since the phone call on Tuesday night. Only for the few hours he'd been in the confessional had he had any respite from her.

The conversation had gone disastrously wrong from the start. He realised that after she'd hung up on him. It had started going wrong the moment she told him she'd been out with Jack the previous night – the same night that Stephen had rung her twice, getting the answering machine each time. He'd suspected that she was out somewhere, enjoying herself, but he had never thought that his brother would make his move so fast. After all, he'd only met her a few days before. He hadn't even got her phone number. Or so Stephen had thought. It turned out that Jack remembered Cathy telling him where she worked, and it hadn't taken him long after that.

Why go over it all again? It only made things worse. Waiting at a red light, his eye was caught by the pub sign farther up the street. He suddenly felt like having a drink. That pub was a sleazy place with a bad reputation, but he knew of a more respectable lounge bar where he and Brendan Hennessy had drunk several times. It would be safe enough to go there on his own. The idea took root in his mind. Why not? A man must have some relaxation. A pint might help take his mind off things. He drove the rest of the way home, only stopping in the house long enough to check his phone messages and change his clothes. Leaving the car parked in the tiny driveway, he headed for the pub, which was on the edge of a housing estate less than fifteen minutes' walk away. Soon Stephen was sitting at the counter, a drink in front of him.

He gazed around the busy pub, surprised at how packed it was. Any time he'd been there before with Brendan, they'd never had any trouble getting a table in a quiet corner. Tonight he'd been lucky to grab a stool at the bar. Of course, that had been during the week, and they'd always gone earlier in the night. The atmosphere had been more leisurely then, the clientele more sedate. Tonight's crowd was younger, more boisterous. Although he noticed a sprinkling of middle-aged people – recognising some as parishioners – most of the drinkers seemed to be in their twenties and thirties. Young married couples, he guessed, out for a good time on a Saturday night. As he eyed the laughing groups, Stephen felt like an outsider. It wasn't his appearance, he told himself. He was in the right age group. As far as clothes went, he wouldn't have stuck out from the people around him. Some of the men wore dark sweaters and jeans, like himself. His leather jacket had counterparts draped carelessly over the backs of chairs. He remembered Cathy's surprise when she'd found out he was a priest. No, there was nothing about him to mark him out as different. And yet he felt different. A man set apart.

It goes with the job, he told himself. *You knew that from the start.* But had he? He thought of the marriage he'd performed earlier that day. The couple had been his own age: sensible, down-to-earth people. Not starry-eyed teenagers. But anyone could see they were deeply in love. The rapt look on their faces as they pledged their vows to each other was still fresh in Stephen's mind. He'd accepted an invitation to the reception afterwards, something he rarely did. The bride was a tireless worker on parish committees and he felt he owed it to her. He left before the end of the meal because of having to hear Confessions, but he was glad enough of the excuse to slip away, telling himself that he'd had enough of watching other people's happiness for one day. Not to mention the fact that he'd had to spend a couple of hours making small talk and sipping mineral water while everyone else was knocking back the booze.

Well, he could make up for it now. He finished his

pint and ordered another. As he waited for it, he was visited by a sudden, unwelcome thought. If Cathy and Jack got married, they'd probably expect him to perform the ceremony. Cathy and Jack! He felt as if a knife had been plunged into his gut. *Don't be ridiculous. Jack's not the marrying kind.* But maybe Cathy was. She was certainly the kind of girl any man in his right mind would want to marry. And Jack was no fool. He seemed pretty smitten. The speed with which he'd asked her out testified to that. Jack was more used to women running after him.

Cathy hadn't wasted any time saying yes, either. So much for his being able to warn her about Jack. By the time he'd managed to contact her on Tuesday night, it was obvious that his brother had got in first with his lies. God knows what damage he'd done. Jack had a way of twisting things. He was a master of the half-truth and the insinuation. He could be very convincing, if you weren't on your guard. It had worked with Cathy, anyway. Judging by her manner with him on the phone on Tuesday, it was very likely she'd never talk to him again. Stephen's heart sank. What was he going to do?

The pub had got busier since he'd come in. The area near the bar had filled up with people standing around, drinking in groups. About a foot away from him, he saw a man caress a woman's back. When his hand reached the waistband of her trousers, Stephen looked away. Suddenly he felt sick of all those flushed, happy faces, those arms thrown carelessly around shoulders, those breasts brushing against arms. Nothing but couples. Everywhere he looked, he was reminded of his own single state. He drained his glass, set it down on the counter and pushed his way through the crowds to the door. Adjoining the pub was a brightly lit off-licence. When he went inside, he asked the bored man behind the counter for a bottle of vodka and something to mix it with. The night breeze felt cool against his flushed face as he walked home.

He drew the curtains across the kitchen window and sat down at the table. The little room was silent except for the whirring of the elderly fridge under the worktop beside the sink. With slow, deliberate movements, he unscrewed the cap from the vodka bottle and poured a generous amount into a tumbler. Then he added just enough white lemonade to take the edge off the vodka. He didn't bother about ice. He lit a cigarette, taking a long, pleasurable pull, and glanced at his watch. Midnight. The witching hour. He tried not to think about what Cathy and Jack might be doing with each other at that moment. Tried. And failed. As images formed in his mind, a red tide of jealousy swept over him, the force of it almost knocking him off balance. He felt his teeth grit, his fists clench. If his brother had been there at that moment, he knew he wouldn't have been able to keep his hands off him.

Shaken, he picked up his glass and took a drink. The vodka burned the back of his throat but he didn't care. *I should have rung her back.* His thoughts hammered at him *I should have apologised, made it right between us. Why did I wait? It's too late now.*

He stared unseeingly at the kitchen cupboards in front of him and lifted his glass again. For the first time since he became a priest, Stephen Brown began drinking with the clear intention of getting drunk.

Five minutes of rapid walking had taken Liz from the quiet bungalow where Jack had dropped her, through several housing estates, each less prosperous than the one before, and finished in a street of mismatched houses, some reasonably well kept, others in varying states of disrepair. The few cars parked along the kerbside looked badly in need of paint jobs. Her footsteps faltered as she stopped in front of the shabbiest house in the street. Even in the fading light it was obvious that the front garden was untended, the grass flattened rather than cut, and in places trampled away to reveal the packed earth underneath. Discoloured net curtains covered the windows. The door needed a coat of paint. The lopsided front gate scraped noisily across the concrete as Liz pushed her way through. At the front step she paused for a long moment. Then, taking a deep breath, she inserted her key in the lock.

Pushing open the door, she went into the bare little sitting room to find her two teenage brothers fighting noisily for possession of the television remote control. Nothing changes, she thought.

'Knock it off, you pair.' Rooting in her bag, she tossed a bar of chocolate to Declan, the skinny fair-haired thirteen-year-old, who was holding on to the remote with grim determination, foiling every attempt by his older, heavier brother to take it from him. She grinned as she saw Declan relax his grip and make a lunge for the chocolate, a look of glee on his pale, thin face.

'Thanks, Liz.' Colm, who was fifteen, with the same dark hair and colouring as his sister, grabbed the remote. He changed channels, threw himself down on the sagging sofa and stretched his feet out, in a series of actions so rapid that it seemed all one continuous movement. 'Did you bring anything for me?'

She looked with distaste at the grubby trainers propped up against the arm of the sofa. God, his feet seemed to be growing faster than the rest of him. 'Not till you take those dirty great things off the upholstery.'

'What upholstery?' Colm scoffed. Glancing at Liz's face, he sat up, lowering his feet to the floor.

'Watch it!' As she threw an Aero bar at him she eyed the balding arm of the sofa. As a piece of furniture, it was a lost cause. Just like everything else in the room. She didn't know why she bothered. 'Mam in the kitchen?'

Colm grunted, popping a square of chocolate into his mouth, his eyes on the flickering screen, where an American sitcom had just started. Declan was hunched in an armchair nearby, his lips moving silently, lost in the programme. Neither of them paid any attention to Liz. She sighed and went through an adjoining door to find her mother slumped at the kitchen table, lighting a fresh cigarette from the glowing butt of another. In front of her on the formica table top, a pile of old newspapers fought for space with soiled plates, teacups and saucers. Liz looked at an overflowing ashtray in dismay.

'Ah, Mam! That won't help.'

'Only thing that keeps me going,' Grace Dennehy said. She was a thin, faded woman with straggly, grey-blonde hair, and a look on her face of perpetual self-pity. When Liz saw that look she was always reminded of the woman in the Beatles' song who kept her face in a jar by the door. Only in her mother's case, Liz thought, the jar must have been beside the kitchen sink, where she stored it in readiness for her daughter's visits. 'What kept you?' Her voice was laden with reproach. 'It must be gone six.'

No, nothing changes, Liz told herself. With a feeling of despair, she looked at her mother's tar-stained fingers. Her narrow, flat-chested figure was dressed as usual in a washed-out sweater that looked like a reject from the Simon shop, and a skirt that bagged at the back. 'Where did they take Da this time?'

'The doctor sent him straight to Dublin, to John of God's.' Her mother dropped the butt into a cup of cold tea, where it sizzled, and drew heavily on the new cigarette. 'It took two men to put him in the ambulance. I needn't tell you, the language was only shocking.' She ran her hand through her straggly hair and sighed. 'I don't think I can put up with much more of this.'

Until the next time. It wasn't the first time Liz had heard her mother say that, by any means. She glanced around the cluttered kitchen, noting the empty shelf unit overhead hanging drunkenly from the wall, its screws protruding from the splintered wood, and the smashed crockery in the overflowing bin. Her gaze flew to her mother's face. No bruises there, thank God. She thought that her mother must be getting quicker on her feet. 'How long do you think they'll keep him?'

Her mother gave a defeated shrug and plucked a shred of cigarette paper from her bottom lip. She looked pleadingly at her eldest daughter. 'Will you go and visit him, Liz?'

'No way!'

'But Liz, he's up there among strangers . . . '

'Best place for him.' She kept her voice firm. 'Hope he stays there.'

'You were always hard,' her mother said.

Hard? Is that what you call it? I just can't face it again, Liz told herself. It was difficult to know which was worse: the drunken bingeing or the pathetic aftermath. She winced at the memory of the last time she'd visited her father in hospital, recalling the shrunken wreck of a man in the new dressing gown that was too big for him, the drawn, blotchy face, the hangdog look. She heard again the excuses, the evasions, the grandiose promises. 'I'll make it up to you, Liz – to the whole family.' Fat chance, she thought. Never again. Meeting her mother's reproachful gaze across the table, she hardened her heart. *Never, never, never.*

'Call me names if you want to.' Liz got up and began

clearing the dishes from the table. She injected a note of briskness into her voice. 'Right, let's get the tea started. What are we having?'

'Who can think of food at a time like this?'

'I can.' Liz went over to the half-empty fridge and was relieved to find a carton of eggs, some rashers and a pound of sausages. 'Right, we won't starve.' There were some tins of baked beans in the press. It was about the only thing you could count on in that house. She could go back on the diet on Monday. She turned to her mother. 'Get one of the boys to go down to the chipper on his bike.' She frowned when she saw the older woman lighting another cigarette. Liz's father was a carpet fitter – a good one when sober – but if he didn't work, he didn't get paid. It was difficult to keep the note of accusation out of her voice. 'Those things must be costing you a fortune.'

Her mother looked defensive. 'Colm has a job after school in the cash and carry, stacking shelves.' She shot Liz a quick glance. 'And your sister would never see me short.'

'Good old Trish,' Liz said abruptly. 'Where is she, anyway?'

'Above in the youth club helping to decorate the room for tonight's social. That girl does too much for them.' The whine came back into her mother's voice. 'They'd never run that club without her.'

Liz smiled wryly. Trish was another martyr in the making. 'Is she still working in the shoe factory?'

'Why wouldn't she be? The money's good.' The self-pitying look was back on her mother's face. 'That's where you should be, instead of up in Dublin, no good to any of us.'

If only she could be back there this minute. Liz thought longingly of the comfortable apartment she shared with Cathy. There was no way she'd ever let her friend know she came from a set-up like this. As she browned the sausages in a frying pan, she wondered what Cathy and that bucko Jack were doing right now. Probably in some pub, drinking an aperitif before heading off for a meal in a good restaurant. Say what you like about Jack, he knew how to give a girl a good time.

'You can send Colm down for the chips, Mam. And get Declan to set the table.' Her friends wouldn't be eating rashers and eggs, that was for sure. She pictured the menu. Grilled prawns to start with. Pink and succulent on a skewer. Mmm. A couple of fillet steaks, cheese and garlic potatoes, a nice bottle of red wine. She eyed the spluttering sausages without enthusiasm. 'Mam, do you want me to do you an egg?'

'If you like.' She saw her mother shrug, her thin face screwed up against the cigarette smoke. 'Don't break the yolk. You know I hate it runny.'

Did she even like food? Nobody could be that thin unless they were anorexic. The cigarettes didn't help, of course, and she had a slight frame to start with. Declan and Trish were made that way too. Liz and Colm took after their father's side. The Dennehys were heavily built, inclined to run to fat if they weren't careful. But Da had been able to carry the bit of weight. He'd been a handsome man before he let the booze take over. She remembered when she was a small child how she'd loved to sit in his lap, playing with his thick, black hair, tracing her finger over the firm curves of his face. Now his skin seemed to be hanging off him in folds.

She shuddered as she cut the rinds off the rashers and threw them into the pan with the sausages. A great example, that pair. One parent drinking himself to death, the other like a famine victim. Cathy didn't know how well off she was. She might scoff at her farming relatives and complain about her mother's lack of taste when it came to marrying again, but at least they all sounded normal. And look at the background she came from. Compared to Liz, she'd been born with a silver spoon in her mouth.

Not that she begrudged Cathy her good fortune. As Liz put the hot food onto the plates, she bit the end off a sausage morosely. It couldn't happen to a nicer girl. But you had to admit that some people seemed to have all the luck. A picture of Jack flashed into her mind. Every girl's dream man. Handsome, sexy and loaded into the bargain. And, at the moment, he had eyes only for Cathy. There was no doubt about it: it was an unfair world.

'Here's Colm.' Her mother broke into her thoughts. 'Sounds like Trish is with him.'

'Well timed,' Liz said as her brother and sister burst in the back door, the delicious aroma of cooked chips filling the kitchen. As she took the warm, greasy parcel from the breathless Colm, she aimed a kiss at the air near Trish's left ear, glancing with friendly contempt at her younger sister, who was clad in an old navy-blue tracksuit and down-at-heel runners, her fair hair scraped back in a ponytail. At twenty-two, how could she bear to be still living at home? And working in a dead-end job into the bargain? 'Sorry, I broke your egg,' Liz said carelessly as she put laden plates in front of the others. 'Want me to do another? There's one left.'

'No time. I'm on the door tonight.' Trish scraped up the runny yellow mess from the pan, threw it on a plate and piled chips after it.

'Still Santy's little helper at the youth club?' Liz asked.

Trish dunked a chip in the congealed egg and shot a sharp glance at her from under pale eyebrows. 'How's the newspaper world? Been made permanent yet?'

Skinny bitch! Liz thought. It was an effort to laugh. But she managed it. 'Any day now,' she said airily. 'Just watch this space.'

It was only a matter of time before she got that staff job, Liz told herself the next day as she prepared to leave in time to catch the lunchtime bus. But there were ways of hurrying these things up. She needed a lucky break. One good story. That was all it would take. Something that would catch the editor's eye, convince him of her worth. She wasn't quite sure what that thing was. But she'd know it when she saw it. A lead on something no one else had. An unusual angle. Some hitherto-unknown fact in an existing scandal. God knows, there were enough of them. Yes, and plenty of journalists already picking over the bones.

Don't lose heart, she told herself. *Something's bound to turn up.* And, in the meantime, she'd done her duty at home. The family crisis was over – if there had ever been one, which she was beginning to doubt. From the looks of it, they were all too used to the situation by now. In a few weeks' time her father would come home, dried out and suitably penitent, and life would go on as before. Until he fell off the wagon again. Her lips tightened at the thought. Then there'd be the frantic phone calls to the apartment. And home Liz would go for a quick visit, to offer sympathy and provide a reluctant listening ear. It was all she was prepared to do. She was determined about that. She had her own life to live. Her gaze fell on the double bed she'd shared overnight with her sister: the faded coverlet, the grubby sheets. Thank God, she'd never have to live in this miserable house again.

Liz was about to leave the bedroom when her mobile phone rang. Cathy? But it was a man's voice. Although it was barely above a murmur, she recognised it instantly. Her heart gave a lurch of excitement.

'You have a nerve.' She kept her voice cool. 'After all this time.'

'Liz, Liz, don't be like that,' Jack said. 'I'm only ringing to offer you a lift home.' His tone was as intimate as a caress. 'You know I'd never see you stuck.'

'Oh?' Her spirits slumped. 'So it was Cathy's idea.'

She heard his soft laugh. 'She doesn't keep me on a string.' His voice was barely above a murmur. Liz suspected her friend wasn't far away. 'Look . . . if you don't want me to come down for you . . . '

She hesitated. She'd sworn three months before that she'd have nothing more to do with him. But her feelings had changed when she'd seen him with Cathy.

'Will *she* be with you?'

Jack laughed again. 'No, Liz, she won't. Satisfied?'

She thought quickly. 'I'll meet you in the main street. At the bank on the corner. Just across the street from the post office.'

'Good girl!' She heard his laugh of triumph. 'Be there around three.'

It's just a lift, Liz told herself. *Don't read too much into it.* Although Jack's manner had hinted that he had more than a car ride in mind. But then, he always had. He'll be lucky, she told herself. Don't forget, there's Cathy to think about. But as she ran downstairs to tell her mother she'd be staying for lunch, Liz's heart sang with guilty joy.

'Wow! I'd forgotten how good you could be.' Jack's body gleamed above her in the fading light. He rolled over onto his back and sighed. 'You're one sexy lady, Liz.'

She gave a lazy smile. 'You're not a bad ride yourself.'

'Come on, I'm the best you've ever had. Admit it, now.'

She ran a hand over the glistening hairs on his chest, caressed his flat stomach. 'Did you know I was Cathy's friend before yesterday?'

'Last person I expected to see. You'd guessed, though, hadn't you, Liz? What an act you put on! "I never forget a face".' He gave a derisive chuckle.

Her hand moved again. 'If we're so good together, why did you dump me?'

'Ouch! That hurt! No need to get physical, Liz. You've got it wrong. Remember, it was your idea to keep it casual.'

'Liar!' She sat up suddenly. 'Any more wine?'

'There's another bottle in the fridge.' He swung his legs over the side of the bed and padded across the carpet to the kitchen. Liz lay back against the pillows and let her gaze follow his naked figure until it disappeared into the gloom of the doorway. What a body! And what an apartment! She turned her head to look at the view through the floor-length window at the city spread out below, pinpricks of light appearing in the dusk. When darkness fell, she knew, it would be a glittering panorama. She gave a little sigh of satisfaction. It was good to be back in Jack's bed.

'You look wonderful.' She heard him put the bottle of wine on the bedside table and click the lamp on. 'You've a beautiful body, Liz.' In the soft light, she saw his face close to hers, felt his hands caress her gently yet possessively. 'See the effect you have on me. I can't get enough of you.'

'Mmm.' She sat up, pushed his hands away and

poured some wine, then held the chilly glass against his flat, naked stomach. 'Better than Cathy, then?' She saw his face go blank.

'Now, now, Liz. You know I'm not the kind to kiss and tell.'

'That'll be the day. Are you seeing her again?'

He shrugged.

'She's not even your type. You like women with more flesh on them . . . '

His face mocked her. 'Don't tell me you're jealous, Liz.'

'Not at all.' With controlled fury, she tilted the glass so that some of the cold wine spilled down his stomach to the dark hairs of his groin.

'You witch!' Taking the glass from her, Jack pushed her back against the bed and poured the rest of the wine over her body, ignoring her shrieks of protest.

'Beast!' Her shrieks soon turned to amusement as she felt his tongue lapping her stomach, probing the creases of her thighs. Despite her anger, she patted his dark head. 'There's a good kitty.'

'There's a good pussy, you mean.' He lifted his head and grinned at her.

'It's not good enough, Jack.'

'I thought it was a quite an amusing trick. But if you'd like something more kinky . . . '

Liz refused to be diverted. 'You know what I mean.'

'I like both of you.' His eyes were pools of darkness in the lamplight. Impossible to read. 'It's too early to choose.'

[404]

'You're a lousy two-timer. She's my best friend.'

His expression didn't change. 'What does that make you?'

We're two of a kind, she thought. Now that she'd got him back, she knew she didn't want to let him go again.

But what would she do about Cathy?

FIFTEEN

On the Monday following his visit to the pub, Stephen rang the priest who was his regular confessor.

'Tomorrow?' The other man was surprised. 'I wasn't expecting you till next week. Anything wrong?'

'Something came up.' Stephen's voice was terse. 'I'll explain when I see you, Brian.'

Brian worked in a busy city-centre parish run by members of the religious order to which he belonged. As always, while Stephen waited for him in the chilly, high-ceilinged parlour in the tall old house next to the church, the austerely furnished room with its echoing, polished floor and unmistakable air of piety brought back vivid memories of his schooldays. When he pictured Brian's calm demeanour, his thinning hair and lined, scholarly features, he was reminded of the dedicated priests he had known in his youth. As the other man's spare, black-clad figure came swiftly through the doorway, Stephen felt his spirits lift. Despite the age difference between them, in the six years he had known Brian he had come to regard him as a friend whose judgement he could trust. If anyone could help him sort out his feelings, Brian was the one. He saw the older man's eyes twinkle as he took an armchair opposite the one Stephen was occupying.

'Now, Stephen, what's all the panic?'

'No panic,' he said stiffly. 'Well, OK, maybe there is.' There was no point in pretending with Brian. It would all come out in Confession anyway. He felt his shoulders slump. 'I've a fair bit to tell.'

He saw the other man's mouth twitch. 'That'll make a change.'

Stephen said nothing. Draping the narrow purple stole around his shoulders, Brian leant forward and said soothingly, 'One thing I know, Stephen – whatever it is, it won't be anything you and I haven't heard before. Many times.'

Yes, but you never heard it from me, Stephen thought. And if that wasn't pride, he didn't know what was. He sighed heavily, then began with the time-honoured words: 'Bless me Father, for I have sinned'.

'That's quite a list,' Brian said when they had finished and he was removing his confessional stole. 'Seems to me you ran the gamut of the seven deadly sins. The only thing missing was sloth.' He placed the folded stole beside his breviary on a polished occasional table and crossed over to the big draughty fireplace to turn up the flame on the gas fire. As he straightened up, his eyes were compassionate. 'I'm not trying to make light of it, Stephen, but aren't you being a bit hard on yourself? I mean, nothing actually happened.'

Stephen resisted the attempt to console him. 'If you call deliberately getting drunk nothing . . .'

'That was regrettable, of course,' Brian said as he

resumed his seat, 'but understandable under the circumstances.'

'Not just the drink. The hangover was punishment enough. But my feelings for Cathy . . . my jealousy, Brian!' Stephen's voice rose in horrified disbelief. 'If I'd had Jack there, I'd have strangled him with my bare hands. Oh God!' He put his head in his hands and felt heavy with despair. 'What kind of an animal have I become?'

'A human animal,' Brian said gently. 'Look, Stephen, we're all flawed human beings. Only God is perfect.'

'I know, I know.' Stephen shook his head. 'But . . .'

'We're men, you and I. Not eunuchs.' Brian smiled wryly. 'Maybe it would be easier if we were. As it is, we've the same needs as any other man. But because of our calling, we have to put those needs aside.' He gave Stephen a searching look. 'Are you in love with this young woman?'

'I – I'm not sure.' Again Stephen shook his head. 'All I know is I don't want to leave the priesthood.'

He saw the look of relief on the older man's face. 'I'm glad to hear it.'

Stephen sighed. 'It doesn't stop me caring about her.'

Brian frowned and shook his head. 'Regrettably, a growing number of priests seem to be having relationships with women these days.' His eyes narrowed, the searching look back on his face. 'I hope you're not thinking of . . .'

'That's not on!' Stephen's tone was vehement.

'Leaving my own views aside, Cathy would never agree to anything like that.'

Brian pursed his lips. 'Have you asked her?'

'I don't even know how she feels about me.' His sense of despair deepened. 'And it's probably too late anyway.'

'Ah yes, your brother.' Brian nodded. 'Bit of a womanizer, you said. But many a man has settled down once he's met the right woman.' He looked thoughtful for a moment. 'You said yourself, she seems to care for him.' His face cleared suddenly. 'Maybe that's your answer, Stephen.'

'No, no!' The words were torn from him. 'I can't believe that.'

'Stephen, listen to me.' The older man's voice was gentle. 'All priests run into this problem at some stage in their ministry. With the majority, it's women.' His face grew bleak suddenly; he gave a shrug. 'And others, for some reason known only to the Almighty, are attracted to their own sex.'

Stephen looked at him in surprise. 'Not you, Brian? I'd never have guessed.'

'We're not here to talk about me,' Brian said mildly. 'But whatever your sexual orientation, it all boils down to the same thing. If you want to remain true to your calling, you've got to stay away from temptation.' He gave Stephen a compassionate look. 'If it's any consolation, it gets easier with time.'

'But it's not just sex.'

'I know.' The older priest nodded. 'There's the need

for companionship, someone to share things with. Living in a community is a help. It has its drawbacks, of course.' He gave a wry smile. 'But you can usually find someone to talk things over with.' He glanced at the crucifix on the wall above Stephen's head. 'But a good prayer life is your best defence.'

'This isn't just about loneliness either,' Stephen said. 'I really like Cathy. We're friends.'

Brian looked dubious. 'Some priests find that friendship with an older woman can be an enriching experience. But . . . ' – he shook his head – 'with someone as young as she is, someone you have feelings for, it's too dangerous. Surely you can see that, Stephen?' His tone grew brisk. 'Take my advice, and don't see her again.'

He felt a sense of anguish. 'But I can't just leave it like that.'

'Sometimes the most honourable course is to walk away.' Although Brian's face was compassionate, his voice was firm. 'You'll be glad afterwards that you did.'

'I can't believe that,' Stephen said. 'Running away never solved anything.' He glanced at his watch and stood up. 'Your advice has been a great help, Brian. But I've got to talk to her and explain. I owe her that.'

'If you must.' The older man shrugged, conceding defeat. 'But whatever you do, remember to keep your distance.' He shot a warning glance at him. 'For both your sakes.'

'Don't worry,' Stephen said. 'I can handle it.'

'Stephen!' He saw the surprise on Cathy's face when she opened the door of the apartment. 'What are you doing here?'

'I came to apologize,' he said stiffly.

She gave him an eager look. Then her face grew wary. 'I'm not on my own.'

He hid his dismay. 'I'll come back another time.'

'No, don't go,' she said quickly. Her expression softened. 'It's not what you think.' She opened the front door wider. 'It's only Liz. And she's going out later.'

'If you're sure I won't be in the way . . . '

'It's OK, Stephen, come on in.'

As he stepped into the hall, he was careful not to brush against her. He followed her into the brightly lit living room of the apartment, where a voluptuous black-haired young woman with a bold, arresting face was curled up on the couch watching television. 'Sorry to intrude,' he said awkwardly, noticing her shoes lying on the floor near the couch and the half-eaten bar of chocolate in her lap.

'No, you're all right.' He saw the interest on her face as she sat up and swung her feet to the carpet. 'It was a crap programme, anyway.' Her voice was friendlier than it sounded on the answering machine. 'Nice to meet you, Father.' As they shook hands, her eyes held his for a long moment. 'Cathy's told me all about you.'

'There you have the advantage of me,' Stephen said. He saw something in Liz's bold stare that made him feel uncomfortable. Something to which he couldn't put a name. 'But please call me Stephen.' He gestured in the direction of the couch. 'Don't let me disturb you.'

'I was going to love you and leave you, anyway.' As Liz crouched to pick up her shoes from the carpet near Stephen's feet, the front of her blouse gaped open, revealing a tightly packed cleavage. She grinned up at him as he hastily backed away. 'I have to go and put on more warpaint.'

'Not that you need it,' Cathy said. Stephen saw the affectionate smile she gave her friend. 'Don't forget to say hello to Justin for me.'

As she got to her feet, the look on Liz's face reminded him of his mother's cat about to put its paw into the milk jug when it thought no one was watching. 'Who said anything about Justin?'

'You're awful, Liz!' He heard the reluctant laughter in Cathy's voice. 'Who is it, then?'

'What you don't know won't hurt you.' Liz grinned, still looking like a furtive cat. She left the room, humming tunelessly to herself. As the door banged behind her, Cathy turned to Stephen, her face showing a mixture of amusement and embarrassment.

'Liz likes to shock, but you shouldn't pay any attention to it. Underneath, she's got a heart of gold.'

You could have fooled me, Stephen thought. But Liz was none of his business, after all. He glanced at Cathy, giving her a hesitant smile. 'Look . . . I think I owe you an apology.'

She nodded, treating him to an unsmiling look. 'I don't understand why you were so horrible to me over the phone.'

'I'm sorry about that.' Her clear-eyed gaze made him feel uncomfortable. 'I think we got off on the wrong foot.'

'It was more than that,' Cathy said accusingly. 'You lost your temper.'

Stephen winced. 'I can't apologise enough for that. I should never have taken my anger out on you.' He swallowed hard as he met her gaze. 'Please forgive me.'

Cathy's expression didn't soften. 'What have you really got against Jack?'

He hesitated. 'I don't want to bad-mouth him, but . . .'

'You already have.' Her voice was stern. 'I think it's about time you explained.'

'Well . . . ' He chose his words carefully. 'Where women are concerned, he's got a bad reputation.'

'So *you* say.'

Stephen sighed. 'Cathy, a girl tried to commit suicide because of him.'

Cathy nodded. 'Jack told me about her.'

He felt a jolt of surprise. 'He told you about Fiona?'

'Poor girl.' She shook her head sadly. 'But you can hardly hold him responsible for that. I mean, you can't make yourself love someone, can you?'

He shook his head, saying nothing. *Clever Jack. He'd got in first again.*

She looked at him earnestly. 'You've got him all wrong.'

'I don't think I have.' When he saw her look of scepticism, Stephen gave an inward sigh. How was he to explain a man like his brother to someone as honest as Cathy? He felt a sense of frustration. How could he protect her from Jack?

'Isn't it time you stopped thinking of him as a brat of a younger brother?' Cathy asked. 'See him for the man he is now.'

'What's the use?'

'No, listen, Stephen.' Her voice was eager. 'I always knew he was a nice guy. But after Saturday night . . . '

'When you were together?' Stephen felt the blood drain from his face. He stared at her tensely. 'What happened?'

Cathy blushed slightly. 'Maybe I shouldn't be telling you this, but I think you should know . . . '

'Go on.'

'Well . . . we were making love – '

'You went to bed with him?' The words were out before he could stop them. As he looked at her face Stephen felt as if someone was squeezing his heart in a vice. 'Cathy! You didn't!'

She looked taken aback. 'Well . . . '

The vice grew tighter. As he pictured her and Jack together, the pain was almost too much to bear. His voice raw in his throat, he said, 'Why are you telling me this?'

Her blush deepened. 'It's not what you think. Yes, I was going to go to bed with him, Stephen. I thought it was what I wanted.' Her eyes widened. 'But when it came to the point . . . ' She shook her head, looking at him in a kind of disbelief. 'I found I couldn't.'

'You changed your mind?' He stared at her, hardly daring to hope. When he saw her nod, the vice around his heart loosened. He gave a long, shuddering sigh. 'Thank God!'

'Another sinner saved from damnation?' She looked at him resentfully. 'Is that what it means to you?'

'No, of course not.' It meant so much more. But it wasn't important at that moment whether she understood this or not. He stared at her eagerly. 'What stopped you?'

'I . . . Jack's a lovely guy, but it just didn't feel right.' She bit her lip. 'This is going to sound weird, but I kept hearing your voice in my head.'

'Saying "Don't do it, Cathy"?' He laughed, masking his relief with humour. 'I can't believe you actually listened to me.'

'I knew you'd think it funny.'

'Sorry, sorry.' He smiled at her. 'Go on.'

Her face grew pink again. 'It was something you said that first night we met . . . after my bag was snatched.'

He looked at her doubtfully. 'We said a lot of things that night.'

'This was after the thieves ran off. I was lying on the ground, not sure if I was alive or dead. And you said, "Are you OK?" Just those three words. But you've no idea how much they meant at the time.' She looked at him, her eyes wide with surprise. 'The other night with Jack, I kept hearing those words in my head, your voice, as clear as if you were in the room with us. And I knew it wasn't OK, knew the time wasn't right.'

He glanced at her hopefully. 'Sure it wasn't the person . . . ?'

'There you go again, blaming Jack.' Cathy shook her head. 'You're not being fair. He couldn't have been nicer about it.' She gave an embarrassed grin. 'It can't have been easy for him. There we were, the two of us . . . I mean, put yourself in his position.'

'Cathy, please!' The words were torn from him. He jumped to his feet and saw her mouth open in surprise. 'Don't you realise what this is doing to me? I can't bear to think of you and him.'

'I'm sorry.' She looked taken aback. 'I didn't realise . . . '

'Cathy, Cathy!' He couldn't keep the anguish from his voice. 'Can't you see, I'm in love with you.'

'You can't be.' He saw the shock on her face. 'You're a priest.' She rose too and looked at him pleadingly. 'Say it isn't true.'

'I can't.' He watched her face carefully. 'Priests have feelings, just like other people.'

'No!' She shook her head. He saw tears start in her eyes. 'I don't believe this.' Her voice was bewildered. 'It can't be happening again.'

Stephen stared at her in dismay. 'Do you want me to leave?'

Get out now, an inner voice told him. *Before you do something you regret.*

He didn't move. 'Cathy?'

She stared back without answering, tears running down her face.

'Oh God, Cathy . . . ' He looked at her helplessly.
Go, you fool.

Stephen ignored the voice. Moving forward, he took her in his arms. 'My sweet, darling Cathy!' He stroked her hair, smelt its clean, flowery scent. 'Please don't cry.' Her tears tasted salty under his lips. As he bent to kiss her mouth, he saw the astonishment in her eyes but she didn't pull away. Instinctively, he pulled her body closer to his. He heard the thudding of both their hearts. Closer still until he felt the softness of her breasts, the curve of her stomach pressing against his. Just before his lips came down on hers, he heard Cathy breathe a little sigh. When he tasted the sweetness of her mouth, his arms tightened around her. Oh God, Stephen thought, oh God! He felt her body respond. Then, as though a match had been ignited between them, he felt its flame course through his whole body, threatening to turn into a conflagration that would engulf them both.

'No!' he heard Cathy cry. They drew apart at the same time.

Stephen's chest was heaving; he felt his sweater and shirt sticking damply to a patch between his shoulder blades. He found it hard to meet her gaze. 'I'm sorry. It was all my fault.' He felt his voice tremble. 'I never meant that to happen.' He looked down at the carpet. 'I think I should go now.'

'It was my fault too,' Cathy said. Slumping down on the sofa, she stared at him, her eyes miserable. 'I needn't have let you kiss me.'

He could still feel the pressure of her lips, the softness of her body against his. 'That's true. But I had a responsibility . . . ' His legs began to tremble suddenly. As he sat down opposite her, he saw that her hands were shaking. 'Cathy, I'm sorry.'

'It was just a kiss,' she said quickly. 'It didn't mean anything.'

To you, maybe.

'It won't spoil our friendship, will it?' Cathy asked. When he hesitated, she looked at him pleadingly. 'There's no harm done. Let's forget it happened.'

'Can you do that?' He knew he never would. He knew also that if he stayed any longer, he couldn't trust himself not to kiss her again. 'I'd better go.' As he got to his feet, he remembered his conversation with Brian. He knew he shouldn't see her again, but he couldn't bear to make his decision final. 'Maybe we shouldn't see each other for a while.'

She bit her lip. He saw the uncertainty in her eyes. 'If it's what you want.'

Please, Lord, let me make it to the door without touching her. He turned away quickly. 'I'll see myself out.'

As he went down the short hallway, Cathy called after him, 'Don't leave it too long, Stephen.' When he heard the break in her voice, he wanted to turn back.

With a sigh, Stephen opened the front door and let himself out of the apartment.

'Maybe we should cool it for a bit.' Cathy pushed away Jack's hand before he managed to open a second button on her blouse. 'You're going a bit too fast for me.'

'Why do I get the feeling I'm back to square one?' Although his voice had lost none of its good humour, she noticed a slight crease in his forehead. 'This isn't the same woman I made love to on Saturday night.'

'I should never have let things go so far,' she said hastily. 'It was a mistake.'

'A tactical error?' For a moment Jack's smile had a wolfish quality to it. 'Is that what you're saying?'

'No.' Cathy was taken aback. 'I don't play games.'

'Neither do I. Not that kind, anyway.' He stroked her arm gently. 'You're hard to figure out sometimes.' His face was thoughtful. 'You blow hot and cold.'

'No I don't!' She felt suddenly defensive. 'Look, Jack, I don't need to explain myself to you.'

'It would help if you did.' His eyes narrowed. 'Cathy, are you telling me to get lost?'

'What?' She stared at him in surprise.

'Because if you want me to go . . . ' He shrugged, turning his palms outward in a graceful gesture.

'No.' Again, she had the feeling of things moving too fast, but in a different direction. 'That isn't what I meant.'

As Jack stared at her, his face grew cold. 'I think you're going to have to spell it out.'

She bit her lip, beginning to feel flustered. 'Don't rush me, Jack.'

'There's more to it than that.' His voice was ruminative. 'Something's happened since Saturday.' With a swift movement, he cupped her chin gently but firmly. 'Out with it, Cathy!'

His grey eyes made her think of two pebbles the sea had polished to a hard gleam. She felt a faint shiver run through her. 'I don't know what you mean.'

'Someone's been saying something about me.' His eyes bored into hers. 'Was it Liz?'

She felt puzzled. 'No, of course not.'

He frowned suddenly. 'Steve?'

'Look, Jack, we've been through that before.' With an effort, Cathy freed her gaze from his. She pushed his hands away. 'It's nothing anyone said. You're a nice guy – I really like you.' Even as the words came out, she wondered if they were true any more. 'But . . .'

'You don't want me to make love to you.'

'Not tonight, anyway,' she said, not wanting to hurt his feelings.

Jack shrugged and moved away from her. He sprawled comfortably against the sofa cushions, his hands thrust into his trouser pockets. 'Bit of a change for me, I must say.' He gave a twisted grin. 'Most women can't wait to get their knickers off.'

Cathy felt herself recoil. 'I don't have to listen to this.'

'Shocked you, didn't I?' Jack grinned again. 'Maybe a bit more dirty talk is what you need. Look, Cathy, I didn't mind too much about Saturday night. I figured you were telling the truth when you said it was all happening too fast for you. But I'm beginning to suspect – '

Her heart gave a guilty thump. 'Suspect what you like.'

' – that you have a problem about sex.'

'What?' She stared at him open-mouthed. 'There's nothing wrong with me.'

'It's nothing to be ashamed of.' He gave her a look that was almost kindly. 'Probably something to do with a repressed upbringing. Country people can be pretty old-fashioned.'

Cathy fought back an impulse to splutter with indignation. 'What was so sexually enlightened about your background, anyway?' She rounded on him. 'From what Stephen told me, things didn't sound that hot.'

'You've been listening to the wrong brother.' Jack's voice was bland. He took his hands out of his pockets and sat up. 'But you can figure that out for yourself another time. Right now, I'd rather talk about you and me.' He moved nearer Cathy and took her hand, pressing it to his lips. 'Your previous lovers probably weren't very skilful.'

'Thanks a lot!'

'No reflection on you,' Jack said smoothly. 'But you're dealing with an expert now.' He smiled at her. 'There's so much I can teach you.'

'God, you're smug!' She stared at him in irritation. How could two brothers be so unlike? She had a sudden memory of Stephen's lips on hers, and snatched her hand away. 'Look, I've told you . . . '

She saw a little pulse beat beside Jack's mouth. His eyes were like hard pebbles again. 'Are you telling me there's someone else?'

'No,' Cathy said. She thought rapidly. 'I mean, yes.'

'Make up your mind.' His voice was impatient.

'Either there is or there isn't.' He gave her a probing look. 'So which is it?'

'It's yes.' Cathy met his gaze without flinching. 'There is someone else.'

Suddenly Jack didn't look handsome any more. 'Anyone I know?'

'An old boyfriend,' she said, improvising hastily. 'I saw him last night.' Better not tell too much. He was like a cat waiting to pounce. But it was difficult to think clearly under that hard-eyed stare.

'Was he here?'

In this very room, Cathy thought, his arms around me, his body pressed close to mine. She shook her head. 'We met in a wine bar.'

Jack looked unconvinced. 'Is that the man you said you wouldn't have back if he came wrapped in fifty-pound notes?'

She'd forgotten he knew about Alan. Cathy tried to remember what else she'd told him. 'Not him. Someone else.' When she saw him raise his eyebrows, she found herself getting angry. 'Jack, this is turning into an interrogation.'

He said nothing for a moment, then shrugged. He gave her a conciliating smile. 'God, Cathy, I'd never do that.' His voice sounded genuinely penitent. 'I'm not trying to give you a hard time. I just wouldn't want you to make a mistake.' For a moment she was tempted to believe him. Until she remembered the way his eyes had looked.

'Don't worry, I won't.' As she gazed at his sculpted

features, she wondered how she'd ever found them attractive. Greek gods were cold creatures at the best of times. Another face came into her mind: kinder, more solid. She felt a wrench of sadness. If only things could have been different.

As if he could read her mind, Jack asked, 'See much of Steve these days?'

'Not really.' She felt her face grow hot. She turned away from his probing gaze. 'I'll make some coffee before you go.'

'Not for me.' He glanced at his watch and stood up, stretching lazily. 'I think I'll drown my sorrows in a pint.'

Cathy felt a rush of relief that he was taking it so well. Maybe she'd misjudged him. On an impulse, she put out her hand. 'No hard feelings, I hope?'

'Your loss.' Jack shrugged. He ignored the hand. The stony look was back in his eyes. 'You're wasting your time with him.' His tone was icy. 'You do realise that?'

'I don't know what you mean.' She heard her own voice tremble.

'And not only because of the dog collar.' His mouth twisted in a sneer. 'The love of his life dumped him years ago. My brother's been hiding from women ever since. Ask him about it some night, when you're in bed.'

She tried to keep her voice steady. 'You've a filthy mind, Jack.'

'With Stephen, a woman is either the Virgin Mary or a whore.' He gave a cold, contemptuous smile. 'Which one are you, Cathy?'

As soon as the front door closed behind Jack, Cathy double-locked it. With shaking hands, she fastened the chain securely. She was probably being stupid, she told herself. He wasn't going to come back, and it wasn't as if he was an axe murderer, or anything, but it made her feel safer. Every time she thought of those hard eyes, she felt shivers run down her spine. She could still see the look on his face, hear his soft words. *Which one are you, Cathy?*

She went to the kitchen to make some tea. But when she tried to fill the kettle, it shook so violently in her grasp that she put it back on the worktop and buried her face in her hands. *Oh God! Oh God!* She'd had a lucky escape, she told herself. Not that it was any consolation to her. She felt nauseated, as if she'd bitten into a shining piece of fruit only to find it decaying inside, the putrid strands still clinging to her tongue. Everything was suddenly tainted: her belief in herself, the way she felt about Stephen, his feelings for her. *With him, she's either the Virgin Mary or a whore.* No, no! I can't believe that! Jack was evil, she reminded herself: he poisoned everything he touched. Stephen was the complete opposite. We're like chalk and cheese, he'd said. A commonplace expression. But she found herself clinging to it.

If only Stephen were here. A few words from him would wipe out the memory of what Jack had said. She knew they would.

'No, I hadn't gone to bed.' His voice was low, hurried. 'As a matter of fact, I'm on my way out . . .'

'Oh no!' She choked back a sob. 'I need to talk to you.'

'I wish I could,' Stephen said. 'But . . .'

'Please!'

His tone changed. 'Cathy, what's wrong?'

'Oh, Stephen, I was a fool for not listening to you.' Her words came out in a rush. 'I've had such a fright. You were right about Jack.'

'What did he do?' She heard the alarm in his voice. 'Cathy, are you OK?'

'It was more what he said.' She was half-crying as she spoke. 'I feel so unclean.'

'The bastard!' The line crackled angrily. 'I know what I'd like to do to him!'

'My own fault,' she sobbed. 'You tried to warn me.' She felt a sudden longing to feel his arms around her. 'I know it's late, but . . .'

'Oh, Cathy, I hate to do this to you.' She could hear the distress in Stephen's voice. 'But I have to go. I've been called out to a dying parishioner. I don't know how long I'll be, but we'll talk again soon, I promise. Will you be OK?'

'Right, sure,' Cathy said dully. 'I'll be fine. Ring me tomorrow.' She put down the phone, heavy with disappointment. She consoled herself with the thought that Liz would be home soon. *I'll have a cuppa while I'm waiting.* This time she managed to boil the kettle without mishap. But several cups of tea later and halfway through a tedious late film on television, there was still no sign of her friend.

Probably making a night of it, Cathy decided. It was happening a lot lately. As she switched off the television, she wondered who the new man in Liz's life was.

She got ready for bed and climbed wearily under the duvet. And stayed awake for most of the night.

SIXTEEN

I should have gone to her. Stephen was filled with regret the next morning as he walked across the churchyard in the thin April sunshine. It was what Cathy had wanted, he knew, but she'd been too proud to ask. Just as well she hadn't; it would have broken his heart to have to refuse. As it was, he'd felt very unhappy about ringing off the way he had. She'd needed him, and he'd let her down. But what choice did he have? His first duty had been to the dying man. Even though it turned out afterwards that the old fellow wasn't as near death as the distracted relatives had believed. Or maybe he was, and he'd rallied after he'd been anointed with the holy oils. Whatever the reason, the patient was propped up, attempting to sip a cup of tea, by the time Stephen was leaving. But that was the way things often worked out. He had still been needed, Stephen told himself. And would be again.

You mean, they needed a priest. The suggestion popped into his head as slyly as a bad thought. *Not you, Stephen. Any ordained minister would have done. But Cathy wanted you, didn't she? The man, not the cleric.* It was true. He sighed to himself at the thought. And he'd wanted to be with her. She'd never know just how badly he'd wanted that. He'd ring her immediately after Mass and arrange to meet that night. It would mean cancelling a couple of counselling sessions. Well, it couldn't be helped. It wasn't as if he made a habit of it. The clients were bound to understand. What if they didn't? It was very short notice. He thought of one couple he'd been seeing over the last few months who could be quite difficult at times. They'd be OK, he told himself. After all, it wasn't in the same category as a sick call. It was still a commitment, though one he'd taken on freely. Suddenly Stephen found himself resenting some of the demands being made on him. He raged inwardly, battling with conflicting desires. Surely to God he was entitled to some kind of private life?

'No time for friends these days?' He heard Sister Eileen's cheerful voice behind him as he reached the sacristy door.

'Sorry. Lack of sleep.' Stephen turned quickly and began to explain about the sick parishioner. 'Probably bury us all yet,' he said with a laugh.

'You, on the other hand, don't look too healthy.' Sister Eileen gave him a shrewd look. 'I'd say now it wasn't only last night you missed your beauty sleep.'

Stephen nodded. 'I've a problem I need to work out.'

'Want to talk about it?'

'I'm not sure.'

But the idea of unburdening himself was tempting. As he eyed Sister Eileen's sympathetic face, he sensed something solid and comforting about her. Standing there, tall and erect in the sunshine, she was like a rock of calm in a sea of uncertainty. The way he pictured

Mother Church, herself. She looked this morning as if you could tell her anything and she'd listen with equanimity. As he thought this, she gave him an encouraging smile.

'What are friends for, Stephen?'

'That's true.' But would she understand about Cathy? He looked at her doubtfully. Why not? She'd shown a lot of compassion where Brendan Hennessy was concerned. Surely she'd do as much for him. One thing was certain: he could rely on her discretion. As he looked at her, Stephen made up his mind.

'I could do with a listening ear. How about a coffee after I've finished Mass?'

Sister Eileen smiled. 'Your place or mine?'

Stephen suppressed a frown. It was an old joke between them. But this morning the words jarred. 'Mine,' he said hastily. The last thing he wanted was that bitch Dolores shoving her oar in. As he hurried into the sacristy to get ready for Mass, he wondered if he'd made the right decision.

'That problem you mentioned . . . ' Sister Eileen said delicately. As she sipped her coffee, she gave him a thoughtful look. Could he have changed his mind? After ten minutes in Stephen's kitchen, she was no nearer to being enlightened than when she'd first sat down. The conversation had covered some minor matters to do with the parish, touched briefly on a lecture on cathetics Eileen planned to attend, and then gone on to discuss, of all things, the type of coffee beans Stephen liked to use in his blender. If they weren't careful, she told herself, they'd be talking about the colour of his socks next. She stared at him in perplexity. He wasn't usually so slow in getting to the point. Nor was it like him to be so restless. That was the second time he'd jumped up from the table to check the taps on the gas cooker.

'All this prowling about is making me nervous.' She smiled, to take the sting out of her words. 'Sit down like a good man and tell me what's bothering you.'

'Sorry.' Stephen obediently returned to his seat. But she saw he couldn't keep his hands still. When he picked up a packet of cigarettes from the table top, she felt herself stiffen. Oh no! Glancing obliquely at the ashtray, with its tell-tale collection of butts, she drank her coffee and said nothing. If it's a help to him, she told herself. Still, it was a relief when he didn't open the packet, just kept turning it over and over in meaningless repetition as he gazed bleakly at the opposite wall.

He had nice hands, she noticed. Large, well-shaped and capable. The nails were clean and neatly trimmed. Sensitive hands for a big man, she remembered thinking the first time she saw them. Hands were important to her. They told you about people. Feet did too. She thought of Sister Dolores with her red, stubby fingers and her bunions. Eileen's mother was fond of saying that breeding will tell. Although she didn't often agree with her mother, this was one thing on which they both saw eye to eye. Eileen was proud of her own slender, patrician hands and made sure to buy good hand cream, even if she had to cut down on something else. As her gaze followed the hypnotic movement of Stephen's long fingers, she felt a sudden inexplicable urge to reach out and measure one of his hands against hers. Instead, she pushed back her cardigan sleeve and glanced at her watch. As she'd hoped, he caught the movement and looked at her.

'I'm sorry.' His face was haggard in the cold light shafting in through the small kitchen window. 'This is much harder than I thought.'

She kept her voice gentle. 'It can't be that bad, surely.'

He gave her a shamefaced smile. 'I'm not sure you'll approve – although you seemed to understand about Brendan . . . '

Sister Eileen felt a thrill of alarm. A suspicion began to form in her mind. She looked at him enquiringly, saying nothing.

'I'm beginning to have some idea what he must have been going through,' Stephen said broodingly. 'Why he made the decision he did.'

She chose her words with care. 'This isn't about him, though, is it, Stephen?' *Please God, don't let me be right*, she prayed. She looked at him keenly. 'We're talking about you, aren't we?'

When she saw his unhappy nod, she knew she wasn't going to get any more joy out of the answer to her next question. But she put it just the same. 'You and that girl?'

Another nod from Stephen.

It was too late for prayer, she knew, but it was hard

to break the habit of years. As she glanced at the anxious face of the man sitting across the table from her, she touched the tiny silver cross pinned to the neck of her blouse. *Dear Lord, don't let him have compromised himself. Don't tell me all is lost.*

When Stephen opened his mouth to speak, she fingered the silver cross again.

'You've behaved unwisely, I have to say that.' Sister Eileen hid her relief behind a judicious frown. 'Left your actions open to misinterpretation. But I don't think any lasting harm has been done.' It was only one kiss, after all. Her own lapse had been much worse all those years ago, and still she'd gained forgiveness. 'The thing is not to let it go any further.' She waited for him to agree. But he just stared bleakly at her.

Was he listening to her at all? She tried again. 'Look, Stephen, Cathy seems to be a sensible girl.' Privately, Eileen had her doubts about that. Most modern young women had no respect for the collar. Some even saw it as a challenge. But it was the plain ones who were the worst, she reminded herself. A girl as attractive as the one she'd met that day in his house wouldn't bother running after a man who wasn't available. She looked at him hopefully. 'Once you explain to her – '

'You don't understand!' His voice was anguished. 'Cathy's not the problem, Eileen. I am.' She saw the misery in his eyes before he turned away to look down at a spot on the table top, his hand shielding his face from her gaze. His voice broke suddenly. 'I'm in love with her. And I don't know what to do.'

'My poor Stephen.' She looked at his bowed head and was visited again by the desire to reach out to him – this time, to take his hand from his face and, with her own fingers, gently wipe away the tears she knew he was hiding from her. Instead, she leaned forward and patted his shoulder briefly. She sank back into her seat, shaken by the strength of her own emotions and the effort it was taking to conceal them. As she waited for him to regain his self-control, she fought down the urge to go around to his side of the table, put her arms around him and draw that dear, dark head of his against her breast. Like a mother, she told herself hastily. Nothing else. All the same, when she saw Stephen raise his head and look at her, she was glad he couldn't read her thoughts.

'I'm sorry.' She saw the embarrassment on his face.

'Nothing to be ashamed of, dear.' Handing him the cigarette packet, she watched patiently as he fumbled with matches and waited until she saw him take a long, shuddering pull. 'Saint Paul says that God never lays a burden on us but he gives us the means to carry it.'

He gave a wry smile. 'Doesn't he also tell us, "It's better to marry than burn"?'

'Not in this case,' Sister Eileen said firmly. 'Why don't we say a little prayer for guidance.'

She would help him, she told herself, as she made the sign of the cross. Together they would combat the wiles of Satan and the snares of the flesh.

'Bye now, take care.' Sister Dolores waved goodbye to the heavily pregnant woman who was leaving her office, two snivelling toddlers pulling out of her skirt. 'Put your feet up and make that lazy sod of a husband do his share.'

Some hope, she thought to herself, closing the door and going back to her desk. With two other kids at home – the eldest on drugs – that poor woman had a better chance of winning the lottery. Things hadn't changed that much since her mother's time, she thought, as she eased her bulk into the uncomfortable wooden chair which was all the parish centre could afford to provide for its social worker. OK, maybe welfare payments were better, but not much. And human nature was just the same. In this so-called millennium year, despite the gains made by feminism and the growth in the country's wealth, women were still getting the dirty end of the stick. There were still men around like her father, who got drunk, beat their wives and abused their children. And the gap between the rich and poor was widening. It was enough to make you weep.

A shrill ringing interrupted her thoughts. Sister Eileen was at the other end of the phone, enquiring about the woman who'd just left. Had Dolores been able to sort out her finances?

'Fat chance, Eileen. The Credit Union were sympathetic. But she's in hock to some scumbag of a moneylender.'

'Would we do any better in the same circumstances?' Eileen said in that sweet-voiced way Dolores loved.

'There but for the grace of God . . . '

'Who do you think you're telling?' Maybe God had something to do with it, Dolores mused, as she put down the phone, but, in all honesty, cousin Hannah, with her generosity and her quick, calculating eye, deserved most of the credit. *And, let's face it, Dollo, a head of red-gold ringlets and milky-white skin had played its part too.* If it hadn't been for Hannah, she reminded herself, she could have ended up with the same kind of life as that poor woman who'd just left her office. Old before her time, husband on the dole, kids on drugs, just keeping one step ahead of the loan sharks. It was Hannah who had rescued her. Hannah who'd taught her, among so many other things, that men weren't the answer.

Dolores would never forget the day she'd first laid eyes on her dashing cousin. Tall, dark and handsome, like the prince in the fairy tale. And successful too. The young girl had never met a woman lawyer before. Never met any kind of a lawyer, if the truth be known. In the area where Dolores lived, people were lucky if they saw a solicitor half an hour before they were due in court on a charge of shoplifting or breaking and entering. Education was a word bandied about by the bogeyman who caught kids mitching from school, but it was not taken too seriously by the neighbours. Why a thirty-something honours-graduate, second-generation Irish-American would want to come looking for her mother's cousins in a dreary block of Corporation flats in one of the roughest areas of Dublin was something Dolores would never understand – and something Hannah could never satisfactorily explain, even when Dolores was older and they were having one of their heart-to-hearts over grilled red snapper and a bottle of Californian Zinfandel.

Not that it mattered one little bit by then. Hannah could do no wrong as far as Dolores was concerned. She was the knight in shining armour who had rescued the skinny, red-haired thirteen-year-old from that stinking block of flats, taking her away from her quarrelsome siblings, from poor defeated Mammy and that disgusting animal who didn't deserve the name of father. Whisking her away on the sixties equivalent of a white charger: a gleaming Boeing jet which zoomed over the ocean, not to a high castle with its spires in the clouds, but to a white-painted frame house in a quiet street. It was in a small-town suburb in New York State, where the neighbours swept the leaves from their front yards and had coffee mornings after church on Sunday. To a house where, for the first time in her life, she slept in a bed of her own, between sheets smelling of rosemary, under a candlewick bedspread that tickled her nose. There was an enormous fridge in the kitchen packed with cartons of orange juice and tubs of ice cream, the shower worked in the tiled bathroom, and she changed her underwear every day. The latter development was one of the first steps in Hannah's campaign to transform Cinderella into the all-American princess.

Not that her cousin had wholly succeeded. Dolores

shrugged to herself as she glanced down at her stocky body in its lived-in tracksuit, and flexed her feet in her comfortable runners. You were never going to make a silk purse out of a girl from Robert Emmet Flats. Never eradicate the memory of her mother's cries on a Friday night, the constant hunger pangs, the stench of a communal lavatory. Not even clean linen, turkey at Thanksgiving and a PhD in sociology from Spokane could do that.

But mighty oaks from little acorns grow. Although she grinned at such a mixture of metaphors, Sister Dolores felt a pang of pride. She hadn't wasted those years in America. OK, so she was home again, living among the kind of people she'd sprung from, sharing the drab backdrop of their lives. The thing was, thanks to Hannah, she was no longer a victim, but a champion. Fighting the bureaucratic social system on behalf of people too ignorant or too defeated to seek the benefits to which they were entitled. A drop in the ocean compared to what the comfortable middle classes raked in, she told herself, but still making a difference to otherwise hopeless existences. And she wasn't alone in her mission. Eileen felt the same way, even if she went on with all that 'there but for the grace of God' shit.

Eileen had said something else on the phone, Dolores remembered.

'Are you coming straight home tonight, Dollo?'

'Do I have to?' She grinned to herself. 'Remind me to get you a cookery book some time.'

'Don't tease.' Eileen's voice sounded strained. 'I need your advice on something.'

As she got ready to leave the office, Sister Dolores wondered what was on her friend's mind. All in good time, she told herself. As poor Mammy used to say, never trouble trouble, and it won't trouble you.

She loved this time of the day. Just the two of them, drinking their after-dinner coffee in a companionable silence in front of the gas fire, Eileen on the sofa, Dolores sitting on the floor. The evenings were still nippy in April; the imitation coals threw out a comforting warmth. She hugged her knees and glanced up at her friend.

'The meal was good.' Although you can't go far wrong with pasta sauce, she thought. Not when it comes out of a jar. But give credit where it's due. 'You're beginning to get the hang of it.'

'We can't all be gourmet cooks.' A predictable refrain with Eileen. 'But I *do* try.'

'Don't knock yourself,' Dolores said gallantly. 'Best spaghetti bollocks-naise you ever made.'

She expected to be pulled up with a gentle reproof about bad language. When it didn't come, she threw Eileen a quick glance. 'What's on your mind, chicken?' She saw the other woman hesitate. 'Come on, you don't have to do your Rock of Ages act with me. This is your Auntie Dollo, remember. What's happened? Is it lover boy?' At the thought of Stephen, she was gripped by a familiar pang, but managed to keep her voice light. 'Have you finally got around to holding hands? Did he give you more than bad thoughts?'

Eileen looked distraught. 'Stephen is having doubts about his vocation.'

'Is that all?' Dolores spluttered with relief. 'You're talking to the queen of doubt here. Every day I ask myself what I'm doing in the last fortress of male supremacy. What's his problem? Not getting promotion fast enough?'

Eileen shook her head. 'There's a woman involved.'

'Isn't there always!' She looked sharply at her friend's face. 'It's not you, is it?' Her voice sounded harsh to her own ears. 'He hasn't – '

'Of course not!' Eileen's face went pink. 'Honestly, Dolores, how can you even suggest that!'

'You don't need to protest so much,' she said sourly, her victory spoiled by the sight of that tell-tale blush. 'So who is it?' A thought struck her. 'Not that gorgeous young one he brought to the parish centre, is it? Well, well, well.' Dolores couldn't hide her delight. 'He's human, after all.'

'What is it with men and sex?' Eileen sighed for the umpteenth time that night. 'Do they ever lose the urge, do you think?'

Dolores suppressed a smile. Eileen could be naive at times. 'How should I know?' She looked at her friend's smooth throat and thought of Hannah, a few years past retirement age, still giving her little candlelit suppers for young women she'd taught in law school. Of course, she'd kept her looks a lot longer than Dolores had. Many years longer. Good early nutrition was probably the answer. Still, one could live in hope. 'Ask me when I'm eighty,' she growled.

'If it was just the – the physical thing,' Eileen said. 'But he thinks he's in love with her.' A shocked note came into her voice. 'He actually spoke of giving up the priesthood.'

Dolores felt her spirits lift. Good riddance to him. The sooner it happened, the better. She patted the other woman's knee. 'It's just talk, Eileen. That fella's in love with the job. You're getting all worked up over nothing.'

'You didn't see him today.' Eileen looked at her doubtfully. 'He seemed to me to be on the brink. It would just take one little thing to tip him over.'

Amen to that, Dolores thought. As she looked at her friend's anxious face, she felt a twinge of compassion. 'If he goes, you'll really miss him.'

'He'll be a loss to the parish,' Eileen said, refusing the bait. 'Father Mulvey was saying the other day how much he's relying on Stephen now that Brendan's gone.'

'It'll be a panic when he finds out he has another defector on his hands.' Dolores chuckled, picturing the parish priest's choleric reaction. 'Maybe he should do something about it before – '

'It's too late?' Eileen gave her a thoughtful look. 'Maybe someone should tell him.'

'That's not a great idea,' Dolores said quickly. *Sweet jeepers, why did I have to go putting that into her head?* 'You said yourself it might only take one thing to push him over the edge.'

'Or to pull him back,' Eileen said eagerly. 'A word

from the right person, at the right time could make all the difference.'

'No, Eileen, no. Take my advice, and say nothing.'

There was a crusading gleam in Eileen's eye. 'You don't want him to leave the priesthood, do you?'

Dolores smiled. 'Now why would I want that?'

'Well, then.'

'Think, Eileen.' Hastily she played her trump card. 'Stephen won't thank you for talking to Dan Mulvey. He told you in confidence, remember.'

'But if it was for his own good?'

'He won't see it that way.'

'Maybe you're right,' Eileen said slowly.

Dolores pressed home her advantage. 'You wouldn't want to lose his friendship.'

Eileen looked startled. 'I never thought of that.' She smiled at Dolores, reaching out an impulsive hand. 'What would I do without you?'

'Any time.' Dolores shrugged.

She looked at Eileen's slender fingers as they patted her own ugly hand. Give him enough rope, she told herself. *With any luck the sanctimonious bugger will throttle himself.*

'Just a flying visit, Mum.' As Stephen crossed the kitchen to kiss her cheek, it struck him that his mother was looking paler than usual, with dark shadows under her eyes. 'Everything OK?'

'I could ask you the same question.' Grainne Brown, startled in the act of putting away her purchases from the supermarket, stared at her son anxiously. 'I don't usually see you on a Thursday afternoon.'

'I'm fine, Mum. But I feel I've been neglecting you lately.' Stephen took the box of Weetabix she was holding, and put it away on a shelf. He grinned as he turned to face her. 'Thought I'd surprise you.'

'Well, it's a pleasant one. But don't bother helping me put away the stuff. I'll only have to change everything around after you've gone.' Her affectionate smile took the sting out of the reproof. 'I haven't kept cereals in that press in ten years.' She picked up a mug, poured coffee into it from a pot that had been keeping warm on an electric plate, and handed it to him. 'Life hasn't stood still since you went into the seminary, you know.'

He sat down at the table and sipped his coffee. 'Sometimes I feel I'm the train left in the siding while everyone else has moved on.'

'I know the feeling, darling,' Grainne Brown said over her shoulder as she moved around the kitchen, putting away the groceries. 'God, do I know that feeling.'

'Mum?'

'Don't mind me, darling.' Her voice was bright suddenly. 'Probably the spring weather.'

He gave a short laugh. 'It's as good an excuse as any.'

'Still counselling, are you?' Her tone was casual.

'Not tonight,' Stephen said carefully. 'I'm meeting a friend.'

'That's nice.' He heard her hesitate. 'You must get tired of dealing with all those broken marriages.'

'Sometimes I help people to stay together.' He gave a rueful sigh. 'It's not always the right solution.'

'I can imagine.' She stopped in the middle of the tiled floor, still keeping her back to him. He saw her shoulders heave slightly.

'Mum?' He got up quickly, touched her arm. 'What's wrong?'

'Stephen!' When she turned to face him, he saw tears in her eyes. 'I should have left your father years ago.'

He looked at her uncomfortably. 'You had your reasons, Mum.'

She nodded. 'But were they the right ones? Even more important, were they the real reasons?' She pushed her hair back from her face with a weary gesture. 'Have I been deceiving myself all these years?' It was the first time he'd heard her talk like that.

'I'll get you a coffee, Mum.' When she was seated at the table, a steaming mug in her hands, Stephen drank his own, leaning against a worktop. 'It sounds like you've been doing a bit of soul-searching.' His voice was tentative. 'What's brought this on?'

His mother sighed. 'I'll be sixty next year.' She gave him a bleak look. 'I think I've wasted my life.'

'No, Mum! You've reared a family, run a home, been a good wife . . . '

'Been a fool, you mean?' He heard the bitterness in her voice.

'Never that.' Stephen was distressed. 'Mum, you're a wonderful person. Sixty isn't old. There's so much you can do.'

'Lose a bit of weight, colour the grey in my hair?' Her mouth twisted wryly. 'Play your father at his own game?'

He said nothing, feeling suddenly helpless.

'I should have taken my chance when I had it.' She sighed, stirring her coffee aimlessly. 'But I was stupid. And now that he's going to retire . . .'

'That's just talk,' Stephen said quickly. 'He's only sixty-two.'

'This year or in three years' time – what's the difference?' The shadows under her eyes grew deeper. 'The two us rattling around this big house . . .'

A thought occurred to him. 'What did you mean, "When you had the chance"?'

She met his eye, then looked away. 'I met someone five years ago. He was in the same situation as myself – he hadn't had a proper marriage for years. He asked me to go away with him, make a fresh start. But . . .'

'I know.' Stephen sighed. 'Gillian was still at college, you couldn't leave your home, marriage is for life . . .'

She bit her lip. 'I think pride had a lot to do with it.'

'That's understandable. Nobody likes to admit they've made a mistake.'

'And I had your father's family to think of, too. Your uncles and aunts are very upright people.'

'You've always got on well with them,' Stephen said. 'They'd have understood.'

'Think so?' Her bitter smile was back. 'To find out the kind of man their precious Henry was? It would have killed them.'

'You wouldn't have had to tell them.'

His mother sighed. 'Then I'd have been the villain of the piece.'

'Oh, Mum.' He stared at her in dismay. 'You've always placed too much importance on what other people think.'

'I know that now.' He saw her eyes fill with tears. 'I've made a lot of mistakes.'

'Did you love him? This man?' His voice was gentle.

She nodded. 'He was a truly good person. And I think he loved me.'

'What a shame,' Stephen said. A thought struck him. 'Is he . . . still around?'

She shook her head. 'Five years is a long time. He found someone else.'

'I'm sorry, Mum.'

'I don't blame him. Life is so short.' She wiped her eyes with a tissue and gave a tremulous smile. 'You have to seize your opportunity when it comes. I realise that now.'

Stephen looked at her intently. 'Are you saying that if you had the decision to make again, it would be different?' Suddenly her answer was important to him.

'Yes.' His mother gave a long, trembling sigh. 'Oh yes.' She shook her head sadly. 'Too late now, though.' She sat up straighter and made a visible effort to compose herself. 'But I haven't asked you how you are, Stephen.' She looked closely at him. 'Was there some reason for your visit today?'

I came home looking for solace, he thought. *And*

found myself being asked for it instead. He smiled at the irony of it. But perhaps it wasn't too late. After what his mother had told him, perhaps she'd have more understanding for his own plight. He glanced at her hopefully.

'Actually, Mum, there was something . . . '

Suddenly, the telephone on the wall behind him shrilled through the room.

'I'll take it in the hall.' His mother ran out of the kitchen as if glad of the excuse to escape, leaving Stephen to pace the tiled floor while he tried to plan what he was going to say when she came back. But the telephone had shattered the intimacy of the moment. When his mother returned to the kitchen, her voice carried the sociability she had worn for the person who'd been at the other end of the line. 'Someone from the altar society.' She glanced out the window overlooking the back garden. 'The daffodils are holding up well.'

Stephen hid his impatience. 'Do you still do the flowers for the church?'

She nodded. 'We're planning a special arrangement for Easter. Of course, there are some beautiful gardens around here. And people are generous. It must be more difficult in city parishes.'

'Mum, about what you were saying – '

'It was a relief to get it off my chest.' She gave him a grateful smile. 'Do you know, Stephen, apart from my faith in the goodness of God, the only thing that has kept me going the past few years has been your example.'

Stephen was startled. 'I haven't done anything.'

'Oh, but you have.' Her voice was earnest. 'Now, I have to admit, I wasn't all that happy when you chose the diocesan clergy. Call me a snob if you will, but with your brains and ability, I felt you should have followed in your Uncle Jimmy's footsteps and joined the Order.'

He grinned ruefully. 'I gathered that at the time.'

'And then I had a few doubts over that business with Barbara.' His mother pursed her lips. 'It made me wonder if you were cut out to be a priest.'

'I was just a kid.'

'But I was proved wrong very quickly.' Her eyes grew suddenly bright. 'You're a wonderful priest, Stephen.'

'Oh, Mum, don't start crying again.'

He saw the pride in her face. 'It will be in a good cause this time.' As she wiped her eyes, she said, 'I don't think you'll find many with your commitment.'

Stephen said uneasily, 'I'm just another flawed human being, Mum.'

'None of us is perfect, darling.' She gave him a fond look. 'But I sometimes think that in an uncertain world, you are the only one who is steadfast.'

He sighed. 'Does that mean you're going to put up with Dad for another thirty years?'

'I'll have to think about that.' He saw her lips tighten. 'You've been a great help, but I've talked about it enough for one day.' There was a note of finality in her voice. He saw her expression soften as she turned towards him. 'Now, was there some problem of yours you wanted to talk about?'

Stephen sighed again. 'Forget it, Mum. It wasn't important. Look, I've got to go. There's someone I have to meet.'

'I'm sorry I'm late, Cathy.' She felt the cool April night air against her face as Stephen stepped into the hallway. 'The traffic . . . '

'I'm glad you could come.' That was the under-statement of the year, Cathy thought. She still felt shaken from her encounter with Jack. The only thing that had kept her going all day had been the prospect of seeing Stephen that night. When they went into the living room, she turned impulsively towards him and felt disappointed when he took a step backwards. 'Don't worry, Liz is out.' She sat down on the sofa and grinned at him. 'I think there's a new man on the scene.'

'Did he hurt you?' Stephen said, his voice harsh.

'No. Jack's a slimy toad. But he wasn't violent. I got a fright, though.' When she saw his look of concern, she thought he would sit down beside her. Again she was disappointed, when he took a seat some distance away. Any further and he'd be out in the hall, she thought. 'Stephen.' She looked hesitantly at him. 'Maybe it wasn't such a good idea to ring you last night.'

'You were upset.' His face still showed his concern as he leaned forward in his chair. 'Cathy, believe me, I'd have come if I could.'

'I understood that.' She felt a sudden longing to feel his arms around her. 'But now you're here, you're behaving as if I had an infectious disease.'

'It's myself I can't trust,' he said in a low voice. 'And I can't pretend the other night didn't happen.'

'Me neither.' She tried to push away the memory, but felt a thrill of excitement instead. 'It was only a kiss, Stephen . . . '

'But it must never happen again.'

'I know that,' she said quickly.

'I shouldn't even be here.' He gave her a distracted look. 'This is how things start, Cathy. It happened to a priest I worked with. She was a widow. It was just friendship at first. But now she's expecting his child.'

'Oh, God!' Cathy's face went hot as she listened to the story Stephen told her. When he'd finished, she asked, 'What are they going to do?'

His face looked haggard suddenly. 'He's leaving the priesthood to marry her.'

'I can see you're upset about it,' Cathy said. 'But at least he's not a hypocrite, like Fergal, who wanted the best of both worlds.'

Stephen shrugged, saying nothing.

She gave him a quick glance. 'But that's not in your game plan, is it?'

'No.' His voice was stiff. 'I was very happy with my life till you came into it.'

Her eyes stung with sudden tears. 'So this is my fault?'

'I didn't mean that.' She saw his face change. 'If anyone's to blame, it's me.'

'How do you make that out?' Suddenly she recalled what Jack had said about Stephen and his attitude towards women. 'Because I'm a slut and can't help myself?' She felt her anger rise. 'You, on the other hand, are a man of God . . .'

She saw his face whiten. 'Don't do this to me.' The words seemed to be torn from him. 'Cathy, please!' He jumped up and began pacing the room.

She watched him resentfully. 'What do you think it's doing to me?'

He stopped pacing and glanced at her in surprise. 'I don't regard you as a slut. How could you even think that?' His face softened. 'Is that why you're angry with me?'

'No,' Cathy said. 'It's because I think you resent your feelings for me.'

'In a way, I do.' He looked helplessly at her. 'I haven't had a minute's peace since the day we met.'

Something melted inside her. 'When you look like that, I want to put my arms around you. Oh God, I'm sorry,' she said quickly. 'I shouldn't have said that.'

'And I shouldn't be listening.' He sat down at the other end of the sofa and gave her another helpless look. 'Cathy, what am I going to do about you?'

His eyes were a lighter grey than Jack's, she thought. But there was nothing cold about them. *If I let him kiss me, I'm lost.* She tried to look away.

'Maybe you'd better go.'

His eyes held hers. 'You feel the same way,' he said. 'I know you do.'

She hesitated. 'Would it make any difference if I did?'

A shadow crossed his face. 'I . . . can't answer that just now.'

Disappointment cut through her. 'I think you already have.'

'You don't understand.' He gave her a pleading look. 'I need time, Cathy.'

'Take all the time you want,' she said bitterly. 'Take forever, for all I care.' She turned her head away. 'Go home, Stephen.'

'But we need to talk. Cathy, please!'

The tears weren't far off, but she held them at bay. 'Come back when you find that answer.'

After he'd gone, she wandered the apartment distractedly.

It was probably a mistake. And I'll never see him again.

Listen, there was no future for us, anyway.

You did the right thing, Cathy.

But the knowledge of that brought no comfort.

Liz opened her eyes and leaned over to squint at the glowing numerals on the bedside clock . 'Nine o'clock.' She gave a gasp of disbelief. 'Do you realise we've spent the last twenty-one hours together?'

She heard Jack's complacent laugh and felt his lips move over her naked back. 'Am I good, or what?'

'Time spent sleeping doesn't count,' Liz said. She pushed his hands away, switched on the bedside light and turned to see his affronted face.

'That's not a complaint, I hope?'

'When I have one, you'll be the first to know.' She leaned against the pillows, stretching herself like a contented cat. 'But you did OK, kiddo.' More than OK, she thought. And the beauty of it was that the whole thing had been so unexpected. The previous night when she'd been out for a drink with Justin and the others, the last person she'd expected to come strolling into the crowded pub near closing time had been Jack. Although he knew most of the places where she and her friends hung out, he'd never come in search of her before.

'You're looking very beautiful, Liz.' He'd bought her another vodka, a brandy for himself. Although his hands were steady, there was a hard glitter in his eyes that made her realise it wasn't his first drink of the night. Under cover of the noisy discussions eddying around them, he put a hand on her knee, and whispered, 'Come back to my place. Now.'

Liz pushed his hand away, looked over at Justin, who seemed engrossed in a discussion on politics with a fellow journalist, and checked that no one else was watching. 'I thought you were meeting Cathy tonight?'

'Cancelled. Had to work late.' His hand was back on her knee. 'How about it, Liz?'

'I'm with someone, Jack.'

He followed her gaze and gave a quick shrug. 'Lose him.' There was an urgency in his manner that excited her. 'I've a taxi waiting outside. Don't be long.' After he'd gone, pushing his way past a group of animated drinkers, Liz stood up and headed for the ladies' room. She noticed that Justin was still caught up in his conversation as she left the pub.

What a night it had turned out to be. While she stretched and yawned between the rumpled silk sheets on Jack's bed, she looked back, savouring the memory of their repeated lovemaking. From the moment she climbed into the taxi, he hadn't been able to keep his hands off her. Once they got to his apartment, he pounced on her with a kind of brutal ferocity that called from her the answering streak of wildness she'd always known she possessed. Neither of them got any sleep that night. It was Jack's idea next morning for both of them to call in sick to their respective offices and spend the rest of the day in bed, alternately sleeping and pleasuring each other.

'I'm hungry,' he said now. 'Ring for a pizza, Liz.' He leaned on his elbow and grinned down at her. 'While you're at it, get more wine from the fridge.'

'I can't stay another night. Cathy will be wondering where I am.'

'Let her.' His voice was abrupt. 'Hurry up, Liz.' He tweaked her nipple. 'I told you I was hungry.'

'Go easy, Jack.' She pushed his hand away and got out of bed with reluctance. Although her body felt slack and sensuous, her mind was suddenly alert. As she waited for the pizza place to answer the phone, she recalled Jack's manner in the pub the night before. She tried to remember the last time she'd seen that reckless glitter in his eyes. While she was ordering the food, her mind was worrying away at the problem. After she put down the phone, the answer came to her. Of course, it had been the time his firm had failed to get a contract they'd been tendering for, to work on an office block. He'd got pretty drunk that night, she remembered. Her face hardened.

'So what sorrows were you drowning this time?' She sat on the edge of the bed beside him and gave him a long look. 'I've a feeling it has nothing to do with work.'

'God, what a body! Voluptuous isn't the word for it!' He reached for her breasts but she shoved his hand away. Jack sighed and sat up against the pillows. 'What's your problem, Liz?'

'She wouldn't sleep with you last night, would she? So you came to me.'

He looked surprised. 'What are you on about?'

'I see it all now,' Liz said. 'That weekend you gave me the lift back. She'd turned you down the night before, hadn't she?' She rounded on him bitterly. 'Don't bother to lie.'

'That little bitch!' She saw a pulse throb beside Jack's mouth. 'I think there's something going on between her and my brother.'

'What? The priest? You're paranoid. Cathy would never . . .'

'Do you not think so?' The look of hope on his face struck Liz like a blow in the stomach. 'You think I'm reading too much into it?

'So you don't deny it,' she said savagely. 'The only reason you wanted me . . .'

Jack shook his head. 'Don't sell yourself short, Liz.' She saw he had recovered his cool. 'You know you turn me on in a big way.' He smiled, glancing down approvingly at his own body. 'Wicked Willie is never wrong.'

'You really fancy yourself.' Liz dashed back the angry tears. 'But if we're so good together, what do you want with *her?*' She frowned as she recalled something he'd told her once. 'Is she some kind of challenge?'

'Could be.' His voice was reflective. 'But it's not just that. Look, Liz, you're one of the sexiest women I've ever met.' His mouth twitched. 'I've a feeling we're going to act out a lot of fantasies together.'

'You *wish!*'

'Cathy, on the other hand . . . ' He shrugged. 'Not to put too fine a point on it, Cathy's the kind of girl you bring home to mother.'

Liz felt as if the ground had opened up beneath her. Her stomach contracted with pain. 'You were thinking of *marrying* her?'

'Did I say that?' Jack chuckled, obviously blind to her reaction. 'But I suppose I'll have to settle down some day. And you're not interested in marriage, are you, Liz.' It was a statement, not a question.

'No way!' Not after her mother's experience. But being someone's bit on the side wasn't part of her game plan either. Despite the room's warmth, a shiver ran through her.

'Better put some clothes on,' Jack said kindly. 'The pizza man will be here any minute. There's some money on the table.'

'I'm not your slave,' Liz snapped. She got back into bed, yanking the bedclothes over to her side. 'Pay him yourself.'

'OK, OK. You want me to be the slave.' He sighed in mock defeat and swung his legs out of bed onto the carpet. As he pulled on a bathrobe, he said, in a wheedling voice, 'Tell you what I'll do. I'll bring you a nice chilled glass of wine. How's that for service?'

'Do what you like,' Liz snarled. But when Jack went into the kitchen, she sat up and gazed morosely through the floor-length window at the blackness of the night sky, the brightly lit city below. Cruel, two-timing bastard. If she had any sense, she'd leave now and never come back. And hand him over to Cathy? She felt a sharp stab at the thought. *You'll have to come up with a better plan than that.*

She's my friend, she argued. I hate deceiving her like this. *You're doing her a favour, kiddo. If Jack gets his paws on her, he'll destroy her. The brother sounds more like Cathy's type. Pity he's a priest. Although, if you ask me, he's playing with fire. God, men are all the same!* As the buzzer on the front-door intercom sounded, and she saw Jack hurry to speak down it, Liz was struck by a happy thought.

Supposing it wasn't just paranoia on his part, and there was really something going on between the other pair, wouldn't it be the neatest solution all round? Not only would it make things right between Cathy and herself, it would be a perfect way for Liz to get even with Jack, while at the same time cementing her hold on him.

First chance she got, she told herself, she and Cathy were going to have a little heart-to-heart.

'So you think you're in love with him?' Liz cloaked her sense of triumph with an understanding smile. 'Don't look so shocked, Cathy. OK, I know he's a priest. But he's a man, after all. And you're one sexy woman.'

'You've changed your tune.' She saw the surprise on Cathy's face.

'Well, I was afraid this would happen,' she said smoothly. 'But now that it has, what's the point in fighting it? And from what you say, he feels the same way. Tell me, have you . . . ' – she rolled her eyes expressively – 'done the wild thing yet?'

'Liz, you're impossible.' But she saw that Cathy wasn't as shocked as she pretended to be. 'You know that's out of the question.'

'Why?' Hoping to shock her into telling her more, Liz was deliberately crude. 'Nothing wrong with his tackle, is there? They don't actually make eunuchs of themselves, do they?'

She was rewarded when she saw the blush spread over her friend's face.

'Aha!'

Cathy gave her a defensive look. 'We kissed, that's all.'

Liz refused to be taken in. 'Sounds like it was one hell of a kiss.'

'Oh, Liz.' Cathy's face crumpled suddenly. 'If only he wasn't a priest . . . '

'But what about Jack?' She feigned surprise. 'I thought you and he were seeing one another.'

Cathy shook her head. 'That was over before it began.'

Yes! Liz hid her joy. 'Poor Jack. I hope he didn't take it too hard.'

'I wouldn't waste too much pity on him,' Cathy said crisply. 'Jack's not all he seems.'

'And you're not just a pretty face,' Liz said in surprise. 'It didn't take you long to find out.' *Shit! Why did I say that?* 'Not that I know anything about the guy, of course.' Her eyes slid away from Cathy's. 'Just a feeling I had.'

Cathy bit her lip. 'I wish my instincts were as good as yours, Liz.'

'Years of experience, kiddo.' She kept her voice airy. 'Tell us, what's going to happen with Stephen?'

'I don't know.' Cathy gave her a quick look. 'You won't say anything about this, will you?'

'Of course not.'

'You see, things are a bit complicated. There's this other priest from Stephen's parish who's thinking of leaving . . . '

'Go on,' Liz said. Although she kept her face impassive, the hairs at the back of her neck had begun to tingle: a sure sign she was about to hear something important. Keeping all her journalistic instincts to the fore, she listened intently to what Cathy had to say. As the tale unfolded, she could almost read the headlines: DUBLIN PRIEST'S LOVE NEST IN SLEEPY COUNTRY TOWN. PREGNANT

WIDOW'S SHAME. It wasn't as juicy as some of the earlier clerical scandals, but handled properly it would have made a good story. No, a great story. A pity she couldn't use it. When Cathy finished speaking, Liz met her eye reassuringly. 'Don't worry, kiddo, my lips are sealed. Anyway, it's not so long since we ran an article on sexuality and the church, interviewing women who'd had affairs with priests. Features wouldn't be interested.'

But the news editor might. This could be the break she'd been waiting for. It'd be a shame to waste it. Liz tussled briefly with her conscience. *I can't break a confidence, can I?*

Use your common sense, she told herself. *If you don't write the story, it's only a matter of time until someone else does.*

She hid her excitement, her brain working rapidly. If she kept Cathy's name out of it and made sure it couldn't be traced back to her, it might be possible. She'd sleep on it over the weekend, she decided. Check it out first thing on Monday morning.

'It's not a lot to go on, Liz.' The news editor frowned, tapping the sheet of paper in front of him with an impatient finger. 'Most of this is hearsay. And you don't even have the widow's name or the town she lives in.'

'That should be easy enough.' She gave him a confident look. 'How many golf clubs are there that distance from Dublin? Besides, I know his first name and where his parish is. Look, Bill, it isn't just hearsay.

My source is impeccable. This is going to break soon and we're the first with it. But I need permission to work on the story. I don't want someone else given it.'

'It'd be worth more if he was a bishop,' Bill said. But she could see he was interested. 'Look, I know you've been trying for a staff job, Liz. And I think you have a nose for news. It's up to the editor, of course, and I can't make any promises, but if this story is as good as you say . . . ' His eyes narrowed. 'You'd better level with me, Liz. My instincts tell me you're holding something back. Who's your impeccable source? You don't have to give me his name, but unless it's someone close to the lovers, I don't want to know.'

Screw him and his instincts. Liz stared back at him. 'Strictly between ourselves?'

'Yeah, yeah,' Bill said impatiently.

Liz sighed. No help for it but to come clean. 'How about a priest in the same parish? Is that close enough for you?' It was gratifying to see his reaction. If his jaw had dropped any lower, she told herself, he'd have cracked it off the desk. He sat up and looked at her with new respect.

'And he told you?'

'Get real, I'm a journalist. No, it was a friend of mine. She told me.'

'He must trust her a lot.'

She could see his mind working overtime, examining all the possibilities. 'Is she a young woman, this friend of yours?' His voice sharpened. 'What's their relationship, exactly?'

Shit. She stared at him in dismay. *Cathy'll never forgive me.*

His eyes were like slits, cutting into hers. 'Come on, Liz. Let the dog see the rabbit.'

'They're just friends . . .'

Bill smiled, showing strong, yellow teeth.

Shit! Too late for caution, she thought. *Might as well be hung for a sheep as for a lamb.* 'Actually, I think it's a bit more than that . . .'

Bill smiled again. 'Two for the price of one. *Now* we have a story.'

SEVENTEEN

'I'm afraid you'll have to contact the parish priest,' Mary Grimes said. 'I can't give out that information.' She glanced over at Stephen after she put down the phone. 'That's the second enquiry I've had this morning about Father Hennessy. It's hard to get through to some of them that he isn't coming back.'

'I hear that all the time,' Stephen said. 'A lot of people were fond of Brendan.'

'That's true. But that last call didn't sound like a parishioner. She was very persistent.' Mary's smooth young forehead creased thoughtfully. 'Do you know, I could almost swear that was the same woman who rang yesterday. But then, you get so many calls . . . '

'True,' he said absently. 'If you've nothing else for me to sign, I'll be on my way.' He sighed as he got up from the table. 'This is supposed to be my day off. I'll be lucky if I get to the gym before lunch.'

'It will be easier once the new curate, Father O'Donohue, gets here.' Mary's face brightened. 'According to Father Mulvey, this guy is a real worker. His parish priest was in hospital last year and, by all accounts, he ran the parish single-handed for a couple of months.'

'Probably coming here for a rest,' Stephen said gloomily.

'Cheer up.' She gave him a sympathetic look. 'Nothing can be that bad. You miss Brendan, don't you?'

'Among other things.' But the one Stephen was missing was Cathy. It was almost a week since the night he'd gone to her apartment, and there had been no contact between them since. Despite this, she was constantly in his thoughts. Day or night, he found himself longing for her company, aching to talk to her, to touch her. But she had told him not to come back until he'd reached some kind of decision, and this he'd been unable to do. He gave an inward sigh and looked up to find Mary watching him.

'Brendan hasn't gone to another parish, has he, Stephen?'

He shrugged uncomfortably. 'I can't really say . . .'

Her gaze didn't leave his. 'There's a rumour going around that he's given up the priesthood.'

'People will say anything, Mary.' He gave an offhand laugh. 'You wouldn't need to pay any attention to it.'

'They're even saying – 'she hesitated ' – that he's getting married.'

'What'll they think of next?' He shook his head and tried to smile. 'Better not tell the parish priest that. He'll have a coronary.'

He could see Mary wasn't taken in by his feeble attempt at humour. She darted a quick glance at him. 'I hope it's true,' she said.

He stared at her in surprise, saying nothing.

'Father Brendan's a nice man. He deserves a bit of happiness.' Although her face went pink, her voice had a note of defiance in it. 'I don't care what anyone says, I think priests should be allowed to marry.' She glanced at the diamond sparkling on the third finger of her left hand. 'We all need someone. It's not natural to expect people to do without love. Even my mother agrees – '

'That we're a bunch of oddballs?' Stephen kept his tone mildly humorous. Although she'd jabbed at an exposed nerve, he was determined not to let it show. 'Think we need certifying?'

'God, no! That isn't what I meant.' Mary's face grew redder still. But she stood her ground, her voice earnest. 'It's just that some people feel that if priests were allowed to marry, there . . . there wouldn't be all this messing around with children and things like that.'

'It's not that simple, Mary.' He felt his own face grow hot and looked at her uncomfortably. 'Don't tar us all with the same brush.'

She threw him a startled glance. 'God, Stephen . . . I mean Father . . . I wasn't implying . . . '

'It's OK.' A thought struck him. 'Tell me, do many people think the way you do?'

Mary's face was crimson by now. She shook her head, avoiding his eye. 'I think I've said too much . . . '

Or not enough, Stephen thought. He'd have liked to question her further but realised it would only increase her embarrassment and achieve nothing. 'You're entitled to an opinion, Mary.' As he turned to go, he said casually over his shoulder, 'Don't pass on that rumour, like a good girl.' Closing the stable door after the horse has bolted, he thought. But what else could he do?

'Father Stephen.' Mary's voice sounded subdued behind him. 'Do you think I should say anything to the parish priest about the phone calls?'

'And put the poor man's blood pressure up?' He shook his head. 'I think there's been enough conjecture, don't you?'

'Whatever you say.' He heard the relief in her voice. 'It was probably nothing, anyway.'

Outside in the churchyard, as he reached his car, he saw Sister Eileen getting out of hers a few yards away. Spotting him, she waved animatedly. Bad timing. If he'd left a couple of minutes earlier, he'd have missed her. Still shaken after the conversation with Mary, he groaned inwardly. The last thing he needed was another of Eileen's inquisitions. Ever since that day last week when he'd told her about Cathy, he'd had the feeling that the nun was hounding him, bumping into him everywhere he went, urging him to talk about his feelings and suggesting joint prayer sessions every chance she got. What a mistake it had been to tell her anything! As he returned the wave, jumping quickly into the car and slamming the door shut, he hoped that she'd take the hint and leave him alone. But no such luck. He straightened up in his seat and saw her tall figure approaching the car with that long, purposeful stride of hers, an eager expression on her face. Feeling trapped, Stephen sighed and rolled down the window.

'I'm running late, Eileen.' He smiled to soften his words. 'Something important?'

She looked slightly taken aback. 'I just wanted to

know how you were.'

'Fine, thanks.' His hands trembled as he inserted the key into the ignition. His foot jerked on the accelerator. 'And you?' Ready for flight, he allowed his words to be lost in the sudden roar of the engine.

Sister Eileen rested her hand on the window, staying his progress, and gave him a searching look. 'Have you thought any more about that . . . problem?'

Reluctantly, he took his foot from the accelerator. As he met her intent gaze, he got the trapped feeling again. 'Look, I haven't decided anything yet.'

'You have to be strong.' For all her compassion, there was a steely note to her voice that told him she was in no doubt as to what his decision should be. She reached her hand in the open window and patted his arm, her dark eyes holding his. 'I'm praying to the Holy Spirit to direct your actions, Stephen.'

Why wasn't He around last week warning me to keep my big mouth shut? Conscious of her hand resting on his sleeve, he had a picture of those long, slender fingers deftly gathering in the strings of a puppet. The image disturbed him. He looked at her uneasily. 'That's very kind of you, Eileen.'

She took her hand away and gave him an encouraging smile. 'You don't have to go through this alone, Stephen.'

'Thanks.' He put the car into first gear, glanced pointedly in his rear-view mirror and waited a moment before letting out the clutch. 'See you around.'

'Any time, Stephen.' She stepped back, a baffled look

on her face. 'Remember, whenever you want to talk . . .'

'Thanks, Eileen. You're a pal.' As he drove too fast across the churchyard, he had an overwhelming sense of release. But at the same time, he was puzzled. He'd never felt that way with Eileen before. He shook his head when he recalled the image of the puppet master his mind had conjured up. People were strange.

Stephen had changed. Sister Eileen stared thoughtfully after the green Nissan until it disappeared from view around the corner of the church. It was difficult to put a finger on how he had changed. She didn't think he was deliberately avoiding her, but ever since that morning in his kitchen, she'd sensed a withdrawal in his manner, a lack of warmth. At first she'd put it down to embarrassment at having broken down in front of her, but he'd had plenty of time to get over that. No, this was something deeper, she decided. Could it be guilt? Was he still seeing that girl, and didn't want to admit it? It would explain his reluctance to meet her eye sometimes. As she was pondering this, the sacristy door opened and she saw the portly figure of the parish priest emerge, followed by another black-suited cleric.

'Sister Eileen!' Father Mulvey called to her peremptorily. 'Come and meet the latest addition to the parish team, Father O'Donohue,' the parish priest said, relishing every syllable. 'A Kerryman like myself.'

The thought struck Eileen that their county of birth was probably the only thing the two men had in common. Unlike the hearty, red-faced parish priest,

Father O'Donohue was a spare, grey-haired man with thin, ascetic features, and a gentle, yet decided manner. Every inch a priest, she thought approvingly. Even after a few minutes of conversation, she could tell he was completely dedicated to his calling. The kind of priest Stephen could be in a few years' time, once he put the present foolishness behind him. Which, of course, with God's help he would. She fought down a pang of unease and tried to give her attention to what the new priest was saying.

'Moriarty's another good Kerry name.' He looked at her enquiringly.

'Her grandfather came from Killarney,' the parish priest cut in, before she could answer. 'She's a Kerry girl at heart.' He smiled at her benignly. 'Isn't that right, Sister Eileen?'

Although she was proud of her Tipperary background, Eileen nodded sweetly. She knew better than to disagree with the parish priest in public. It just wasn't worth the aggravation. Even Stephen had reluctantly come to accept that fact. Stephen! Her smile faded. She felt a pang of anxiety every time she thought of him. Maybe God's help wasn't going to be enough to resolve his problem. Something had to be done. But what?

'You'll find I run a tight ship,' she heard the parish priest say to the new curate. 'But if you pull your weight, we'll have no trouble.' He gave an approving smirk as he glanced at Sister Eileen. 'This lady here is a valued member of our little team.' As she gazed back at him, an idea came to her. Although Dolores had warned her not to interfere, there could be no harm, surely, in looking for guidance. In a general kind of way, that is. Father Mulvey was in unusually good form this morning. It might be the right time to approach him. As the two men were about to turn away, she quickly made up her mind, putting out a hand to detain the parish priest.

'Can I have a word with you later, Father?'

'Well, of course, my dear.' He glanced at his watch. 'I'll just finish up the tour with Father O'Donohue.' He gave her a jovial nod. 'See you in the parochial house in half an hour.'

'Nice to see a real coal fire.' Now that she was there, Eileen found herself casting around for something to say. 'Although it's a lovely day outside.'

'It can never be too warm for me.' Father Mulvey rubbed his hands vigorously. 'I'm a martyr to bad circulation.' As he sipped his tea from a china cup, he cocked a bushy eyebrow. 'Now, what was it you wanted?'

Eileen hesitated, thinking again of Dolores.

'It's just something that came up in a recent discussion,' she said carefully. 'Is it ever lawful to betray a confidence?'

Father Mulvey frowned. 'Can you be more specific, Eileen? I haven't much time for hypotheses.'

'What I mean is, if someone swore you to secrecy about something but you thought it was for their own good to tell someone else.' She found herself stumbling over the sentences. Why was it so hard, she wondered.

The parish priest seemed to be having equal difficulty. He drew his untidy grey brows together and sat, lost in thought. Eileen studied his face as she waited. The whites of Father Mulvey's eyes were slightly bloodshot, she noticed, and the merciless spring sunlight showed up a threadwork of veins on his fiery cheeks. Eileen was surprised. As a publican's daughter, she knew enough to read the signs of the seasoned spirit drinker, but she'd always assumed that the bottle of whiskey and glasses that stood on a tray on the small sideboard were there for visitors. A quick glance at the bottle revealed it to be about a third full. Well, who'd have thought? But what was wrong with him taking a drink, anyway? The poor man had to have something to while away his evenings. Better than entertaining women, she thought. As she glanced back at him enquiringly, his eye met hers.

'You're not talking about professional confidentiality, are you, Eileen?'

'No, Father.' She hid her impatience. Had the drink addled his brain? 'It's more a matter of conscience.'

'Ah, I see.' His face cleared, then grew grave. 'Now, Eileen, girl, if your friend is engaged in wrongdoing of some kind, you couldn't keep quiet about it. You know that.' A shocked note came into his voice. 'It would be your duty to tell.'

Put like that, what was she waiting for? But still she hesitated. 'You'll lose a friend,' Dolores had said. But could her advice be relied on? She didn't even like

Stephen, and made no secret of the fact that she hadn't much time for people from what she called privileged backgrounds, even if she was willing to make an exception in Eileen's case. If Dolores was out in the Third World, Sister Eileen told herself, she'd be an exponent of liberation theology, supporting revolutions, denouncing the wealthy. She wouldn't lift a finger to prevent Stephen from leaving the priesthood. She didn't care enough. Eileen was the only one who did. And it was up to Eileen to save him from himself, and from the wiles of that Cathy creature, who was far too attractive for her own good. Stifling her doubts, she made up her mind.

'I want to prevent wrongdoing, Father. Before it's too late.'

'Gotcha!' Liz grinned to herself in triumph as she hurried down the steps of the clubhouse, breaking into a trot to reach the battered Toyota parked carelessly on the tarmac in front of a sign that read 'Members Only'. She had her story, she thought excitedly. And not just the usual counterfeit kind you saw in a lot of papers, promising more than it delivered, written with one eye on the libel laws and based on rumour and studied innuendo. No, this story was 100 per cent solid, straight from the horse's mouth. Or rather, the mare's. Before starting up the Toyota's noisy engine, she hugged herself in glee at the thought of the interview she'd just come from. *Am I lucky, or what?* In her most optimistic dreams, it had never occurred to her that when she finally ran down the right golf club, one of the waitresses serving lunch in the bar would turn out to be the woman who was carrying Brendan Hennessy's child.

It wasn't all luck, though, she reminded herself as the exit from the club grounds loomed up. It had taken nearly two days of patient enquiries, trekking up and down unmarked, tree-lined roads in an unfamiliar car, to be met with blank faces and, in one club, downright hostility from a suspicious golf steward, before her hard work had paid off. In her excitement, Liz took the turn too fast, spraying a hail of stones in the air, almost colliding with a small truck crammed with bleating sheep that had pulled in near the gateway.

'Country gobshites!' she cried out, shocked. Hauling desperately on the steering, she saw triangular sheep's faces poking out through the slats in the truck, while from the cab an equally bucolic face under a peaked cap gazed curiously at her as she shot past. What a place to park, she fumed. Luckily the road ahead of her was clear. All it would have taken was a car coming against her and the career of Liz Dennehy, ace reporter, would have come to an untimely end. Not to mention creating a lot of lamb chops in the process. Fools like that truck driver were a danger to everyone. And the old rattletrap she was driving was no help. It might be Justin's pride and joy but you'd need to be an all-in wrestler to cope with the steering, while the whole car began to shudder violently once the needle went up to seventy.

All the same, don't knock it, kiddo. Liz was a realist, after all. OK, so it was a heap of junk, but it was transport, and she couldn't have done the job without it. And considering that Justin was barely speaking to her since that night in the pub when she'd left without him, she'd been lucky to be able to borrow it. He hadn't copped on about Jack, fortunately, but he'd got into a snit because she hadn't told him she felt sick and needed to go home. 'You made me look a right eejit, Liz.' It had taken a lot of fast talking from her to soothe his offended dignity, while at the same time persuading him to lend her his car, without actually specifying what kind of assignment she needed it for. But when it came to pulling the wool over people's eyes, Liz knew she was an expert. She chuckled to herself as she recalled how she had prevailed upon Stella Gibney to agree to an exclusive interview on her relationship with the priest.

'It's going to be all over the papers, anyway,' Liz had said. 'And everyone will have their own slant.' She smiled encouragingly at the flustered woman with the streaked blonde hair who sat across the table from her in the empty dining room where she'd been laying tables for a function later that evening. Without seeming to, she rapidly made an inventory of Stella Gibney's appearance, mentally jotting down telling details like the lines of strain on the white face, the dark roots showing among the bedraggled blonde streaks, the slight bulge at the waistline of the white blouse she wore outside her short black skirt. 'This way you'll be sure that your side of it will get told,' she continued.

'I don't know.' She saw Stella hesitate, twisting a paper napkin between irresolute fingers. 'Maybe I should talk it over with – '

'There's not enough time for that.' Liz gave her a look that was nicely calculated to fall between urgency and compassion. 'You want people to know the truth, Stella, not some cover story put out by the clergy.' When she saw the wavering doubt in the slightly prominent blue eyes across the table, she knew she'd won.

You can get people to fall for anything, Liz thought, grinning to herself as the rusty old Toyota shuddered its way back to Dublin. *All you need is an air of conviction.* She'd interviewed enough gurus and con artists in the last few years to have learned that. Not that Stella Gibney had needed much persuasion. That woman had her own agenda. She'd a real thing about the clergy. Wanted everyone to know the shabby way the bishop and his representatives had treated her boyfriend. There were some beauties of quotes. Liz could see them on the printed page: 'The Inquisition is alive and well and living in Ireland.' And what about: 'Left penniless after over thirty years' devoted service to the Church'? She couldn't wait to get back to write the story and slap it on Bill's desk in the morning.

She reached the outskirts of the city and got caught up in the early-evening commuter traffic, the gearbox protesting at the constant stopping and starting. Once the paper gave her a permanent contract, she'd buy herself a decent car. Better keep Justin sweet till then. Although she was going to have to dump him as soon as her relationship with Jack was more established. But maybe not. There was no sense in putting all your eggs in one basket. It would be a way of keeping Jack on his toes. If he thought he could take you for granted, his attention might begin to stray. That's why it would never have worked out between him and Cathy. She might be the kind of girl to take home to Mother, as he'd said, but he'd never have stayed faithful to her. And Cathy had a thing about fidelity.

And not just from lovers, either. For the first time, after all the excitement of chasing the story, it occurred to Liz that her friendship with Cathy might be in danger. No. She pushed the thought away. They'd known each other too long. Through thick and thin. They were closer than sisters. *Look,* she told herself, *concentrate on getting that copy written up. That's the priority.* Once it was safely with the editor, she could put her mind to concocting a believable explanation for Cathy.

I'll find the right words, Liz thought. *I always do.*

'I won't have it!' Father Mulvey shouted. 'I simply will not tolerate this.'

The parish priest wasn't skinny enough to look like a turkeycock, Stephen thought. But his complexion had taken on the same hue as a Christmas bird's neck. He wondered what was causing this current outbreak of rage. The last occasion he'd seen Father Mulvey this worked up was when a Communion wafer had been discovered lying on the carpet under one of the kneelers in the front row of the church, most probably dropped there by some child or a feeble old person. The parish priest had put it down to the work of an Antichrist, ranting from the pulpit about blasphemers and threatening to excommunicate the offender if detected. The only effect of these fulminations had been to cause embarrassment to the priest whose Mass he'd interrupted, upset to babies and elderly people in the congregation, and an outbreak of sniggering among the few teenagers present. As Stephen recalled this, he was glad there was no one else in the parish priest's study to witness his latest eruption of bad temper.

'Take it easy, Dan,' he said soothingly. 'You don't want to burst a blood vessel.'

'It wasn't my health you were thinking of . . . ' – The older man's tone was scathing – ' . . . when you decided to take up with that floozie!'

Stephen felt the blood drain from his face. 'What did you just say?'

'Don't you play the innocent with me,' Dan Mulvey said. 'I know all about it. You and that . . . that Jezebel. How could you do it, Stephen? After all I said to you?' His words poured out in a torrent, impossible to stem. 'First Brendan, now you. Have you no shame, man? And you an ordained priest. God's anointed, consorting with loose women and – '

'Hold on a minute, Dan – '

It was very hot in the little room. A blazing fire in the middle of April, for God's sake. No wonder the old man was puce in the face. Stephen eased his collar, with its white plastic insert, away from his neck, and felt droplets of sweat against his skin. As the flow of words began to falter, he said gravely, 'These are very serious accusations you're making. You'd need to be sure of your facts.'

Father Mulvey took out a crumpled handkerchief and wiped his glistening cheeks. Although his paroxysm of rage seemed to have spent itself, his eyes were seething with anger. 'Well, are they true, or aren't they?'

'No, of course not,' Stephen said.

'So the parish sister is a liar, then.' There was a hectoring note in the older man's voice.

For a moment Stephen was bewildered. Could Dolores have been stirring up trouble for him? 'Do you mean the parish social worker?'

'No, no,' the parish priest said testily. 'I see as little of that woman as possible. These bloody feminists are the cause of all the problems in the Church. No, I'm talking about a dedicated sister who knows where her duty lies.' His voice rose sharply. 'Which is more than I can say for you.'

'You can't mean Sister Eileen.' Stephen's bewilderment grew. *No, not Eileen. She wouldn't. She couldn't have.* 'But we're friends.' He shook his head. 'She'd never betray a confidence.'

'Sometimes we have to put the greater good first,' Dan Mulvey said self-righteously. 'That poor woman had to do a lot of soul-searching.'

Stephen stared in confusion at the parish priest. He

heard the words, but his mind refused to take in their meaning. 'Eileen wouldn't . . .'

'Nevertheless.' The other man shrugged. His expression didn't soften. 'I notice you're not denying it, Stephen.'

'For God's sake, Dan.' With an effort, he found his voice. 'I haven't done anything wrong. An innocent friendship, that's all it is.' Even as he said it, he wondered just how true this was. 'Nothing happened,' he said stiffly.

For a moment the parish priest studied Stephen's face. Whatever he read there seemed to satisfy him. 'Maybe it's not too late, then.' A grudging note of conciliation crept into his voice. 'No life is free from temptation, after all. And if there's been no harm done –'

'It's not as simple as that, Dan.' The words were wrenched out of Stephen. 'Did Eileen . . .' He found himself wincing as he said the name. 'Did she also tell you I was thinking of leaving the priesthood?'

'Goddamn it, man!' Dan Mulvey frowned. 'What kind of wild talk is this? You're not the first idiot to have his head turned by a bit of fluff.'

Anger gripped Stephen. 'I'll thank you not to refer to Cathy like that.' His tone was suddenly icy. 'Despite what your . . . *informant'* – he spat out the word – 'may have told you, she is an honourable young woman deserving of respect.'

'Ho!' Fury glinted in the parish priest's bloodshot eyes. 'Don't you take that tone with me, my lad.' When Stephen stared back at him, refusing to be intimidated,

Dan Mulvey's expression changed. 'The parish is falling down around me, Stephen.' Suddenly his voice was full of self-pity. 'What will the bishop say?' As he slumped down behind his desk, his face was suddenly haggard, his eyes tired and old. 'What in God's name am I going to tell him?'

Despite his own anger, Stephen felt a twinge of pity for the older man. 'I haven't decided yet, Dan. I need time to think.'

'Thanks be to God.' The parish priest straightened up, a look of relief on his face. 'I knew you'd see sense.'

'I'm not making any promises.'

'I'll tell you what you'll do, Stephen.' The light had returned to Dan Mulvey's eyes. His bluff, hearty manner was back in place. 'Take a few days off. Go away somewhere on your own and think things over.'

'This isn't a good time, Dan,' Stephen said reluctantly. 'Have you forgotten that Monday is the start of Holy Week?'

'You're the one who should have thought of that.' The older man gave him a sardonic look. 'We should be able to manage without you till Wednesday. We have Father O'Donohue on the team now.'

'But . . . '

'Just be back in time for the Easter ceremonies, Stephen.' The parish priest waved a dismissive hand. 'For God's sake!' His voice was airy. 'Two Kerrymen should be able to run this place between them.'

If one of them does all the work, Stephen thought. But he didn't really care. Let someone else worry about that. All he wanted to do was crawl away to a safe place and tend his wounds. Right now, the parish, and the people in it, could get on without him. He felt a wave of nausea every time he thought of Sister Eileen's treachery. He knew it would take him a long time to come to terms with it, but he had more important things to think about and urgent decisions to make. As he listened to the parish priest, it struck him that, for once, the old man was talking sense. What he needed was a few days on his own to think, to pray, to consider his choices. He thought of several likely places and got to his feet.

'I'll make a few phone calls, Dan. Go this evening.'

Thursday afternoon. Coming up to finishing time, Cathy stood up from her computer and eased her cramped back and shoulders, before leaving the office to go out onto the shop floor.

'All set for tomorrow, Jason?' She glanced at the young salesman, who was stacking up cartons of software accessories in a display gondola at the end of one aisle.

Glancing up, he pushed his floppy brown hair back from his flushed face and gave her a cheerful grin. 'Just about, Cathy. Martina's going wild with the price-gun back there, doing the last of the floppies.' He chuckled as he went back to his task. 'Then it's all systems go for the big spring sale.'

'Good work.' Jason was a real dynamo, Cathy thought. Nothing was ever too much trouble for him.

Her own arms ached from opening cartons and stacking shelves, but she accepted it as part of the job. With only a small staff, at busy times everyone had to pitch in. Even Martina. Cathy smiled to herself as she noticed her assistant, down on her knees, repricing stock with grim determination. When it came to it, the older woman would lend a hand and do what was necessary, even if she grumbled at every opportunity.

We make a good team, the three of us. Going back into the office to finish up for the day, Cathy thought of what Paul Kinsella had told her earlier. The shop was doing so well, he planned to take on another assistant. And they'd all be getting a bonus at the end of the month. As she shut down her computer, she felt a glow of satisfaction.

It wasn't just the money, she told herself, putting on her jacket. She really loved her job. OK, the last few days had been tough and the pace probably wouldn't let up till the sale was over, but as her father always said, hard work never hurt anyone. Besides, there was nothing like hectic activity for keeping your mind off other things, like the dull ache in her stomach since last Thursday, and the way her heart beat faster every time the telephone rang.

Forget Stephen, she told herself firmly. *It wasn't meant to be. Pick up a nice, slushy video, send out for a pizza, and put your feet up for the night.* Despite this appealing prospect, her spirits were low as she walked home. When she reached the apartment, she was delighted to find Liz there before her.

'Hello, stranger.' Cathy sank wearily down on the living-room couch and kicked off her shoes. 'Did you get that story you've been chasing all week?'

The other woman said nothing for a moment, but sat staring fixedly at her, a solemn expression in her dark eyes.

She felt her heart give a little jump. 'Is anything wrong?'

'Cathy,' Liz said gravely, 'you are looking at someone who's just been offered a permanent contract.'

'But that's wonderful!' Forgetting her tiredness, Cathy jumped up to embrace her friend. 'I'm so happy for you.' She waltzed Liz around the room, laughing with excitement. 'That's the best news I've heard all week. Sit down and give me all the details.'

'Not much to tell.' Liz shrugged. 'Keep knocking hard enough and a door will open eventually.'

'You're very cool about it.' Cathy was puzzled. 'If it was me, I'd be dancing on the ceiling!'

'I'm a bit tired, kiddo.' Liz's gaze slid away from hers. 'Had to cover a lot of miles. This story I've been working on . . .'

'How did it go?' Her interest was aroused. 'Did you get what you wanted?'

'It went well,' Liz said. 'It'll be in tomorrow's paper. Front page.'

'Wow!' Cathy was impressed. 'A double celebration. Want to go out later for a drink?'

'I can't. I'm meeting someone.' Liz looked at her watch. 'Time I got ready.'

'Not Mystery Man again?' Cathy joked. There was no answering smile from Liz. The solemn expression was back in her eyes. 'Something's wrong, isn't it?'

'Well . . .' Liz said.

'Uh-oh!' Cathy studied her friend's face. 'Don't tell me he's married.'

'That's not it.' She saw Liz's mouth tremble. 'Cathy, about this story in tomorrow's paper. There's something I need to tell you.'

'How could you?' Liz saw shock, disbelief and horror chase in quick succession across Cathy's face. 'Everything I told you about Stephen's friend is going to be in the newspaper? I can't believe you'd do such a thing!'

'Cathy, it's not my fault, I keep telling you. The editor had the story already . . .'

'But how?'

Liz shrugged. 'You know what these places are for gossip.' She injected a note of persuasion into her voice. 'Cathy, the woman was out to *there* – you'd have to be half blind not to know she was pregnant. Telling people he was her lodger,' she sneered. 'As if anyone believed that.'

She saw tears in Cathy's eyes. 'But why you?'

'It's my job. I can't turn down an assignment. You know that. Look, Cathy, I'd no choice.' Liz had repeated this so often she was beginning to believe it herself. 'If I didn't cover the story, someone else would.'

'Liz, that was the excuse given by the pilot who dropped the first atomic bomb. He could have refused, but he didn't.'

Trust her to take the moral high ground. 'I'd have said no, if I thought it would do any good. But my chances of being made permanent would have been zilch.'

She saw the shock in Cathy's eyes. 'You sold Brendan's story in exchange for your contract?'

'What do you take me for?' Liz was indignant. 'I don't even know the man. At first I wasn't even sure if it was the same one you told me about. Look, kiddo.' She lowered her voice in an effort to be persuasive. 'I can understand you being angry, but you've got the wrong person.'

'Well, maybe . . . ' Cathy looked doubtful. 'But I still think you shouldn't have.'

'That's where you're wrong, kiddo.' Liz had a sudden inspiration. 'Just think. If someone else wrote the story, God knows what they'd have dug up. There's no way I could have kept your name out of it.' She watched Cathy intently. 'Or Stephen's.'

'Oh my God!' Cathy sat up straight, a look of horror on her face. 'You didn't tell them about us?'

'You've nothing to worry about,.' Liz said soothingly. 'And there's only a vague reference to Stephen.' *They should be thanking me,* she thought. 'But I felt it was better to warn you.'

Cathy's lips tightened. 'It's a bit late for that.' She got up from the couch and bent to put on her shoes. When she straightened up, a slight frown creased her forehead. 'Something puzzles me.' Her voice was calm as she looked at Liz. 'Are you the same person I've lived with for the last four years? Because I just can't tell any more.'

'Come on, Cathy.' Liz tried to laugh. 'Would I lie to you?'

To her dismay, Cathy walked out of the room without answering.

'Are you going away?' she asked when she saw the packed bag on the floor of the tiny hallway.

'Just for a few days,' Stephen said. 'Cathy, what are you doing here?'

'We need to talk.' She couldn't keep the urgency from her voice. 'Are you alone?' When he nodded, she gave a sigh of relief. 'Hang on a moment. I'll just pay off the taxi.'

As she hurried breathlessly into the kitchen, she saw a look of concern on his face. 'Has something happened?' he asked.

She hesitated, not sure of where to begin. She glanced at a pot that was bubbling on the gas cooker 'That smells good,' she said.

'Spaghetti carbonara. I was just about to . . . ' He glanced distractedly around him, grabbing up a wooden spoon. 'Have you eaten?'

'No. But don't mind me.'

'I always make too much,' Stephen said easily. He drained the pasta and tossed it back, steaming, into the saucepan. 'There are more plates in that cupboard and cutlery in the drawer by the sink.' He turned to give her a quizzical grin. 'I'd have done garlic bread if I'd known you were coming.'

She bit her lip. 'Stephen, I – '

'Look.' His voice was gentle. 'Let me get this on the table. Then we'll talk.'

It was a relief to be able to sit down and catch her breath. It was her first time in Stephen's kitchen, and her gaze took in the shabby floor covering, the cheap wooden furniture, the cracked worktops. Not the kitchen of one's dreams, she thought. Yet at that moment, there was nowhere else she wanted to be. Despite the droplets of condensation that ran down the wall behind the gas cooker, and the darkening window fogged with steam, the room seemed to her to be perfect, a haven of security. But even more comforting was the sight of Stephen's broad shoulders and his dark head bent over the worktop. Watching his intent face as he deftly broke eggs and stirred them into the spaghetti, adding herbs and seasoning in an almost ritualistic way, it struck her that she would always feel safe in any room where he was present.

'Not as good as Luigi's.' His face was apologetic as he put the steaming plates down on the table. 'And we don't have any wine.'

'This is every bit as delicious as the pasta we had in the Italian restaurant.' As they began eating, she smiled at the memory of their first meal together. 'That was a great night, Stephen.'

'Until Jack barged in.' His face was rueful.

'I can't think what I saw in him,' Cathy said. A

thought struck her and she glanced at him in alarm. 'There's no danger he might show up here?'

Stephen's face had darkened at the mention of his brother, but he gave her a reassuring smile. 'We're safe enough. Jack doesn't believe in slumming. Of course, if he thought you were here . . .'

She shook her head. 'No, that's definitely over. Even he must know that.'

'So he's not the reason you came?' He looked puzzled. 'I thought maybe he'd done something else to upset you.'

'He hasn't been in contact since.' She put down her fork and gave him a quick glance. 'Maybe you should finish your meal first.'

'That bad, is it?' He studied her face for a moment. 'Come on, you can tell me.'

'This is harder than I thought it would be.' In her frantic haste to rush over to his house and warn him, it hadn't occurred to her until now to consider the effect her news might have. 'Stephen, something's happened . . .' Her mouth went dry and she had to take a drink of water before she could go on. 'I'm afraid you'll never forgive me for it.'

'Try me.' He gave her a smile that caused Cathy's heart to turn over.

'I don't deserve your trust.' She gripped the edge of the table to keep her hands from trembling. Forced herself to meet his gaze. 'I'm afraid I betrayed your confidence.'

'It must be something in the air,' Stephen said wryly.

He gave a resigned shrug. 'My parish priest has already heard about us. Who did you tell?'

'Only the whole country,' Cathy said falteringly. 'Liz has an article in tomorrow's paper. It's not just about you and me.'

His face went white. 'Brendan?'

She nodded, felt her voice choke on a sob. 'She even knows about Stella's baby. And it's all my fault.'

'Cathy.' Stephen's gaze met hers across the table. He reached out and took one of her hands in a warm clasp. 'Pull yourself together,' he said quietly. 'And start at the beginning.'

'It's not your fault.' His face was grave in the weak light cast by the single bulb dangling from the ceiling. While Cathy had been speaking, the garden outside the kitchen window had grown dark. They were drinking coffee at this stage, their meal congealing, forgotten, on their plates. 'If anyone broke confidence, it was me. If I hadn't told you about Brendan in the first place . . .'

'It was one thing to tell a friend.' She shook her head. 'But to tell a journalist –'

'She was a friend, too,' Stephen said. 'Look, Cathy, there's no point in torturing ourselves. The thing is, what are we going to do?'

'It's too late to stop the story.' She gave a resigned shrug. 'Liz said they'd already started printing the paper.'

'Tomorrow morning this parish will be overrun with reporters,' Stephen said thoughtfully. 'Maybe it's just as well I'm going away.'

'Tonight?' Cathy stared at him in surprise. As she remembered the weekend bag she'd seen in the hallway, she said reproachfully, 'You were going without telling me?'

Stephen looked embarrassed. 'I hadn't made up my mind about that. It's because of you I'm going. I have some decisions to make.'

'About us?'

He nodded. 'And my whole future.'

She felt a leap of hope. 'Does that mean what I think it does?'

He hesitated. 'I'm not sure yet.'

'But you *are* thinking of leaving the priesthood?'

'It's on the agenda,' Stephen said. 'But I haven't decided anything.'

'I see.' A thought struck her. 'Will tomorrow's story make a difference?'

'To what I do?' He shrugged as he got up to replenish their coffee cups. 'My parish priest will have a fit, of course. Nothing new about that. But Brendan's story would have leaked out sooner or later. From what you say, his girlfriend was keen enough to talk to the press.'

'If Liz was telling the truth.'

He threw her a quick glance. 'Does that mean she might not have kept our names out of it?'

'I'm not sure.' Cathy frowned. 'I don't know if I can believe anything Liz says any more.'

'If that's the case,' Stephen said, 'I can't leave you to face things on your own.'

'I'll be OK.' She hid her doubts under a confident

smile. 'Even Liz wouldn't be mad enough to lead the other journalists to me. But the sooner you get away from here, the better.'

'I've had an idea.' She saw his face brighten. 'A friend has lent me his weekend cottage in Wexford. A few miles from the town, overlooking the river. It's quite isolated and doesn't have a phone. Come with me, Cathy. We'll be safe from reporters there.'

'I'm working tomorrow and Saturday.' She looked at him in dismay. 'It's out of the question, Stephen.'

'Don't you see?' His voice was urgent. 'It will give us time together. We'll never get a better opportunity to discuss our relationship.'

'No, I can't.'

'Just to talk.' He looked at her earnestly. 'I promise you'll be safe with me.'

Could she trust herself, she wondered. Yet the idea was tempting. 'Let me use your phone. But I can't promise anything.'

She found her employer at his home number. 'Are you out of your mind, Cathy?' Paul Kinsella said. 'The sale starts tomorrow.'

'I hate to do this to you, Paul.' She crossed her fingers. 'But I wouldn't ask if it wasn't important.'

'I know that,' he said grudgingly. 'I'll send someone from the other shop to cover for you. Get your crisis sorted out. I'll see you on Monday.' His voice was suddenly harsh. 'And Cathy . . .'

'Yes, Paul?'

'Don't ever do this to me again.'

As she went to tell Stephen she would go with him, she found herself wondering if she was doing the right thing.

EIGHTEEN

It was late when they got to the cottage. They left the car at the side of the road, near a cross-barred gate, and had to walk the rest of the way through almost complete darkness, stumbling up a hilly, pebble-strewn path, unseen foliage brushing against their shoulders and legs. As they rounded the side of the cottage, which, Stephen had told her, faced out over the estuary, Cathy heard the gentle lapping of water and saw lights glimmering in the distance. Suddenly, a raucous cry overhead shattered the peace. She gave a nervous start and felt a warm hand clasp hers briefly.

'Things that go squawk in the night.' She heard Stephen chuckle. 'Nearly there, Cathy. There's a key around here somewhere.' He left her side and began rummaging in the darkness. A door creaked. Then a light went on. As Cathy followed him into the cottage, the pungent smell of burnt wood greeted her nostrils. Her eyes blinking in the sudden light, she saw that they had stepped straight into a low-ceilinged room with rush mats scattered on a flagstoned floor. A table and plain wooden chairs were at one end, and an old-fashioned straight-backed settle faced a brick fireplace at the other. A couple of unpolished pine doors were set into the far wall. As he set down their bags, Stephen pointed to one of them.

'Kitchen and bathroom thataway.' She saw him hesitate. 'And . . .'

'Are the bedrooms upstairs?' Fighting back a yawn, Cathy headed over to the other door and opened it eagerly, feeling around for a light switch. But instead of the staircase she expected to find, she saw sprigged wallpaper, a bed with rolled-up bedclothes on its mattress, an old-fashioned wardrobe and a chest of drawers. 'Is this all there is?' She turned to look at Stephen in dismay. 'Why didn't you tell me?'

'Don't worry.' She saw the embarrassment on his face. 'I'll sleep out here.'

She glanced with disbelief at the wooden settle. 'On that?'

'It pulls out to a bed. A bit makeshift, but it'll do.' As he glanced around the room, he shook his head ruefully. 'I should have remembered how simple this place was. The thing is, it never mattered before.' He gave her a sheepish look. 'I've made a bit of a mess of it, haven't I?'

'Oh, I don't know.' Cathy smiled wryly. 'Seems to me it has all the basic requirements for a love nest. Privacy and a small double bed.' As she sat down wearily on the settle, she gave a light laugh. 'What more could an accomplished seducer want?'

'Cathy!' She saw the horror on his face. 'You don't think I planned this?'

'I mean, it's a really romantic set-up.' A careless sweep of her hand took in the floor, with its rush matting, the ashes in the fireplace, the half-empty fuel box beside the hearth. 'No doubt you'll be out chopping logs at first light.'

He looked at her uncertainly. 'I don't blame you for being angry.'

'I suppose I should be. But I haven't the energy.' Trying to find a comfortable position against the hard-backed settle, Cathy felt herself being overtaken by a huge yawn. 'But I may as well tell you, I wouldn't have come if I'd known.' She stood up and looked sternly at him. 'I suppose that's why you didn't tell me?'

'Please believe me.' Stephen's voice was earnest. 'This wasn't some kind of ruse. I meant what I said before we came. You've nothing to fear from me.' He glanced at the bedroom door. 'I'll just give you a hand with making up the bed. Then I'll get out of your way.'

'OK.' Cathy felt too tired to argue. All she could think of was the prospect of crawling under the covers and closing her eyes. When they went into the bedroom and began dressing the bed with a pair of cotton sheets they'd found in the bottom drawer of the chest, she let Stephen do most of the work. As she watched him carefully tucking in the blankets on his side, she wondered what Liz would have said if she'd seen the pair of them making up a bed in which only one of them would sleep. 'What kind of an eejit are you, kiddo?' But what Liz thought didn't matter any more. Every time Cathy remembered what had happened earlier that evening, she felt a sense of disbelief. How could she have done it?

'Things will look different in the morning, Cathy.' She glanced over to see Stephen watching her. 'And hopefully you'll have forgiven me by then.'

'I'm not angry with you.'

She saw him smile. 'That's a relief!'

'And I do believe you.' Cathy hesitated, choosing her words. 'But that settle doesn't look too comfortable.'

He shook his head. 'Don't you worry about me.' She saw him cross the room and take a pillow from the top of the wardrobe. 'It won't be the first time I've slept there.'

'You don't have to,' she said. 'The bed's big enough for both of us.'

'You've a kind heart.' Stephen looked gravely at her over an armful of blankets. 'But I'll take my chances outside. Something tells me that it will be a lot easier.'

'But Stephen . . . ' She looked at him doubtfully.

'Cathy, I know you mean well.' She saw a shadow cross his face. 'But don't make it any more difficult for me than it is already.'

'Maybe you're right.' She was aware of her own feeling of disappointment. 'If the settle gets too hard, don't be afraid to change your mind.'

As he turned in the doorway, their eyes met. Stephen was the first to look away.

'Thanks, anyway.' The door clicked. And she was alone.

The room was chilly, with a faint smell of must. Cathy was racked with shivers while she undressed. As she slid gingerly between the sheets, she pictured Stephen in his nest of blankets in the outer room. All at once, her arms ached to hold him. She found herself longing for the feel of his body lying against hers. She thought of the way he had looked at her before he left the room. If she had called him back, would he have come? Suddenly there was the sound of feet outside the door and her heart beat faster. Was he having second thoughts? But a hinge creaked somewhere and the footsteps moved away.

We have the whole weekend, she thought, as sleep overcame her. Then she was travelling through the countryside, along dark twisting roads, under tall, interlacing trees, while the car's headlamps swept briefly over woodland copses, lighting up gates and the roofs and gable ends of wayside dwelling houses. Beside her in the driving seat sat Stephen, a warm and comforting presence.

Just before dawn Cathy dreamed she sat with her mother in the farmhouse kitchen. On the table in front of them was a stack of children's copybooks which Louise had brought home from school to correct. 'Look, Mum.' She picked one up in surprise. 'This has my name on it.' Inside the cover, the neat lines of childish handwriting soon gave way to a jumble of unfinished sentences, snatches of nursery rhyme. 'Pussy cat, pussy cat, where have you been? I went to London to visit the . . .'

'That wasn't the real reason, was it?' Louise smiled knowingly.

How had she found out? Cathy stared at her in dismay. 'I would have told you, Mum, only . . . '

'I suppose you thought you'd got away with it?' Her mother's face was cold.

'It wasn't like that.'

But why had she gone to London? She struggled to find the words, attempted to explain. But the more she tried, the more her mother refused to listen, shaking her head and humming a little tune until Cathy wanted to scream with frustration. The dream paled into greyness and she was surrounded by the tenuous shapes and contours of a barely familiar room. For a tense moment she thought she was back in the farmhouse. Then the memory of last night's events rushed into her mind and she heaved a sigh of relief. Sitting up, she swung her legs over the side of the bed and padded barefoot across the linoleum to pull back the curtains from the old-fashioned sash window. The leaf-sprigged wallpaper emerging from the gloom reminded her of the spare room in the farmhouse, and she thought of her dream again. Some things are better left untold, she thought. And she banished the memory of her mother's face.

Was Stephen awake? There was no sound from the outer room, even though she leaned against the adjoining door and listened. On a sudden impulse, she gently turned the handle and peered around the edge. The front room was brighter and she was able to make out the dishevelled pile of blankets on the pulled-out settle. But of Stephen, there was no sign. Hesitating in the doorway, she noticed a shaft of light quivering on the dark stone of the floor, and realised that the outer door was ajar. As she watched, the light grew brighter. Cathy crossed the room. Pulling back the door, she looked out, to see the sky suffused with pink streaks. Below it, the broad estuary lay spread out, a white mist dancing over the surface of the water. A few yards away from the house, a man stood at a low wall with his back to her, his shape silhouetted against the growing brightness.

Cathy felt her heart lift. Snatching up her jacket, which lay on a nearby chair, she pulled it on and stepped eagerly out into the dawn.

When the bright curve of the sun rose above the rim of the horizon, Stephen caught his breath. A daily miracle, he thought. Yet one he so seldom witnessed. As he stood watching the white mist lift from the water, listening to the sounds and stirrings of the river bank and the call of the birds greeting the new day, he felt his taut nerves relax. The memory of his sleepless night began to ease. He stretched his tired limbs and allowed the peace of the place to envelop him. Whatever the next few hours might bring, he had this brief oasis of time between the agonising self-questioning of the small hours and the decisions of the day to come. If only one could always live in the moment. How much simpler life would be. And then his heart gave a leap of excitement as he heard the sound of a pebble being dislodged by a footstep on the hilly ground behind him.

'I thought you'd be out picking early mushrooms.' He saw a glint of amusement in Cathy's eyes. The blue shadows he'd noticed under them the previous night had gone. Her face looked smooth and rested.

'You're the country girl, not me.' Stephen hid his joy at seeing her. As she came up beside him, her jacket swung open to give him a glimpse of soft curves under the red satin kimono. He pulled his eyes away, peering further along the estuary at the rooftops of the town emerging from the mist. 'I might be able to do something about firewood, though.' When he looked back, he saw her yawning, stretching her arms and lifting her tousled hair. For a moment, he imagined her face beside him on a pillow. 'Did you just wake up?'

'Actually, I think I'm sleepwalking.' She stifled another yawn, her eyes examining him with curiosity. 'Did you go to bed at all?'

'Not really,' he said ruefully. 'You were right about the settle.'

She laughed. 'You should have taken me up on my offer.'

'Maybe I should.' His tone was equally light. But something in her eyes caused him to turn away and gaze down at the water, where a heron had begun a stately quest for food, its stalk legs stepping through the shallows, its long beak dipping rhythmically. 'Looks peaceful, doesn't it? But there's a lot going on underneath.'

'Yes,' Cathy said behind him. He felt a touch on his arm, light but insistent. 'Why did you bring me here, Stephen?'

Taken aback by her directness, he looked again at the heron but it offered no help. Reluctantly he turned to face her. 'I've been asking myself that all night.' He shook his head. 'Without much success, I'm afraid.'

Her eyes didn't waver. 'Come off it, Stephen.'

Stung by the accusation in her voice, he said, 'Do you know what I thought the first time I met you? You were like a cactus my mother has, all prickly outside leaves but with a beautiful flower in the centre.'

'Well, if you want to know' – Cathy's chin went up – 'you reminded me of my father.' He saw her frown. 'I don't need to feel that safe, Stephen.'

Again he felt stung. 'Do you think I wasn't tempted?' He couldn't keep the bitterness from his voice. 'Talk about being between a rock and a hard place. In and out of the kitchen all night, drinking coffee. Standing outside your door, forcing myself not to open it.'

She looked impressed. 'Your commitment is that strong?'

'No.' As he spoke, his realisation grew. 'What I feel for you is stronger than any vow.' He heard his voice break suddenly. 'But I gave you my word.'

'That was last night.' She gave him a candid look. 'I told you, I don't need protecting.' Taking his hand, she guided it under her jacket. 'Sex is no big deal, Stephen.'

'For me it is.' As he felt the soft swell of her breast through the shiny stuff of her dressing gown, he began to be aroused. Gently taking his fingers away, he clasped her hand instead. 'But it isn't the whole story.'

'I know.' Cathy nodded. 'It has to be with the right person.'

They stood very still, only their hands touching. Yet they were so close that Stephen could feel the beating of her heart and the slight tremor that ran through her as a cold breeze started up from the river.

'Cathy!' He drew her jacket around her and pulled her against him. 'I don't want to be your father. Or your counsellor.'

'Nor I your sister.' She put a finger to his lips, tracing their outline with a questing finger. 'Come to bed, Stephen.'

He held his breath, his eyes seeking hers. 'Are you sure?'

She pulled his head towards her and kissed him on the mouth. As they drew apart, he saw her smile. 'Are you?' she asked.

'Yes,' Stephen said. 'I'm sure.'

He took her hand, and together they walked up the pebbly track. At the cottage door they stopped and he pulled her into his arms again, smiling down at her upturned face. Then they stepped under the lintel and across the hushed outer room, their feet echoing on the flagstoned floor.

'I hope you've kept my brother out of this,' Jack said.

'Why should you care?' Liz was surprised.

'It's my name too. I don't like the idea of dirty linen

being washed in public.' He frowned suddenly. 'I hope you'll remember that.'

'What's that supposed to mean?'

'Nothing. Just marking your card.'

'There's nothing newsworthy about you,' she scoffed. 'And if your performance last night is anything to go by . . . '

'I'm surprised you remember.' A touch of malice in his voice. 'I wasn't the only one drinking, you know.'

Liz shrugged. 'I have the better head.' The one thing she could thank her father for, she thought. 'Besides, I had a lot to celebrate.'

'It's not all joy, though.' The malice still lingered in Jack's voice. 'There's the little matter of Cathy.'

'You're enjoying this, aren't you?' Liz sat up suddenly and swung her legs over the side of the bed. 'I think I'll give her a buzz – catch her before she goes to work.'

'It's too early.' Jack groaned, pulling the bedclothes back over him. 'While you're at it, get me a couple of aspirins.'

'You should keep them on your bedside table.' She frowned as she put down the phone. 'Cathy must have left. I'll try her mobile.' It was switched off. 'That's strange.' And the shop was still on the answering machine. On an impulse, she consulted the phone directory and tapped out another number. A recorded voice said, *'Father Brown is not available for the next few days. Father O'Donohue will be taking his calls. His number is . . . '*

'They're probably off somewhere, shagging like bunnies,' Jack said gloomily. 'I knew there was something going on.'

'I don't know your brother.' Liz shook her head. 'But I know Cathy. She'd never do a thing like that.'

He gave a malicious smile. 'She probably thought that about you.' His voice rose to a falsetto. '"Liz is *such* a good friend. She'd *never* betray a confidence."'

'Knock it off, will you.' She chewed her lip thoughtfully. 'I may have to look around for another apartment.'

'Good idea.' He closed his eyes and burrowed his head into the pillow. 'I was never crazy about that one.'

'Why? Does it bring back unhappy memories?' She looked at him sourly. 'Good apartments are hard to find. The thing is . . . I'll need somewhere to stay while I'm looking.'

'No, Liz!' Jack's eyes shot open. He sat up in bed and stared at her. 'No way!'

'You're not the only one who likes their space,' she snapped. 'But it would only be for a while.'

'Nobody puts a ball and chain on me.' Jack gave an affronted laugh. 'Better make your peace with Cathy.' He sank back against the pillows. 'What about those aspirins?'

'Don't tempt me,' she growled. 'I know where I'd like to ram them.' She glared at him as she hastily pulled on some clothes. 'I'll ring her from the office.'

So she has *gone away with him.* Liz put the phone back on its cradle and glanced thoughtfully around the busy newsroom. Who'd have guessed Cathy had it in her? And the priest was just another horny shagger like the rest of them. She smiled cynically to herself. It would almost restore your faith in human nature. One thing was clear, though: they weren't expecting Cathy back in the computer shop till Monday. It gave Liz a breathing space. And a lot could happen in three days. Cathy might have forgiven her by then. And even if she hadn't, she was far too soft-hearted to throw her out of the apartment. Unless, of course, she planned to move the priest in. That could be awkward. Liz frowned. Cathy's name was on the lease. *Worry about that when it happens,* she told herself. In the meantime, she was going to enjoy her new status in the office. She glanced up and smiled as yet another colleague stopped by her desk to offer congratulations.

'Good story, Liz. Heard you're going to do a follow-up.'

'Just waiting for a photographer.' She grinned at him. 'Then it's over to Saint Mary's to hit them with questions while they're still in shock.'

'"The female of the species is deadlier than the male",' the other journalist said in mock admiration. 'I'd better keep on the right side of you, Liz.'

'Very droll.' But she was in no mood for repartee. She thought of Cathy and sighed. She found herself hoping that her friend had gone somewhere no Irish papers would be available.

When they awoke, the sun was high in the sky and their stretch of the estuary was alive with the sound of seabirds and the occasional rhythmic cough of an outboard motor. After a breakfast of sausages, which Stephen cooked for them in the small but surprisingly modern kitchen, they walked the half-mile to the nearest shop, bought a copy of Liz's newspaper and read it outside in the thin, April sunshine. The story wasn't on the front page, but it took up most of an inside one.

'Liz never said anything about photographs.' Cathy was surprised. As she studied a shot of a couple hurrying towards a car, she was relieved to see the faces of strangers. In another picture, an anxious blonde woman stared straight at the camera. 'Thank God, they've none of us.'

'That's Brendan all right.' Stephen sighed. 'And I recognise Stella from a snapshot he showed me. But there's something here about me. Listen to this: *"Rumour has it that Cupid has struck again in this particular parish. Locals are hinting at a friendship between one of Father Hennessy's colleagues and an attractive young woman. Is it something in the air?"* I suppose it could be worse.' He folded the paper and looked at her. 'At least they've kept your name out of it.'

'Would it matter that much?' Cathy asked as they headed back along the road towards the cottage. 'People are going to find out sooner or later.'

'Not that way.' She saw Stephen frown. 'What about our families?'

Why did other people always have to complicate things, Cathy thought. 'You're right, of course.' She smiled at him and linked her arm through his. 'Let's forget about it for the moment and enjoy this nice spring day.'

But the sky had darkened, with a cloud covering the sun. The hedgerows began to rustle. 'Come on!' Stephen grabbed Cathy's hand. As the first large drops fell, he quickened their pace to a run. They arrived breathless and drenched at the cottage. 'It's down for the day, I'm afraid. There goes my plan for our walk on that beach I was telling you about.'

'There's always tomorrow,' Cathy said. 'Besides, there's something about being cosy inside when the rain's falling. And once the fire's lit . . .'

'We'll be snug as bugs.' As he knelt in front of the hearth, Stephen began tearing the newspaper they'd bought into strips. He grinned at her over his shoulder. 'I knew there had to be some use for this.'

'The fire's the best place for it.' She frowned as she thought of Liz's treachery. 'But I suppose it'll be all over the other papers tomorrow. Not to mention the Sundays.'

'We don't have to read them.'

'You're right.' Cathy laughed. 'Just send them up in flames.' While she towelled her damp hair, she marvelled at the ease they felt in each other's company. Everything they did together was such a pleasure. Watching him as he carefully built up the fire, she recalled his tenderness when they'd made love earlier.

'It was wonderful,' he'd said afterwards. She'd heard the awe in his voice as he held her close. 'I never thought I'd have a woman I loved in my arms again.'

'When was the last time?' she asked softly.

'There was a girl once. But that was a long time ago . . . Before I entered the seminary.'

'And nobody since?' She couldn't hide her surprise. 'A man as loving as you?'

'I've met women I liked over the years. But that's as far as it went. Celibacy is a state of mind, I suppose.' As his arms tightened around her, she heard him sigh. 'No one has ever got under my skin the way you have.'

'I've been in love before,' Cathy said, 'but this is different. It's hard to explain. It's deeper, somehow. And yet . . . it's like having something so precious that you're afraid it could be taken away.'

'Like a rare jewel?' His voice was eager.

'No.' Despite the warmth of his body against hers, she felt a tremor go through her. 'Something more fragile.'

Now, looking at him as he bent over the fire, her doubts returned. When Stephen got to his feet with a satisfied nod, dusting down the knees of his jeans, Cathy said, 'All this is real, isn't it?' She heard the anxiety in her own voice. 'We're not just playing house.'

She saw the surprise on his face. 'You think my feelings for you are some kind of act?'

She shook her head. 'That isn't what I meant.'

'I think I understand,' Stephen said. 'I can't quite believe it's happening either. Sometimes I want to pinch myself.' He came over and put his arms around her. 'Look, feel me. I'm real. It's not a dream.'

'That isn't it, either.'

'Don't look like that, my darling.' He cupped her face with gentle hands. 'You know I would never do anything to hurt you.'

'Love doesn't work that way,' Cathy said slowly. 'There are no guarantees.'

'Tonight there are.' His voice was confident as he bent to kiss her. 'I'm going to cook one of my mother's tried and true recipes for you.'

'Not pasta again!' She pushed her doubts aside and tried to smile. 'Your mother must have had an affair with an Italian sailor.'

'Show a little respect,' Stephen growled.

'I hope your cooking's better than your accent.' She gave a reluctant laugh. 'Look, maybe I'm being foolish . . .'

'No, Cathy.' His face grew serious. 'I know we need to sort things out. I'm not avoiding it. But I've only just found you.' He looked at her pleadingly. 'We have so little time together. Let's give ourselves today.'

'OK,' she sighed. 'Tomorrow, we talk.'

The rain blew away during the night. Saturday turned out to be a bright, breezy day, with a hint of warmer weather to come. In the afternoon, they drove to a long, sandy beach a few miles away, and walked arm in arm, braced against the wind, with only the gulls for company. The tide was out; the sight of the waves in the distance brought back memories for Cathy of childhood summer holidays. For Stephen, who had grown up near the sea, there was the sense, as always, of slipping back into familiar shoes. Listening to Cathy as she told him stories of trips to the seaside with her parents and sisters, he found himself talking about his own father.

'Do you know, I actually admired him once. At one time, I even thought I'd follow in his footsteps and become an engineer.'

'Why did you change your mind?' He heard the interest in her voice. 'Was it something he did?'

'No, it had nothing to do with him,' Stephen said. 'You don't pick the priesthood, Cathy, it picks you. Look, you asked me once what I had against my old man – '

'And you got angry with me.' Her voice sounded subdued.

'I'm sorry about that.' He gave her arm a comforting squeeze. 'Let's just say he hasn't made my mother happy.'

'I see,' Cathy said. To his relief, she didn't pursue the subject. 'I never wanted to be a teacher like my parents. From an early age, I knew I wanted to make lots of money and live in big cities. I saw myself in a penthouse in London, or New York, maybe.'

'When did *you* change?' Stephen asked jokingly.

Cathy didn't smile. 'I don't think I have. But after my trip to London' – her voice faltered – 'I never wanted to go back there again.'

'Maybe it's time you did.' A thought struck him. 'Why don't I go with you? You could show me that view of the city you told me about.'

'Revisit the scene of the crime?' She gave a short laugh.

'You don't mean that,' he said gently. 'It could be a healing process for you. Although we mightn't be able to do it for a while. I have to think about getting a job, finding a place to live.'

He saw her look of surprise. 'What about your house?'

'Belongs to the parish.' He gave a rueful shrug. 'And I've no savings, either. What they pay us only covers the essentials, the odd holiday and the loan on the car. I'll have nothing once I leave.'

'You can stay with me.' She smiled at him. 'And they're taking on staff in the shop. I can put a word in with Paul. Of course, the money wouldn't be great.'

'It'd be better than the dole, I suppose.' He hesitated. 'Working together mightn't be such a good idea, though.'

'It's not really your scene, anyway.' He saw Cathy frown in concentration. 'What about your counselling?'

'In the long term, maybe. I do it on a voluntary basis for a charitable organisation. To get paid, I'd need a professional diploma.' Stephen was struck suddenly by the irony of his situation. 'If I'd taken my mother's advice at the time and joined a teaching order, I'd have academic qualifications, job prospects.' He checked his stride, picked up a pebble and skimmed it across the waves, which had gradually come nearer as they walked. His shoulders slumped as he turned back to her. 'All I'm trained for is working in a parish.'

'You'll think of something.' He felt Cathy's comforting touch on his arm.

'You're right.' As he looked at her, his spirits began to lift. 'I'm beginning to get a few ideas already. Let's go back before it gets dark.'

As they turned to retrace their steps along the beach, Cathy gave him an impish smile. 'I'm going to treat you to some pub grub tonight. I don't feel like trying out that kitchen.'

'As kitchens go, I've seen worse,' Stephen said. 'The cottage belongs to a friend I've known since we were in the seminary together. An aunt died and left it to him a few years ago. He's always talking about extending it, but apart from making a few changes to the kitchen, he's done nothing.' He gave a rueful laugh. 'Whenever he invites any of us down, it's a choice between spending a night on the settle, or in a sleeping bag on the living-room floor.'

'He must get a lot of visitors,' Cathy said.

Stephen grinned. 'To be fair to him, he's very generous about lending it out. The other day, when I needed to get away, he was the first person I thought of. And he agreed straight off. "Stay as long as you want," he said.'

'It sounds like you priests stick together. It's a bit like a brotherhood, isn't it?' Cathy's voice was thoughtful. 'You'll miss all that when you leave.'

Stephen felt a sudden pang. Abruptly, he tightened his grip on her shoulders, pulling her around to face him. 'I won't need it any more,' he said, kissing her hair. 'I'll have you.'

'That's true.' As she gazed up at him, it was hard to read her expression in the fading light. 'But you'll need friends too.'

'I'll still have those,' Stephen said quickly. 'They won't all desert me.'

'Not if they're friends,' Cathy said.

He gave her a troubled look, but before he could speak, she reached up and kissed him on the lips. Forgetting what he had been going to say, he kissed her back. As they clung together, a cold wind came gusting in on the tide, sending shivers through both of them. Cathy pulled away from him and linked her arm through his. 'I think we should go.' When they resumed their walk, she said, 'About that meal . . . '

'I think it's a great idea.' Stephen was relieved at the change of subject. 'But we'll go somewhere decent. And you must let me pay. I'm not on the poverty line yet.'

'We'll argue about that later.' He heard the smile in her voice. 'And you can tell me about those ideas you have.'

'OK,' Cathy said as they sat across the table from each other in the small, dimly lit restaurant. 'You've had enough time to mull it over since this afternoon. Out with it.'

'As I see it,' Stephen said, 'there are other avenues we could explore.'

'Such as?'

'Well, they're always looking for people to work on projects in the Third World . . .'

Cathy frowned. 'As lay missionaries, you mean?'

'The emphasis is less on religion and more on self-help programmes. They teach the villagers how to sink wells, plant crops, all that sort of thing.'

Her saw her look of disbelief. 'You want to go to Africa for a year?'

'Maybe two,' Stephen said. 'But I don't mean alone. I want you to come with me.' He looked at her eagerly. 'It's worthwhile work, Cathy.'

'I don't doubt it.' Her tone was dry. 'But I thought you said you didn't want us to work together?'

'Not in a computer shop, Cathy. This would be different.'

'I'll bet it would.' She gave a faint smile. 'You said you had another idea?'

'Which you'll receive with equal enthusiasm.' He felt deflated suddenly. 'Look, don't laugh, but I've thought of a way we could be together and still practise my ministry.'

'Join another religion?' Her voice was flippant.

He was surprised. 'How did you guess?'

'I'm psychic.' She gave a wry laugh. 'I hope it doesn't involve having to shave our heads and chant in the streets.'

'Nothing so exotic. Look, Cathy, nobody's surprised when a Protestant clergyman becomes a Catholic priest, but it's been known to work the other way, too.'

'I thought you'd a thing against Protestants.' He saw her quick glance. 'Or was that another of Jack's lies?'

'Half of my relatives are members of the Church of Ireland,' Stephen said mildly. 'If I'd been brought up as one, I'd probably be a vicar in some quiet parish.'

'Or an archdeacon, like your great-uncle?'

'A dean, actually.'

'Well, it's an idea,' Cathy said.

He watched her face. 'But not a great one?'

'What do you think?'

He sighed. 'You're probably right. Although the two churches have a common faith, there are doctrinal differences.'

Cathy laughed. 'Can you see me as a clergyman's wife?'

'You'd be wonderful,' Stephen said. 'You care about things like poverty and injustice.'

She shook her head. 'That was my father, not me.'

'But what about that homeless beggar the night we met?'

'He was so young.' Her face was wistful in the candlelight. 'I kept wondering what kind of a mother he had.' He saw her expression change. 'But this isn't solving your problem, Stephen. How do other priests who leave manage?'

'I've never really thought about it.' He stared at her in surprise. 'Brendan is the only one I know of. And he went on being a priest for a couple of years after he met Stella.'

She gave him a clear-eyed look. 'Lived a lie, you mean.'

'If you want to put it like that,' Stephen said uncomfortably. 'Look, Cathy, it's easy to pass judgement but maybe he'd no choice. It would be difficult to get a job at his age.'

'It's not too late for you, though.'

'You're right, of course.' Yet he was filled with doubt. 'It's just that everything has happened so fast.'

'For me too.' Her expression softened. 'Let's not talk about it any more.' As she reached across the table to take his hand, her eyes looked suddenly bright. 'We don't want to spoil our last night together.'

At her touch, all his senses came alive. He lifted her hand to his lips. 'There'll be other nights. This is just the start.'

'Yes, of course,' Cathy said.

But when he looked at her, he saw his own doubt mirrored in her eyes.

Although they kept up a light-hearted banter on the drive back to the cottage, they made love that night with a feverish desperation that neither of them had known before, touching each other's bodies hungrily, unable to get enough of each other, falling at times into a fitful sleep, only to wake again and again in the darkness, clinging together like victims of a disaster. At last, as the night sky began to pale outside the window and an occasional bird note signalled the new day, Stephen dropped into an exhausted slumber while

Cathy lay dry-eyed in his arms, devoid of consolation. Mercifully, sleep overtook her too. When she awoke, the room was bright and the space beside her empty. Running barefoot over the cold floor of the outer room, she peered out the front door into the morning sunlight to see Stephen, head bent, pacing the stony path as he read from a small leather-covered book, his lips moving in prayer. Unnoticed by him, she went back to bed and wept despairingly into her pillow.

'Leave the dishes,' Stephen said when he saw Cathy begin to clear the table. 'I'll do them later.' She'd been very quiet during the meal, he thought. Her face was paler than usual, and the blue shadows were back under her eyes. 'Are you sure you won't change your mind and stay on till tomorrow?'

Cathy shook her head. 'My job is important too.'

He felt a sense of anguish. 'But nothing has been decided.'

'Hasn't it?' She gave a wry little smile. 'You're going back for the Easter ceremonies, aren't you?'

'Cathy, no matter how I feel about you, or what we've done together, I'm still a priest. They're depending on me.'

'It's not just duty, though, is it?' Again that little smile.

'I've said I'll give up the priesthood.' As his eyes searched her face, his distress grew. 'Do you not believe me?'

'I don't want you to do it just for me,' Cathy said.

He stared at her, baffled. 'You're not making sense.'

'It has to be right for you too. Let's face it, Stephen, if you hadn't met me, it would never have crossed your mind.'

'Someone else might have come along.'

'It's too big a sacrifice, Stephen.'

'Cathy, it's the only way I can keep your love.'

'How soon would yours turn to hate, though?' She gave him her clear-eyed look. 'How soon before you'd start resenting me?'

'I'm not saying it'd be easy, Cathy. But I could live with it.'

She shook her head. 'It could destroy you.'

'No!' He gave a despairing cry. 'We'll work something out.'

As they faced each other, he saw a strength in her he'd never noticed before. 'Can you honestly say that the priesthood doesn't matter to you?' she asked.

He stared back at her without speaking.

'Look at me, and say it.'

'I can't.' He sat down at the table and buried his face in his hands.

'I won't live a life of deception, Stephen.'

'I won't ask you to.' He lifted his head. 'It would destroy you.'

He saw the relief on her face. 'I knew you'd understand,' she said.

'What good is that?' All his certainties abandoned him then, and he was overcome with despair. 'Cathy, you've left me nothing. Not even honour. Because of you, I've betrayed my vows, lost my vocation.' He gave a sob of anguish. 'And all for nothing.'

'It wasn't nothing.' Cathy's voice was firm. 'It was beautiful.' Again he saw that new maturity in her face. 'Nothing has changed. You're still a priest. And a good one.'

'How can you say that?' He gave a bitter laugh.

'Because I know you,' she said. 'Don't torture yourself, Stephen. God will understand.' She smiled faintly. 'He created sex, after all.'

'Yes.' Despite his pain, Stephen returned the smile. 'It *was* beautiful. Oh, Cathy!' His voice broke suddenly. 'How will I manage without you?'

'No better than I will, I suppose.' As she turned away, he saw her mouth tremble. 'I think I'll go and pack before one of us does something foolish.'

'I'll wait till the bus comes,' Stephen said as the Nissan nosed its way through the narrow streets of the town. He pulled into a parking place in sight of the stop, where people had already begun to assemble. 'I'm sorry you won't let me drive you back to Dublin.'

'This is easier on both of us.' Cathy kept her voice light. 'Besides, you wanted to stay on for another couple of days.'

He nodded, his gaze fixed on the windscreen in front of him. 'I've a lot of thinking to do.'

As she watched his bleak profile, she had a sudden image of the grey clouds scudding low over the estuary and heard the call of the seabirds. Funny how a place she'd known such a short time could create this sense of loss. 'I think I'd better go and join that queue.' She managed a laugh. 'All those people trying to escape Sunday afternoon in a country town. Can you blame them?'

There was no answering laugh from Stephen. When he turned towards her, she saw the pain in his eyes. 'I was wrong when I said it was nothing, Cathy.' He touched her hand gently. 'These last few days have been everything.'

'For me too.' She bit her lip. 'I'll say goodbye now.'

'No, I'll walk you to the stop.' He got out, took her bag from the boot, and came around to her side of the car. As he opened the passenger doo,r Cathy thought, *I can't do this*. But then she was out on the pavement and they were looking at each other and smiling.

'Take care of yourself.' He pulled her into a close embrace. She smelled his aftershave, felt the strength of his arms around her, and then they were apart. He bent to kiss her lips. She put her hand to his face and felt it wet. And then the bus came. She saw the queue move briskly ahead of her. Another, quicker hug. Then she was on the platform, paying her fare. She found a seat at the back, craning her neck to catch a glimpse of his tall figure through the window. The bus gathered speed and quickly left the town behind.

It was only when they were a few miles out on the open road and she looked up and saw the low cottage perched against the skyline that she realised she would never see him again.

The flagstones in the living room echoed emptily under his feet. He looked at the dead grate and began to clear out the ashes. When he went to the outhouse, he saw that there was just enough kindling for the fire and noticed more logs neatly piled against a wall. He'd need to chop some if he was going to stay on for another few days. But the estuary, with the wind whipping over the sunless water, had lost its appeal, and the cottage itself had a comfortless air, even after he'd got the fire going and had cleared the table of the signs of their last meal together.

He went into the bedroom but could find no trace of her presence. The bed was neatly made, the dressing table cleared of her possessions. Yet she was everywhere. Wandering the empty rooms, he half expected to hear her laugh, to turn a corner and meet her clear-eyed gaze. And he couldn't get her voice out of his head. He hoped he never would.

That night, as he sat fruitlessly trying to read a book, he spotted a small, delicately coloured silk scarf, half hidden down the side of the uncomfortable settle. She'd been wearing it around her neck, he remembered, the morning they'd got caught in the rain. She must have taken it off while she was drying her hair and forgotten about it. He held its silken folds to his nostrils, inhaling the subtle yet unmistakable scent of her.

'I'll love her forever.' Although he spoke softly, his voice seemed loud in the empty room.

Forever is a long time, he heard Cathy's voice say.

That's something I have plenty of, he thought. *A*

lifetime of it, year in, year out. He looked at the scarf in his hands. She might need this. Maybe he should post it to her. But he knew he wouldn't. He also knew he would never come back to the cottage.

I'll leave tomorrow, he told himself. *Spend a day or two with my mother. She'd like that.* But he wouldn't tell her about Cathy. Not yet. Maybe not ever. And then he would go back to his parish, take up the broken strands of his priestly life, and try to knit them together again. Next week was Holy Week. The week of atonement. On Good Friday the Sacred Liturgy would retrace the Saviour's footsteps to Calvary, but Stephen knew that his own agony had already begun and would go on even after the Paschal Flame had been lit.

In time, he hoped, the longing would ease. And maybe some day he might become a priest worthy of the name. The kind of priest Cathy believed he could be. In the meantime, he would go through the motions: say Mass, bury the dead, absolve the living and lead the faithful in prayer. He knew this was what God wanted him to do.

EPILOGUE

'Cathy, I can't believe how grown-up you've got,' Noreen said. 'When I saw you waiting for me this morning at Heathrow, I had to look twice to make sure it was you. I thought I must be suffering from jet lag.'

'I was a kid when you first went away six years ago. But you've been home a couple of times since.' Cathy looked enquiringly at her eldest sister. 'Have I really changed that much in two years?'

'Not in looks.' Noreen said. 'But there's a serenity about you I've never seen before.'

It was a hard-wom serenity, Cathy told herself, remembering the pain-filled days after the break-up with Stephen and hte end of her friendship with Liz. 'I've been through some difficult times, Noreen. But you know what they say. "What doesn't kill us makes us stronger." Whatever happens in the future, I know I can cope.' Her chin lifted proudly. 'I'm my own woman now.'

'I can see that,' Noreen said. 'But what you said about "difficult times" . . . ' She hesitated, glancing around the hotel bar, and then back at Cathy. 'It was only a flying visit that time. We hadn't a minute to talk properly. But I felt in my bones there was something troubling you.' Her face showed her concern. 'Tell me, dote, was I right?'

'Your instincts are never wrong.' Cathy smiled fondly at her. 'Something bad happened six years ago, Noreen, just after you went to Saudi. I couldn't talk about it for a long time. But someone helped me sort it out a few months ago.'

'Thank God for that,' Noreen said.

'Yes.' Cathy gave a faint smile. 'When you rang me from New York and asked me to meet you here in London to look for a wedding dress, I jumped at the chance.'

'I'll probably end up buying the dress in Dublin. But it was a good excuse to have a few days' shopping. When Gavin comes home, wild horses couldn't make him set foot in a clothes shop.'

'And they won't be able to drag us out.'

'I'm counting on that,' Noreen said.

'But it's not my only reason for coming to London.' Cathy took a deep breath and looked at her sister. 'This isn't my first visit. I was here six years ago.'

'When something bad happened?' Noreen looked into Cathy's face and touched her arm gently. 'Tell me about it, pet.'

When the two young women came up from the Underground, the morning air touched their faces with a chilly sweetness that held the promise of later heat. Not many people were about. The trendy boutiques and bistros on the high street were shuttered still, but a shop selling newspapers was open, and the aroma of freshly baked bread wafted tantalisingly from another as they passed. Outside a florist's, they saw a man arranging bright splashes of scented lilies, carnations and majestic gladioli in containers on the pavement. On an impulse, Cathy went into the shop and bought a single red rose.

The same pub with mullioned windows was on the corner. And the houses and gardens on the quiet avenue looked much the same as they had six years before. When they came to the turn-off and saw ahead of them the hilly road with the drab houses on one side, the trees and open parkland on the other, she felt Noreen's hand clasp hers comfortingly.

'If only I could have been with you, Cathy.' Her sister's dark eyes were sorrowful. 'I'd never have gone to Saudi if I'd known.'

Cathy nodded. 'But you're coming back for good now, that's the main thing.' As they started up the hill, she recalled the air, sharp with autumn, the path strewn with fallen leaves, the low October sun. Now the trees were bright with summer foliage and daisies speckled the grass. Like the last time, there were few people about. It was too early in the day for the crowds of picnicking families or the young couples lying in the sunshine, trying to make the most of the hot weather. As she'd hoped, they found the viewing park deserted. The nearest figures to be seen were a couple of men walking greyhounds across the lower slopes, while, far below them, the city lay in a dreaming haze.

'Do you still think you did the right thing?' her sister asked.

'I had no other choice.' Cathy gazed downward, her eyes seeking to distinguish between rooftops, spires, domes, cupolas and the spaces where trees grew. 'I still regret it had to happen. But I couldn't bring that baby into the world.' She turned and looked at the other woman. 'Wherever she is, I think she'd understand.'

She saw her sister's eyes glisten. 'Maybe she's in heaven with Dad.'

'You were always religious.' Cathy gave her an affectionate hug. 'But this time, I hope you're right.'

'God is good.' There was a wealth of meaning in the other woman's tone. 'And life goes on.'

A little smile played around Cathy's lips. Her fingers traced the slight curve of her stomach under the light T-shirt. 'This time, it will.'

'I think you're doing the right thing,' Noreen said. 'But it'll be tough, bringing up a child on your own.' She frowned. 'I still feel you should have contacted Stephen before he went to Namibia.'

'I think he has enough to worry him out there,' Cathy said. 'Maybe when he comes back in two years' time . . .'

'*If* he comes back.'

She felt sadness press down on her suddenly. 'I can't think about that now.' And then, without warning, Cathy felt a sensation in her stomach that was as delicate as the flutter of a butterfly's wings. She caught her breath in surprise and then turned to smile at her sister. 'I'll be OK.' As she felt the tremulous flutter again, she was filled with awe. And gratitude. 'Don't you see, Noreen, I've been given a second chance.'

The two women stood for a few minutes longer, gazing down at the city shimmering in the summer heat. As they turned away, Cathy walked over to the edge of the viewing area. Taking the long-stemmed red rose from its cellophane wrapping, she held it to her lips and breathed a silent prayer. Bending down, she laid it reverently on the grass.

Also by Dee Cunningham

and published by Marino Books

A Very Private Affair

A beautiful woman who is reunited with the son she gave up for adoption more than twenty years previously.

A young man who finds more than a mother.

A story told straight from the heart that grips the heart of all its readers.